Vekon (candy shop)

You're a rock solid dude
& a true, true friend!

Keep on rockin' bro.

Cheers,

CRESCENDO

a novel

by

Jonathan Brown

This book is a work of fiction. Names, character, places, and incidents either are the product of the author's imagination or are used fictitiously, and any resemblance to actual persons, living or dead, business establishments, events, or locales is entirely coincidental. All other characters, and all incidents and dialogue are drawn from the author's imagination and are not to be construed as real.

ISBN 9780988544208

This book is dedicated to my mother Rosemary.

Shout Outs!

All of the 'good stuff' comes from the support of others-a team effort if you will. This means that I have thousands of people to thank. If I miss you here it doesn't' mean that you don't occupy a place in my heart but on the day I scribed this thank-you, you may have been dancing towards the back of my mind's dance floor.

Having said that: First and foremost I'd like to thank my beautiful wife Sonia. Thank you for talking me off the ledge the many times I wanted to take pen, paper and laptop and gently slide them into the wastebasket. Your love and support has been immeasurable. Love ya madly babydoll!

Dad, thank you for allowing me march to my own drum. I know it's difficult to corral us artists let alone raise us. My super-siblings: Gary and Cleta, you two never let me quit. Thanks for believing. Thanks for pushing. Huge love and thanks to Kat, William a.k.a. 'Billy Slice', Ashten, Gizelle a.k.a. Zellybear, Jonathan a.k.a. Youngblood, Jackson a.k.a. Rocky and "Big Bad" Louis y'all are the best nieces and nephews an unhinged uncle could ever hope for.

Julia-from drum student to good friend, to editor thank you to the tenth power. Tony, thanks for being a buddy and guy who takes care of all things technical…the stuff that makes me want to snap! Chris a.k.a. The Bear you are a dear friend. Thanks for the support and for tuning up my blogs. Mathew a.k.a. The Cutter, your support has been grand. I truly enjoy our libation infused writing symposiums…such as they are. Thanks to the great author Bjorn a.k.a Bourgenion much oblidged for paving the way and passing the wisdom on down. Jay, thank you for your friendship and massive generosity. Oslyn, welcome to the family baby and thanks for being you. Janet, you prop me up more than you can ever know—thank you for that. Jennifer a.k.a Jenny Brasco your friendship keeps my writing fires burning while your laughter takes me right back to grade 9. Carl a.k.a. Rhino my closest friend thanks for always having my back and ah, sorry about that trick I played on you at my wedding. Marty a.k.a Marny, man…you are the greatest. Elide, what can I say except a million thanks for everything. Diane and Gwen you made the good years, great. Vekan a.k.a Candyshop nobody backs a Cat up like you do brother—thanks man. Paul and Charlene I love you two more than cold beer on a hot day...o.k. maybe it's a tie but the love is truly there. To Master Kwon thank you for sharing your wisdom and for your patience. And sorry if some of my moves carried with them a touch of Hollywood.

To all of the Browns and Wedderburns thanks for the truckloads of laughs! I am truly blessed to be part of this crazy family. Thanks for the love and support and keep those laughs coming or I may have to write our story...I'm just playin' y'all. To the Mauros, you are the greatest family a poor sap could marry into. Thanks for making me an honorary Italian.

Thank you to all of our California brothers and sisters. You're warm smiles and rich characters have made the last 15 plus years quite a ride. To all of my Vancouver friends and family who make my visits home feel like Christmas, new years and my birthday all wrapped into one—thank you.

A big thank-you to Gina Welch, editor extraordinaire. Merci beaucoup to Karen Phillips for the lovely book cover.

To one and all I hope you enjoy Lou Crasher's first adventure at least half as much as I enjoyed writing it. By the time you read this Lou's next rockin' romp should have hit the shelves. If not feel free to give me a gentle shove. And remember, all of the world's problems can be solved with love!

Chapter 1

The day it began started out differently than usual. I was getting ready to head to work when Michael, my immediate boss, called to send me on an errand. I am a musician, a drummer, but to pay the bills I work for Michael at a place called the LA Practice Joint, which sits a stone's throw from Hollywood High School in West Hollywood. "The Joint" is a place where bands, mostly the rock and roll kind, come and rehearse for gigs, demo tape recordings, and new CD releases. We also have the hobbyist type that comes down to drink beer, smoke pot and "Jam, dude." Ninety per cent of the bands that come through The Joint are seconds away from signing the big recording contract, or so they'd tell it. It is my job to let them into their rooms, take their money, keep the place clean and flash them a phony smile when they inform me of their impending fame. We charge a low rate and they treat the place accordingly. When they've completed their jam session I make sure that the pile of crumpled single dollar bills adds up, kick them out and let the next soon-to-be-famous group through the gate, easy as pie.

When Michael called early this morning it was to tell me to run by his parents' house to pick up the business phone, a four hundred dollar iPhone. Seldom does a minute go by that Michael does not remind me and the rest of the staff of the phone's price, although depending on his mood the price varies.

"No problem," I told Mike and with apartment number, buzz number, address and parking situation locked down I was on my way.

My boss' parents own the business. They are a sweet elderly couple who flop over at the Knickerbocker Apartments on Hollywood Boulevard. I eased my 1965 Mustang into a roomy spot in a three minute loading zone outside their place. I didn't have to worry about the time limit as the building was empty and a pleading For Lease sign hung in the window. This was no doubt another location where the businesses gave it the old three month college try before having to pack it in—a sign of the times.

After repeating my name twice into the speaker I was buzzed in. I wouldn't have put money on the elevator's chances of getting to the twelfth floor but she managed. Eddie, the owner, was waiting for me in the hall outside his door.

"You must be Louis," he said in a powerful voice that belonged to a younger man.

"Yes, and you must be Mr. Eddie Carruthers," I replied, pressing his flesh.

"Come in, come in, we've heard good things about you."

"Well, I'm glad to hear that," I said, stepping into the warm room.

The apartment was pretty much what I expected. It was very clean, too hot and overrun with knickknacks. What really caught my attention amid all of the old ornaments was the oversized flat screen television. It was three sizes too large for the room but I didn't protest, as Eddie had the football game on. The Denver Broncos were battling it out with the Oakland Raiders. Oh, how I wanted to call in sick, put my feet up and watch these rivals go at it but how one calls in sick from his boss' abode is a mystery to me. The Miller Genuine Draft bottle at Eddie's elbow and its golden delight within didn't make things any easier.

"Here, sit down a minute. So my useless son left the phone here and now you had to come out of your way and meet his old coot of a dad and the old battleaxe of a mother. Ain't that right, Evie?" he called.

"You know I don't respond to that kind of talk, Edward," his wife called from the kitchen.

"What the heck are you doing in there while we've got the whiz kid out here?"

As if on cue, Evie entered the room with a tray of milk and cookies. Eddie jolted forward in his La-Z-Boy.

"Milk and cookies," he blurted. "Come on Ev,' he's a man, for heaven's sake, not a boy."

"No, no that's fine. Mrs. Carruthers, milk and cookies are my favorite," I said, standing as I remembered my manners.

"Liar," Eddie mumbled with a grin.

Eddie couldn't remember the "darned" score so I got to perch on an ottoman until the score flashed on the screen. During that time Evie tried to get acquainted with me but Eddie continuously shushed her.

Minutes later I was in my ride, not ten blocks from work. I rolled to a stop at a red light where Cahuenga meets Hollywood. I watched the steady flow of traffic from my left as I waited for an opening. I ignored the few pedestrians passing in front of my car, which turned out to be a mistake. A tall pimply faced kid with a nose ring reached in through my open window and snatched the iPhone from my passenger seat. Four hundred dollars flew out my window quicker than I could select my favorite cuss word. I was going to get it back, plain and simple. I cranked my car hard to the right and pulled in behind a flatbed truck loaded with shopping carts. Sliding my old school steering wheel club into the locked position I hefted it and hit the ground running. Up until my early twenties I played football at the free safety position up in Canada. That was, let's say, a few years ago, but I still had wheels.

How long my cardio would hold out was the big question as I put the three punks between 17 and 20 years of age. I gained on these kids immediately and it was then that my heart filled with hope as I remembered that kids today are raised on video games, junk food and cheap marijuana. They didn't play countless hours of kick the can, manhunt, and red rover like my generation had. It seemed that as children we ran non-stop from morning until the street lights came on. Cardio be damned, I was going to nail these suckers!

They made a right at the first street they hit. Pushing as hard as they could the motley trio moved down the sidewalk, pausing occasionally to check my progress and to pull up their baggy pants. When one kid with a shaved head and a Green Day T-shirt abandoned the posse and darted into the street, a woman in a BMW 3 series with shocking red hair was forced to lock her brakes up. The kid was lucky she hadn't been on a cell phone or he'd have been one with hood and pavement. She leaned on her horn, and the kid responded with his middle finger.

"Run him over next time," I shouted as I sprinted past.

The pimply faced kid still had the iPhone so I kept up chase on the remaining two. If I appear to be a fool rushing into a fight I promise that this was not entirely the case. I have a background which consists of a variety of sports. In this case, a moment no doubt destined to end in fisticuffs, my years of playing football were sure to help. I played that game up until my 21st birthday. One thing I took away from my coaches was that even if you play on a losing team you've got to just drop your shoulders and run through a guy and never stop driving those legs. Being on a losing team tends to toughen one up some, as it's often the other guy running over you. Also, I used to go a few rounds with a crazy uncle of mine, but more on that later.

An alley opened up in front of them to their right. The pimply face kid took it while his partner (unaware of the plan) overshot the drive and fell to one knee. I caught up to him as he tried to gain his feet and threw a firm elbow into the small of his back. I could hear a tooth chip as his face made contact with the pavement. He yelped like a wounded poodle and let me know how he felt about it in Spanish. It was one of the three Spanish curse words I knew.

It was getting close to mano-a-mano time. The kid with the iPhone looked back to check on his cronies. Shock registered in his eyes as he saw how close I was. He tried to accelerate but it was too late. I pulled up beside him and swung the club at his legs behind the knees. He screamed as he went down. The iPhone popped out of his hand and slid on the ground ten feet before coming to rest beside the wheel of a garbage dumpster. I was panting heavily from the chase. My veins overflowed with adrenaline. I put a knee in his back and laid the club across his neck the way a snake handler would position a lethal cobra. As I was telling him what I thought of him with choice words the Latino with the newly chipped tooth tackled me off of his buddy. I suppose it served me right for trying to play tough guy/street lecturer. I now lay a few feet from the iPhone still with my club in hand. The Latino was up first and kicking me in the ribs or wherever he could. I got off a lucky swing that caught him on the shin.

It was not a fatal blow but it was enough to make him change his plan. He leapt on me and tried to wrestle the club away. He spat in my face. I spat back in his but was not satisfied in the least. If possible I was going to kill this man. The pimply faced kid was on his feet now and yelling orders at his buddy while calling me a "dead nigger" every five seconds. I decided I'd kill him too. Pound for pound the stocky Latino was probably stronger than me but I was far more passionate. I tend to get that way when my ass is about to be kicked. He drew back to head butt me. He was in perfect position to break my nose. I tried to get the jump on him and threw my head first, and our heads met, well, head-on. His face was now surrounded by pretty little stars. He rolled off me with a moan. The pimply face kid stepped over his friend and started kicking at me. I rolled away as fast as my aching head would let me. At one point he landed a kick at the base of my spine that sent a shock wave of pain from my toes to my ear lobes, ending on the tip of my tongue. If he kicked me again I didn't feel it. Certain that I was about to pass out, I was about to make myself comfortable when a loud voice commanded me to "get up". Whether it was the pimply faced punk or my ancestors I know not, but next thing I knew I was upright with wobbly legs beneath me. As my head cleared I remember what my uncle used to say when we goofed around at boxing: "If something comes at you get out of the way, then return the favor with something twice as hard as he was going to hit you with." Wordy, but I got the gist.

The Latino was up too, and back in the game. His twisted mouth raised on one side revealing a bloody, confident grin. He slowly took off his plaid shirt exposing large biceps covered in nasty tattoos. By nasty I mean he was covered in ink about death, guillotines, Rottweilers, pit bulls and bloody knives. I would have liked to have attacked while he was overdramatizing the plaid removal but I still needed time to recoup.

"Rather than spend all that time in the chair getting ink done you should have been in the gym learning how to fight," I said, stalling, hoping for my legs to stop shaking.

"Is that right?" he asked with a smirk. "Why don't you drop that club and fight me like a man, tough guy?"

"Keep your girlfriend out of it and maybe I'll consider it."

The pimply faced kid's face reddened. "You're a dead—"

"Nigger, I know," I interrupted. "You mentioned that all ready. Is that all you've got, you little bastard?" My legs were nearly back.

"Listen, bro," the Latino piped in. "Let's stop bullshitting and get it on."

"Why don't you take her home and you two get it on?" I said.

That was the last straw for the man in the tattoos.

He charged me straight on. I held my ground as if I were slow to react and at the last second swung the club down in an overhand swing as if I were splitting a cedar stump. The club connected perfectly with my attacker's collarbone. All three of us heard the bone snap. He went down on one knee with a grimace but didn't cry out. He was definitely a tougher hombre than me. He was, however, officially out of the game. I walked over to the iPhone and bent to pick it up. The pimply faced kid summoned up his courage and made a play for me. Again I feigned unawareness. At the last moment, I stepped aside, letting the kid's own momentum carry him into the side of the dumpster. As he used the edge of the can to hoist himself up I brought the club down hard on his right hand, breaking it in at least two places. He screamed and slumped into the fetal position. He looked up at me with tears in his eyes and threatened me one last time. I considered tossing him a two dollar line like "Crime doesn't pay," but decided against it. With club and iPhone in hand I walked out of the alley and back to my ride, which had a bright yellow parking ticket on her windshield.

Chapter 2

The LA Practice Joint is a dump. And for the record I don't write home about it. The low pile blond rug is now almost charcoal gray, and the eggshell walls are scuffed and gouged from floor to ceiling. The battle scars are not entirely visible to our clientele, as each wall is blocked top to bottom with rental amplifiers, drums, speakers and so on. An old slab of three-quarter inch plywood sitting atop two short file cabinets serves as our desk. I'm the only employee of The Joint who keeps the clutter on top of the desk somewhat organized.

When I got back to the office, a pair of shiny red cowboy boots were kicked up on top of the clutter. The boots belonged to Gladys, Eddie Carruthers' 72 year-old sister. Two things I learned early on about Gladys: one was that to judge her book by the cover was a mistake. This woman had more spunk then I did at 18 when I thought I had the world by the tail. Two was that she had a mouth on her that would put some of my old football buddies to shame.

"What the hell happened to you, ya little bastard?" Her voice always sounded full of cigarettes mixed with vintage pennies.

"A couple of punks stole this damn iPhone. Rather, this four hundred dollar iPhone, from me. We tussled and I stole it back. I won and they lost but now I have sore ribs, a sore head—hell, I'm just sore. How are you doing?"

She gave me her sandpaper on sandpaper laugh before taking her boots off the desk to lean forward. "That's a load of crap, Louis, and you know it. Do you want to know what I think?"

"If I say no do you promise not to tell me?"

"Show some respect, you son of a bitch. I still pack a pretty good left, you know, and from the look of it you're not too good at getting out of the way." She paused and lit a cigarette. "Now here's what I think went down. You probably made a play for one of those two bit skirts you're always drooling after and she said 'no.' But you persisted like the horny little bastard you are until she finally kicked your little ass silly." Her deep laughter turned into a cough which seemed to make her laugh harder. I tried to look pissed off but couldn't help joining in with her. After grabbing some ice and applying it to the back of my head I sat down opposite her.

"I'm bloody choking over here, Louis, get me a drink, for Christ's sake. I'm an old broad!"

It was harder to get out of the chair than I expected but I managed and handed her a Diet Coke. "You're welcome," I nagged. She waved me off.

"Seriously though, did she hurt ya?"

Even though Gladys kept up the "she" angle I knew she was concerned. "I'm fine. She doesn't kick very hard." We smiled at each other as she butted out her smoke. "So what brings you by the shop, Granny?"

"Oh yeah," she said, riffling through the file cabinet drawers. "I'm looking for some god damn Tylenol. I've got a hangover big enough to raise the Titanic."

It was my turn to bust her chops. "Is it really a hangover or did one of your sick little boy toys hit you over the head with a sex toy while trying to escape or something?"

She picked up the Louisville slugger we keep under the desk and came at me like a tornado. "Listen to me you little shit. My men beg for it. They can't get enough of me. *Comprende*, you little prick. Go ahead. Say something else. Go ahead."

"Okay, okay! Calm down. It was a joke. You're so sensitive."

"Well shit, I told you I was hung over, you little..." She sat down heavily in the chair. "If I didn't feel like crap you'd be begging me to pull this thing out of your ass."

"Hey Gladys, I've got some Tylenol but you have to say please."

"Screw it. Gimme."

"Nope."

"Please then, you little prick," she asked, pinching the bridge of her nose.

"Just the please, lady." I loved this. Gladys and I were close but she was always abusive and I was beginning to worry that I liked the abuse. She picked up the bat again slowly.

"Okay you big baby, here." I tossed the little pack to her. She knocked a handful back and chased them down with the Diet Coke.

"Hey, go easy on those things. I'm going to need a few myself."

She closed her eyes, put her boots back up on the desk, and with a sigh she spoke in a low tone. "All right, handsome, tell me about this donnybrook of yours, with the details this time. Because I'll be honest with you, you don't seem too bad off but I just don't see you as the brawling type."

"Fine, but here's the deal. I'll give you the whole story but I don't want any interruptions. No bull. And for the record I am as tough as I need to be, got it? Good."

And so I laid it out for her like a picnic blanket, omitting nothing. She interrupted me about twenty times, which was half her usual number. In the middle of my reconstruction she opened her blue eyes and put them intently on me. Her look was graver than a no-nonsense Supreme Court judge. When I was done she glanced up at the faded ceiling tiles—the ones that remained anyway. Half a minute crept by before she lit another cigarette and took a long drag. She mumbled something I didn't catch before pulling the filter off the cigarette. Her tanned face worked into a smile as she took another deep drag.

"Son, what you did was just plain dumb. But don't feel so bad, your whole generation behaves asininely all the time. You risked your life for a damned piece of technology. A piece of ass I would have understood, kid, but hell, a cell phone?"

"It wasn't the phone so much as they pissed me off. I forgot to mention that one of them spat in my face, which reminds me, I've got to wash my face."

"Butt in like that again and this bat goes you know where. Those punks could have been packin' heat, you moron. I'd be sitting here without any Tylenol listening to the story from some low rent flat-footed cop—and then what? I'd have to notify your kin? And brother if you put that on me I'd resuscitate your butt and choke your lights out. Caesar's ghost, my head hurts! Now get out of here, take the day off."

"No can do, I need the dough. Besides tough guys always work on fight days," I teased.

"Hell, work. I don't care. I just wanted to see how big your stones were. A sissy would have taken the day off. I'll see ya, handsome. I'm going up the road and see if I can't take this edge off."

"You want a drink now? Give it a rest, Glads."

"Stow it, you little pissant. These Tylenol ain't doing Bo Diddley. Whoever heard of buying regular strength Tylenol anyway? Not to mention Diet Coke?" She threw the pack of Tylenol at me, sneered at the drink and headed for the door. At the threshold she stopped and turned back to me.

"Hey kid, I hope you did what you said you did with that steering wheel club. If society is a giant body then those guys must be from the asshole."

"Thanks, Glads."

"So what are you?"

"Excuse me?"

"You know, what part of society's body are you? Are you the arm? Or the leg maybe?" She had a kid in a candy store grin on her spa-tanned face.

"Why the heart, of course."

"Hm. Well, old Gladys here is the pu-"

"Okay, okay, I get it, I get it. Go get your drink, girlie and leave the little boys alone." She cackled all the way down the hall. After she was gone, I got up and washed my face—twice.

With Gladys out of the way I eased into the old office chair and put my own weary dogs up on the desk. I sat and stared at the iPhone, which slumbered happily in its charger despite the new scuff mark from the pavement. I let my mind digest the recent episode. My mother would have killed me had she known what I did. The same would go for my old man, though he would have better understood my actions. I suppose men can dig why other men do dumb things in the name of pride or bravado. I could just hear it. My father would argue with my mother that I acted on principle and my mother would have pointed out that it is interesting how often principle has to do with money or material things. Not a chance would I mention this ordeal to them during our next Sunday night call. The phone's ring startled me even though I was looking right at it.

"LA Practice Joint." Business voice.

"Yeah, uh, hey. Do you guys have rehearsal time over there... like available time, dude?"

"Yeah man, when did you want to jam?"

"Next Monday. No Thursday. Yeah, no, Monday."

"So, Monday the 10th then?"

"No, dude, Monday as in tomorrow, dude, like man-ya-na, man." He giggled the oh-so-familiar pot smoker's giggle.

"Tomorrow isn't next Monday, tomorrow is tomorrow, pal." I reached for my Tylenol.

"You're wrong, dude, you're so wrong. If today is Sunday and tomorrow is Monday then tomorrow is the next Monday we're going to have or encounter or whatever so I'm right, dude."

"Okay, smart guy, then Monday the third?" I said with a sigh.

"Hey, hey, hey I can hear the condescension in your voice, dude. Don't think I can't. 'Sides, the customer's always right, dude."

After playing musical days with the client for another five minutes it turned out that he was calling the wrong rehearsal studio. I enjoyed twenty minutes of peace until the office door opened slowly, the doorknob fitting into the hole in the wall behind it. Filling the doorway was a six-foot-two inch blond transvestite in a pink tutu. The giant stubbed out her half smoked cigarette under one of her four inch stiletto heels. She leaned over the plywood and fed me Audrey Hepburn eyes.

"I'm here for the Pippy Longstocking audition. You see Pippy is smart. Pippy is sassy. Pippy is coy and oh, definitely sexy. And that's me. I'm going to be Pippy, the lead singer."

"Well yippee for Pippy. Let me check the book."

"Um hello, you haven't said a thing about my look. Let me break it down for you sugar. The tutu is from Aardvark, a secondhand store on Vine. The shoes were my mother's, may she rest in peace. The body is what Pilates can do for a girl with gumption, and the hair tie..." She paused to flip the wig. "Saks."

"Saks Fifth Avenue?"

"Oh no, sweetie I'm talking Saks Fashion Outlet. I don't go near those bitches on Rodeo, honey. Thank you, but no... Thank...you! Now the stockings, my favorite little accessory are from Benny's Bunker on Melrose." She gave me a slow 360 degree turn. "So? Don't leave a good girl hanging. What do you think?"

"Well, I suppose you'll make about the best Pippy they've ever seen."

"Oh you are too kind." She put her index finger to her bottom lip. "Say, do you...?"

"I have a girlfriend," I lied.

"Figures. So where do you want me?"

"Studio B. You're the first one here so I'll just let you into the room." I walked her down to the studio through a perfume cloud thick enough for three women and let her in. I then turned on the P.A. system. "Good luck with the audition, big guy. I mean big... little girl."

I made my way back to the office and cracked myself a Pepsi. Pippy's band was the only one scheduled for the next three hours, which gave me plenty of time to relax, barring more intelligent phone calls. Sleep snuck up on me unannounced. The smell of a sweet perfume, not Pippy's this time, brought me out of it. I opened my eyes to see one of the most beautiful African-American women that I'd ever seen standing in front of me. But who was I kidding? She was the most beautiful woman I'd ever seen, period. Her dark ringlets cascaded over her slender shoulders like a gentle waterfall. Her eyes were a sharper green than mine, and much prettier. When she smiled they nearly disappeared into tiny little slits. Perfect teeth beamed through slightly parted sensuous lips that danced up to her dimpled cheeks. This was pure insanity. She had the kind of face that I wanted to see more of. It was also a face that made fashion photographers cancel the makeup artist before a photo shoot. Into their cell phones they chuckle, "She doesn't need any darn make up. Take the day off."

There she stood, more beautiful than Nefertiti. Her tank top exposed tight abs and toned arms. A tiny lime green cell phone poked out of the pocket of her nice-fitting faded Levi's. She laughed as I stood and knocked my Pepsi into the garbage, which naturally hadn't been emptied, so the drink bounced off the debris, hit the floor and soaked into the dirty rug. Her laugh, which was another part of her I could get used to, rang out. It was like an intro to a Chopin piece played upon a finely-tuned Steinway.

"I'm sorry. I didn't mean to laugh. I'm Angela," she said, offering a hand.

"It's okay really. I'm Louis or Lou, whatever you like... better. Welcome to the palatial Practice Joint. LA's hottest..." she raised one of her perfectly sculpted eyebrows at me. "Okay, well then, welcome to a joint with totally reasonable rates."

"May I?" she motioned to the seat across from me.

"Of course, yeah, stay as long as you like." I sat without looking and nearly missed my chair. She grinned but held the laugh back. Bless her heart. We sat looking at each other. What I thought was a moment between us was merely a moron forgetting what his job was. If she hadn't cleared her throat I'd have kept staring until Christmas.

"Oh right. So are you interested in jamming here? I mean is that why you're here? Of course it is."

"Why don't you tell me what your rates are?"

"Rates, rates are good." Somehow I managed to rattle them off without bumbling them up. Amazing, seeing as there were two whole different rates. She wanted a tour so I gave her the best tour I could, elaborating, embellishing and elongating at every possible turn like a true business man. And boy, did I want to make this sale. In fact this was the first time I ever looked at this job as a sales job.

We have six rehearsal rooms at the Joint. By the fourth room I'd already dropped my keys twice, banged my head on a speaker, sneezed, stuttered over the cancellation policy segment of the spiel and turned on a sound system before checking the volume which caused the P.A. to scream like fifty tea kettles in our ears. I'd have had a better chance with Angela if I'd given the tour drunk on whiskey in pink boxer shorts. Who knows, maybe the court jester type would be her thing. The fifth room was the Pippy Longstocking auditions. This would be a great opportunity to take the idiot light off of me and shine it on the giant Pippy contestant. At the end of one of their songs I knocked once and we entered.

"Sorry to interrupt, fellas, I just wanted to give Angela here a quick look at our largest room."

"Angela?" the transvestite asked.

Angela replied, "George? Get out of here is that you?"

"Yeah, well, actually, it's Pippy now. Right guys?"

The three other band members nodded with grins on their faces. The audition was over. They had found their Pippy in George. Apparently George and Angela went way back. They hugged and laughed and when Angela introduced us George mentioned that he'd already met the delicious chocolate gent from the front office. Angela smiled at me as if I'd just been let in on an inside joke. The pleasantries zipped around the room for another five minutes before we made our exit.

"So what do you think of George?" she beamed.

"Pippy can sing, and this chocolate gent is proud of him."

She put her hand over her mouth and giggled. They said their goodbyes and 'I'll call you's' and we moved to our final room. With a six month old paint job and a ten month old carpet room number six was our cleanest room. It also had the best PA system.

"...You mean I didn't tell you the story of this system? Allow me to introduce to you the system that once belonged to J. Lo. That's right. The story goes like this. J. Lo had this system in her Miami Beach home where she wrote 'Jenny From the Block.' When she was about to go on tour one of her dancers sprained his baby toe and claimed that the P.A. system was the wrong color according to feng shui. J. Lo agreed and that's when I got the call and passed the word onto my boss who picked it up for a song...no pun intended.

"J. Lo didn't like the color?" she asked.

"Yup, kooky huh?"

"It's black, Louis."

I shrugged my shoulders. "So what do you think," I asked.

"Tightest little piece of bullshit I've heard this year."

"I've got to fix that story. At what point did you know I was, you know, fabricating?"

"Actually, the part when you opened your mouth was where you lost me."

She shook her head with the kind of grin on her face that women get when they've decided in their minds to go on at least one date with you, though they'd never vocalize it. We trod back to the office to wrap up. The Joint became a go for Angela. I could barely contain myself. She paid for a month's worth of rehearsals up front, cash. I'd never seen this type of business during my short stay at The Joint. The boss would do cartwheels, I was sure.

"Is there a problem?" she asked.

"No, I just...well, no, this is great news," I said. I wasn't sure where to put the money as there wasn't a chance in hell I was going to let her see the pathetic 1940's shoe box we use as our cash box. I decided to leave the money on the desk and just write out the receipt, which also was embarrassing as my boss bought the cheapest receipt books that Sav-On carried. To add to this mess we'd run out of them. I could only hope that she'd say 'nevermind' as I searched for what I knew I wouldn't find.

"Umm, you know what?" she said. Great I was saved. "I think I'll go ahead and pay for two months right now."

"Wonderful," I said, "more money." I counted it and resumed my search, accidentally pinching my finger in the filing cabinet. Being fleet on my feet I amended my curse word to 'Free Society.' This Angela woman had knocked my compass off its hinges, jerked the rug from under me and set my inner pinball machine on tilt in under an hour.

Chapter 3

I wouldn't dare be so bold as to say that Angela liked me, but I was fairly sure I hadn't turned her off completely. Until. The transaction complete, she left with a smile. I was basking in her lingering perfume when I began doodling absentmindedly. My artistry became focused as I attempted to draw symmetrically perfect hearts with mine and Angela's names within. Silly, I know, but who'd see? As it turned out, getting both sides of the heart even proved to be more difficult than I thought. Then her perfume grew stronger in my nostrils and there was the sound of a throat clearing. I dropped my pen and moved my horrified eyes slowly upward. She was back.

"Sorry to interrupt your, um, work. I just forgot my keys," she said reaching down to pick up a set of keys that lay not two inches from my art work. I was so far gone that I hadn't noticed them. I hadn't felt like a little school boy since the days when I was a little school boy and even then I thought I was a teenager. As quickly as this nightmare began it ended and once again I heard her tiny footfalls moving down the hall. Depression set in.

Angela's band ended up booking three practices a week. Our rendezvous carried on much the same way as our first meeting; Angela the flawless damsel never in distress, and Lou the ever-bumbling buffoon. I was nearly as smooth as an intoxicated three fingered ten-pin bowler. The night of her first rehearsal, Angela came in wearing faded jeans and an oversized Dodgers jersey. The smell of roses, or maybe tulips surrounded her as she politely asked that I fix the mic stand in her room.

"It just seems to be stuck. I don't know if you have another one or if you want to try to adjust the one in the room."

"Let's have a look. I'm sure it's nothing a little elbow grease can't fix." I got up from the desk and came around, trying to appear larger than I am. I said hello to some of the band members as I entered. The stand was stuck with the mic at waist height.

"As you can see it's too low. Do you think you can get it up?"

"Almost every time," I responded, soaking with wit. A few of the guys chuckled. I loosened the clasp with minimal effort but hoisted the mic with a little too much zeal. The mic collided with the underside of my chin at close to sixty miles an hour. The boys more than chuckled this time. At least Angela had a sympathetic look on her face when she laughed.

The next rehearsal was not much better. I simply had to have another glimpse of her fine figure in her black jeans and cashmere sweater. It was an old school look, but she made it work. Having upped my workout program to three times per week, I decided rolling up the sleeves of my plain white T-shirt was a necessity. I crept into the rehearsal room to empty the garbage can. I jerked the bag out of the can with exaggerated ease making sure her view of my biceps was not obstructed. The arm held, but even with minimal contents within the bag did not. All I needed was the red clown nose. I made a note to thank my boss for the no-name garbage bags.

Friday rehearsal came along and Lou was ready for it. Not a chance was I going down in flames again. How is it possible that one can be semi-cool until the object of one's desire arrives on the scene? Today I was going to be Mister Nonchalant. I could take her or leave her. Easy come, easy go. Out of the corner of my eye, I spied her in a sharp blazer and slacks number. The color was one of those puce or magenta types that I always get wrong, and it really brought out the beauty of her eyes. I kept my feet on the desk and took my time moving my eyes from my novel.

"Oh, is it rehearsal time already?" I muttered with phony sleepy eyes.

"Yup," she smiled. "How you doin,' Lou?"

"Oh you know." Bored. She frowned at me, but I pretended not to notice. I hauled myself out of the chair as though it was the last thing I wanted to do.

"Late night, Lou?"

"Yeah, you know how it is." More boredom. "Late nights, late days, what can you..."

"Are you all right? You seem kind of, I dunno..."

"No, I'm good. I'm okay... fine. I mean, a little tired but not sick or anything. Not that you said I was sick. I'm cool. Yeah, I'm cool."

She grinned like she was holding back a laugh. I'd tipped my hand and she'd busted me. Refusing to put eyes on her as I held the door for her, I noticed that what's left of our ceiling consisted of 8"x8" perforated white tiles, with three ball point pens lodged in a tile above the desk. I wondered how long they'd been there.

I let the band into their room, flicked on the lights, turned on the PA, made my exit without catastrophe, and returned to the office in time to catch the phone.

"LA Practice Space... hello?"

"Oh. Sorry hi. What time do you guys close?"

"One a.m.," I answered.

"But I thought I saw a sign that said you were open until two, man."

"On some weekends we do stay open until two but it's slow tonight so we're closing at one."

"But the sign says two, dude."

Annoyance was building like a wave at my end. "Well sir, there's the sign and then there's the guy answering the phone. Me. And being that I'm the only cat here tonight we're done at one, son."

"Well maybe I should come down there and we can settle this."

"Excuse me? What did you just say to me?" The telephone was near crumbling beneath my tightening grip before a familiar raspy laugh hit my ears. "Gladys, you little...Who was that guy? He sounds too young even for you!"

"Lou, you're such a loser. 'The guy on the phone says.' My god, man, you're a twit. Don't you know the customer is always right, you rude s.o.b.?"

"You're looking at a statutory beef, Gladys. Who's the infant?"

"Hush up, you dizzy pervert. He's my useless grandson. I put him up to it. He didn't want to do it. You kids today wouldn't know a good prank if it bit you in the ass. So you're off at one then, sweetheart?"

"Yeah, why what's up?" I asked.

"Meet me at the Cookie Jar. I'll buy you a cheap pint seeing that your girlfriend put the boots to you this week."

"Gladys, last call will have come and gone."

"What a sissy generation you belong to. Don't you know anyone at all? I can get hooch 24-7 anywhere in this empty town."

"Just promise me you won't tell me what you do to get that hooch."

"Piss off. You coming or not?"

"Yeah, I'll be there."

"Good. Come around back."

"Nope, you tell your friend over there that segregation is over, no more back of the bus. Lou's coming through the front door and I'm comin' in hot." I hung up.

The Cookie Jar is one Hollywood's many hidden little hole-in-the-wall places; small stools, tiny round tables and lots of hanging deep red velvet curtains with gold ropes. From the front the place looked closed, so despite my witty declaration to Gladys I was forced to go around to the back. Eve, the club's bouncer stood a half inch taller than me with a frame that carried fifteen more pounds than mine. We always got along and I was glad for that. She was no joke when it came to doing her job.

"Well hello Louis, Gladys said you might be dropping by."

"Hiya, Eve." There was no cover charge but I always slipped her a fin as if it were some kind of sad person's protection money. High Roller Lou, that's me. She put a firm hand on my chest, barring my path.

"Ah, Gladys said you were coming but her instructions were to not let you in. And she was firm on that, bud."

"Have a good Eve... Eve." I turned to go.

"C'mere you big sissy, she was only joking! What a pushover. Would you actually have left me with the five spot?"

I stepped close to Eve. "You rock my world, Evie baby, and there's plenty more five spots where that came from. You see. I tip you because you're you."

"You can lie to me anytime, drummer boy. Have fun...and behave."

I did as exactly as I was told. I had two beers worth of fun and I did behave myself. Not once did I rise to Gladys's childish taunts. I just nodded my head, winked occasionally and let her fans enjoy the Gladys show. A boy scarcely a day over twenty one was completely smitten with Gladys. I could tell by his seat shifting that he was about to make his play. I'd seen this show too many times. This was my cue to exit. Don't get me wrong, I'm happy the old broad gets her groove on. I just don't need to bear witness.

Chapter 4

My old gal, the 1965 Mustang, got me over the hill and into north Hollywood all on her own. It was as if somebody else turned my steering wheel and worked the pedals for me. It's like that sometimes when you meet someone new. Angela was the only thing on my mind. I was picturing us way too far into the future and it didn't bother me one bit. I knew I had it bad, but I loved it.

Once home I had to push my electronic garage door opener eleven times before the ton of rust reluctantly opened.

"Someday it's going to be me and you, pal," I threatened.

This open threat took me back to an old memory. When I was about nine years old I was up in my bedroom raising all kinds of hell. I was making such a racket that my mother came bursting into my room ready to break up what she thought was a fight between myself and some friend of mine.

"Boy, who are you yelling at like that?"

"This stupid Gameboy doesn't work. And it doesn't work cause it's a stupid son of a..."

"Don't you curse boy, not in this house. Not anywhere. Now why are you hollering at an inanimate object?"

"It's not inanimate, it's stupid. And now it's personal."

My mother spent half the day laughing at me after that one.

Now, I rode the elevator alone up to my apartment. When I got into my place I tested a theory. I took the battery out of my garage remote and swapped it with the one in my television remote. The television came on but it wouldn't change channels no matter what angle I pointed it at the tube. I shook my head. All those years ago when I was upset with the "stupid" Gameboy, my mother came in and changed the batteries in the unit and had it working fine. A little over two decades go by and I'm still the same dumb chump cursing inanimate objects.

I got up from my love seat, which has had so little loving since it has been in my possession that I actually just call it a seat. I called the voicemail number and put her on speaker. I got a pen and paper ready to write down my one to nine messages. The first message was that of my big boss's wife Evie, Gladys' sister.

"Louis, we heard about what happened after you left our place on Sunday. Sorry it's taken us so long to call. We meant to; the memory just isn't what it used to be. Anyway, are you okay? We hope you're all right. Next time just give them what they want. They're just, just bastards is all. Pardon my language, dear. Anyhow, you call us later and tell us how you are and..."

Her voice was interrupted by her husband Eddie's. He was saying something in the background about how women are the only creatures on earth that can have conversations with answering machines. She called him an old grouch and hung up.

The next call was from the *LA Times*. Some cat was offering a great deal on subscriptions. They usually call every two weeks.

"... So if you're interested call us back and ask for Damien, that's me. And by the way your voice sounds very...um, warm. Bye-bye."

The next call was from Bobby.

"Lou! Lou! Lou, you old sausage, what's up? It's Bob, the object of every broad's desire. Listen man that was heavy shit you laid on my cell about those suckers in the alley. If you want to go have a beer so you can cry about it while I pick up women, give me a shout."

Hmm, maybe tomorrow night, I thought. I knew at some point I'd have to listen to how my buddy Bobby would have handled the fight situation as well as the meeting with Angela better than I did. It might as well be over a few beers. The next message caught me off guard by starting off with a soft woman's voice.

"Um, hi it's me. It's, ah, been awhile, I know, but I had to call."

Suddenly Angela moved to the rear of my brain. Well, not the rear. Just back a bit.

"Oh god, I hate these voice mail thingies. Anyway, I was just thinking back to the way you used to do that thing I like," she giggled. "I miss you."

Who are you, sweetheart? What thing did I do? My mind was racing like a game show contestant's, hand poised over the button.

"I was hoping we could hook up. Call me if you want. My number is the same."

Which is? Which is... what? I was losing my marbles.

"... In case you forgot, it's area code 818-555-3241. Call me, baby. I miss your touch. Bye, Geoffrey."

Geoffrey! That was all I needed; a wrong number. I considered calling her and telling her that I wasn't her intended man but I was sulking too much. Moving Angela back to the front of my pea brain cheered me up. In fact I felt as though I'd stepped out on her for thirty seconds. I heated up some leftover spaghetti and downed two beers watching a Jay Leno rebroadcast. After doing the dishes I hit the sack with a smile on my face. I dreamed that Angela and I were guests on the Jay Leno show. We had a slamming funk band and we played some really hot tune and then got interviewed. Jay directed all of his questions at Angela and during one of the commercial breaks I gave him a mean look which he completely ignored.

My ringing phone brought me out of it.

"Hi Lou, it's Mike. Sorry to wake you."

Mike, my immediate boss, is the fine young son of Eddie and Evie.

"No problem, man. What's up?"

"We were robbed last night. They ripped my new security door right off the damn hinges. Then they came in and grabbed a ton of gear from rooms D and E."

My heart sunk as he told me that Angela's room had been hit.

"You're kidding me," I replied.

"You booked that new band in E, didn't you?"

"Yeah, I'll give them a call."

"It's okay. Their singer is already down here."

"Angela?"

"Yeah, pretty girl." He said with a sigh as if it is a bigger shame when bad stuff happens to pretty people.

"Put her on the phone please, Mike."

I didn't know what to say except sorry. Sorry for losing your gear in your first month of rehearsals. Oh man, I was bummed.

"Hello?"

"Hi Angela, it's Lou. Are you all right?"

"Oh Lou, I can't believe this. I'm so pissed off!"

"Angela, I am so sorry about all of this, really. How much of your stuff did they..."

"All of it. They cleaned us out." Her voice had a quiver in it.

"I'm on my way down there; I'll see you in twenty."

I grabbed the world's fastest shower then headed over the hill into Hollywood. Coming south on Highland I was forced to make a left after Peach Street into the short driveway that puts you in the lot behind the building. This maneuver annoys motorists but I was in too much of a hurry to go all the way around the block. I ignored the burst of angry horns. A police cruiser took up two spaces at an angle. Next to it my boss' Nissan Pathfinder. A uniformed cop stood over what was left of our metal security door and spoke into a radio. I nodded and was about to walk past when he said, "hold on" into the radio.

"Can I help you?"

"Yes, I'm an employee here. My name is Louis."

"Go ahead, but I want to talk to you before you leave." He went back to his radio conversation.

Inside, Angela got up from my boss' chair when she saw me and gave me a quick hug; a fit body with a nice smell. Stay focused, Lou.

"Hi, Angela, Mike."

"Did you see the door Lou? Did you see what they did? That door cost me close to eight hundred installed. Man, I'm so sick of Hollywood."

"You and me both," Angela added. "I can just kiss my band's equipment goodbye. Timing couldn't be worse; we're due in the studio in less than two months."

She put her elbows on her knees and buried her face in her hands. I looked from Angela to my boss. They were quite the miserable pair and there was nothing I could do about it. A different uniformed cop came into the office.

"Lou, this is officer Taggs. He is here with officer Rollins who you probably met out front."

We nodded to one another but we didn't shake. Mike explained that I worked the day before but that Randy the late night maintenance/security guard was the one who closed. Officer Rollins came in at that moment but let his partner handle the questions.

"You probably can't help us, but did you see anyone hanging around that looked like they shouldn't? You know, like they were trying to scope the place?"

"No, not really," I answered.

"Not really?" he asked unable to keep a career cop's suspicion out of his eyes.

"Well there was the usual couple o' three Latino dudes that hang out on the sidewalk but they're always there. They're harmless as far as I can tell."

"Any prank or threatening calls?"

"Just my boss' aunt," I chuckled but nobody else found the humor. Officer Taggs stood motionless with pen poised, waiting for something useful.

"Any bands here that you think capable of something like this?"

"If there was a riot and a music store window was smashed, sure there are a few guys in here that would step in and lift something. But rip that door off and rush this place? Nobody I can think of."

"You seem certain of that." Taggs shifted his weight to his opposite foot. Either his feet hurt or he was getting bored. I'm no master of body language.

"I'm just guessing like the next guy."

"What next guy?" He was staring hard now.

I returned his hard stare slightly confused by my own 'next guy' statement. I could tell Taggs didn't like me. His partner's frown told me he shared the sentiment.

With a sigh Taggs folded over his notebook and put his pen away. He told us that they'd do what they could, but it was a long shot that they'd turn anything up. Consider the valuables gone, in other words. They left us sitting there in silence. Mike finally excused himself past Angela and reached for his phone. Angela and I walked into room E and looked at the damage. Although it looked like a smash and grab the thieves found enough time to trash the room. There was graffiti on the walls and floor and garbage everywhere. This meant that Randy hadn't emptied the trash at the end of his clean up. I hope the boss made a note of that. They had some kind of carpet cutter that allowed them to slice the carpet up. Someone even got up on a chair or something and pulled down a handful of ceiling tiles. After taking this in, we looked into Angela's storage locker. Her lock, still in the locked position, dangled loosely from the latch.

"A lot of good that lock did, Lou."

"They must have used a crowbar or tire iron to pry that lock latch off. It would be easier than trying to crack it open."

We stared a few moments longer, as if hoping the stuff would just materialize on its own.

"What are you doing now, Louis?" Angela asked.

"I suppose I'll help the boss clean up and then chill until my shift later."

I could tell she wanted to say something but didn't. When we got back to the office my boss was red faced, talking into the phone.

"... No you listen to me, man. My parents have been with your company for twenty five years. So don't tell me that because my payment is past due you're not covering me.... What?.. Oh really? You'll be hearing from our lawyer! What's that? Never mind what my lawyer's name is smart ass, you'll know soon enough!"

His attempted confident tone told everyone in the room and the person on the other end of the phone that there was no lawyer. Mike nearly slammed the phone down until he remembered it was an iPhone. Not good for slamming. It also would've defeated the purpose of my previous knuckle skinning.

"Those A-holes at my insurance company don't want to cover me."

He sat down hard with a curse.

"Tough break, boss. Do you want me to start cleaning this crap up?"

"No, this fight isn't over yet. Dad's coming over and we're going to photograph the place. If they do eventually cover us we'll need to show damages. Besides, I'll get Randy in here when clean up, time comes. You see he didn't take out the friggin' trash again."

He pulled off his baseball cap and ran his fingers through his gray-specked hair, then replaced it. "This fight isn't over yet, as I said, Lou. Take five—a long five. I'll call you in a few days."

"Where are you parked, Angela?"

"I'm on the street, around the corner. Why?"

"Here, let me walk you to your car."

"Thanks."

The morning smog cloud hadn't burned off yet. On days like these tourists often assumed that the day was going to remain overcast or even rain. By noon the sun would be out and tearing through LA's thin ozone. Angela had a BMW, 3 series. I was impressed with the shape she kept the car in. She'd upgraded the rims but didn't go overboard with the flash, which in my opinion ruins most cars' aesthetic.

"So you dig German engineering, eh?"

"Eh? That's Canadian isn't it?"

"Yes, 'Eh' is Canadian and 'huh?' is American."

"Well I don't use 'huh.'"

She crossed arms pretending to be mad. I took a step closer to show I was no pushover.

"And you will never hear me say 'eh' again... lady."

"Come on, let's go get breakfast, Scarface. I'll drop you at your car later."

She punched me lightly on the shoulder. I walked around the car trying not to grin too hard.

As embarrassed, as I was to admit it, I confessed that I was craving IHOP pancakes. To my delight she was on the same page.

"Okay," I said, "If you had to pick—say, on a desert island, what would it be: IHOP or Denny's?"

"I love my Grand Slam breakfast, but it would have to be IHOP."

"Right on! You're the best."

"How would you know about that?" she inquired with serious eyes.

"Well, I don't mean anything. I mean the IHOP. I wasn't being sexual. Not that you said or even thought—"

"Relax, brother, I'm just playing."

"Girl, you should be an actress. You scared the-you-know-what out of me. Give me a minute to catch my breath."

"Now who's the actor? Catch your breath, my foot."

We drove along Fountain Avenue as far as we could before easing down to Santa Monica Boulevard where the IHOP stood proudly. A friendly Latino man with a twenty mile wide grin valet parked the Beamer. Angela gave the hostess the name of Louis-Louis.

"Now you're trying to be cute," I said.

"Don't you think I'm cute? I thought that little heart you were drawing was, I don't know, because you thought I was cute."

"I categorically deny drawing any such thing," I pouted. "It was simply a cross section of a leaf magnified one hundred times. I have a thing for biology."

"Biology, I'd have thought you had a thing for women. Oh well."

"Vocalist and a comedian are we?"

I tried not to look at her as she smiled at me.

"And yes, you are cute, I suppose."

Just then the hostess called my new name. "Louis-Louis. Party of two? Louis-Louis?"

Angela nearly fell over laughing when I raised my hand like a student, acknowledging that this ridiculous name was mine. An elderly couple waiting for their table looked at me with pity in their eyes.

I ordered the Passport Breakfast, which has been one of the top three breakfasts in North America for decades. I may not be able to show any valid documentation, but I truly believe it in my heart. The Passport has pancakes, sausage, bacon and eggs the way you want em.' It is paradisiacal, to say the least. Angela ordered the Rooty Tooty Fresh and Fruity, no doubt unaware that she looked as cute as a mouse's ear when she said it. It was basically the same as the Passport, only you got to choose a fruity topping for the pancakes. She went with blueberries.

"Good choice. You know, blueberry pie is my favorite type of pie."

"Do they actually have blueberries in Canada? I thought it'd be too cold."

"Oh I can hardly contain the laughter over here Angela, please stop."

"I like that you call me Angela and not Ang' or Angie."

"I'm glad you like."

"What about you? Do you like Louis or do you prefer Lou?"

She sat low in her chair with her elbows on the table leaning forward so her chin hovered two inches above her clasped hands. It gave the effect that she was hanging on my every word. What a doll.

"I prefer Lou, except when you say 'Louis.'"

"Oh a charmer. Momma told me to watch out for boys like you."

"Boys?" I reply with raised eyebrows.

"Oh pardon me, men like you."

"That's better."

She rolled her eyes and shook her head. We smiled at each other over our coffee mugs.

"Again, I want to say how sorry I am about your equipment Angela."

"It's all right. It's not your fault. Besides, I've had a brainstorm."

"Oh yeah?" The fog of guilt that surrounded me began to lift.

"Oh yeah, I have a proposition for you."

"Proposition is a good word."

"Why don't you find my gear for me?"

"Excuse me?"

"Hear me out. You have connections; bands that come in, other practice studios and so on. Why not use those resources and track down our stuff?"

"Angela there are trained professionals that do that jazz. I'm just a drum kit drummer. I can't even play the bongos."

"Huh?"

"You said huh?" I smiled.

"Whatever, but what do the bongos have to do with.. ?"

"Nothing, I'm just saying I wouldn't know how to find..."

"I have money. Well, I can get money from my producer and he can go to the label and get you some money. We'd hire you as a detective... dude."

It was dangerous how well she could sell.

"No offense, brother, but I know Mike isn't paying you what he should be paying a brother."

"I won't argue with you there."

"Play P.I. for a few days until you go back to work. What do you say?"

"I say that with those eyes of yours you could crack any witness on any witness stand any day, talk any jumper down from a building, and smile a rich man out of his money."

"Okay, okay slow your roll. So you'll do it. How much scratch do you think you'll need?"

"Jim Rockford use to charge two hundred a day plus expenses. I love that you say 'scratch.' I do too by the way."

"Do you mean Rockford Files? Aren't you a little young for that reference? My older brothers use to watch that show."

"I've always been a fan of things late 60's and 1970's. I may have been born in the wrong era." I smiled.

"Retro brother, huh? Now having said that you ain't getting no two hundred a day."

"Plus expenses," I added.

"Sorry, Bub. Bring it on down."

"One twenty a day flat...and I'm firm on that."

"Done," she said. We shook across the table.

"Cool, but one last thing; you did say 'huh' earlier. What's up with that?"

Chapter 5

I rolled out of bed around 9:30 a.m. After a short jog followed by push-ups and sit-ups, I hit the shower. I tend to exercise more nowadays seeing as I'm not playing any organized sports. Next I called Angela and asked her for an equipment list plus serial numbers if she had them. I also asked for any distinguishing features: stickers, dents scratches, marijuana butts or roaches in any hidden compartments. She had more information than the average musician would. I took the insert map out of my Thomas Brothers guide map and spread LA out on my coffee table. With a black marker I put an X over the LA Practice Joint. Then I circled what I believed was a 25 mile radius around the shop. Although being raised on the metric system I may have been looking at kilometers. Within this area were a dozen or more pawnshops I was going to hit.

I added a little water to the old gal before moving over the hill back into Hollywood. The first five shops turned up zip. It was now early afternoon and the sun was fully making her presence known. I moved westward at a crawl along Santa Monica Boulevard as it was difficult to read some of the businesses signs. Sadly for the working transvestite hookers my pace and roving eye gave them false hope that I was a customer. A few would pout coyly while others threw mock tantrums as I rolled by.

Not long after this I found my mark. A flop by the name of Jim's Pawnshop sat wedged between a lingerie shop and a bakery. A little bell sounded as I entered. I imagined that I was on a game show and the bell signified that I'd successfully made it through the transvestite gauntlet. The shop was not much different from her cousin stores; all kinds of stuff piled all over the place with ridiculously high price tags attached to it. If I were looking for gear dating back to 1972, Jim's would be the place to shop. I'd have to make a note of that. Behind the counter stood a 6-foot 150-pound Japanese-American woman with no incisor teeth. I put her at thirty-eight years old.

"Hi, handsome, welcome to Jim's. I'm Jimmy. You probably thought Jimmy was a man, a white man, right? Yes you did, I can tell. This is my place. I have the best prices in town. Yes I do." She took a short breath.

"We've been here 12 years me and my husband Frank. Frank is the white guy that everyone thinks is Jim." Her laugh was a high pitch cackle.

I wanted her to stop talking so I could look the place over and move on but I noticed something odd about her. Sweat gathered at her upper lip yet the air conditioner was blasting just fine. The corners of her mouth trembled as did her hands. Her eyes seemed to plead for something. I missed this at the outset as her glasses had the thickest lenses I believe a lens company could possibly manufacture. Jimmy was just short of terrified. I haven't been in this city long but I've seen enough news programs and movies to know a robbery in progress when I see one. The overhead mirror revealed a hooded figure below the counter at Jimmy's knees. Poor Jimmy. I winked at her and then took over the dialogue.

"Sorry, lady, you talk too much, I'm outta here." I winked at her again hoping she caught my act. A quick visual sweep told me volumes. The back door to the shop was bright red. More importantly it was ajar. I went back out the way I came in. I grabbed an elderly black woman by the shoulders and calmly but with some heat said, "Call the police. There's a man in that store with a gun to the clerk's head."

"What? Let go of me."

"Just do it. I'm a cop. I'd call it in myself but my cruiser is two blocks from here."

"Good place for it," she said and pulled away from me.

"Please!" I yelled and hit the ground running. I passed five store fronts before I got to the corner. I took a hard right and accelerated toward the alley. I was horsing it now. Another hard right put me into the alley's heart. Five store backs and I was at the red door. I approached like a man walking a tight rope. I spied through the opening. The hooded man stood the same height as Jimmy but he had seventy pounds on her. If I were a sniper I'd have dropped him right then and there. I am not a sniper, so that was out. I lied to the woman in the street about being a cop, but I wasn't lying about the guy having a gun. He held in his left hand what I'd guess was a .38 Special and was poking Jimmy in the lower back with it. Here was Lou; not a cop or even a real private investigator and totally unarmed. But I liked Jimmy, so I was going in.

The two of them were roughly twenty feet ahead of me at the cash register with their backs partially to me. A quick turn of the head and I'd be made. I'd have to risk it. Jimmy finally got the cash drawer open. The thug pushed her aside and went ferociously at the loot. With his attention elsewhere I crept in and pulled the door to, but did not close it. I flattened myself between two floor-to-ceiling bookshelves that held everything but books. Cash spilled in and out of the gunman's pockets. He turned to Jimmy and shouted at her.

"Not much here, bitch. D'ya gotta safe?"

"No, no safe," she whimpered.

"Bullshit! Where is it?"

I knocked on the wall beside me. "Who's that? Who the hell is that lady?"

Jimmy screamed that she didn't know. "Come on," he yelled, grabbing her by the hair.

I inhaled and waited. When they got to me Jimmy walked past without looking at me. I jumped in between them grabbing the gun with both hands. I'd hoped he'd give it up because of the element of surprise, but the element wasn't heavy enough. With my back to him we wrestled. I put my foot against Jimmy's back and shoved her through the red door. She let out a yelp and tumbled to the alley's pavement. Jimmy was safe and I had a lock on the gun. The gun went off. It was particularly loud in the tight area. A shiny trombone sang as the bullet tore into her. Shame, I like trombones. I smashed his wrist over my knee four times before the gun hit the floor and slid to the back door. He figured I'd try to turn and fight so he threw an arm around my neck. Before he could get a good purchase there, I ran us back toward the cash register. Away from the gun, Lou, that's it. I could smell hard liquor on his breath. We'd traveled fifteen feet when the back door swung open. Hooray, some Law, I thought. But it was Jimmy cussing and skip-running down the hall toward us, firing at will. Like Siamese twins we dove over the counter and hit the ground rolling. Jimmy kept firing in our direction. Bullets whizzed over our heads and tore into the floor around us. Over the gun chatter I heard my wrestling partner shout, "Crazy bitch."

I tried to count how many shots she'd taken but lost track in the excitement. The fact is in between shots, me and the hooded guy threw short punches and elbows at each other. Finally the pleasant clicking sound of a talked out gun reached my ringing ears. We panted in unison on the floor. I now had a clear view of his acne-covered face. Two seconds passed before we exchanged that universal look that men and dogs exchange just before trying to resume the fight. We locked on again and rolled over the splintered floor. Just then some Law came barreling through both doors.

"Police! Drop it, lady, and you assholes freeze!" We were already frozen.

"Drop it, lady!"

Jimmy stared at me but I know she didn't see me. She shook slightly as she held the gun.

"Drop it, lady, I won't tell you again!"

"Don't shoot her!" I yelled.

"Put a sock in it brother, and stay down."

The slightest movement on Jimmy's part and I was afraid they'd put her down, seriously.

"Jimmy, do as they say, honey," I said calmly.

"Whack the bitch, she's crazy," my wrestling partner shouted. He 'was met by a chorus of 'be quiets.'

"Jimmy, is that your name?" the lead officer asked. "Put the gun down, Jimmy. Come on, that's it."

She moved the gun hand slightly as if to raise it. The room filled with shouts. I joined in, in a last ditch attempt. "Guys, she's out, she's out! Don't shoot!"

A big cop bursting out of his uniform around the middle crept up behind her and took her gun easily while another cop subdued her. A couple other cops folded me and the gunman into various shapes before moving us outside. The gunman swore that it was me that tried to knock over the store but when Jimmy came out of her stupor she backed me all the way. As the cops were stuffing the hooded man into the cruiser he resisted long enough to call to me, "Hey hero, how did you know I was going to whack the chink?"

He received a nightstick in the ribs for the comment. An onlooker voiced her approval at the cop's action. The cop who earlier disarmed Jimmy came up to me and put a heavy hand on my shoulder.

"It's nice to see people getting involved once in a while. But your play was plain suicide. Did you just react or are you one of those bungee jumping, skateboarding thrill seeker types?"

"I don't trust bungees or their jumpers and skateboards are for kids, silly rabbit. I'm just a guy that likes to play drums, officer." I don't think he knew how to take the drum part of my response. When he took his arm off of me I thought I might float away. After some thought he asked me how I came to be in the shop at that time and what was I shopping for. I told him I was interested in trombones. He asked why not drums and I told him I already had drums. He told me that there was a trombone in the back but that it took some lead during the robbery. Jimmy overheard the conversation and disappeared into the store. Two seconds later she came skip-jumping out the door with trombone in tow.

"Here, here take it for saving my life," she squeaked.

"Do you boys need to take this down to the lab?" I asked.

"Lab? What do you think this is, *C.S.I.*? We already dug the slug out of her. She's all yours if you want her."

I turned to Jimmy. "Thanks, Jimmy. We had fun didn't we?"

She hugged me, giggling and jumping up and down. The cop walked away shaking his head. "Only in LA, only... in...Los-friggin'-Angeles."

After the cop trudged off, I quickly asked Jimmy about my list of gear. She didn't need to look at the serial numbers to know she didn't have what I was after. Ten minutes later, having pried Jimmy off of me I was driving east on Fountain Avenue instead of Santa Monica this time. My new trombone sat on the passenger seat as proudly as she could what with having taken lead earlier. I'd clean her up when I got home... after two beers and a clubhouse sandwich. Then I planned to document the day's events and plot out the following day. As I snaked through the traffic I visualized the page. I'd write case number one at the top and across from it I'd write Angela's name as she was the client. I wouldn't even consider drawing any hearts this time. A few lines down I'd write 'pawnshops' in block letters and list the ones I hit under that. Across from that I'd have a progress report column with comments. For today I'd write the letters S.F.A. which stand for: sweet f*** all.

Chapter 6

With yesterday behind me and today in front of me I was ready to rock. I added a few extra push-ups and sit-ups, seeing as I skipped a run. I sang excerpts of various Commodores and Earth, Wind & Fire songs, as I don't know complete lyrics to any one song. This whole private eye business was far more exciting than my regular gig. I had to keep reminding myself that beyond watching *Rockford Files* and *Magnum, P.I.* re-runs, I knew precious little about this business, and that I'd soon have to return to my regular nine-to-five, if you could call it that. I called Angela to catch her up. Always keep the client informed, I should think. I got her voicemail. I was about to hang up but ended up leaving a half-baked message.

After a homemade power shake I was out of the gate like a greyhound pooch. I'll never admit to being afraid of pawnshops after what went down yesterday but I thought today I'd search a category a little more familiar to me. I'd wrestle the pawnshop alligators tomorrow...maybe. On the docket today: rival rehearsal studios. I personally don't consider them to be rivals, but my boss is always carrying on about them in this way, so like a team player I went along with it. I decided to do the San Fernando Valley before working my way into Hollywood. The farther I motored out the 101 freeway the stronger the needle in a haystack feeling I got. However, I was doing something as opposed to doing nothing, and that's saying... something.

The first stop was the city of Woodland Hills. A healthy amount of studio musicians and rising star actors flop in this area. The neighborhoods are quiet and clean and many homes sit on properties the size that a gardener can make a decent buck. The musicians' union operated the first space I went to which meant the place was nice and the prices were high. The guy running the counter was obviously an English literature major, maybe even unpublished writer frustrated by his station.

"I haven't the slightest notion as to what you are accustomed, young man, but I assure you that at this establishment we do not entertain artists who would even consider possessing stolen equipment."

I wouldn't put money on it but that sure sounded like a run-on sentence to me. Best not to bring it up at this juncture, was my thinking. I did, however, need to relate to this scholar on his level, or at least close to it.

"Dear sir, I am accustomed to the known fact that some artists are not unlike a few bad apples in that they come by their instruments, or gear, if you will, ah, ah, dishonestly. I mean, this is Los Angeles after all, man." Take that, I thought. Either I had him on the ropes or he was appalled at my verbiage, for he said nothing. I trudged on. "Am I to understand that your claim is that you know the origin of each, every, and all pieces of equipment that cross that threshold and into this burgh?"

My tongue now had a headache.

"Precisely, and this is no 'burgh,' as you put it."

I needed another way in. It was time to take myself down a notch. I needed to relinquish power, as talk show therapists say—kissing ass, in other words. "Look, I'm sorry, man. I didn't mean you or this fine establishment any disrespect. It's just the pressure of the job. You see, I work in a place like this in Hollywood. Of course, my place is non-union and quite dumpy compared to all of this." I spread my arms and looked around wide eyed as a child might upon entering the gates of Disneyland. "You and I aren't so far apart. We're in the rehearsal space trenches, man. They don't appreciate what we do. We're underpaid and often waylaid. Hell, listen to your elocution, not to mention diction! You should be on the lecture circuit doing book signings, the whole nine yards...my good man!"

'My good man' meticulously removed his wire rimmed spectacles. He tucked them gingerly in his breast pocket. From the depths of his pomposity rose a minute smile. I got him.

"A thankless job it can be. I most certainly will not argue that." He sighed. "Be thankful you don't work with some of this lot. One would expect decent behavior from symphony musicians and respected jazz practitioners. Such is not the case. What do you mean you're out of Yamaha music stands?' 'Why don't you carry violin strings?' 'The Steinway piano in room two has a sharp E key.'" He raised his voice. "As if you could tell, you Berkelee School of Music bastard!" He paused, deflated, and then pounded the table with a bony fist and a curse. He'd feel that later. With an apology and another sigh he walked to the back dragging his feet as he went. When he re-emerged he carried a leather bound log book. We found only one band that had rented a storage locker that would jive with my search. He popped the lock and let me have a look. One amplifier was the right make but the serial numbers were way off. I thanked him and gave him a copy of my list as well as a contact number. He spoke to my back as I was leaving.

"This business of ours can ruin a man. If you have dreams, young man, I suggest you follow them."

I promised that I would and made a hasty exit as his eyes were filling with water. I'm not particularly good at the grown men and tears gig. As the drumming detective my next stop was Valley Jam House which sat on the Sherman Oaks/Van Nuys border. As I walked through the door I was slapped in the face by such a strong marijuana smell that I was forced to grab the counter for stability. A sturdy gent in a black and blue plaid hooded sweat shirt with cut off sleeves sat at the helm. Dirty stubbed feet in five-year-old Birkenstocks sat atop a messy knotty pine desk. It appeared that in the 1990's he'd taken a dull knife and made his favorite jeans into cut-off shorts. Long black greasy hair splayed over his heavy shoulders. His mouth and left eye were smiling. Good pot. I couldn't tell what the right eye was doing as it had a navy blue pirate patch over it. The smile remained fixed so I threw words first.

"Excuse me man. The name's Lou and I work down in Hollywood at the-"

But that's as far as I got before he burst with laughter and exhaled a huge cloud of smoke.

"Sorry dude, I'm not laughing at you, or the fact you live in Hollywood."

"Work in Hollywood."

"Right, sorry it's just this killer weed man. Whoooo!"

"I can dig it."

"You like?" Offering me a pull on a joint he had hidden beneath the desk.

"In my youth I like. Anyway the reason I'm here is we had a robbery at the Practice Joint and I'm stuck with running down some of this gear."

"It sucks to be you, Mack. That's a job for someone like..." He looked at the ceiling and waved the joint around in a circle searching for an example. I got tired of waiting.

"Columbo?"

"Who? Ah, Nathan Fillian, dude who plays Castle on the show of the same name." I'd totally baffled him. He knew what to do with the joint, however. He took another pull. I handed him my list of gear. He lifted the patch off his eye to read the list. After far too much scrutiny he handed the list back to me.

"I got nuthin.' But I will tell you this though, Mack; I heard about what happened to you guys down there. At least I think I did..." Both Birkenstocks now moved in unison like windshield wipers. "No, that was Greg's in Long beach. Oh yeah, it was—no that was Vinny's up in Bakersfield. I'm sorry, Mack, the memory's shot. All that bad weed in the early 2000's. I got good shit now though. Are you sure you won't..."

"Retired," I responded. "And what's with calling me Mack every three seconds?"

"Isn't that your name? You said it was." He waved it off as if a fly was buzzing around him. "Suit yourself on the non smokeage. Say... there is this, though. If I were looking for stolen stuff I'd look at Dave Abbott."

"Is that the guy who used to play keyboards with Napoleon's Fallopian Opus?"

"That's the same dude, dude. Dy'a ever hear about what he really does to make dough? He steals and fences the very kind of jazz you're talking about."

"No kidding?"

"Hey, on hemp's honor. If I lie, stick a reefer in my eye."

"Nice little poem." I say keeping it friendly.

"Thanks," he said, proud.

I told him that I didn't think Abbott would add up to much and thanked him for his time. This was not entirely true, but I didn't want him remembering me if asked. The fact of the matter was I knew of Dave Abbott's reputation quite well. He's every musician's public enemy number one. Even if only half of the rumors are true he's still responsible for ripping off thousands of dollars' worth of gear over the years. Why he has never been caught is a mystery. Some say he's connected. This is why I blew off Mr. Birkenstocks. I don't need any connected heat on my case.

Back in 2007, Abbott's band was on their way up. They just got signed to a new record label with heavy financial backers. They had limos, radio play, wine, women and lousy songs, in my opinion. Just before going on tour the band started fighting and called it a day. The record label wanted their invested money from the band and put the squeeze on Abbott. It is believed that Dave began selling off gear to pay his debt. Running out of his own supply he began ripping off other bands' gear and selling it. The kicker is that the record label had two other main artists that simply weren't putting up the numbers. Investors got nervous and pulled out. The label threw in the towel. All bets were off and nobody came collecting. Abbott was a free man. But greed does what greed does and Abbott became accustomed to the stolen property bullion. He kept making our tough lives tougher. Mr. Abbott was now my prime suspect and would have been from day one, were I a real private investigator.

Chapter 7

In addition to all the types of music one can choose to play, there are also different types of musicians one can choose to be. For example, one might be a studio musician and just cut CD's, jingles and soundtracks. Or one might decide they only play live, or play four string ukuleles at house parties. One might be a songwriter (where the real money is) and never perform. For the most part, I myself am a sideman. Somebody has some material and they have shows coming up or a recording date and they need a drummer, they call someone like me—or me, if I'm lucky.

Guys and dolls like me are the guns for hire. Line up the show and we'll knock em' down. When I get hired for a new show I like to get my hands on the songs as soon as possible and get to work. I'll fly through the tunes quickly and start with the hardest piece. It's often the one they'll ask for, in an audition situation. The most exciting part for me is when the most difficult piece is committed to memory. No chart necessary.

I now had that same sideman adrenaline rush, in that I could feel in my bones that Dave Abbott knocked over my work place. This drummer was going to burn him down.

Musicians and crime fighters all over Southern California would thank me and lie about knowing me. The old gal was on automatic pilot all the way home as I was busy grinning like an idiot through traffic. Even my cantankerous garage door couldn't pry the smile from my mug. As I waited patiently for the door to rise, a shape flashed across my rear view mirror. Kids; always up to something, or appearing that way at least. I pulled into my usual spot next to my neighbor's 1966 Cougar XR7. I'd only seen her once when Lexington, the owner, pulled the car cover off her for me to see. She was cherry, as they say. Windows up and steering wheel club fixed I stepped out of the ol' gal.

A strong perfume hit my nostrils. When I got out an attractive Asian woman in her mid-twenties stood by the trunk of my car.

"Whoa, you startled me. Hi I'm Lou."

She held a pink purse shaped like an old army trunk only it was so small that when she held in both hands only four fingers and two thumbs fit on the strap. Her pink sweater was ribbed and hadn't complained once so far about the torso it was housing...And that made two of us. I couldn't make the brand of the jeans but I think the company should offer her a modeling contract.

"I'm Hi," she said, "and I don't mean stoned. It's short for Hyacinth." A petite hand left the trunk and shook like a much bigger hand. "I'm sorry that I startled you."

"Oh no, no it's fine. I'm fine," I said giving her hand back.

"My car won't start. I wonder if you could help me."

"Your wish is my wish."

"Excuse me?"

"Never mind." I tell her. "Which way is it to your ride?" I ask.

Naturally Angela is the only one for me, even if she doesn't know it yet, but the way Hyacinth clicked along in her little pumps just-so was really putting the pressure on my loyalties. The beat up 80's Chevy Caprice Classic she claimed to own should have sent off some sort of warning bell in my head but no such luck. A half step before the car a half stick of dynamite went off in my skull. My bell was ringing. Someone sapped me from behind like the true sap I was. I vaguely remember the pavement rushing quickly toward my face. Somewhere between the conscious and subconscious lay Lou Crasher totally unconscious. Totally crashed.

A bump in the road woke me. I didn't have to be a real P.I. to know that I was in the trunk of the Chevy. At least it wasn't a Smart Car. I decided not to attempt picking the lock or tunneling through the back seat. Knowing one's limitations saves pride and prevents panic. I'd wait it out and see who my captors were and what their plan was. I could hear the muffled voices of three to four people mixed in with obnoxious punk rock music. The car rolled over some rough terrain like pot holes or train tracks briefly then skidded to a stop. The music quit. Two doors open. Two doors close. Footsteps. No dialog, just the sound of dancing keys. I closed my eyes and the trunk opened. There wasn't much difference in light through my lids. Hands grabbed at me and I feigned grogginess so I could count numbers and hope for an opening.

"Come on, bitches get him outta there."

"Shut up, Travis, we are. He's heavy, man."

"You wimps, I'd do it myself but this prick busted my hand. Okay, good, hold him steady." "Hey there, asshole," he says to me.

The pimply faced kid from the alley, now known as Travis, slapped me with his good hand. "Snap out of it, man. I want you to see what you got comin.'"

I kept up my dizzy act as Travis pulled his hand back to slap me again. Using the two guys holding my arms back as leverage I kicked Travis square in the family jewels. He went down chirping like a budgie. The man on my left reefed so hard on my arm I thought my shoulder was going to pop. The other guy fed me a solid punch to the gut. I doubled over. A familiar pink trunk purse came rapidly into view and caught me on the nose. My eyes watered as my heart pounded angry blood into my veins.

This in turn fueled my adrenaline motor. I was categorically pissed. Pitching forward forced them to let go of my arms. I fell on Travis, my hands having no problem finding his throat. My grip tightened on his neck as though it were an orange I intended making into fresh squeezed juice. His eyes popped open wide with terror. I began to chuckle as I tasted the blood from my bleeding nose. The trunk purse came in for another shot. I released one hand from Travis's throat and easily pried it from Hyacinth's hand. My plan was to drive the purse through Travis's face and out the back of his skull when Travis's other two pals pulled me off of him. I rolled away from their kicks as best as I could. Travis was crying and cussing in the dirt. A boot made by the Caterpillar Company caught me in the stomach. I was able to hold onto it. Twisting the foot back and forth I heard three cracks before he got loose. He limped toward the car. The other guy and Hyacinth helped

Travis over to the Caprice.

"This ain't over, asshole. I know where you live! I fucking know where you live!"

I closed my eyes against the tire-spent gravel. Travis just made a huge mistake: he left me alive!

Chapter 8

I felt like finding the coziest looking rock I could lay my hands on, using it as a pillow and catching as close to forty winks as possible. Ah, but I decided against it. I had a home and all I had to do was get to it. I knew I was still in the San Fernando Valley because there are some things a guy just knows. Exactly where in the Valley was something a guy didn't know. I started to make tracks downhill toward the freeway lights. Once close enough to read the off ramp sign my eagle eye told me I was in the city of Chatsworth— California's pornography capital, is what some people claim. True or not this little tidbit wasn't going to help me any. Barring any freeway traffic the old gal would have me home in fifteen minutes. She wasn't here, so that was out. Although never a math whiz I managed a quick count of all my fingers, toes and more precious body parts. The math added up. My watch was gone (all twenty five dollars' worth of it), but to my surprise I still had my wallet with all its contents content—including my sixteen bucks. I was livin' with an apostrophe 'n.' This was now the smart money and the smart money said for me to walk to the nearest gas station and have a taxi pull me out of this porno town.

Hopefully the walk was no more than twenty minutes in length as my weary bones would have me searching for the comfortable pillow rock if I tried to push it past minute twenty. Moving slightly faster than a snail in her teens I'd been mobile nine minutes when a late model Dodge Ram truck passed me from the rear then skidded to a halt thirty feet in front of me. Reverse lights piped up and the truck rolled slowly back to stop beside me.

"Lou? Is that you?"

"Mackerel! Are you ladies a sight for sore bones."

"What are you doing out here? And who tap danced on your pretty face?"

"A couple o' punks who don't see things the way I do. Oh and there was a woman with them too."

"There usually is, Lou. Hop in."

"Kat, Tami you guys are looking awesome as usual."

"Well Lou, you've looked better."

"Tell me about it. So what's up? Are you gals any closer to opening up that gym of yours?"

"Three weeks tomorrow, babe," Kat said with a high five slap to Tami. "In fact, that's why we're out here. I recently bought a two bedroom condo down the road. Tami is renting a room from me."

"That's right, Lou. It's awesome and we're within walking distance from the gym," Tami added.

"Right on, right on girls, I'm proud of you."

"Never mind your pride, just be there for the opening."

"Oh for sure, Kat, you make it sound like I'd miss it or something." My phony grin hurt my head.

"Well who knows, maybe you'll be wrestling with your new friends," she teased.

"You're gonna pay for that, don't think you won't." I shifted so I could stretch my arm across the bench seat back. "So the Derby twins are finally going to open up shop."

"Don't start, Lou. You know how we hate that Derby twin crap," Tami said, punching my shoulder, to which I overreacted with a painful wince.

"Oh my god, I'm sorry Louis."

"I'm just playing. I'm all right."

"Fool," she said, to which Kat agreed. "So are we taking you home or are you going to grace our couch with your presence?"

"Well since you used the 'c' word—couch— I think I'll head home if you don't mind the extra miles."

"Don't you mean kilometers, Canadian boy?"

"Oh you dames are hilarious. Are you guys going to start with a little standup at your opening?"

"Ooh, somebody's a little testy," Tami said.

"Easy Tami, he did get his ass ki—I mean he did have a tussle tonight."

"Thank you, Kat. You always were the more sensitive twin." That got me an even harder punch to the shoulder.

Katherine and Tamika were not twins. In fact neither of them had 'Derby' as a surname either. Furthermore they didn't look related, as Kat is Asian and Tami is African-American. However their body types are practically identical; thick black hair flows to the mid-point between the shoulder blades; and rarely is one seen without the other, as they are kickboxing personal trainers who train together. Back when the movie *Swingers* was out and swing dancing had its resurgence, Kat and Tami often spent Friday and Saturday nights cutting a rug at the Derby night club in Hollywood. This was how they came by their detested nickname.

We were working out at a family workout gym in Burbank two years back when the girls first hatched the idea of opening their own place. The three of us were each pedaling our stationary bikes to nowhere when almost in unison the girls whispered the gym idea. Voices were kept low as the girls were employees of the gym at the time. I threw out all of the necessary support words until my cardio level prohibited further dialogue. When I showed up the following day for a back and biceps workout I found the girls with a handful of other staff members gathered around the front door looking bewildered and angry.

"This movie doesn't look good. What's up?"

"Take a look. See for yourself, Lou," Tami mumbled. I shaded the glare and looked through the window to see what looked like an empty warehouse. I took a step back to check that I had the correct address. I had. The gym was completely empty, save a single ten pound barbell.

"Holy shit, ladies."

"That's what we said. This entire gym was a scam. Now I know why these bastards pushed us so hard to hang clients up on the long term memberships."

"Um-hm. How could we not see this coming?" Kat asked.

"Because you're honest," a tiny lady with dreadlocks replied. "I live upstairs from the gym. At around 4 o'clock in the morning two big semi-trucks pulled up and a bunch of guys, big guys, loaded all of the equipment into the trucks. They were done in under an hour. I thought maybe they were repo-men or something but from what I'm hearing now is that they move all over the country set up shop, get memberships and haul ass in under a month. I bet you ladies had a check or two coming to you?"

"No, we got our checks two days ago."

"Well I suggest you line your birdcage with it 'cause if you took it to the bank the bank's going to have news for you."

Nobody said anything as we knew the woman's words to be true. "Well if this isn't a sign for you gals to go ahead with your gym I don't know what is," I said as cheerily as possible. The dread-locked lady said she'd become a member in a heartbeat.

For the rest of the drive home I filled the girls in on what I'd been up to. Naturally they were worried, especially when I told them about Dave Abbott, who incidentally they had heard of. As we pulled in front of my building, Kat shoved the truck into park and asked me what I planned to do about my friends who kidnapped me.

"I'm not really one for the revenge game, girls, but I do need these guys off my back if I'm going to play Magnum P.I." They waited for me to elaborate. " Magnum was a television show in the 80's shot in Hawaii—"

"We've seen a re-run or two, Louis. What about the kidnappers?"

"I'm going to have to call on an old friend," I finished.

Chapter 9

I don't know if I'd exactly call Jake a friend, but he is definitely someone who can be counted on. Reliability is certainly one element of friendship, but I doubt that also living in slight fear of a friend is a normal element. I know very little about Jake, and to be honest, I think it's best for me that way.

I met him over a year ago. I'd only just completed music school when I had a gig forty five minutes north of LA. After the show, I pulled into Bart's Liquor store for some freeway munchies, just next to a black Kia something or other. A slim Latina woman of about nineteen sat looking nervous in the Kia's passenger seat. I nodded to her for no other reason than courtesy. Her nervous eyes left the storefront for under a second to meet mine before swinging back to the front door. I tried not to think of the countless horror stories I'd heard in Vancouver about Los Angeles before moving here. Two large garbage cans propped the front doors open. As I was stepping past them the horn of the Kia honked four times rapidly. "Shit!" I said as the man with a gun in his gloved hand moved the gun off of the counterman's face to level it at me. Suddenly the horror stories came flooding into my brain. I raised my hands automatically. "Down on the floor, asshole," the gunman shouted at me.

The counterman, a thickly built brother who looked far too calm shook his head at me to ignore the command. I don't know why but I began to feel calm when I saw the counterman's eyes. In fact, this dude seemed so cool that I felt that it was he who was in control of the situation.

"I said down on the floor, *brutha*. And you, fill up this fucking bag, counter boy."

The opposing counterman yelled for me to get out. He didn't have to tell me twice. A shot went off. I sprinted to the old gal and fired her up. When I looked up the Latina girl had a gun of her own leveled at me. I raised one hand and feigned raising the other when I slammed the automatic gear shift on the floor into reverse. I was now gunning it toward the front doors with no real plan. The gunman raised his gun toward my back window but was forced to hesitate. I'd just nailed both garbage cans and sent them his way. He jumped over one and half stumbled over the second. As he was gaining his balance, the clerk cleared the counter and tackled the gunman. I was forced to lock my brakes up so as not to run both men over. The store linoleum was slick under my '65's shoes. I was hardly in control. One or both bodies stopped my tires' momentum. I was half in half out of the store.

As I got out the Kia came to life and accelerated backward. She screeched to a halt perpendicular to me. She screamed in Spanish to whom I guessed was her boyfriend or husband. Bonnie and Clyde they were not. She waved the gun but wasn't really pointing it at anyone or anything in particular. I ducked down to see the gunman pinned beneath my back tires. I couldn't have planned a better outcome. He called me what I believe in Spanish translates to 'homosexual' in English. Who I didn't see was the cashier dude from the store. The woman's screaming became louder and then stopped abruptly. I popped my head up to see the counterman walking around the Kia toward me. He carried two guns in his hands. That would be the gunman's and his gal's. It was safe to get up. He helped me to my feet.

"The name's Jake. Thanks for the help. Are you hurt?"

"No, not at all. My heart's beating two hundred miles an hour but that's about it. My name's Lou. Lou Crasher." He gave my hand a shake that made me wonder if I'd ever play drums again. Jake only had ten or twelve pounds on me but he looked far more dangerous than even Hollywood could make a guy look.

"What did you do to my Marianna, you pigs? Marianna! Answer me! Get me the fuck out of here," the gunman shouted.

"Better pull forward slowly Lou."

When I sat back in my car the gunman screamed in pain. I pulled off him slowly as directed then shut the old gal down. Jake hauled the man to his feet, and then came through his jaw with a right. It was effortless but the man's head flew back and forth as if it were held to his shoulders by a rubber band.

"Jesus, that's one hell of a hook, Jake. Ouch!"

"Hmm," was all he said as he let the man slump to the ground. He went in and called the cops. I checked on the girl who was sleeping peacefully on the seat. When Jake got off the phone and came back out I told him I'd hoped he didn't take the girl down the same way he had her man.

"Pressure point," was all he grunted. "The cops will be here soon. You don't have to be in this if you don't want to. I can spin you out of it—tell 'em you took off."

It felt odd to just leave the scene but at the time I was technically an illegal alien so I took the free pass. I ran over the events about ten times before I got home. With my feet up and half way into my second beer there was a knock at my door which meant someone either let this person in or the downstairs door wasn't shut all the way.

"Who is it?"

"Jake."

I opened the door. He walked past me and took a seat, scarcely looking around the place although he seemed like the type of guy who managed to take in the whole place in one glance.

"Hey, how the hell did you know where to find me?"

"Your plate."

"License plate? So you're a cop?"

"No."

I waited for him to explain but he said nothing. He just sat looking at me blankly. Thick forearms rested on his legs as he sat with military posture.

"Okay, so you're one of these secretive brothers. Mind telling me why you're here before I throw your ass out?" I was bluffing. I wouldn't know where to start in a tussle with this bull.

His eyes, although still on me, seemed to drift away. "Bart, the owner of the liquor store, has been hit three times in the last four months by the same guy. The last time he received a nasty cut to the forearm. The cops always show, but after the fact. I told Bart I'd stand in for him."

"Ah, like an undercover sting. But you don't work there, then."

He frowned at my interruption and carried on. "Tonight was my twenty-third shift and bingo, home run. You just happened to walk in at a bad time. The garbage cans were a nice touch." There was no need to tell him it wasn't entirely premeditated.

"The cops showed and took em' down. I kept you out of it, like I said."

"Didn't our buddy or the girl mention me?"

"Yes, but I told the law not to worry about you."

"Really? Just like that you can tell the cops their business? How?"

He locked up again and gave me a hard look. Social skills just weren't this cat's thing, I gathered. He handed me a card with an 800 number on it and nothing else.

"You ever get into a jam, call this number and I'll get back to you."

"Well thanks, but I don't think—" His look stopped me again. "All right thanks. And thanks for keeping me out of it." I paused. "Oh and again, nice hook, by the way."

He got up to leave.

"Hey Jake, you got a last name?"

"Yup," was all he said before letting himself out. I poured myself a double Canadian Club and Coke as is Canadian custom after surviving a friendly visit from a deadly tiger.

I kept Jake's card but never needed to use it, since he gave it to me some sixteen months back. I did hear from him on two occasions though. Once he left me a voicemail saying that he was at a gig I'd played on Sunset Boulevard at the Cat Club. It was a simple message:

"You guys are too loud for that club and you played too many notes."

It was so bizarre I played it back three times. The second time he called me at work and told me I wasn't going out on enough auditions. When I asked how he knew what I was up to he kept silent on his end. I told him that I was going to hang up as the conversation was far too stimulating. The line went dead. He beat me to it.

So now I sit here with an ice pack on my ribs, a beer at my elbow and Jake's card in my hand. I exhale deeply and dial the number. All I get is a beep. No greeting of any kind. I punched my number and hung up. After staring at my phone for ten minutes I decided I was losing my grip. Then it occurred to me that I hadn't checked on my old gal since my abduction. When the girls dropped me off I came straight upstairs. I threw on my Adidas and opened my door to see Jake standing in my hall.

"Motherf—damn, Jake! You scared the hell out of me! Are you trying to get yourself killed?" He grunted and walked past me into my place.

"I guess you got my page. It's kinda creepy you showing up so quick."

"I was around the corner. What's stirrin'?"

"I was going to check on my car."

"It's fine, I was just down there."

"So you know I was kidnapped today."

"How's does me being in your garage add up to me knowing that?"

"All right, wise guy, sit down and I'll run this thing down for you."

I gave Jake a beer, of which he drank only half, and laid out the story for him. He didn't interrupt once and had only one question.

"What do you want done to this Travis guy?"

"I just need him not to snatch me again, at least not until I find the stolen booty. And I don't mean killing anybody either, Jake. Not to suggest that's what you do, or have done, and if you have, which I'm sure you have, don't tell me about it."

"Scare him."

"Yeah, scare him like you scare me, only more so."

"Done. Three days tops."

"Really? That's it and I won't owe you anything, and you'll stop telling me how to be a drummer every six months?"

"Are you through?"

"Essentially."

"You think finding this gear will get you this girl Angela. Keep your eyes and ears open."

"Meaning what?"

He let himself out.

Chapter 10

It was eighty one degrees and clear with a slight breeze. Jake felt that any breeze at all helped clear LA's smog. Finding Travis's residence was child's play for him. He began with the Chevy Lou was picked up in. You ask enough people and somebody remembers a car, especially classics and high-end late models. Once that is established, the plate is usually the hard part except in the instance when one owns a personalized plate: KICKAZZ. Punks always find ways to put a 'look at me' label on themselves, Jake thought. Jake parked his 1967 Barracuda convertible three quarters of a block from the three story apartment building. Normally he'd have ridden his motorcycle, but today he'd be moving cargo. The peach colored building's front door was propped open so the Cort Furniture delivery men could load in easily. Two delivery workers came out as Jake approached. Their bandannas and shirts were soaked with sweat. One passed the other a water bottle. When their eyes met Jake's they nodded nervously at his menacing gaze. This was one of two common responses to his look. The other was an averting of the eye. He stepped by them, got into the elevator and pressed three. The hurried footsteps of a woman met his ears.

"Hold the elevator please. Thanks," she said, breathless as she jumped in. When she saw the muscular black man with the mean look she wanted to jump back out of the elevator. Too late. Jake raised his eyebrows and gestured to the button panel.

"Ah, one, I mean two, please. Sorry. Thanks." As they rode in silence Jake looked straight ahead so as not to frighten her. The box stopped and the door opened at the second floor.

"Ma'am, if you don't mind me saying so, you look a little like Patricia Arquette, only prettier."

She could have sworn that her legs were going to buckle when she heard the boom of his deep smooth voice with a touch of rasp. Most Hollywood leading men would kill to have a voice like that, she thought. "Thank you, I—"

But her words were cut short by the closing door. Jake cracked a quick half smile as he rode the rest of the way. He turned serious as the door opened at three: Time to go to work.

Who was that guy from the elevator? Elaine thought to herself. She played the whole thing back in her head. She'd kept her eyes ahead, as had the mystery man, but she did sneak a look out of the corner of her eye. He didn't just look strong, he looked powerful. Heavy shoulders, wide back and all kinds of veins crawling on those chiseled forearms. Ooh, and those hands. They looked like they could bend steel one minute and paint a beautiful portrait the next. She loved men's hands. She hoped she'd see him again. But who was he visiting on the third floor? She knew it was a visit, seeing as she was the building manager. Suddenly her heart sank as she thought of that slut Debbie in 302—a different guy each week. "God, I'd love to evict her," she said out loud.

He couldn't be going to see any of those elderly Russian couples could he? She chuckled as she pictured him being friends with that little shit Travis in 300. No, it had to be the slut. "I hate men," she said.

As he stepped into the hall, Jake heard the blaring music. He didn't need to be a scientist to know whose apartment it was coming from. When he got to 300 he held the door handle in his right hand and put his shoulder to the door to test its strength. This door was not going to give him trouble. He let go of the handle did a quick stretch of his shoulders and neck and resumed his position. He took a deep breath, closed his eyes and applied gradual pressure to the door. He got lower for leverage. His legs now completely flexed. The door began to creak as he was about to take another deep breath. The sound of splintering wood could not be heard over the blasting rock music. Jake walked the five steps down the corridor which brought him into the one room bachelor. He peeked into the bathroom. It was empty, good.

The punk Travis sat on a beige beer stained two-seater with his back to Jake. His greasy hair bobbed in rhythm with the music. The 26-inch television showed a porno movie with the sound off. Jake shook his head as an underage looking woman was about to satisfy two men. He walked around the couch to the television and pulled the cord out of the wall. After which he killed the stereo. Travis was out of his chair like a shot with a switchblade in his left hand.

"What the—who the fuck are you?"

"Button up your pants, Travis," Jake said calmly.

"Fuck you! What the hell are you doing here man? I'll cut you up." The way this black guy didn't seem to care about the knife scared Travis more than a little.

"Button your pants and I won't hurt you...much," Jake again calmly.

"Do you want to die, asshole? You don't think I've done guys before? Well I have, and I will again, man."

Jake stood perfectly still, perfectly relaxed; his patient look becoming impatient. Travis began to tremble. Quickly he buttoned his pants, careful not to drop the knife. "Okay, okay maybe this blade is making you nervous. I'm putting it down, all right, ya bastard, there's no more knife. Are you happy now?"

Jake walked slowly to stand in front of Travis. The smell of stale beer and cheap cigarettes met his nostrils. Travis's forehead was wet with sweat in the air conditioned room. In a quick movement Jake slapped Travis in his temple with the palm of his left hand. Travis was out before he hit the sofa. Jake walked over to the television and popped the porno DVD out of the machine and snapped it in his left hand. He then scooped Travis up, tossed him over his shoulder and carried him out. He took the stairs this time. In the lobby, the Cort Furniture guys nodded with confused looks on their faces. Jake stopped. "You guys work out of the Glendale store by the tracks?"

"Yeah, why?" the younger worker responded.

The older delivery man sighed, "That's exactly where we work, young man and we haven't seen a thing here today except the furniture on this here truck."

Jake dropped Travis into the back seat of the '67 . A large woman carrying a Chihuahua said with some sort of European accent, "What has happened to zee little man?"

"He's had too much to drink."

Her little dog growled at Jake's voice. Jake and the woman both looked at the dog, then at each other. She didn't believe the man in front of her but she wasn't going to say anything. She did like his voice though.

Chapter 11

The Percussion House is the small music school that romanced me down to Los Angeles in the first place. When I attended, the school held six hundred students, and counting. It was founded in 1995 by two local studio musicians. Sheila Moore, a talented backup singer and ghost lead vocalist, sang many a high part for metal singers in the late 90's. Her partner, and later husband, Joe Styles played dozens of lead guitar solos for big name cats on days when the big name rocker couldn't cut the big time solo for the record. Players like Joe and Sheila were paid handsomely for their silence, which is why few people knew of them, or believed musicians like them existed.

One June afternoon Joe and Sheila met and hit it off. Although vocalist and guitar player they both shared a passion for percussion. Before either could play, sing or tap a note they were shacking up in Pasadena. They loved to stay up late, sit naked on the floor and play various Latin and African drums as a sort of rhythmic foreplay, if you will. Their favorite night was Saturday when they could play louder and longer with limited neighbor complaint. It was also the night they'd allow themselves to indulge in the pleasures of marijuana and red wine. Next, out would come the big drop sheet, body paint and so on. A few years later they tied the knot and began hunting for just the right instructors for their school. With all of the ducks lined up, the school was born. All who attended knew of the weed, wine and drop sheet ritual, as the instructors weren't shy about mentioning the nights in their lectures. They were going for a sort of New Age/early 1970's type of hippie atmosphere. After all, the best players played from the heart. *Rimshot Magazine* did a piece on the school, which was how I discovered it many years later. Drums in a free love, friendly environment—sign me up.

While going to the Percussion House I became tight with one of the receptionists. Her name was Stacy Krunch. I tumbled head over it for her but she insisted that I was too young. I liked her for letting me down easy like that; what with her three puny years on me. Perhaps it was a maturity thing. I mean I was all bug-eyed, buck-toothed and pigeon toed when I stepped on LA soil those few short years ago. We keep in touch from time to time, but not like in the days when I was a student. Lives get in the way.

Stacy leapt to the forefront of my brain after I learned about Dave Abbott and his criminal activities. She had umpteen million connections. She also ran a musician's referral service on the side and rumor had it she was kicking butt. I still had the phone number from when I copied it out of the magazine. I could still see the excitement in my chicken scratch writing.

"How's my milk chocolate-y Crispy Krunch?"

"Sweet Lou Crasher, as I live and as I breathe."

"In the flesh, baby, and I'm older now. How are you?"

"Good, good." I could see her smile. "How're you doin' Lou? You must be working 'cause you haven't called my service."

"Ah, but it's never enough."

"I hear that. So what's up?" she asked.

"Have you got a minute?"

"Lou, for you I have a minute and a half."

"Ooh baby. Here goes. I don't know if you know it or not but I'm working at the LA Practice Space."

"I do now. I heard you guys got hit the other night though. How bad was it?"

"Not good. Question."

"Shoot."

"Who hit us?" I thought I might get lucky.

"What am I, a detective?"

"No, but I'm pretending to be one."

"Oh, Louis." Here it comes. "I hope there's money in it as well as the woman you're chasing."

"Stacy Krunch, I'm shocked."

"So snap out of it. Who's the broad?"

I paused, busted. "You don't know her."

"Um-hm," she said.

I proceeded to lay the meat and potatoes of the story out for her. In addition to the pawnshops and rehearsal spots, she suggested I frequent the jam session circuit as well. When I mentioned that I would keep an eye open this weekend while I was out hitting the circuit with Bobby Flye she guffawed.

"Do you still roll with that fool?"

"What can I say? He's like a brother to me."

"Yeah, a redheaded stepbrother. If you keep hanging with him you're going to be in a world o' hurt." I joined her in a laugh.

"So Stace, what do you know about Dave Abbott?"

"He'd sell his mother if he hasn't already. And if you're hangin' with him, this conversation is over."

"Settle down. Nobody's hangin' with anybody. Girl, I can't believe you'd think—"

"So believe it," she said. "What's the deal?"

"He's suspect numero uno so give me what you got."

And with a sigh she gave me Abbot's story—the abridged version.

"He had a bunch of projects on the go. He was a wheeler dealer of musicians and equipment. He got his fifteen minutes with a group named Napoleon's Fallopian or whatever they were called. You know how he stiffed his band and all that?"

"Yeah," I tell her.

"Anyway he's still around and some folks believe he's got protection."

"What do you think?" I asked.

"He's never been caught. He's never been busted. And no one's ever beat him like he deserves. And all the while everybody knows he's dirty. How do you spell connected baby?"

I whistled quietly thinking I might be in over my head.

"You be careful, Lou. If the walls start closing in you call in the serve and protect fellas, ya hear?"

"That hurt."

"So toughen up. Let me see if I have an address for him. Here, he signed out some ACDC videos back in the day and gave his girlfriend's address. Write this down, Mr. Dick, I mean detective."

"Oh you're hilarious."

"And I'll be here all week. 2055 Digby Drive over in Silverlake. Don't ask the apartment number because it's a house."

"That's it? You just give any address and you get videos?"

"He may have been shacking up there. Besides you know this is the school of love and trust."

"I thought it was love and body paint. Hey thanks so much, Stacy, you're the best."

"Don't worry about it. I was only working."

"Well, I appreciate it."

"Lou?"

"Yes dear," I say, putting some bass to my voice.

"I'm jealous."

"But I thought I was too young for—" I began, but I was talking to a dead phone line.

Chapter 12

Dave Abbott's girlfriend's place had plenty of parking out front. I eased my ride in and threw the club on the wheel. Still inside the three day period that Jake said he needed to deal with Travis and his gang of fools, I approached like a rat would a slumbering boa constrictor. I checked up and down the block two times before I made my way to the house. Set two thirds of the way back on the small lot was a tiny bungalow. Neighbors on both sides owned identical homes. The only difference was that Abbott's gal owned three large hanging baskets over her front porch. I avoided the third step in my climb as I noticed a full length split down the center of the board. The song *Poker Face* by Lady Gaga could be heard faintly through the door. I knocked and waited—nothing. I tried again, putting more knuckle into it. The door opened a few inches, the way it does in bad horror movies.

"Candy?" I called. Still the only sign of life was Lady Gaga.

"Candy?" Louder this time. I felt a little foolish shouting this into a stranger's home, but that was her name. I double checked by calling ahead and asking for her. When she said "Yes?" I hung up and made tracks over here. Now that people can take their phone numbers with them it makes it easier to reach out and touch someone. Candy Striper was her full stage name. Some four years before my arrival Candy was one of LA's hottest exotic dancers. She often made headlines in those days as her show often flirted with the obscene. Various arrests added to her fame. She rarely danced today as Jack Daniels and Father Time teamed up on her and softened her marketability. Nobody's heyday lasts forever, which is why they call them 'heydays.'

"Candy, the name's Lou. Lou Crasher. I'm looking for Dave Abbott." The door opened all the way. With one hand on top of the door Candy stood falling out of a black and red kimono. A mini Cuban cigar of the Cohiba brand jutted out of the side her mouth. She spoke out of the other side.

"What do you want with him?"

"I'm a drummer and I'm looking for a gig, actually."

"Who told you to come here?"

"A bass player."

"Cute story. This bass player have a name?"

"A dude named Colby Stakes."

"What kinda name is that? Sounds like a stage name or something," she said, taking a pull on the cigar.

"I think it's the name his mommy gave him, Candy Striper." I smiled like I was playful. She smiled back. I could see how this woman once caused scores of men to take long business lunches and rush the stages she danced on. Sadly I could also see the wear and tear the life had taken on her. She invited me in. Her place was bright and cozy.

"You sit in the love seat and I'll sit here." I got the better end of the deal as she walked over to a lime green bean bag chair. I've never looked cool sitting in those things. Before descending onto it she opened the kimono and let it fall to the floor.

"Well?" she asked.

"Ah, Miss Striper, you've dropped your robe."

"Oops," she said with a giggle and molded herself into the waiting beans. "So do you like the view or not, handsome? Don't leave a good girl hanging."

"Candy, I don't care if you were born with it, worked out for it, or paid for it. That body makes me glad to be a man." Flattery gets one somewhere was my plan.

"Ooh baby, don't stop there. Go on."

"Okay, but just one more. Dollface, I haven't seen a body like that since Pam Grier starred in *Coffy* back in the day!"

"Oh my god, can I just tell you how huge a Pam Grier fan I am? I so love her, my God." She stared at her ceiling fan, no doubt watching a movie memory.

"So what are you doing here again, ah—"

"Lou. I was actually looking for Dave. I was a big fan of Fallopian as well as Sons o' Bitches' Sons." The S.O.B.S. was another one of Abbott's early bands, which miraculously leapt into my head. "Is he here or is there a number I can reach him at?"

"Yeah, I preferred the S.O.B.S. to Fallopian myself." Her gaze returned to the ceiling fan. Just then a Jack Russell terrier burst through a cat door in the kitchen and headed straight for me at mach one speed. Five feet away from the love seat, the dog took flight and landed in my lap. Candy told me the dog's name was Josey. Josey ran up my arm and began gently nipping at my small hoop earrings.

"Ever since he was a pup he's been in love with earrings."

"He totally drives Dave crazy. It serves him right for wearing such big ass silver hoops. See I like your earrings—not too big. Just say 'no' if he bites too hard, Lou."

"How'd you come up with the name Josey," I asked?

"I named him after Clint Eastwood in the—"

"Outlaw Josey Wales, my favorite Western," I blurted.

"Ooh first Pam Grier, now Josey Wales! I could just kiss you." She struggled to get out of the bean bag chair then skipped across the floor to me.

"No, that's okay," I pleaded, but it was too late. She leapt Josey style and landed in my lap. She kissed me all over my neck and cheek. The more I tried to explain that this wasn't a good idea, the harder Josey worked at tearing the earrings out of my head. I've lived in LA awhile now, but I still wasn't ready for the dog and stripper act.

Just then Murphy of Murphy's Law kicked in. "Candy, what the fuck is this?" bellowed Dave Abbott from the threshold. Sometime during the excitement Candy's cigar had fallen on the couch and was still burning. She put her hand on it.

"Holy shit, that hurt," she said climbing off me. Dave still demanded to know what was going on.

"Oh lighten up, Dave. He's just a Pam Grier fan. You could take a page or two out of his book of taste." She marched past him to the kitchen to get ice. Her head barely came up to his sloped shoulders.

"Who the fuck is he?" he asked from an inflated chest.

I got up and stretched out a hand. "Name's Lou. I'm a drummer looking—"

I was cut short by a short little punch that sat me back in the love seat. Candy screamed an obscenity from the kitchen. Josey had now completely destroyed the cigar butt and was barking at all three of us. Candy came back to the living room and stared up at Dave. Without looking at me she tossed me a pack of frozen peas. It felt good against my jaw.

"Damn it, Candy, I ain't going for this crap no more, I told you."

"Look, he's just some dumb drummer looking for a gig. And he's a Pam fan too. Hello, you know about me and Pam."

He scratched his chin and appeared to be looking at his pigeon toes for answers. He looked like Frankenstein's scolded monster, the way he towered over his beloved.

"So, so you're like a Pam fan, man?"

"Pam all the way."

"Sorry, dude, it just looked like you and my gal and the dog were getting it on." I couldn't believe my hearing. Candy slid a little closer to Dave.

"Were you jealous, babe?"

His breathing got heavy. Hers did the same. They grabbed each other and began kissing each other madly. The dog kept barking. Dave's hands explored her body like he'd been at sea for eighteen months. On the one hand I was glad Dave wasn't trying to take my head off. On the other hand this alternative was sure to make me vomit. With the grace of a pair of camels they hit the floor. I knew where this going. I handed the bag of peas to Josey who tore it apart instantly.

"Don't make a mess," Candy shouted at the dog. As I crept past, one of Candy's hands that were running through Dave's hair shot up with a business card for me to grab. I took it reflexively. It had her name and number on it.

As I was pulling the front door closed behind me, I heard Abbott's Harley Davidson belt buckle hit the floor. I cringed at the thought. I took the steps two at a time forgetting about the third step with the crack in it. My leg disappeared to the thigh. Somewhere behind me on a higher step was my other leg. This was clearly a position for a yoga instructor, not me. After prying my leg loose and massaging some life back into it I noticed that Dave and Candy had come outside on the porch to stare down at me. Candy was once again sporting the kimono and was sucking on a fresh cigar. Her expression read boredom.

Dave said, "I been meaning to fix that step." Candy just 'hmphed.' Josey came out and licked my face.

Searching for something to say, I offer," Quickie?"

"Yup," they respond in unison.

"You almost got caught in the middle of that one, huh?" Dave added.

"Yeah, but the stair caught me instead." That got me a laugh. "So Dave, any of your projects need a drummer?"

Chapter 13

Jake casually maneuvered the convertible up Laurel Canyon Road, into the Hollywood Hills and over to Mulholland. He knew of a large pullout where if one was to drive back far enough he would be barely visible from the street. The day before, Jake had visited the crew of city workers in the area, posing as a laborer looking for a gig. From the tattooed Native American guy named Joseph, Jake learned that there wouldn't be a crew at the site until the following Monday. Travis woke up a few minutes before arriving at the pullout and threatened to jump out. Jake ignored him, knowing he was bluffing. It's not in a coward's nature to jump from a moving car.

Jake skidded to a halt at the end of the dirt drive. Travis coughed, exaggerating the extent of the dust. "Jesus man, take it easy. I got bronchitis."

Jake shut the ride down and spun in his seat to look at Travis. Travis did his best to hide his fear.

"I'll make this brief. The little kidnapping stunt that took four of you to pull off is the last time you'll see or have anything to do with my friend. He doesn't exist to you. If you gain some misplaced courage in that coward heart of yours and choose not to heed this warning, you will see me again, and I'm the last person you'll ever see."

Travis screwed up his face, searching for something slick to say. He leaned forward in his seat as if to whisper in Jake's ear. "Tough talk, but you've fucked with the wrong guy, asshole."

Before he completed his last syllable Jake was out of his seat, over the backseat and onto the trunk of his car. In a quick move he jerked Travis by the collar of his denim jacket and hoisted him onto the trunk beside him. They were now face to face. Without thinking, Travis spat squarely into Jake's face. Travis would have been better off insulting

Jake's mother, for Jake is a man from the old school where to spit in a man's face is never done. There is no higher insult. Jake gave Travis a short seven-inch punch to the solar plexus but before Travis could crumple back into the seat, Jake got under him as if to lift him in a fireman's carry and raised him right over his head and threw him as far as he could. Travis flailed in the air in a vain attempt at landing on his feet. 'Cats only territory, pal,' Jake thought as he leaped down from the car. He walked slowly toward the pathetic looking punk, giving himself time to rein in his rage.

"Okay, okay, enough. Look. My name is Travis MacBeth, nephew to one Bernard Outlaw. He's my uncle, dude, and he's going to be pissed. Here, check it out."

Travis reached for his back pocket. Jake grabbed his throat and cut his air off in the event that Travis had another concealed blade. Turned out he was going for his wallet. Jake looked at the driver's license and the ID checked out.

"MacBeth is a common name, featherweight." But even as he said it, Jake knew in his gut that this punk was Bernie Outlaw's nephew. It would explain how a coward rolls around LA acting the cowboy without suffering consequence. He obviously felt that his family lineage allowed him to behave with impunity. Jake cursed himself. It wasn't like him to make a move such as this without more in-depth research. One more day and he'd have uncovered the family tie. Travis saw Jake's mind working and chuckled.

"You're a man, Travis, and a man's got to do what a man's got to do. But know this. If the bullets start flying it will be you that I'm going to kill."

"Ha! Tough talk from a—"

Jake cared little for what Travis thought was going to be a clever insult. This time Jake knocked him out with a palm to the nose, which broke easily. He walked casually back to the car and wheeled it toward the road. Once again he cursed himself for not researching the target better. It was not necessary for Jake to break Travis' nose, but the man had spit in his face. It was a matter of ethics.

Chapter 14

I ended up with a three-inch-long bruise on my shin from the busted step at Candy Striper's. No sweat compared with everything else that had happened the last few days. I also hit a home run with Dave Abbott. Turned out, one of his bands did need a drummer. It was a sub gig, which meant the job was mine until the regular drummer came back from his vacation. The slight pressure of the deal was that we were only going to get two rehearsals before a show at the Dragonfly Bar on Melrose this Saturday night. Before I left Candy's, Dave gave me a CD of the eight songs I was going to have to learn. They had a brief argument over which songs I was to get down for the show, which escalated to a shouting match. As before, the shouting led to baby talk and soft voices. I got the hell out of Dodge before being caught in the middle of another one of their 'quickies.'

I was proud of myself for my slick getaway briefly until I realized I hadn't taken down Dave's number. Pounding my steering wheel. I suddenly remembered the business card Candy snuck to me earlier. Wonderful, I was going to have to call Miss Striper to get to Abbott. We learn as we go. I'd call her when I got home.

"Hi Candy, its Lou."

"Wow, calling so soon. I'm glad to see you're as enthusiastic as me." I could hear cigar smoke floating from her lips.

"Ah, actually, sweetheart, I was hoping to get ahold of Dave. You two were getting close to it and I split so fast I forgot—"

"What, you didn't have thirty seconds to spare?"

I didn't know what to say and I told her so. "Candy I...I don't know what to say."

"You don't have to say anything. Just come back over here. You'll be glad you did."

"Sorry, doll, I can't come over. Could you just give a brother a break here and give me Dave's number...please?"

"Oh, you're such a bore. Men are boring. Here's the cell number. I can't give out his home number."

That added up as far as my suspicion of him. Maybe he kept the stash at his place. I wrote the number down and thanked her. I lied and told her that the only reason I didn't take her up on her proposal was because she was seeing Abbott. She told me I could lie to her anytime.

Going after Dave the way I was had its risks to be sure. If he had knocked over my place of work then there was a good chance he knew me if he was the one who cased the place. I was gambling that he didn't. Maybe he had scouts or soldiers who did the casing. Either way I told myself that if he 'made' me he would have tipped his hand at Candy Striper's house. He had not, in my opinion, so I kept this drum roll a-rolling.

Dave answered his cell before the first ring was done. We set up a rehearsal for the following afternoon, which meant I was going to have to haul ass as far as getting these songs locked in my brain. I reached for my ghetto blaster as we spoke and cued up the CD. The practice was scheduled at a place called Riley's, which as it happened was on the bottom of my list of places in the San Fernando Valley to investigate. After Abbott hung up I grabbed my staff paper and got busy writing up song charts.

Once the charts were done I listened to each song twice. The first time through was to check my chart. The second time through was just to listen and absorb. Time flew by as it does when I'm in that mode. When I checked my watch it was too late to call Angela and give her an update. But I was in that musician's fired up pre-gig mode and there was no way I was going to squawk about missing a phone call to a fine sister.

When I woke I was still in the same mode. The call to Angela would remain on hold until my last four eggs became a sweet cheese and mushroom omelet. I backed this up with seven-grain wheat toast and orange juice. Abbott's CD played in the background at a low volume. The tunes were fairly straight ahead, which meant there were no odd time signatures, sudden operatic segues or mandolin solo surprises. All was going to be well because the material was officially locked.

I called Angela, got voicemail and left a non-damaging brief message. I thought about calling Jake's cell but decided against it. He's not the 'Check in with me when you have something' type. He would contact me when he felt the need. Besides, I was sure the creepy bastard knew what I'd been up to anyway. I had a rehearsal to get to.

"Alex, the keyboard player?"

"Yeah."

"Nice to meet you, I'm Lou." We shook hands. We were the first ones to arrive at the rehearsal space. We engaged in the usual musicians' small talk, which is basically an exchange of each other's resume. The key to this game is to bring an attitude of total nonchalance while making sure the key points of your musical past are heard by the other party. If it is done correctly, it comes off as a casual job interview. You just want the other guy to have confidence in you. If this ritual is done with too much attitude then you come off as a desperate guy who probably hasn't done half of what he says he's done. If both parties bring too much 'tude then the pleasant interview becomes a dog pissing contest, or a 'My drums are bigger than your keyboard' situation.

The rest of the guys dragged in as coolly as they knew how. When I asked about the trudging, although not in those words, they explained that they'd been out drinking the night before.

We slammed through the tunes for seventy five minutes straight before some of the boys demanded a smoke break. We were all happy with the break, for it wasn't the length of time that was getting to us; it was the non-working air conditioner in a tight room that was doing it. Fresh air was a nice slap in the face. I couldn't imagine throwing cigarette smoke into my lungs at this point...or any point, but to each his own. The general consensus was that I was doing a bang-up job on the tunes. A couple of my tempos were a tad fast but I assured them I would reel it in come show time. They hardly seemed convinced because as rockers we all knew that if anything, songs tend to move on the fast side once adrenaline is tossed into the mix. I took the spotlight off myself by paying some of the guys compliments. It worked like a charm. Always does with the fragile artistic mind. I told them I wanted to check out one of my charts before we got back to the rehearsal. Alex was the lead smoker as far as having half a cigarette butt left to smoke, while the others were at two-thirds. This gave me more than enough time for what I really had in mind. Sonny, the guitar player, had a dark red guitar unit made by the Line Six Company. It looked exactly like the one Angela's guitar player used at my studio. The truth is they all look the same, but I had my serial number page with me. As I saw it, Alex's remaining half cancer stick gave me plenty of time. I banked on none of any of the other guys coming back into the furnace any sooner than they had to.

Bull's eye! The numbers matched. I was looking at the unit that belonged to Angela's guitar player. What was his name again? It didn't matter, because my name would be Hero.

"What the fuck are ya doin' man?" Sonny must have butted out his cigarette early. I hadn't considered that possibility. It would have been too obvious to hide my serial number paper so I acted as though it was a music chart. If he caught sight of it I was done.

"Huh? Shit, you scared me man. Hey, is this one of those processors that makes your amp sound like the actual Line Six amplifier?"

"Yeah, it is. What the hell are you doing with it?"

"Ah, my brother's always talking trash about these things, but damn, man, your amp is straight up killing, man! I can't wait to tell Grady." Grady being my imaginary brother.

"Yeah, it's sweet all right, but you don't want to be touching other people's shit, man, seriously."

"You're right, dude, sorry." I moped over to the drum set and added the serial number page to my charts.

When Sonny's back was to me I casually took the page off the music stand and shoved it into the bottom of my backpack. When he turned to look at me, my hand came out with my Gatorade bottle. His suspicion seemed to be subsiding.

If he didn't buy my cover he didn't let on. The rest of the guys sauntered back in, refreshed by air both of the fresh and the nicotine variety. We launched back into the heavy rock-and-roll tunes for another thirty minutes.

"So will we be squeezing in another rehearsal before the show?"

"Naw, Lou, I'm satisfied. Just listen to the CD I gave you a few more times. It'll be cool."

"Cool."

Smokes took flame once again as we stood in the studio parking lot.

"Is this your mustang, Lou?"

"Yeah, Alex, that's my ol' gal."

"Sixty-six?"

"Sixty-five, actually."

"Right on. You should pound out those few dents and slap some paint on her."

"Yup." I promised. "When I get around to it."

"Which in musician speak, translates to, 'I'm broke and it is never going to happen,'" Abbott laughed. The boys dutifully followed suit.

"Exactly, you know the deal."

Cigarettes were butted out and replaced by a bowl. The bowl was in fact a glass pipe shaped like Star Trek's Enterprise packed full of marijuana. I declined, they puffed. Once satisfied they piled into the bass player's cargo van. It roared to life but the music of Black Sabbath roared louder from its speakers. Over the heavy metal anthem, 'Ferries Wear Boots' Abbott shouted, "Alex, drop me off at home first, you pissant."

"Yeah sure thing fuck-o," Alex replies. This is what is called male bonding.

His screeching tires were a call to action for yours truly. I hopped into the old gal and turned her over. I was about to embark on my first real life tail.

I heard countless voices from countless classic films call out, "Follow that car!"

Alex's tire squealing was the only speed to the pursuit. The pursuit wasn't quite as slow as O.J. Simpson's white Bronco police chase but it was in the snail's pace category of chases. What should have been a ten minute drive from Riley's to Abbott's took almost 25. They did however, stop at a 7-Eleven and bought beer. I must add that they purchased light beer, which for a Canadian-born lad such as me seemed utterly...pointless. American light beer is no more than flavored water and those who drink it may as well admit that they truly don't fancy beer on the whole. I found this to be a grave insult to the institution of beer, and I nearly blew my mission by getting too close.

I followed the van down Abbott's street. They stopped in the middle of the block at a quaint little white house with red trim. I couldn't risk driving by, as not 30 minutes earlier my car was a brief topic of discussion. As luck would have it, a tiny alley to my left jumped out of my peripheral. I ducked in and waited anxiously, eyes glued to my rearview mirror. If this turned out to be some sort of shortcut out of Abbott's I was screwed. The van drove past. My heart slowed. The guys without a doubt were stoned because the same Black Sabbath song was blaring out the van windows.

I backed out, and this time I did chance a drive-by of Dave's house. I pictured millions of dollars' worth of gear stashed inside. I was going to enjoy burning this guy down, as they say in movies. The end of the street was a dead end. I hadn't noticed the sign that was no doubt at the street entrance. Rather than go right to the end I elected to do the three point turn in and out of a neighbor's driveway. As I wheeled the ol' gal to the left she stalled. She never stalls. I turn her over. She breathes life briefly then quits again. "What is it, doll?" Before trying a third time I notice my gas gauge sitting so far below the E sign that the needle would need binoculars to see the E.

I shout, "Mother of pearl, Lou, you moron!" In all your years of driving in this country and that (Canada), now you choose to run out of gas. *Sugar*, I shout once again. I don't like to cuss in the ol' gal. I was now smack-dab in the middle of the street, blocking traffic that was sure to come according to Murphy and his darned laws. I leapt out and started pushing. Traffic was not my only worry; Dave could easily decide to walk his dog, or take out the garbage or come outside to take the training wheels off of his bicycle. My '65 was heavy as they don't make em' like they used to. That and the slight uphill grade had sweat gathering at my temples. A Latino boy of about ten jumped behind the car and helped me with the last few feet to the curb.

"Thanks little man, I ran out of gas."

"How about a tip, mister?"

"Shouldn't you be in school pal?"

"Shouldn't you have put gas in your car?" he said cheekily.

"All right, here's two dollars, ya little hustler. And make sure nobody messes with it."

"Gracias, homes," he said and ran off laughing.

I dug a gas can out of my trunk and started walking, but stopped after three steps. I was met by the same problem: how to get past Abbott's house without being seen. I shook, rattled and rolled my brain until a plan emerged. I walked a few houses away from Abbott's and knocked on what my sixth sense told me was the friendliest door.

A man with a deep voice and a trace of a Spanish accent called through the black security door. "What do you want?" I knew he could see me, but I couldn't see him.

"How's it going man?"

"I asked you what you want, man? You can't just roll up on me like this. And I sure hope you ain't selling anything 'cause I ain't buyin' shit."

"No, I need a favor, which I'll pay you for."

His voice was right against the door now. "Sorry, dude, I ain't got any gas, man. But hey, if you need any body work done, shit, I'll hook you up, bro."

"That sounds good. Ah, but today I just need to cut through your yard and I'll pay you ten bucks." I held it up to the screen. The door opened and a stocky Latino with a purple goatee came onto the porch.

"What the fuck did you do, homes, that you gotta bring your shit to my yard?"

"Let me put it to you this way. Somebody on this block has been getting with my girl. Now I don't know the dude but she's with him right now and I don't want her to see me creeping by with this stupid gas can."

"Dude, sorry. Dude, that's rough man. Sure I'll take your ten and I'll take another ten too."

"What? Why?"

"Cause your story's bullshit so I need compensation if any shit comes down on me."

"Fair enough pal." I gave up the twenty before his price went up again.

"Hold on, storyteller. My cousin's in the guest house in the back of the property. I gotta tell him you're coming through. You don't want to get shot, do ya? Ah come on I'm just playing dude. Relax." He grabbed a cell phone out of his pocket and called his cousin.

"Ortiz, wake up, fool. I gotta a buddy coming back. Let him through. Huh? Because, I said so. Plus he's got ten bucks for you." He folded the silver cell closed and smiled at me with a shiny gold tooth in the front of his grill.

"This also covers my return trip man," I say.

"Okay, okay, take it easy. Just give Ortiz the ten spot. He was sleeping but he'll be up now that there's beer money coming."

"Right. Hey, you got a card or something? I have a '65 Mustang that needs body work."

"Hell yeah I do here. We'll give you a good price too, bro, no doubt."

"Thanks. Oh, and I hope Ortiz doesn't buy light beer with this scratch. I'd never forgive myself."

"I'll bitch slap him if he does."

Ortiz could have been the twin brother to the guy I'd just done business with. His hand was out long before I got near to his little stoop.

"This is a return fare, Ortiz."

"Cool."

I was now back in the narrow alley I'd pulled into earlier and heading toward Burbank Boulevard. The nearest gas station wasn't far. Not that I had a lot of dough to put in the gas can. Abbott's street, Lilac, cost me 32 dollars. If I weren't on Angela's payroll I'd be steamed to say the least.

Chapter 15

Back at home I checked my mail box before heading up; two bills and a whole heap of junk mail. I cracked a much needed beer, grabbed my phone and dialed Bob. It was time to put his 'bad ass' truck to good use. I called him up and broke down the situation for him. Forty minutes later he showed and called me from the truck on his cell. As per usual, he told me to get my ass downstairs. He got a kick out of that. Growing impatient with the elevator, I took the stairs. The two-year-old metallic Chevy Avalanche idled at the curb. Bobby had his exhaust system modified to get him a few extra horsepower. I don't know about all of that, but I do know she sure has a nice loud rumble to her since he sunk the money into her. I agreed that his truck went from being 'bad' to 'badass,' but I rarely voiced it. He squealed away from the curb like a teenager once I was barely in the cab.

"So what's ol' Bobby need to get you out of this time?"

"As if." We both know that if anything the opposite was true.

"Here's the deal. We're headin' to Sherman Oaks to a cat named Dave Abbott's."

"Is that the dude that knocked over your business?"

"The one and only."

"I know that bastard. Oh, dude, we need to make a stop first. We need to get us some ski masks and baseball bats and do this guy right. Do you know how much...Oh man don't get me started on this maggot!"

"Right, so you know the cat. Well, we're going to bring him down."

"Cool. But I'm serious. We need to do him right—the violent way like we used to."

"Man we never 'used to' anything. Stop talking foolishness."

"Oh, I forgot you Canadians wouldn't know about violence or retribution or anything confrontational."

"Oh, we know all about violence, pal. We just let you guys spend all of the money and expend the majority of the human lives on all the wars you start and we sit back and enjoy a slick lifestyle."

"That's right. See? You said it."

"Yeah, I said it. Now tell me who's smarter in this little equation, the warrior on the front line or the cat sittin' pretty? And let us not forget, Bobby-o-pal o'mine, that we backed you guys on the Afghanistan front, just not Iraq, which was the illegal war." This was about the millionth time Bob and I had this discussion.

"Look, all I know is that Canadians are pussies."

"Always remember one thing, Bob." He made his eyes thin slits before looking over at me. "This Canadian can kick your narrow ass anytime he wants to and take your little truck and sell it on eBay to any Canadian pussy I want to. So keep your eyes on the road before I have you sleepin' the long sleep."

Bob held my stare for eight seconds before his laugh lines showed up.

"So which way, then?"

"Take the 101. Woodman is going to be your exit."

Bob then asked me all about Angela and the whole ordeal. I noticed he paid most attention when I spoke about Angela. Boys will be boys. I finished my yarn by the off ramp. Bobby had only two comments.

"First of all, no woman, movie soundtrack or bass guitar solo can be as fine as you're talking up this broad to be. Secondly, the only way I see for this to the end is if you give me a month of Sundays on the jam circuit."

"That's a bit excessive, don't you think?"

"Excessiveness is in the eye of the beholder, Cymbal Crasher. Deal or not?"

"Deal. And Angela is that fine."

"Oh wait, Lou, that's a month of consecutive Sundays."

"Not a chance."

"You're a pussy, Lou."

"Sissy."

"I bet Angela is really some Cat named Alan."

"If she was a he I'd give him your number like always."

"I still think you're an idiot, Lou, for thinking that returning this broad's gear is going to get you this broad. You need to grow up. Now Bobby over here would just *tell* this girl what time it is and she'd know for herself what kind of man she'd be getting. You want to get her something, buy her flowers. You don't drag your coolest friend into the deep valley on a fool's errand."

In his cumbersome way, Bob had a point but I was going ahead anyway. The things we do for love...

"Turn here," I instructed, all business now.

Bob shut the truck off and killed the lights, allowing it to roll to the curb a few houses down from Abbott's place. "Okay, rock star, which one is the asshole's?"

"Little white one... Red trim... Classic Datsun 510 in front."

"Fine, let's creep over to the neighbor's, go in back and see what's doin' over the fence."

"Let's do it."

We moved like prison inmates scurrying across the yard, hoping to avoid the search light.

"Pay dirt," Bob whispered.

An old palm tree grew at an angle from the backyard we stood in, snaked over the fence and into Abbott's property. We peeked through the fence but saw only thick vegetation. Bob suggested we climb the 'leviathan,' as he put it. He held an upturned palm for me to lead the charge. I didn't squawk as this was my party. We were able to do a graceless duck walk for the first section. After that it was a hug and shimmy sort of dance. I knew I should have joined the circus when I was a kid. Below me was an oval shaped pool that hadn't entertained a swimmer since George W. Bush was President.

"I can almost see into a second floor bedroom."

"Can you see him?"

"I said almost, Bob."

"Lou, a woman ever let you hold her like you're holding this tree?"

"Quit playing the fool."

"Move a little higher, Lou."

"I don't know Bob, I think we're at the—"

Without as much as a creak, the old palm snapped. A moment like this gives you just enough time to utter a curse word, make a funny face and take a deep breath. We were heading for the murky waters below. It was only natural to try to distance ourselves from the tree in the interest of future family planning. The noise must have been heard down the block. Palm leaves everywhere. The water reeked. I wondered if this was where the phrase dirty pool came from. The pool lights came on. Abbott had obviously heard the rumpus.

Bob grabbed my arm. I could barely make out his bulging eyes. Bubbles escaped his mouth—panic. Looking up I noticed an area thick with huge palm leaves. We swam to them. I was now close enough to see that they formed a sort of makeshift tent over the top of the water. I poked my head up and sucked air in quietly, not wanting to alert Dave Abbott. I pulled Bobby into the tent by his shoulder and immediately slapped a hand over his mouth.

"Shut up," I whispered. "Breathe through your nose."

We could hear Abbott losing his marbles, parading around the pool.

"Son of a bitch, I told that piece of shit landlord. I ain't got time for this. It's fuckin' contraband time, shit."

A sliding glass door slammed. Moments later a car roared to life with a backfire.

"Datsun 510," we said in unison.

"Move, Bob, move. And let go of my arm."

"You let go of mine. Hey, what was the word he said?"

"Contraband. It's Latin for stolen shit. Or at least he thinks so anyway."

"Dang water messed up my lizards."

"Bobby, stop playing and give me your hand. Lizards? I saw those Polyesters at Payless shoes in '99."

I hauled him out of the pool. Two sets of squeaky shoes tore down the path. I was horsin' it with Bob somewhere trailing behind. I waited at the truck.

"Come on, grandma," I said.

Bob slammed on the brakes at the main road.

"First instinct, which way?"

"Left, Bob."

"Good call. Man, are you going to have a huge dry cleaning and truck detailing bill, Cymbal Crasher."

Ignoring Bob, I did my best to fight the spinning roulette wheel feeling in my stomach, wondering whether we made the correct turn.

After four long blocks, I could tell Bob had the same feeling.

"Hey Bob, do you think we—"

"Lou, why the hell did you climb so high on that damn tree?"

"What?"

"You heard me."

"You told me to, Bubba."

"Yeah but you were the lead dog, dog. You should have been testing that thing for stability as you climbed."

"Oh right because palm tree stability botany was my major at friggin' music school. Don't be an idiot, Bob."

"Hey man, I'm helping you out, Party Crasher, all right."

"Shut up, there's the Datsun, at the Shell station. Pull over to the air and water station."

I crouched down in the seat as Bob moved in. Abbott had just flipped the gas lever down as we entered and was done in seconds. He couldn't have tossed more than three bucks into his ride.

"Probably not going far, assuming he was on empty."

"Cool, that'll save you some gas money, Lou."

I told Bob to put a sock in it. Abbott led us on a straight path from Sherman Oaks to a little dead end street in Panorama City near the Budweiser brewery.

"Smell those hops and barley, Lou?"

"Yup."

"I'm going to stop here. I don't want to get pinned down. You run down there and see what the bastard is doing."

"Sure enough," I said with a sigh as I climbed out of the truck. On one side of the street birds of paradise grew the length of a wire fence. I hugged this as I kept low and sprinted down the block.

The block ended in a half circle with ten yards of gravel which butted up against railroad tracks. Two plain white five-ton cargo trucks were parked one behind the other on the circle's curve. Abbott was parked in front of the first truck. As I closed in on the rear truck I heard the roll-up door of the first truck fly up.

"Okay, what have we got to fence this fine evening?" Abbott was talking to himself. I could see the back of his left shoulder. He moved a flashlight over the truck's spoils.

"Son of a bitch," I whispered.

There was a rustling sound at the fence behind me. I looked to see a tiny black and white rabbit hop from the birds of paradise.

"Who's there?" Abbott called. His light flew past the truck. He could not see the rabbit from where he was, so naturally he had to investigate. I didn't have time to slither under the truck. Not soundlessly anyway. Up was the only solution. One foot on the tailgate, the next on the side handle and I was on top of the truck lying flatter than a Denny's pancake on my belly. Abbott moved below.

"I said, who's there? Fer chrissake! Aw shit, a fuckin' rabbit. You're fucking lucky I don't have my thirty-thirty with me Bugs-friggin'-Bunny."

He went back to work. I quietly rolled onto my back, took in the stars and drank in the brewery's pleasant odor. Soon after the door rolled down, Abbott's ride fired up and he was gone. Moments later Bob's truck barreled down the street. He locked his brakes up causing his back end to swing out slightly. I climbed down from the truck roof.

"So where we at, rock star?"

"You got bolt cutters for that truck full of stolen booty?"

"I know you ain't suggesting I show up for a gig unprepared." Bob slid his seat forward and came up with black and yellow bolt cutters.

"Dang, Bob, those look like police issue to me." Bob ignored the comment.

Bob popped the lock on the truck with ease and turned to me with empty eyes. "Say Lou, will you be doing anything on this here job?"

"I don't like how you say 'this here job.' Just so you know this is our first and last job of this nature. Dig?"

"Sure, you're right... until the next hot dame shakes her tail feather in your face."

Bob whistled at all of the merchandise in the truck. "Lou, you need to rethink this."

"Meaning?" I asked.

"Okay, we do high end furniture, cars, exotic animals, jewelry whatever. We just got to get into the repo biz, cuz.' Come on. Come on. Ah, come on. Come on. Come on, Lou. Don't poop the party, Party Crasher, come on, seriously. Come on."

"I'm a drummer, and you? Well, you're a brother with a half decent truck. That's where it ends, Bubba."

Bob waved me off and set to the gear. We lucked out as most of Angela's gear was at the back of the truck. As we tightly packed Bob's truck I thought of all the musicians whose gear we were looking at, like the kids who saved their allowances to buy an amplifier. I thought of the street performer who after collecting a million soda cans buys an acoustic guitar. My thoughts then moved to the female drummer. She has it bad enough being in this traditionally man's business, and then she has to ask two hundred times a day through a six-inch speaker if she can take our order at the local In-and-Out Burger. Finally seven months go by before she buys a priceless vintage snare drum. Stories like these and more could easily be attached to this equipment.

I realized that I wasn't home yet. I would still have to do the gig with Dave just to be sure he didn't put two and two together. Gear gets stolen; sub drummer doesn't show up for gig. If he was just a thief I wouldn't worry, but there were the rumors of his 'protection.' I ran it by Bob and he agreed with me. Besides he wanted to go to the show as he heard that hot-looking Hollywood babes frequented the club. It was not going to be easy to lay down solid grooves with a plastic smile on my face. My only hope was that I didn't hop my kit and drop Abbott like a bad cold.

We popped the lock of the other truck but it was empty. Only Abbott knew when he planned to fill it. We moved like crustaceans attempting to avoid the steaming pot of water down the road to the second nearest pay phone. It was a miracle that we found one at all in this day and age, but that's the Valley for you. I jumped out and called the law to report the truck. The operator wanted my name and other details but it was time to fly. We chanced a police cruiser in the area might see us with our truck full of booty but thought it a necessary risk seeing as the five-ton was now without a lock. No telling what the black and white rabbit might do with all of that gear.

Chapter 16

We decided that Bob would store the gear at his place as he rented garage space from his landlord. Tomorrow I'd speak to Angela and set up the rendezvous. I was busting at the seams with excitement at the thought of making the call. Back at my pad, another thought grabbed me. I would not only have to do the gig to maintain appearances and so on, but I also needed to snag that guitar processor back that belonged to Angela's guitar player. Complete the job. Accomplish the mission. That's what Jim Rockford would do. Now I needed a plan. A-snatch and-grab operation would not be my first choice. Subtlety, that's what I was looking for; a sting, a three-card Monty, maybe a bait and switch. The more clichés and scenes from films that played in my head, the faster the fog lifted.

"Kat."

"Wrong again, Louis."

"Tami, I knew it was you girl, I was just playing," I lied.

"Um-hm. What's up, Lou, you didn't get rolled again, did you?"

"Only once in this lifetime, baby. Listen, I've got a gig coming up this weekend and was wondering if you dolls wanted to stop by?"

"Cool. Where?"

"Dragonfly."

"Cool again. Wow, twice in one week Louis I feel blessed."

"Ah, great to hear you feel that way because—"

"Here it comes," she sighed.

"Do you see how connected we are? Anyway, I do actually need your help. I promise you it's legal and not dangerous. Honest."

"Mother always said that when a man ends a sentence with the word 'honest,' he's lying."

Kat came into the room on Tami's end and made it a mock conference call, with Tami feeding Kat excerpts of my dialogue. A few minutes later we hatched a plan to secure the processor. After I hung up with them I called Jake.

"Jake, it's Lou. The gear is in the nest. The show must go on. That's a ten-four, and may democracy be safe. Over and out, rubber ducky." Imagining Jake scowling at my cryptic message, I smiled.

Chapter 17

I gelled with the crowd for most of the opening band's set. I always like to see what is going on with other bands. There was a lot of buzz about Dave's band floating through the throng. The neat thing about being a sub drummer is that nobody knows who you are and you can hear what cats have to say in a fly-on-the-wall sort of way. Two tall girls in matching pairs of three-inch heels and identical fishnet stockings that ran up to similar black miniskirts talked about Abbott.

"Yeah, it kind of sucks though because I heard the regular drummer Randy or Andy or whatever quit and the new guy sucks."

"Oh my god really? That blows. I loved Andy/Randy what's-his-name. Let's do a shot so we can stomach this."

"Not true girls, the new guy rocks," I pipe in.

"Excuse me?" one of the girls responds.

"Yeah, his name's Lou and I hear he went to Harvard."

"So what, they don't teach you how to rock-and-roll at Harvard." They both had screwed up looks on their faces.

"That's just it ladies, he taught *them* how to rock at Harvard and now one can get a Master's in rock at Harvard. No lie," I lied.

"No shit. Is he cute?" the girl who had been silent up to this point asked.

"Well, I hear he's a black guy who kinda looks like James Garner."

"Who's that?"

"Picture Johnny Depp, only hotter, and you've got a young James

Garner. You dames enjoy the show."

"Wait, come and do a shot with us."

"No can do, fishnets, I've got a show to do." I winked Sinatra-style and oozed into the crowd.

I heard one of them say 'Huh?' to my back as I walked away. I went backstage and started warming up. I have a little practice pad that has a thick rubber surface and on this I go through some snare drum rudiments—which are to drummers like scales are to a pianist.

Ten minutes later I was counting in the first song. My adrenaline was way up, which I expected. As soon as I heard the tempo of the first lyrical line, I knew I was moving this train too fast through a narrow pass. To slow down too quickly is amateur because even the most lay of listeners can feel that. So the choices are either carry on at the speed you are moving and apologize to the boys in between songs or gradually pull the tune back a few notches. I chose the latter and got a nod from Sonny the guitar player.

They had me go straight into the second song over the applause from the first song. These types of transitions aren't always easy when you're playing new material but the switch came off hitch-less. If only the same thing happened moving from song two to three. I was to play a huge Phil Collins-style drum fill over the big toms by myself and then boom—the boys come in on beat one. I dropped my stick just before the fill and was forced to do it one handed. In the blink of an eye, what should have been the thunderous drums of Navarone became more like the sound of a one-legged mouse tip toeing across highly tuned tin pots. However, with my free hand I did manage to throw up the rock-and-roll sign.

I recovered fairly quickly and finished out the set. Obviously with more rehearsal time I could have murdered Abbott's tunes but such is the life of a sub. Bottom line; it was me in the chair on that night not some other Cat. Respect it and move on, I always say. We were the last band and the club still had another hour of booze peddling time left so there was no rush for us to haul our gear off the stage. I walked through the crowd and received as many sneers and head shakes as I did pats on the back and glass rises. Ah, the life of a sideman. A short person in a loud satin shirt on his way out of the bathroom held the door for me.

"Thanks man," I say.

"Sure. Nice set, brother."

"Thanks again." I now had the bathroom to myself. After doing my business and washing my hands, I splashed cold water on my face. When I looked into the mirror a stoic Jake stood motionless behind me.

"Jesus, Jake that is so Hollywood. What are you, the Grim Reaper or somebody?"

"If I was, do you think you'd have time to ask that question?" Jake replied.

"Yeah, whatever. So what's up?"

"Good set. You're improving."

"Thanks. Wow, it's the first time I've physically seen you at one of my gigs."

"How could I resist such a deep message drenched in espionage and intrigue?" He paused a moment before continuing. "We have a problem. Your little playmate is Bernie Outlaw's nephew. I see by your look you've heard of Bernie."

"Oh fuck a duck on a Sunday. Are you sure? What the hell am I supposed to do? Don't answer that. I'm on the next plane back to Canada."

"That is one option, yes," Jake said.

"Well, what other option is there? Outlaw is a small time gangster, fast becoming not-so small time."

"Stay and fight, and I'll help, seeing as I may have had a hand in this." Jake was referring to the fact he hadn't fully checked Travis out before bouncing him around the Hollywood Hills.

"A hand in it? What do you mean a hand in it?" I asked.

"Does that matter at this point?"

"Shit Jake, now don't get all...well, you know. Look, how do I fight this cat?"

"With difficulty."

"Yeah no s-h-i-t." I pinched the bridge of my nose as if that would help me think. "Do you think together we could—I mean, I don't want to leave LA, man. It's like the song says, I love LA." My voice cracked like a teen in mid puberty.

"Stick it out and I've got your back. Leave and I've got your back, until your classic ride leaves Los Angeles county." Jake still hadn't moved a muscle during this whole conversation.

"Well, what about you Jake? If you put the screws to this snot nosed nephew then Outlaw is going to be gunning for you as well. Dig? Wait, you didn't kill him or anything did you?"

"If I had, this conversation would be going a lot differently."

"Oh yeah, different how?" I asked.

"I don't like to waste words." That was the end of that. Finally he moved to the sink and washed his hands. I was relieved to hear that I wasn't going to be hauled in for a conspiracy to commit beef.

The door flew open and crashed against the wall. My first thought was that this war I just found myself in was now in play. I got into a fighting stance. Jake stood still. Thankfully it was just a tottering girl feeling the effects of booze. Jake caught her before she hit the floor. I'd have thrown my back out if I'd caught her the way he did. Jake picked her up slowly from their tango style dip. Once the woman gained her balance and focus she moved in to kiss Jake. He gracefully spun the woman around avoiding the kiss and leaning her against the sink.

"Don't like girls, Jake?" I teased. He glared at me.

The drunken woman moved her fake weave to the side. "Are you like a black action hero?" she asked.

"No ma'am. I hope you're not driving tonight."

"Oh my, that's a voice that could make me do things," she said.

I could see Jake was becoming uncomfortable. "I'll leave you two alone."

"Hey, you're the drummer, right?" she giggled.

"Yes, ma'am," I said, using Jake verbiage.

"Not bad for a first show, or whatever. I love all of Dave's bands. Listen, guys, can you watch the door while I go potty?"

"Potty?" I said.

"Potty?" Jake grumbled.

She stumbled into a stall. Jake and I stepped out of the room to barricade the door. One of the club's bouncers told us he'd heard a girl was in the guys' can. Jake told him it was true and that she'd be right out. The bouncer clearly didn't like being told what was what in his house but decided against voicing it.

"Maybe you are an action hero, Jake."

"I see you still have your sense of humor what with Outlaw on your tail," Jake said, killing the party vibe. Just then, I saw Kat.

"Hiya Lou, nice set. Dang I didn't know you could hit that hard."

"Thanks, Kat. And thanks for coming out tonight. Oops, this is my buddy—"

"Jake," she said with a half grin. They hugged like old friends.

"Oh, let me guess," I said disgustedly. "You two go back before the war. Kat, you were fresh off the bus outta Kansas and Jake happened by the bus station in a nice classic Coup de Ville and Armani threads. It was pouring rain, which you both found odd. But there was just this little something in Jake's voice and his psychotic eye that told you to trust him. Within three weeks, Jake put you in touch with all the right people and you never looked back. Kansas was suddenly a distant memory. How am I doin'?"

"My god it was like you were there, Lou," Kat chuckled.

"Sure go ahead and laugh, but you know what? We've all heard it before, Sunshine."

"Sunshine?" they said in unison.

"Forgive him, Kat. I've just been the bearer of bad news," Jake said.

Kat folded her arms and looked concerned, awaiting an explanation. I took a breath and was about to launch into the short version when the drunken woman in the bathroom pounded on the door to be let out. Apparently she'd forgotten that the door opened inward, poor lass. Jake opened the door slowly so as not to smack her with it.

"Hello you," she said through half closed eyes. This time Jake let her hug him, briefly, of course. When she saw Kat her eyes turned cold. "Who's she, baby?"

"I'm his pregnant wife, now take a walk before you have an accident." The woman turned tail as quickly as she could on wobbly heels. Kat giggled after she was gone. "I can be such a guy sometimes," she smiled.

"Kat, is Tami holding a table for us?"

"Yup, right this way. Take my arm, Jake. I don't want you doing one of those mysterious brother disappearing acts you do."

Jake was reluctant, but he came along without a fight. I patted him on the back like we were pals, which I knew he would hate.

"Jake, you know, the disappearing brother act is like so 2002, dude. You need a new act."

Without my noticing, Jake quickly pulled a chair in behind his path. Naturally I stumbled over it. Kat looked back in confusion. We joined Tami at her table. After quick hugs and hellos we sat.

"So are we ready to drop the hammer on Sonny the guitar player?" I asked.

"You pick a hell of time to doubt us, drummer boy."

"Nobody doubts anybody, Tami," Kat said, rushing to my defense.

"It's almost time to rock, so pay attention, Lou. When you load your gear down the hall and out the back door, if you're moving too fast you'll miss our little friend who is kickin' it beside the garbage can. As long as you do what you're supposed to do, when the time comes it'll all be gravy, as you often say. You know the rest." She rose up from the table. "And now if you're through with your panic attack..." Tami winked and moved as if in a slow motion music video toward the bar.

Kat shook her head at my appreciative countenance.

"Hey, let a man be a man, baby. Heck, I'm a man on borrowed time here, baby, so again, please, let a man be a man."

"Whatever. Now Jake, what's this bad news you dropped on Lou? It's not going to screw with tonight's deal is it?"

"You know of his current enemies?"

"Yes."

"There is a connection by blood to a Bernie Outlaw."

"The way the press tells it this man is soon to gain federal interest. Do you mean *that* Bernie Outlaw?"

Jake nodded, I'm sure to save excess words. Kat made a 'holy crap' whistle. "Louis, I am so sorry. But hey, how bad can it be? When we saw you they'd had their fun."

"That was before."

"Before what, Louis?"

"After you guys picked me up I put Jake onto them. Shit, you know what they say about fighting one's own battles," I said pathetically.

"Aw, now come on, Lou, don't start that macho bull, even if it is nice to see some male toughness in this state of male bikini waxes."

As if the waitress in a black bra, black ripped jeans and heavy eye liner read my thoughts, she put a beer and a shot of tequila down in front of me. On her left breast was a tattoo of a woman who looked a lot like the waitress herself with a dialogue bubble coming from her lips that said, "Take me."

"Well thank you kindly, how much?" I ask.

"No charge," she said. Tami had sent it over. I did what came naturally with the shot and chased it with a healthy portion of beer. It was at this time that it dawned on me that I'd gone a heck of a long time between finishing the set and tasting such a paradisiacal treat.

"Ah, that's better," I burped. Jake scowled. Kat called me a pig.

"So Louis, what do you plan to do?"

"Well, Kat, having just received the news of this impending sunny day, at this point I'll finish the plan that we've hatched to get this final piece back and then I'm heading back to Rainier climbs. Vancouver, that is." I took another pull on the beer.

"Jake, what do you think he should do? I mean this Outlaw is a bad you-know-what. I don't buy everything the media says, but I do believe the rumors. Check this. Tami and I were looking at a site for our gym in Canoga Park. Prime square footage with a view to match, and so on. We're all set to meet with the landlord for a second or third time, I'm not sure. Anyway, the landlord doesn't show, but some slick dude in a nice suit with a very impressive vocabulary shows up instead with lease papers. The papers are in order, and why shouldn't they be? It was a standard lease. And then ever so gradually, dude starts telling us about an extra maintenance fee, not on the lease."

"Did you point that out to him?" Jake asked.

"In freaking triplicate, as lawyers say. He never lost his smug grin as he maintained that in order to do business—look, it was extortion plain and simple!"

"And you think he was one of Outlaw's boys?" I asked trying to be smart.

"Canoga Park is the birthplace of his LA turf, so you tell me," she said, capping her story off with a swig of her cocktail.

"That kind of strong-arming never worked in the days of Jim Rockford. What makes Outlaw think it's going to work today?" I asked.

"Amateur," Jake said. "If Lou stays or goes I'm in his corner, either way." He didn't look at either one of us. I wondered if the guy ever relaxed. He was definitely reading the room, a guy always ready to react. Maybe someday I'd convince him to take up an instrument. Ah, but knowing the bastard he probably already plays violin, piano and Hungarian kazoo beautifully. He's always watching. He had to be ex-military, possibly Navy Seal.

"Louis, if you decide to stay, Tami and I are in that same corner with you. But I'll tell you what, you need a plan, like yesterday."

"Thanks, Kat, I never—"

"Just have another sip. Your thanks will do. Besides, your beer is going to get warm. Or is that the way you like it?" she chuckled.

"No, that would be the British," I clarified proudly.

"Vancouver is in the province of British Columbia, isn't it?"

"Familiar with our provinces...say, for an American you're kind of smart."

Jake caught my eye and motioned for me to turn around. Kat caught the same look. We turned to see Tami doing a shot with Sonny the guitar player. After slamming the empty glass on the table she giggled and stumbled into his arms. He seemed proud of the fact that he caught her, and he seemed excited that she liked being caught by him. Kat pointed out to Jake and me that Tami was actually shooting water while Sonny, clear tequila. They'd come in early and set the whole deal up with one of the Chippendale-looking bartenders. He didn't want to play along until the gals threw a little green his way, backed up with soft voices and eyelash batting. I was impressed, and told Kat I'd reimburse her for it.

Alex the keyboard player bolted out of the club the minute we were done. He was none too pleased, as his sound kept cutting in and out during the show. In between songs I'd spy him wrapping and unwrapping cords frantically. Poor sap.

Our plan was moving full steam ahead. After my beer disappeared I moved to the stage and started tearing down my drum set. I had what they call a six piece drum set: a snare drum, bass drum, three rack toms and one floor tom.

Your standard drum kit usually consists of five pieces. And back in days of the American jazz cats, one would usually see four drums to a kit. The hard rockers of the late seventies and eighties bumped it up to seven, eight and sometimes nine piece and more. Keep in mind the drummers of those sets usually had drum techs, roadies, managers and a gal in every port. At my level, with the music I play and the size of my classic ride, a six piece is just right.

As I tossed each drum into separate cases I glanced as inconspicuously as I could manage at Tami and Sonny, who were also now on stage with me packing up his gear. Abbott didn't pack his gear up. Instead he had some wide eyed fan that must have had fake ID do his grunt work. He seemed happy to be getting what I'm sure he thought was a foot into rock world. He totally ignored us, pausing only to push his wire rimmed spectacles back up his nose as they repeatedly headed south. I packed all my stuff onto my dolly and set it by the side of the stage. Sonny swayed slightly as he asked me to help him lift his amplifier off the three-foot high stage. He brought his side of the amp down on his toe and cussed. Tami tried to stifle a giggle. Sonny, red-faced, smiled at her, telling her she was cute. I wanted to puke, but felt this was not the time. As I walked down the narrow hall which lead to the alley I heard Sonny instruct Tami to leave the rest of his stuff where it lay. Musicians are typically protective about their gear even if recently and illegally acquired. No doubt he envisioned Tami taking a dive with his new toy.

The heavy metal door at the end of the hall was closed but not all the way. I used the front of my dolly to push it open. The door swung open to the left, and to my right was a blue dumpster, which, to the careless eye, was pulled up snugly against the building. To those who cared, were in the know, and perhaps, birds of prey, there was just enough space between the dumpster and building to house an exact replica of the guitar processor case that Sonny had in his possession. Although the bag weighed the same as Sonny's would with processor within, the contents differed. Earlier in the day Kat purchased the case from the world famous Guitar Center and loaded our case with old San Fernando Valley phone books. Tami came out the door like a woman attempting to not appear drunk, with Sonny's guitar in tow. Either she had an acting or a drinking background or both, because she was good. Sonny hurried up from behind her with short little steps.

"Baby, watch the axe. You shouldn't have brought the—"

Tami planted a big kiss on his lips to cut him off. He broke free from her when he heard his 'axe' hit the pavement. The guitar was okay, as it was in a hard shell case. I was already back from my car. I pulled the fake case from the dumpster and met Kat in the dark hallway, where we switched cases.

"Anyone look funny at you when you snagged this from the stage?"

"Huh, these drunks probably thought I was Tami," Kat replied.

"What about bouncers?"

"They're too busy watching Jake like he's a Rottweiler off leash with no owner in sight."

"Sounds like my house when he comes to visit," I add.

In the middle of the hall, I found an ice cooler, the kind you might find in a Motel 6. I slid the real processor underneath it. Tami came in just then from the alley, fake giggling. You could hear Sonny yelling after her to not bring anything else. I handed her the replica.

"You're doing great, kid."

"Try calling me that again and see what'll happen to you, Louis Crasher!" She gave me a sly grin. I could tell she was enjoying this. She hurried back toward the stage. A tenth of second later she did a one-hundred-and-eighty degree turn. Sonny came into the hallway, so it appeared to him as though she'd skipped back to the stage and grabbed his processor and was heading back out to his car. I'd taken a knee as if just tying my shoe. It was lame, I know, but I needed some way to explain, if asked, as to how Tami beat me back to the stage from the alley, and what better way than to behave like a moron who's slow at shoe tying. Having completed shoe lace number two I walked past Tami without comment. Looking back over my shoulder, I could see the back door closing behind them. I crept back down the hall and retrieved the real guitar processor from its hiding place. Peering out the back door, I saw Tami get into Sonny's car. Once his car fired up and the lights came on, I put the processor behind the dumpster. Back inside the club I hopped back on stage and did what we players call an idiot check, where we make sure we haven't left anything behind...like an idiot. Satisfied with the check, I turned to see our table was empty with chairs up. I spotted Kat and Jake at the bar. Jake hugged Kat and he made his exit. Let the record show that I was not hurt that he didn't say goodbye. I'd see him soon enough.

"Hey Kat. Well, the switch came off without a hitch. Now I guarantee Sonny's going to want to keep the party going with our gal, so how do we get her out?"

"We've got that all worked out."

"Oh yeah? I'm listening."

"Well you can listen outside," a bouncer interrupted, "'cause we're all closed up. You don't have to go home but you can't stay here."

"Awesome movie wasn't it man? The *Blues Brothers* movie. That line, John Belushi said it," I said.

"Dude," the bouncer said. "I've only see it like fifty times. It's a classic. Hey, nice playing tonight bro. Try to wrap it up in five."

"Cool."

"Let's move it outside, Louis," Kat said, "and I'll give you the plan."

"Right, the plan, I forgot."

We moved out back to my car. No sign of Tami or Sonny. I grabbed the prize from behind the dumpster. I now had all of the pieces to Angela's inventory. I was feeling good.

"They've split, now what?" I asked.

"She's going to take ill, puke in his car, call me, and I'm going to pick her up."

"What? Is she going to stick her fingers down her throat? Man, you guys are tough."

"No, she's going to pretend to take a mint or something, I don't know, and the pop a trilosintaxitol."

"Try to do what and where?" I asked.

"She's going to drop a trilo. They make you puke instantly. Doctors and nurses sometimes use them if a kid swallows something he shouldn't have. Failing that, they pump the stomach, I guess. Problem nowadays is they're easy to come by."

"Who the hell would want...ah don't tell me, supermodels?"

"Supermodels, regular models, teen age bulimics, you name it."

"Man, your country is a mess. So Tami's going to do this? You guys have gone way beyond the call of duty for me."

"And don't you forget it," Kat said with a grin.

"Um-hm. Well listen, Sonny lives in the valley so let's head down Santa Monica in our rides toward La Brea, where he'll probably head north. It'll take us closer to Tami when she calls. I'll follow you."

"Anywhere?" she flirted. Clearly she was enjoying this cloak and dagger stuff too. I squeezed the processor into my trunk beside my cymbal bag. Kat's Dodge Ram roared to life with a deep rumble. I loved that sound. She backed up quickly and swung the truck around so she was beside me, her tires squealing to a halt. Show off. Her passenger side window came down.

"What's wrong with this picture: me with a big empty truck and you with a Pinto chock full of drums?"

"You little brat, this is classic 1965 family muscle car. Do you know that when they built this car…"

"Try to keep up, Mister Family Muscle. Tami just called." She held up a glowing cell phone. "La Brea and Third, you were right."

Kat had really put the pedal to the metal. When I pulled in behind them they were both in the truck with Sonny nowhere to be found. I shut the ol' gal down and came to Tami's window.

"Hiya doll, how you holding up?" I ask.

"Fine Lou," she said chewing on what I guessed was a Tic Tac.

"Tami, Kat, thank you both so much. Tami, you really dropped a trilo as the kids say? Did it hurt?"

"It doesn't hurt. I'd sure like to brush my teeth though, dang."

"I owe you ladies big time." I looked around. "I can't believe Sonny's into the wind already."

"Well, even though I upchucked in his ride, he still wanted a piece of this, if you know what I mean. So when he tried to stop me from getting out he might have met with a shot to the solar plexus."

"He might have, might he?" I smiled.

Chapter 18

It took me three attempts at dialing Angela before I succeeded in getting a ring signal. It wasn't that the line was busy or that I kept reaching a fax machine, rather it was just yours truly getting four numbers deep and then abandoning ship for fear that my pre-planned dialogue blew...which is to say sucked. Finally, I decided to just make the call and get to the point. Most women liked the direct approach, or so I had read.

"Hiya, Angela, it's Lou. How are ya?"

"Who?"

"Not who, Lou," I responded with humor to mask disappointment at her non-recognition.

"Just kidding. I've got call display."

My rock-and-roll chest billowed with confidence. "Aha, so you've got my number memorized. Now we're talkin', sister girl."

"Ah sorry, my display just says Louis Crasher. No memorization here, hon. Say, anyone ever call you cymbal-crasher, what with the drums and all?"

"For the past hundred years at least, Angela. Yeah."

I could hear her quiet laugh. "So what's up, P.I. Guy?'

"Funny you should apply nomenclature that way because it just so happens that this PI has recovered your gear." I was beaming at my end of the phone until the silence continued a little too long. I cleared my throat, and continued with passion. "All of it has been...I have it all in my possession." Still more silence, so I threw more words at it. "So all that needs to be done is the drop, okay? Angela, are you there?"

"Yeah, sorry Lou, I've got a bad connection. That's great! I mean, my God, that's awesome. You did it, really?"

She used the right words only her delivery was a little forced. Either that or I was too into this investigative jazz and was reading too much. Heck, maybe I threw her off with my use of the word nomenclature, it's happened before. Regardless, I suddenly felt that it would be best for me to stay in LA and ask for Jake's help with the Bernie Outlaw business. I just had to see how this played out.

Angela seemed to recover somewhat as the conversation moved ahead. I suggested we grab a bite before doing the exchange but she'd already eaten and besides, she had a few things to take care of. When a relative stranger tells you they have a 'few things' to take care of it could mean up to two million different things. As time marches on and you get to know them, that number decreases significantly because after all you know the kind of person they are so you know very well what kind of job, hobby or chore might fall under a 'few things.' But for now, my mind was left to torture itself with silly guesses and suppositions. I should also point out that if a man such as myself is interested in the other party, then the number of possible 'few things' is even greater than the normal one million things, hence the aforementioned 'up to two million things.'

So once I was off the phone I was left trying to figure out what she had to do before seeing me and figuring out if I was going to slide down to IHOP on my own or construct one of my world famous club house sandwiches. I walked to my living room, opened the blinds and let the sun in. I had to settle for instant coffee. I could visualize my mother shaking her head. She never drank the stuff and always made sure you knew about it. The flashing light on my phone caught my eye. I dialed into voicemail. The stock recorded voice told me I had no messages even though the number said I had one. I walked back to pour the coffee when suddenly Bob's voice came out of the phone.

"Hey, loser, what's up? Didn't you have a gig tonight or is that tomorrow? Just kidding, I was there for most of the set. You sounded like shit so I left. You owe me a cover charge pal. No seriously, I made a friend if you know what I'm talkin' about, and had to get her out of there. Hey, hey when they're beggin' for big Bob, Bob delivers. And that's what I'm talkin' about." He was then cut off by voicemail.

Naturally he had to call back to get the last word in.

"Hey asshole, nice try cutting me off. Anyway, it's about one a.m. and I'm about to rock this girl's world. Say hi to Lou, baby." There was a pause.

"Hi, hi, Lou, I'm Chastity. Sorry we had to leave. You sounded great." There was a rustling then Bob was back. "Call me tomorrow and tell me what's up. I saw Jake there...that scary motherfucker. Oh, gotta go, it's time to work Chastity's belt. And that's what I'm—"

I deleted his message, and spared myself the last of his overplayed catch phrase. I shook my head and moved to the kitchen. It was clubhouse sandwich time. I whistled some non-descript tune as I went to work and was amazed that even whistling a tune not yet written I could manage to do it off-key. I was running low on roast beef but made up for it in the turkey and ham departments. Having only traversed but a third of the way into the loaf of twelve grain bread it was still fresh. My lettuce snapped back at me and the tomato was crunchy. Both jumped from the crisper into my hand as if dying to be part of the magnificent sandwich to come. I could tell this sandwich was going to be a real party. The hot mustard jar was close to extinction but she gave everything she had left, a real trooper. The next part, and this is where I have lost fans in the past, was the Miracle Whip.

The jar was practically brand new and accepted the plunging knife with a pride second to no other mayonnaise. When all occupants rested quietly on their twelve grain mattress I threw cracked black pepper and a touch of hot sauce into the mix before fixing the roof atop the creation. I put the blade in position, applied slight pressure with my other hand and halved the treat with plastic surgeon-like care. Even though it was before noon, to scarf down such a masterpiece without a long neck Miller Genuine Draft beer would be sacrilege, if not treason. Lucky for me I had sixteen or so in the fridge. I felt bad abandoning the coffee but I'd get over it. My friends and I bee lined for the couch. We had an appointment to finish the last twenty minutes of an old *Rockford Files* episode I'd borrowed. I hit play and sunk my pearly whites into what was quite possibly one of the world's top three sandwiches ever made. The beer chased the bite down and was moving fast. As I'd taken a big bite I was forced to send more beer down my gullet for backup. Just then there was a knock at Jim Rockford's trailer door. As he was about to open it there was a knock at my door. What were the odds?

Normally I'd have ignored it but this last week was not a normal week. I promised the sandwich I'd be right back.

I opened the door without checking the peep hole. On the other side of the threshold were two Caucasian males carrying a combined weight of well over five hundred pounds. The tops of their brush cuts put them each just under six feet four inches tall. Their tailor did fine work using miles of Armani fabric to fit these lads snug but not uncomfortably so. They both took two steps back from my door as if choreographed. They either didn't want to intimidate or they needed more room to breathe.

"Howdy, boys. You're going to have to be brief as I'm watching the last half of a *Rockford* episode," I said, appearing casual.

"Sorry to intrude, my good man. Whereas I am not a huge fan of Mr. Rockford my brother Xavier here is, so I'll advance to the point. My name is Oliver. Pardon me if we don't divulge our last name at this time. At any rate, our employer wishes to speak with you, which would explain why we stand before you now. I haven't many more details to give at this juncture, however I do possess a few. Perhaps we could continue this conversation somewhere other than this splendid corridor."

I was immediately thrown by his upper crust British accent, but like a good P.I. I possessed a poker face made from onyx. I gave nothing away.

The brother who I took to be Xavier spoke. "What, not expecting two big lads in quality suits to be educated Brits?" So much for my poker face.

"Au contraire, Xavier. I just didn't think the elevator would have held both of you. You guys aren't huffin' and puffin' so you didn't take the stairs, I'd wager. I knew you two spoke the Queen's perfect English before Oliver uttered a word."

Oliver became intrigued. "Would you mind terribly explaining how you knew such a thing so early on, my good man?"

"I could tell by your knock," I lied. I moved aside opening the door as wide as it would go, motioning for them to come inside. Oliver thanked me as he came in. Xavier thanked me too, but in what I believe was an attempt at a John Wayne impression.

With a huge eye roll Oliver said, "Please forgive my brother. He's abandoned his roots for pathetic American film and television. I say that meaning no offense to Mr. Rockford."

"Jimbo and I take no offense. Have a seat there or there, but not in front of that delectable sandwich." They sat accordingly. "Either one of you want a beer?"

They both declined. I took a big bite and a bigger pull on the beer. I picked up my remote with a slightly shaky hand and hit pause. "Okay, what's going on?"

"Mr. Crasher, we work for a gentleman who requests an audience with you."

"Who's the gentleman, Oliver?"

"He's a man who, were I to mention his name, you would know."

"I would know him by reputation or personally?" I asked, appearing clever. I don't know why I was playing cat and mouse, other than it seemed the right thing to do.

"Reputation, to use your word."

"So who is he?"

"Yo, you ask a lot o' questions there pal," Xavier piped up in his best Sylvester Stallone voice. It was awful.

"Xavier, for the love of God, man, enough with the tawdry, unpolished..." Oliver sighed. "Let us do what is in accordance with our employer's wishes, please, man!" He turned back to me. "Again, please accept my apologies, Mr. Crasher. Now then, I must politely insist that you come along with us for a meeting that should not take more than one hour and then you will be brought back here, unharmed."

"You cats are asking a lot, so I ask again, who is your boss?"

"A businessman..."

"What kinda businessman needs five hundred and sixty pounds of muscle from Piccadilly Square on his payroll?"

Xavier shot me a hard look as I began working on the second half of my sandwich. "Are you calling us goons, Mr. Crasher?"

"Xavier please, you know how I feel about intimidation!" Oliver barked. With that Xavier eased back into the corner of his seat and I was glad about it. I was raised to never back down unless of course "it means your ass," as grandma always said. Either one of these heavies could have picked me up by my pinkie toe and thrown me over his shoulder. However, I had to flex a little muscle at least so as not to be a complete ponce, which is a British term for sissy.

"Here's the deal. I don't want to mix it up with you guys, not here with all my fine possessions and so on. So, I'm going to trust you when you say you'll bring me back in one piece. Who knows, maybe I'm a sucker for your impressive verbiage. Having said that, I won't step foot one out of this place without finishing this sandwich and watching Jimmy take care of the bad guys. And that's non-negotiable, lads."

They conceded to the terms, which I thought was neighborly of them, and Xavier accepted a beer after all. Oliver did not approve. It turned out that Xavier was a Jim Rockford fan but preferred Magnum P.I. I too was a Magnum fan but was more loyal to Jimmy. Xavier and I argued back and forth on the matter like friendly sparring partners. Oliver checked his watch. I needed to call Angela but wasn't sure how to do it with my new guests present. Then when I thought about it I remembered she was going to call me after her few things. Why hadn't she called? As I was pondering this Jimmy solved the big case and yet again was not paid for it by the client. Poor Jimbo. I hit stop. Oliver was first to his feet, anxious to get on the road. I grabbed my wallet and keys and followed the giants out the door. With the three of us in the elevator it was cozy. Mrs. Wiggins from the second floor took one look at us and decided to wait for the next car. But as the doors were closing she jammed her cane in between the doors preventing them from shutting.

"Are you all right, Lou?"

"Oh yes, I'm fine, Mrs. Wiggins. How are you holding up?"

"Nevermind that—who are these men?"

"Allow me, my lady. I am Oliver and my brother here is Xavier."

"Where are you taking Lou? Because it looks like you're taking him somewhere, you know."

"My good lady, Mr. Crasher is coming to visit our modest lodgings in the Topanga Canyon," Oliver explained. "We should have him back in and couple hours."

Mrs. Wiggins considered the men closely with a frown. "Well I don't like it. ID, boys. Get 'em out or Louis, me and this cane will get busy, as the kids say."

I couldn't believe my ears when I heard little old Mrs. Wiggins, who had to be in her early eighties demanding these large lads break out their identification—with a threat, no less. An even greater shock was that Oliver and Xavier complied without complaint. The elevator tried to close but I pushed on the little center portion which lets the door know that it shouldn't close yet. Satisfied with the twins' driver's licenses Mrs. Wiggins let us go, instructing me to call her when I got in.

"Will do, Mrs. Wiggins. Oh, and by the way, we just watched the *Rockford* DVD you loaned me. It was great."

Down on the main floor, Clarissa from my floor was waiting with a scowl on her face. "What was going on up there? Were you having a convention?"

"Sorry, Clarissa, we ran into Mrs. Wiggins."

"Oh for God's sake Lou, you know the hours I work. I don't have time for this." One side of her hair had fallen out of the hair clip and covered part of her eye.

"I know Clarissa, you've mentioned your hours before."

"No need to be snitty, Lou."

"Clarissa?"

"What?"

"Now you're holding up the elevator and Mrs. Wiggins is waiting for it upstairs." She got in the car and reminded me that she didn't have time for this.

"She's a bit tense, is she not Mr. Crasher?" Oliver asked.

"She is, at that, Ollie. Can I call you Ollie?"

"If you must," he said with a sigh.

Xavier chuckled quietly. As the sun greeted us at around 83 degrees I was feeling better. I told myself that these lads wouldn't have shown their ID so easily to my neighbor if they planned to eliminate me. Sure the ID could have been faked but the fact that they showed in broad daylight with witnesses added to my cheery mood. We stopped walking near the end of the block at a black Range Rover.

"Would you mind driving, Louis Crasher?"

"Why not, I love these modern heaps." Why Oliver mentioned my full name I didn't know. It couldn't have been a veiled threat because they'd already shown they know where I live. Hmm. I was sure all would be revealed later.

"Oh yeah, I almost forgot," I said. "Who's your boss again?"

The British bruisers got in without answering my question, Oliver in the front and Xavier in the back. Like a little kid, Xavier flipped down the rear DVD player and queued an old John Wayne movie.

"Is that *The Cowboys*? The movie where the Duke helps out those young kids?"

"Good ears, Mr. Crasher, indeed it is," Xavier said with a congratulatory pat on my shoulder. Oliver rolled his eyes and mumbled, "Nonsense."

Miraculously, the 101 heading north was fairly light. The Rover owned a smooth ride at 85 miles an hour. As I shoved her over 90 gingerly, Oliver gave me the disapproving eye. I eased her back to 85 and got us to the church on time. The tires chattered as I rolled up the red cobblestone drive. Impressive black gates opened a yard before the Rover reached them.

"Just like in the movies, huh fellas?" Their silence told me it was quiet time. I'm no expert at pricing real estate in southern California but I knew I was looking at four million bucks in property, minimum. This also gave me hope. What would a big time criminal like Bernie Outlaw, who I was positive I was about to see, want with a small time honest dude like me? Guys making his type of juice were sure to be too busy counting, stealing and hiding money to notice me. We have a few drinks maybe, he'd warn me to leave his pissant nephew alone and send me on my way. I pulled up to the front steps and shut the Rover down. Getting out, I put the keys in my pocket. Oliver stepped around the car to face me. The sun was now gone.

"Planning a quick getaway Mr. Crasher?"

"Excuse me?"

"Keys please, my good man."

"Yes of course, must have been—"

"Habit. I understand, Louis."

As I gave up the keys, the front door swung inward. Out bounced a loud little man dressed as a cowboy. This was Bernie Outlaw, small time hood fast becoming known to the 'protect and serve' badges downtown. Bernie wore a powder blue suit with all kinds of white fringes. The suit was cheap, no question but the plain white shirt underneath was expensive. Just one of those things, I suppose. At the neck was an over-sized cowboy tie of the gaudy variety. It was a silver and bronze Texas longhorn that weighed no less than three hundred pounds. Seven hundred dollar alligator skin boots brought him down expensive travertine tile steps to meet me. At first, I put Outlaw in his early thirties but at handshake distance he moved into mid- to late-forties.

He did what many little-bigmen do upon meeting you, and that is attempt to break as many bones your hand as they can. This always confused me because an overly firm handshake does not gain them any height, it only says, 'Hey, I'm short but look how hard I can squeeze.' I could easily squeeze back and play that game, or relax, wait it out and save my hands for drumming. Occasionally, if a guy won't let go, one is forced to deliver a quick punch to their face. In that case I would be saying, 'You are short with a firm grip, but now how does your face feel?' Thankfully Bernie let go of my hand so we didn't have to dance further. Bernie was all Texas with a slice of LA present in the form of three earrings in his left ear and two in his right and a small diamond stud in his nose.

"Hey, hey, hey! There he is. Pleasure to make yer acquaintance, Mr.

Crasher. What do ya think of my two oil tankers Oliver and Xavier? Were they nice to ya?"

"Yes, fine young lads. Hell, they even let me drive your Range Rover here." I gestured with an open hand to the vehicle like a game show hostess. Bernie's face turned grim.

"Say what now?

"They let me drive. I was gentle though and everything."

Bernie turned slowly with a glare fired at his employees. "You let him drive my car?" he said, shouting the last two words. Oliver and Xavier showed mock fear at their boss who immediately burst into laughter. "I'm just kidding, Mr. Crasher. I told them to let ya drive. Ya see I've been taking these here acting classes—doing pretty good too. Anyway in film when everything is going along just dandy and then without warning a fella just plumb loses it they call that a, ah—what do they call that, Ollie?"

Oliver responded with a sigh, "a beat or a transition." Oliver grumbled up the steps and into the house.

"Right, a beat. Ain't it a hoot? I just love them classes. I'm pretty good too." He then slapped me hard on the back, which is another in the fun bin of little-big-guy antics. He moved toward the stairs suggesting we go inside and have a drink and 'gummin,' which I quickly learned meant conversation.

I regretted not bringing ear plugs as the combination of high ceilings, lots of glass and more travertine tile floors really helped Bernie's voice carry.

"What'll you have there Mr. Crasher? Beer? Scotch? Vodka? I got pretty near just about everything except Perrier water which in my belief is just plain old homosexual water from France." I told him that heterosexual beer from the good old United States would be fine, unless of course he had stronger Canadian beer. Apparently he liked me already. Then as an afterthought he decided to try another acting beat.

"I'm afraid scotch is all yer gonna git, Crasher!" It was my turn to show mock fear which got me a laugh. "Ollie," he yelled at the closed door that led to the kitchen. "I did it again. What the hell was that thing called again when a fella just—"

"A beat," Oliver exploded from the kitchen. We then heard what sounded like a magazine sail through the air, connect with a wall and then hit the tile floor. Bernie leaned close and whispered that he loved irritating his big tankers. My mother would say that Mr. Outlaw was tired of living. Bernie got up from the couch we sat on and opened up what I thought was merely an antique looking credenza used for fine plates or even books. As it turned out it was a bar equipped with a mini fridge. From it he handed me a blue labeled beer which happens to be brewed in eastern Canada and is actually called Blue. Bernie was turning out to be a decent man. He came back around the bar knowing I was impressed and sat down.

"How do you like them apples, Mr. Crasher?"

"Blue apples, my favorite!" I responded.

"Good. Now then, we need to have a little chat about a little outstanding debt between you and me." When a guy uses the word 'little' too much my antennae go up. Just then Oliver came in with a Perrier bottle in his big fist. "Pardon me, gents, but Mr. Outlaw, I've just been on the phone to your brother and—"

"Dammit Oliver, now I told you how I feel about that sissy French piss water. You know I can't stand the sight of it. I mean, it's queer. Not to mention how at every turn of the world stage they try and corral us like God knows what. No, just let me finish. What you hold in yer claw there is goddamn un-American!" Bernie's face was a shade lighter than a Red Delicious apple. His little chest heaved up and down in his powder blue suit.

Oliver paused, as if choosing his words with care. "Would that be a beat, Mr. Outlaw?" he asked.

"A what? No goddammit! Xavier, get in here and deal with yer moron of a brother, please."

Oliver's face showed boredom as he pressed on. "As I was saying, it appears that Mr. Crasher here has recently been engaged in a brawl with your nephew. I do not possess all of the details, as they are not easy to come by where your nephew is concerned. However, I gather that young Louis here delivered quite the beating to the little whelp."

With very little thought I was out of my seat like a cat out of a cold water pond full of dogs. "That son of a bitch jumped me. And not without help, I might add. He had four buddies with him. They jumped me for a $400 phone, which wasn't even mine to lose. I gave chase and I got lucky, that is all. Either one of you guys would have done the same. And that's all I'm saying on that." They didn't say anything. Xavier rolled in through a different door like a massive fog. All exits were blocked. I was pinned down for sure. Still no one spoke, so I kept going. "Listen, Bernie, all cards on the table. I came here willingly today. I could have made it rough for the two tankers there but I didn't. I was jumped by that idiot and I didn't go to the cops, which I could have. Hell, that's gotta be cool, to say the least in the eyes of a Texan. Not to mention honorable in the eyes of upstanding Brits." The verbal diarrhea kept flowing so I let it. "Furthermore Bernie, you're moving up in this town and everybody knows it. And mark my words the one thing that is going to bring you down just when you think you're at the top of your game is going to be that little whelp as Ollie so aptly put it. I did you a service." Here I was again talked out. I sat down and took a long hard pull on the beer, hoping it wasn't my last on this earth. It was Outlaw's turn to stand up.

"Ollie just walked in and informed me of this little dust up o' yers while you sat here drinking that fine beer. Am I correct on that?"

"Yes, sir."

"Now then aren't you wonderin' what I brought you out here for in the first place?"

My heart sank. I hadn't thought of that. I now waited like the accused on trial for the verdict to come down. Still, I remembered—Never let them see you sweat.

"This is LA. Fifteen million dudes; I figure this was a case of mistaken identity at best," I lied.

"I haven't moved up the ladder by making mistakes, Mr. Crasher, you can be sure o' that. No, the reason I had the fellas bring you out to this fine estate of mine is because you've been caught with yer hand in the cookie jar."

"Meaning what?" I asked.

"Meaning you stole some musical equipment, son, which didn't belong to ya."

"Well, no sense denying seeing as I'm a guy who talks straight. However you've been misinformed, or informed incorrectly, whichever way the grammar goes."

Oliver piped in, "Either will suffice, Master Louis." Outlaw frowned at Ollie's interruption.

I carried on. "I recovered stolen goods; goods that were stolen from my place of business."

Outlaw grinned as he rubbed his chin. "Mr. Crasher, an associate of mine—well, he's hardly an associate. Let's just say the man who came by this equipment allegedly from your place of business works for me."

"Wait a minute." Now I was hot. "Do you mean to tell me that musical public enemy number one a.k.a. Dave Abbott rips off every hard working musician, sells the gear, and you get a piece of that action? So in fact you—who claim to be a fan of film and theater— would steal from your entertainment cousin, the musician?"

"I never looked at it that way, but yeah, that'd be about right, "Outlaw answered.

"Well, home of the brave and land of the free, and here I was thinking you were a decent criminal," I said. Outlaw was on his feet with cheeks flushing.

"How dare you come into my house, my estate, and call me an un-decent criminal." Oliver pinched the bridge of his nose at the bastardization of the word *decent*.

"I didn't ask to come here, Bernard!" I was on my feet now too.

Bernie looked like he'd been slapped in the face. With a whisper and a faraway look in his eye he told me no one called him Bernard but his dead grandmother. He shook off the memory and lunged at me. One heel of his cowboy boot hit the glass table sending a spiderweb crack from end to end. He was on me punching short little punches. I blocked most of them with a Muhammad Ali style rope-a-dope technique but one of his fists slipped through and fattened my lip. Xavier pulled him off me easily. I apparently wanted it to be my turn. I stepped onto the table and put one of my old school Adidas right through the table. It was a miracle I didn't slice my leg up. I hopped out of the bronze table frame and got one shot into Bernie's nose before Xavier wrapped a massive bear paw around my throat. My reaction was to pry his fingers off individually. When he knew of my plan he cocked his other hand back in a hammer fist and aimed it at my face. The message was loud and clear...I struggled no more and he let me go.

As if nothing transpired, Oliver walked into the kitchen and returned with an ice pack for Bernie's nose. It was bleeding but not broken, which I decided was a good thing. Expecting a tantrum and then an order to have me killed, I was pleasantly surprised when Bernie gave Xavier hell for letting me get a shot in. He promised to make Xavier pay for the table.

Bernie tilted his head back and applied the ice pack. Suddenly he started laughing. Ollie, Xavier and I looked on, confused.

"Mr. Crasher, I cannot remember the last time somebody socked me, let alone took a poke at me. Huh, I forgot how good it feels to trade blows with a fella. Nothing like a good dust-up." He laughed a moment more and then brought his head back down, checking the ice pack and then his nose for blood. Satisfied the blood tide had ebbed, he got down to business.

"Now then, I am about to make you a proposition. An offer I suggest you take. You've cost me money on the Abbott thing, you've busted up my nephew, albeit he's about as useful as a bull tit but he is family just the same, and you've skinned a knuckle on me, which as you are now aware is not entirely your fault." He glared at Xavier, who feigned pulling lint specks from his trouser cuffs.

"You throw all these into the pot and it's a hell of a shit stew there, Mr. Crasher. So here's the deal. I got a brother by the name o' Chet MacBeth. Travis' old man. If you're wondering about our different last names it's because my daddy was a son of a bitch and I wouldn't keep his shit name for two minutes past my thirteenth birthday. My brother Chet there, he kept the name because he didn't have the stones that I did to do what is or was right. Are you gettin' the picture here, son?"

I said I was.

"Good. You and my twin towers there are going to break into his home and get me something he owes me. Well, I suppose I can give you a little more detail. Yer going to get me a photograph. It ain't particularly expensive and there's no great espionage here but it does have a what you might say is a sentimental value to it, if you get my meaning."

I considered asking if it was a portrait of his grandmother who called him Bernard, but now wasn't the time to crack wise.

"Now you boys are going to take a few other things too—make it appear random like so he won't suspect me. You're going to do this tomorrow night while he's up at Lake Tahoe with his mistress. Other than that y'all can plan the finer details, of which I care not to know."

"Question," I interrupted. "What's to become of me if I refuse your offer?"

"Well hell, Mr. Crasher you can go on your merry way and enjoy the rest of your incredibly short life."

"I thought as much but I had to ask. I have another question then. Does your brother have any other kids, a nanny, overzealous talking magpie, anyone or thing that might be there?"

"Negatory on all that. Ollie says the wife has gone to some bullshit convention in Vegas. My boys here will answer any other questions you have and they'll see ya home." With that he stood and shook my hand over the broken coffee table. Once again he gripped too hard then gave me a wink like a Hollywood producer might who's just screwed you out of a deal...or into one. As he clip-clopped away in his snake skins he told me over his shoulder that I could have another beer before I left. Once through the giant entrance way and up a half dozen steps he shouted down to us that Xavier had better get that table replaced by sun-up.

"I didn't know they called it sun-up in California," I said to Xavier.

Chapter 19

Xavier insisted on driving for my trip home. No doubt he and his brother felt I was in no shape to drive after having my destiny handed to me by their boss. Beyond agreeing to get together late tomorrow night an hour before the caper, dialogue was limited. Curbside to my apartment Oliver rolled his window down, "It's just a spot of bad luck, old boy. You'll manage."

I wasn't in the mood for any of that cheerio British bullshit, however Oliver did seem sincere. Before getting to my place, I stopped by Mrs. Wiggins' to let her know I was back safe and sound. She looked me up and down like a medical examiner before finally commenting on my lip, which was still slightly swollen. She didn't buy my story about sneezing so hard while sitting in the back of the twins' car that my face collided with my knee. As that was a lie, I didn't blame her for not believing me, but sometimes people just have to just take the crap they're shoveled.

"Well," she said, "at least you're back in one piece. Come by in a day or two and I'll give you another *Rockford* episode."

"It's a date, Mrs. Wiggins," I beamed.

I glanced at the phone and saw that there were no messages waiting, and was disappointed that Angela hadn't called. I cracked a beer and began trying to put everything together in my mind when a single knock hit my door. One sound and I knew who it was before opening the door.

"Jake, come on in. Whoa, that's a sweet tuxedo, man." He moved straight to my tiny kitchen table, pulled out a chair and neatly placed his jacket on it. He then sat in a different chair.

"How did it go with Outlaw?" he asked, getting right to business.

"Man, I am through being surprised by you. Anyway it went fine. He made me a Don Corleone type of offer." I slid out my other chair and sat across from him. I held my beer and raised my brows but he declined. I continued on and spread the whole story out in front of him. As per usual he didn't speak until I was done.

"So they know about what you did to Travis, but do they know what I did to Travis?" It was a good question.

"Damn Jake, I forgot to ask. Something tells me they do know but just didn't play that card. In fact, the way they showed up here—" I paused, searching through the fragments of dialogue and events. "I bet they know we're connected but they don't know much about you yet. Sorry to drag you in, but I bet Outlaw is checking you out. I mean look at the way they just show up and grab me." My head was beginning to spin.

"Sounds right. How do you think they figured out the gear situation?"

"Another mystery to this string of unknowns," I answered.

"Not really. Use your head. Be Sherlock Holmes and use the process of elimination."

I stared at Jake. Why was he testing me? His face showed nothing, so I thought I'd play along for the hell of it.

"Okay, there's me and Bobby, we pulled off the scam. No way he talked to anyone, not even under torture. He's too stubborn. The girls wouldn't have said anything, and you? No. Maybe the guitar player in Abbott's band figured out the scam; shit, he almost busted me at rehearsal and then we stung him."

Then like a ton of bricks I figured out why Jake wanted me to figure out what he already suspected.

"Oh no way, you mean Angela? No way. It doesn't make sense. Jake, she hired me to find the stuff. She—it was her stuff that was ripped off. Wait, wait. Bernie said that Abbott essentially pays a chunk to him, and..." I paused. My head started swirling like a tilt-a-whirl.

"Louis, assuming you told Angela that you recovered all her stuff, what was her reaction?"

"Not the hip-hip-hooray response I was looking for, I'm afraid," I said, peeling the beer label off my bottle. "Okay, let's say she ratted me out. What's the connection with Bernie? And why would Abbott steal her stuff?"

Jake changed his mind and grabbed himself a beer from the fridge and sat back down across from me. "Who can say? My guess is Abbott pays protection but he's not exactly on the payroll. Hitting your place was the plan, but grabbing her gear was an accident."

"Hm, do ya think?"

"I said it was a guess, remember? Anyway, forget that for now. What about this Don Corleone type offer?"

I took another sip before answering. "Short version: the twins and I have to break into Outlaw's brother's pad and steal a photograph for him. He claims it's sentimental or some bullshit but that's the gist of it. No one's supposed to be home. It goes down tomorrow night. He claims that if I do this we're square."

"Are you gonna do it?" Jake asked.

"Yup, I don't think he needs a fall guy. I think he just needs to flex some muscle."

"You mean you hope that's all this is. I'll back you up."

"Forget it, Jake, you've done enough, man, really."

But of course, Jake gave me one of those looks that said he did the things he wanted to do on this earth and it was going to stay that way. I didn't argue, I just thanked him again.

"What time does the hammer drop, Louis?"

"I'm supposed to meet the twin tankers at one a.m. at some all-night diner in North Hollywood...off of Lankershim and—"

"I'll be there," he said and started to get up.

"Jake, you haven't finished your beer. You Americans never finish your beers. It's insulting." He ignored me and put his tux jacket back on.

"Listen," I said. "I'm pretty certain Bobby has already dropped the stuff off with Angela. I mean she probably called Outlaw after she got her stuff back...or I don't know, maybe before. The point is...what do I do about her, man?"

"Are you asking me if I think she'll still go to the prom with you?" And with that Jake left with a disgusted look on his face. After the door closed, I called after him inquiring where he was going in that spiffy tux. I got no response.

Chapter 20

I downed the rest of my beer and dumped Jake's. He was right and I knew it. Angela was connected to this whole racket and probably was the one who rolled on me. Sadly, I can't say it's the first time I've been a sucker to a dame. I took a step back and looked at my situation. Outlaw had me over a barrel, sure, but who's to say he didn't have Angela in the same kind of spot? A ray of hope was shining through. I had to talk to Angela and get to the truth. I am a detective, after all.

Those who work the halls of psychotherapy might say that I was about to call Angela out of a need for some type of closure. Let me start by saying that I hadn't learned of the term 'closure' until I moved to Los Angeles. Therapists coined it, soap operas adopted it, and talk radio wore it out like teenagers wore out the word 'like.' Personally, I can't stand the word *closure*. I don't need it and I ain't seeking it. I am merely a drumming private dick trying to complete a job and save his skin, period.

As luck would have it I got Angela's voicemail after the first ring, which meant that someone else was leaving a message at the same time or that she was in the middle of dialing somebody. I decided to leave a message rather than call back and risk missing her if she stepped out.

"Hiya, Angela," friendly mixed with business, "it's me, Lou. A Lou that is in one piece. Ah, let me get right to it. The twins picked me up. I met Bernie and now I'm on the hook for trying to be a Good Samaritan. Shit, was that too whiny? Anyway, I'd like to talk to you. It's like Ozzy Osbourne said, 'I'm going off the rails on a crazy train.' Call me."

So that was done. The ball was in her court now. The phone rang almost immediately. I grabbed her before the second ring, heart pounding. It wasn't Angela, it was my boss.

"Hi Lou, how's it going at your end?" he asked.

"Oh, hey boss. Good, it's going good. I've got good leads on the gear. Wait, I'm not going to bullshit you. I found the stuff, all of it."

"You're kidding me! That's great. When we have more time you'll have to tell me how you did it. Listen, things at my end aren't going so hot. The construction guys I hired really blow, when they're here that is. I never should have gone through the ex-wife on this shit. Anyway, we've got two rooms going but that's it at this point."

"Well, that's some dough coming through the door anyway, boss," I said, being a cup half-full kind of guy.

"True, but the bad news is that I won't need you for another week or so. You see, I have to pay these useless jerks out of my pocket until insurance kicks in, which also means I have to mind the store while this happens."

"That's okay; I got a little gig going on the side. Thanks for the heads up." We both sat silently a moment on our ends of the phone, and then I remembered something. "Hey, I thought your insurance company dropped you, late payments and all that."

"They did, but luckily dad opened a policy I hadn't known about."

"Good man, your old man."

"No kidding. Going through the Great Depression taught his generation a lot about responsibility. Of course, he and mom won't stop reminding me of it, especially now. All I learned was how to get stoned and protest in the sixties. Anyway, got to go. Keep in touch."

The next day I got up early and took a drive to the tiny drum studio I rent off Burbank and Lankershim —technically North Hollywood, although as with many neighborhoods around LA, the people of this area sought to carve out their own identity. This area was now renamed 'vista something' or 'something playa.' The idiocy is that the neighborhoods don't change, the zip code stays the same, but the area gains a pretty little sign. It is a way for the inhabitants to kid themselves that their property values will go up. That and they gain a cute name to drop at boring cocktail parties. And people say musicians are wacky.

Friends of mine often ask why I don't just practice at my place of business. And in fact I do, but there are other advantages to having your own space. The first thing is that my lockout gives me 24-hour access, no neighbor complaints or anything. The second advantage is that it is my studio with my drum set. I suppose you could compare me to the artist with the personal loft versus the artist who only has access to classroom paints and materials during class time.

I opened the double lock and climbed into my tiny room. As usual, I nodded to Gabrielle Union, Mohammed Ali, Jimi Hendrix and jazz great Tony Williams. I had other small photos on the walls but most of them were old band promos of my previous bands. I don't usually greet those. The best thing for me to do when I have a problem is to sit down and work it out behind the drum kit. I start out with rudiments. Some cats dread working on rudiments because it can often feel like the homework part of drumming. I don't see them that way, for two reasons. First is, I look to the history. The snare drummer used to be one of the top gigs during the civil war. The drummer was the cat who marched the troops forward, backward, sideways, you name it. They had a decent salary, the nicest tents, gourmet food, everything. They had to be creative with their rhythms so the enemy couldn't know what the plan was. To me, that's heavy. The other thing is Buddy Rich. He was without question one of the greatest drummers of all time. His drum solos, like others' of his time, often began on the snare drum. He stated that if you could not play a decent musical drum solo on the snare drum alone then he or she had no business playing the rest of the drum kit. To me, that's also heavy.

After fifteen minutes of this, I was warmed up. Normally, I'd crack one of my music books, but I wanted to play from the heart. I reached down and put the $55 Radio Shack headphones into position. I scroll through my iPod Nano with one hand with only one band on my mind: Earth, Wind & Fire. I needed Philip Bailey's sweet voice and that killer horn section. The second the band's horn section hit my ears with *In the Stone*, all my troubles were gone. From time to time I thought of my upcoming caper with the twins. I wished that I could see the house before we robbed it so I could know where all the escape hatches were in case the twins decided to hit me over the head with a brick, or worse one of their fists, and leave me holding bag. Occasionally, I wondered what was so important about a photograph that Outlaw had to steal it from his brother. I always forced this question out of my head, because all of that would be his business. The less of that I knew, the better.

As the last of the greatest hits faded, I reached for my bottled water.

Up next was to be Led Zeppelin's *Houses of the Holy*, but just then my studio door swung in. Jake stood on the threshold in jeans, a black T-shirt, black leather jacket and a motorcycle helmet in his hand. I never knew he rode.

"Hey Jake, I don't remember telling you where my studio was. What's up?"

"I checked phone records—Travis's, Outlaw's and his brother's. They know about me but only have a description of me from the idiot. It won't make much difference in the near future, I suppose. Just came by to let you know that initially I was going to be in the diner. But now I won't. Eyes will be on you, so don't worry. I'll follow you to the house. If they decide to cook you, I'll pull you out of the fire...after you've burned a little bit."

A giggle came from behind him, then a woman who could have been the queen of an uncharted African country poked her smile into my room. "Hi Lou, I'm Sondra."

I stood up and came out from behind my kit. We shook hands and then stepped outside into the back alley where the air was fresher. "Nice to meet you, Sondra, and may I say wow! Look at you."

She laughed and told me she would have liked to say she'd heard a lot about me, but you know how Jake is. We walked over to Jake's bike. It was a cherry number made by the Ducati Company.

"That's a pretty ride, Jake. Italian, right? I'd have thought you more of a Harley type of guy."

"Then it is a good thing you're paid to play drums and not to think," he said testily.

"Jake," Sondra said punching him in the arm, "Be nice. What was that you were playing along to in there Lou?"

Jake answered for me—Earth, Wind & Fire. In unison, Sondra and I asked how he knew seeing as I had headphones on. Jake didn't answer us. We smiled, shaking our heads.

We had as much small talk as Jake would allow before they climbed on the bike, fired her up and rolled down the alley. As Sondra's back disappeared I realized just how much juice Jake really had, for it's not everybody who can get ahold of phone records. Who the hell are you,

Jake? I asked myself. And more importantly who is Sondra and does she have a sister? Well, will you look at that, I thought, I'm getting over Angela quite nicely. Oh, who am I kidding? I was totally jazzed about that girl. Now I wondered why I was staring down an empty alley. I went back inside and got the Led out, as rockers around the world would say.

Chapter 21

"Mr. Crasher, nice of you to show up. Both Oliver and I figured you'd show up, truth be told. That is, if you were still in town."

"Oh, come on fellas, I always try to do what I say I'm going to do. Besides, why would I run? I have Bernie's guarantee that no harm will come to me if I do this. Is there something that doesn't add up with our arrangement? And if Outlaw was going to screw me, would you big lads tell me anyway?"

"Settle down, Louis. You pose question after question without the benefit of acquiring answers. It is far too American of you, and you, a Canadian, tsk, tsk." Oliver opened a napkin and spread it on his lap. I pulled into the booth and sat beside Xavier. Oliver and Xavier wore black pants, black boots, and thick black turtlenecks. We all looked at each other in disbelief, for I was dressed exactly as they were.

"So much for subtlety, huh, boys," I said.

A waitress named Destiny came by and asked if I wanted tea like my two friends. "Tea, certainly not," I respond, "I'll have coffee, please, and I take it refills are free at this burg?"

"Yes, sir, coffee as well as hot water refills are free at this—what did you call it?"

"Ah, burg, I said burg."

"Hm. Cute word, never heard it before. I'll be right back with your coffee, green eyes."

"Well, well, young Louis, I think the lass fancies you. Sakes, I never even noticed that you possessed green eyes," Oliver chuckled.

"I, on the other, hand did notice," Xavier commented. "Still, I think there is also just a dash of hazel around the outside of the eye."

Oliver leaned across the table slightly. The table groaned under his weight.

"Smashing, you are correct, brother, he does have a slight—"

"Guys, guys," I interrupted, "Enough already. I am not comfortable with six hundred pounds of British beef inspecting my eyes. It's creepy."

The twins laughed and clinked their tea cups together. They both had difficulty holding their cups as their fingers were too thick for the handles. Destiny came back with my coffee and some creamers. "Here you go, handsome. Careful, it's hot."

"Sarcasm, I like that," I said.

"Good, because I like you," she said and walked away only this time she put a little music in her walk.

"Just think, young Louis, once we've done this bit of unsettling business you'll be free to live out your life and chase your...Destiny." He and his brother shook our booth and the next one over with their rolling laughter.

"Okay, okay, let's get into it, shall we, dudes?"

They wiped their eyes in identical fashion and then Oliver went to work at a crude drawing of MacBeth's house. Once done he spun it around and showed it to Xavier and me. The layout didn't seem to contain anything out of the ordinary. A short walkway with two small patches of grass on either side ran up to the front door. We'd move down between MacBeth's and the neighbor to his east and make our way in through the back door.

"Is there no back alley to approach from?" I asked.

Apparently there wasn't. Oliver and I'd go in while Xavier kept the car close but not too close. The twins had cell phones that doubled as walkie talkies. After some discussion we'd decided not to use them. I teased them that if Outlaw was so heavy how come he didn't have state of the art ear pieces and stuff like Jennifer Garner used on the television show *Alias*.

"Oh, do not suppose that for one moment our employer doesn't have such gadgets. We were just not allowed to use them on this episode due to somebody allowing you to slug our boss," Oliver said, annoyed.

"I'm not following you," I said.

Xavier interjected, "Bernie is punishing me for letting you smack him."

I laughed. "I see. So you haven't fixed the glass table yet. So much for sun-up."

"So much for sun-up indeed, master Louis," Oliver said, irritated.

"Damn it, brother!" Xavier said, pounding the table, "My man at Cort Furniture dropped the ball. Must I hear this nonsense from you as well as from the Napoleonic cowboy?"

We continued to work out the finer details. The next hour wasn't filled with planning for there wasn't a whole lot of planning needed for this deal. We were actually just waiting for time to pass so neighbors could put heads to pillows. Part of the time the twins talked about their childhood days back in England. They argued a lot about minor details but for the most part the conversation was upbeat. If we weren't dressed like cat burglars onlookers would have taken us for long lost friends. The twins had a close family. Their mother was sweet and their dad, although tough, loved his family. They grew up very poor but their parents made sure they had what they needed. In fact, the twins agreed that it wasn't until they were well into adolescence that they discovered how poor they really were. By that time it didn't matter. They were happy.

Destiny kept checking on us, with the two of us exchanging playful banter. The Brits got tired of teasing me, finally. We'd been there just over an hour when Destiny pulled up a chair and joined us.

"So what exactly is the deal? I haven't heard about any turtleneck conventions going on in this part of the Valley. What gives, fellas?"

The twins looked more nervous than I thought they would have, so I took the reins. "We are Chippendale dancers, and this is our uniform when we're off duty."

"Good God, Louis, please," Oliver blurted. I wasn't happy that he used my real name.

"Oh come on, Skip, don't use my dance name when we're off duty.

Call me Risky, my real name," I said cleverly.

Destiny took a cigarette out of a pack, stuck it in her mouth but didn't light it. "Chippendales, huh. I heard all their dancers are gay," she said with bored eyes.

"Oh enough of this," Xavier couldn't take it anymore. "My brother and I are twins and twins often dress the same and it's a mere coincidence that our friend here," he pointed at me, "dressed as we are dressed."

"Okay, so indulge me a moment, boys. Your name is Louis and you use humor to help tell your lies, and you," looking at Xavier, "when under pressure tell the most logical yet lame lie that comes to mind." The unlit cigarette bounced up and down between her lips as she spoke.

"A word of advice to you guys. The next time you plan to rob somebody or something, don't dress the part and then meet at an all-night diner half full of witnesses." She took the cigarette out of her mouth and held it in her fingers. She tapped it over the floor as if dumping ash then put it back in her mouth.

"Oh, and any schematics that need going over will need more than a meaty hand covering it when the hot waitress comes by with tea and coffee. Get it together, boys." She got up to go.

"Destiny, you are it. You're all aces with me, doll. I see you are in the last stages of quitting smoking so why not distract yourself with me, for example?" I was bouncing back again from the Angela tragedy.

"Check your check, Louis." Her hips played an even nicer song as she walked away this time. At the kitchen door she looked coyly back at me over her shoulder. It was pop music poetry in motion.

We sat there exactly like the three played out little boys that we were. Nobody spoke. We'd been handed our hats. We barely looked at each other. I'm sure that the lads were having the same doubts about successfully pulling off our plan as I was. Finally, Xavier checked the bill. The grand total was zero. She'd picked up the tab. There was a little note:

Drinks on me fellas. Try not to get caught.

Louis: call me at 818-555-1243 and don't

wait the standard three days cause by the third

day I'll be into the wind...XO D.

It was time to go. As we stood we began leaving tip money. Somehow it became a tip festival; every dollar one guy put down was matched if not topped by the next guy. We were idiots. Xavier finally grabbed Oliver and I and pushed us toward the door. We'd just been made by a savvy waitress who picked up our check and made herself twenty three bucks for tea, coffee and conversation. Ain't life grand!

Chapter 22

The plan was to ditch the old gal and ride together to MacBeth's in the Rover. There was slight contention as I wanted to park far from MacBeth's in a different neighborhood all together. I had visions of pulling off the job and then being followed by a nosy neighbor or security guard with a cell phone right back to the old gal. It would be one thing if I get caught but hell, I refuse to get my '65 'stang hauled down to the roller's impound lot. She would not be amused. The twins finally relented and followed me from the diner to another vista something-or-other neighborhood... still within the North Hollywood city limit. I shut the ol' gal down and told her I'd be right back, but if not I'd have somebody come and get her. I climbed into the back of the Rover.

Xavier drove the eight minutes to MacBeth's. I, unlike Oliver, had no problem with his driving. Oliver backseat drove the whole way there. Xavier was obviously accustomed to his brother's protestations. But to make matters worse, Xavier responded to each comment in his terrible John Wayne impression. We finally pulled to a stop barely around the corner from the house so that if Xavier leaned forward in his seat he could just see the front of the two story house. Once the vehicle was shut down, Oliver said, "Lads, a word if I may. The waitress back at the diner basically pulled our knickers down. We would be well advised to take her words to heart, especially you and I, brother, for future reference."

His voice trailed up a few decibels with the last word. Something was going on between the two of them but I wasn't sure what. Thoughts of double cross entered my mind but I pushed them out. If they were going to tank me Oliver wouldn't have lacked such subtlety. No, there was something else at play, I hoped. Nevertheless I was going to be like Spiderman and keep my spidey senses about me.

Oliver and I opened our doors to get out. I was easing my door closed when it appeared that Oliver was going to slam his door. Xavier and I loudly whispered 'no.'

"Brother, please. All it takes is for one of MacBeth's neighbors suffering from insomnia to hear you slam that door and check his bedside table and note the time. Please, for the love of Lady Diana God-rest her...don't slam that door!"

"He's right. Or maybe the not-so-happy couple has had an argument. The man can sleep because he's pig headed and selfish. He's said his piece. But the wife, no such luck. She stomps downstairs to finish off a small tub of Ben and Jerry's, hears your car door slam and then bingo; tomorrow when the cops canvass the neighborhood she remembers her kitchen clock read two thirty a.m. Ease the door closed like I did," I said, briefly.

"Good Lord!" "Why don't the two of you get a flat together, get 400 cable channels and watch telly until your eyes explode," Oliver said hotly.

Oliver feigned slamming the door to make us nervous and then eased it closed. The two of us moved down the sidewalk and carried on a fake conversation the way background actors in a movie would, without sound. We had hand gestures and everything so that if we were observed it would look normal. However we remained quiet so as not to wake anyone. At the house we carried on the same way up the narrow walk and then down along the side between the two houses. Two steps in, the neighbor's motion sensor light came on. We immediately flattened ourselves against MacBeth's building. We both breathed hard, but not from exhaustion. A light came on from a window next door almost directly above us. I gauged it to be a kitchen window. A voice came from within.

"Hush up Martha; somebody's set off the motion detector." The man's voice had booze, cigarettes and close to fifty years in it. From somewhere else deep within the house came a similar voice, only female. Martha.

"Oh, you old paranoid fool it's probably just a cat. But hey, since you're out there I'll take another bourbon and put some love into it this time."

I was wedged nicely in a crook made by the house and the chimney with Oliver beside me. The motion light shined within inches of our toes. The man cupped his hands over his eyes to block out inside light. Oliver squeezed closer to me fearing our goose was cooked. Sadly, he didn't know that the move put most of his near three hundred pounds on my foot. I'd will the pain away. Mind over matter, I told myself. Surely the light would go out any second. I was losing the battle of convincing my baby toe that it wasn't feeling excruciating pain. Then Oliver let out a sharp little bark sounding like a small dog. He sounded good too. He covered every species from Pekinese to Poodle. The motion light went out. We let our breath out. I nudged Oliver off my foot.

"Sorry, chap," he whispered.

The man in the window told Martha it was a dog and yelled at her to make her own damn drink. We crept down the rest of the way and huddled near the back door. The motion light came back on but wasn't investigated this time. We surveyed the back door. The window in the door was a thick double paned variety. It would be too much trouble. We moved to the sliding window beside the door. Silently Oliver motioned a slow palm to the center of the two windows. He pointed to the right window and then at himself then he pointed to the left side, the sliding side, and then pointed at me. I caught his meaning. He pulled his hand back barely three inches from the window base. He whispered one, two then three and smashed his palm into the window frame. Both windows popped off the track. He grabbed his window with his other hand while I just managed my side with a fingertip catch. I was impressed with myself. Sweat beaded on Oliver's forehead.

"Nice one, Ollie," I whispered.

It was a tight squeeze, but I made it through the window then came around and unlocked the door for Ollie. I closed the door behind him quietly. We stood silently in a spotless laundry room. Well, spotless except for the broken latch and bits of metal from the window. Oliver placed the two windows neatly in a corner beside a laundry basket. He had gloves on so there'd be no prints on them.

"Lead the way, big Ollie," I whispered.

The house was a perfect fit to Oliver's earlier diagram. We came out of the laundry room, down a short hall and then rounded a staircase and started creeping upward. Ten low rise stairs, a landing, turn the corner, climb six more steps and we were upstairs. I don't know why I counted the steps. Maybe I was in 'young private dick taking in useless as well as useful information' mode. We had decided not to use any flashlights for the twins shared my paranoia about neighbors spotting the light. It was a good call because as it turned out, the street lights gave us enough light. We passed one room to our left then entered a room to our right. It was MacBeth's den. Oliver had me move to the desk while he watched the door. Other than a few neatly stacked papers, the desk held three framed photographs. It was just as I was rounding the large teak desk that we heard a faint jingling sound. Boys to men around the world know this sound, whether heard on the sand lot, playground, barnyard whatever. It meant K-9 incoming. A sturdy Doberman Pincer carrying the weight of a Rottweiller stood on the threshold and stared at me, then Oliver. Oliver braced himself for impact. The dog growled then leapt at Oliver. With his beefy open hand Oliver clapped the dog on the side of the head just before its teeth reached his neck. The dog hit the ground, rolled, and was on its feet. With a quick head shake and a longer growl the dog attacked again. This time Oliver caught the dog in a bear-hug. The Doberman snapped at his face but in one motion Ollie drew his head back and squeezed the dog around his rib cage. The dog yelped briefly then was silent. Ten seconds later the dog's eyes closed.

"Holy shit, Ollie you killed it!" I shouted.

Ollie eased the dog to the floor as if putting an infant to bed.

"I've done nothing of the sort. I've merely put the poor chap to sleep, I may have cracked a rib though, poor thing—bloody hell."

"I thought you guys said there were no animals here. No surprises, remember? Dang it, Ollie."

"I am perfectly aware of what was said, Louis. Just grab the photo and let's be off."

"Okay, but Outlaw said to make it look random. Are you perfectly aware of that conversation too?" I was being a tad testy at this point. "All right Ollie, which one of these pictures are we supposed to—"

My voice got stuck in my throat when I saw one of the three photos. Angela stood leaning against her car with a provocative smile on her face. Oliver didn't seem to notice me stammer. He was still consumed with the dog.

"Ah, Ollie which one of these pictures?" I asked.

"The photo with the pretty girl in it, yes that's the one, tuck it away and let's grab a few things on the way out."

Oliver produced a black sack and began tossing trinkets inside. An ornate candle holder, an African carving, a thin high tech looking DVD player and so on. I was behind him all the way with the photo of my one time dream girl under my sweater. My eyes darted side to side and in back of us for other dogs, baboons or rabid rats. Thankfully we made it back to the laundry room without ambush. Another plus was that Oliver didn't knock me out and leave me to greet the cops. He had his hand on the back door when he suggested we go back and out the front door. He didn't feel confident that his tiny dog impression would work a second time. I agreed and gave him a wide berth to pass so he could lead the way out the front. He gave me an odd look as I did this.

He swung the front door open quickly. I was on his heels. He stopped a moment, uttered bloody hell, and then continued. His back was too large for me to see what caused the utterance. When he started moving again I pulled up beside him. It was my turn to utter something similar to bloody hell.

Parked at a forty five degree angle to the curb was a private security vehicle belonging to the Protek Company. The passenger side door was open with the interior light burning bright. What was more alarming was the Protek employee lying on the ground on his back. He was sawing logs. The car's radio was ripped out. Oliver and I took it all in quickly and then moved with a brisk walk down the sidewalk. Gone was the pantomime act from before. We couldn't resist running the last twenty yards to the Rover. Xavier fired up the ride and we took off. Oliver cursed him for driving too fast. We zigzagged through various side streets until Oliver commanded his brother to park.

"Bloody, bloody hell Xavier, are you a complete boob? Shall I begin with you not doing the proper research and forewarning Master Louis and I that MacBeth is the proud owner of a top form Doberman Pincer? Or shall I chastise you for brutalizing a security guard in front of the house without so much as peep of warning to us at all. Honestly man, have you taken full leave of what little senses you currently possess?"

"Brother," Xavier shouted, "I caution you to curb your tone and tell me what the hell you are carrying on about." As Oliver was gearing up to give Xavier another dose, I chimed in.

"Hey, who the hell is this girl? And what the hell is going on?" They both ignored me.

"Xavier, dear brother," he took a deep breath. "A fine specimen of K-9 crept up on Louis and me and attacked. Because of your blunder I was forced to put the animal down. Not permanently, mind you, but you know what an animal lover I am. Oh, how this upsets me."

He squeezed his eyes shut as if blocking out a nightmare.

Xavier spoke softly," Louis, Oliver I apologize to you both. I believe that events came down as you have said. MacBeth must have picked up the dog as recently as today or yesterday, I swear it. Again, my apologies." He shifted in his seat to get more comfortable. "Now then, pray tell me of this security guard business."

Oliver was still into his thoughts, no doubt about the dog. "Xavier, do you mean to tell me that you honestly don't know anything about the security guard?" I said.

"Scout's honor, as they say in this country."

"Allow me the short version. We came out the front door. There was a Protek car, passenger side door open. The radio was gone and the guard knocked out cold by you... or so we thought."

"Great Scott, it wasn't me I swear but what is more amazing is that I frequently checked the house—that is to say when I wasn't changing the radio stations or what have you."

Oliver glared at his brother and then told him to take me to my car. As we drove to my car I had two thoughts. The first was that Angela was way into this Outlaw/MacBeth business. The second thought was that only one person I know could take out a security guard while under the sometime watch of a lookout man. Jake had done it again.

Chapter 23

"Louis, this is no time to play silly, you know exactly who the young lady in the photograph is. In fact judging from your actions prior to this I expect you quite fancy this lass." Oliver was very matter of fact, in fact.

"If by fancy you mean that I thinks she's cool, well, I'm not so sure anymore."

"Understandable," Xavier said.

"Indulge me lads; it would appear that this woman, Angela, told Bernard that I returned her gear to her. And it also seems that something is going on between her and this attack dog owning idiot MacBeth?"

Oliver cleared his throat, "To 'indulge you,' as you say, Louis, can only be done so as far as our employer would permit, you understand. Having said that, firstly, Angela is in fact as you have said the one who informed Bernie that you returned the property. She is in a bit of the soup, however."

"Meaning what, Ollie?" I was more focused than an observatory telescope.

"Meaning Bernie didn't have a problem with a stranger, a non-officer of the law, searching for Angela's belongings as no doubt a simple drummer, no offense, would doubtless find anything. Fact is Angela convinced Bernie that having you look for the gear would cover her fanny if the police were close to making a connection between Mr. Abbott and her. He did, however, have a problem with the money."

"Hm, convoluted," I said. "Money, What money? The money the gear would have sold for?"

"Ah, no master Louis, the money Angela paid you for the search."

"What would Outlaw care? The money came from her record label. At least that's what she told…" My focus was seriously sharp at this point. "Are you saying Outlaw is the record label?"

"Quite. Out and Out Records, to be exact."

I slumped down in my seat a little, my brain digesting to me a perverse story. My gal-to-be had played me like a worn out 33 1/3 piece of vinyl…the B-side. And as great rock and rollers Led Zeppelin once said, 'it's nobody's fault but mine.'

"But hold up here fellas, Bernie's got the big house, fine ride, a record label, as you say, and whatever else I don't know about. Why's he care about a few shillings to me? We're talking peanuts."

"Well, is it not often the case, young Louis, that the wealthy are wealthy because they hang on to every precious penny?"

"He's cheap, in other words. Okay enough about that. What else, Ollie, you started out by saying 'firstly.' Is there a secondly?"

"Ah, yes secondly, or rather, second. Angela has been involved with Bernie's brother. Initially she was to spy on him, which ultimately would lead to this evening's events. However I have a suspicion that originally the relationship was of a phony nature on Angela's part but time has managed to twist things a bit. Ah, that is to say, I believe the lady currently fancies Mr. MacBeth. Sorry, chap. Also within the confines of my suspicion are that Bernie picked up on this development and pushed up today's caper for fear of his brother taking precautions."

"Like zipping out and picking up a killer Doberman to lay in wait for two cool burglars," I added, showing my powers of detecting.

"Possibly. Again I am compelled to remind you, young Louis, that this is only a suspicion at this point."

It seemed to fly with me. "So when you or Bernie or whoever said that MacBeth was out of town with his mistress, you cats meant Angela?"

The twins nodded in unison. I felt like the village idiot, and then I laughed like the village idiot for a moment.

"So why then would MacBeth have a picture of his mistress out in plain sight when the dude is married?"

"I'm afraid Bernie fudged the story a bit there Louis. You see, MacBeth and his wife have been separated for quite some time now. She actually lives in Vegas."

"Well, hallelujah for her and everybody else but me. Shit. Okay, last question. Tell me why we have risked jail time for this friggin' photo? She looks better in person by the way, but again, why the risk?"

"And now young Louis, I'm afraid we have come to that point where we can no longer share any more information with you. Surely you understand."

"Oh, I understand all right, but my upbringing prohibits me from using the kind of language I'd like to, to explain just exactly how well I understand."

The twins gave me confused looks. To be honest I wasn't sure myself what I'd just said.

"At any rate when we get to Bernie's he'll fill in the blanks for you," Xavier said.

"So we're going to Outlaw's then, huh?"

"Yes, once we get to your car Xavier will ride with you just to make sure you don't get lost along the way."

Lost, my backside, I thought. "Well Bernie had better have some seriously cold beers waiting." I was in tough-guy threatening mode now.

"Oh, not a problem, young Louis, I picked up flat of beers just this afternoon, knowing we would be celebrating!"

"Canadian beers?" I asked.

Chapter 24

I had to show Xavier with my seat how he could slide his seat back for more leg room in the old gal. He appreciated the simplicity. He didn't have to give me any directions back to Bernie's. I don't claim to possess amazing directional senses or anything like that. It's just that when I'm in thinking mode the old gal just seems to know where to go. It's as if the 1965 Mustang came with the first invisible G.P.S. system.

I couldn't believe how in just a few short days my life had spun in a direction so far from that of a struggling musician. I missed the boring life of being an underpaid rehearsal space cat. I wondered if Pippy the transvestite singer ever found her/himself in spots like this. What about Abbott's guitar player? Was he bummed out over losing what wasn't really his? Had he figured it all out and did he want revenge on the girls and me? Questions.

I sure liked my '65. She was simple. Simple seats, simple dashboard. No bells for open doors, no talk back voice telling me to buckle up or any fancy altimeter telling me I was about to tip over. She's simple like me, and together we rock.

"Hey Xavier, you and Ollie seem like regular Joes. Intelligent, nice guys too. I could almost trust you big tankers. Tell me, why the hell do you cats work for a mental midget like Bernard Outlaw?"

His mass rippled in the passenger seat as he chuckled softly. "Mental midget, I shall have to borrow that one. Louis, to answer your question you must know that there is more at work here than what appears on the surface. You know, like in American television shows."

"Yeah, I gathered that from something Oliver said earlier. You two just don't seem to fit into Outlaw's cowboy movie... with the exception of your stellar John Wayne impressions, of course."

He smiled as if he'd just gained another fan. "Now then, here we are. Just park behind Oliver. He's left the gate open for you."

Oliver was already seated with a glass of wine at his elbow when we came in. Xavier headed for the kitchen and came out with two lovely Molson Canadian beers. The former glass table was replaced but not with a replica as I expected. Instead, sitting in the glass table's place was a heavy table, probably teak, which appeared to have dated back to the Ming dynasty.

"Well whadoyaknow? There's a table after all and heavy too." I remarked.

Bernie explained that the table showed up after the twins headed out.

"What gives, Ollie? Xavier couldn't find the glass variety?"

"I shall let Xavier field this one," he said with a casual open handed gesture to his brother.

"Oh, it's not much really, I merely convinced our illustrious employer that if he was bent on fisticuffs we had better possess furniture that can withstand the rows."

"I heard what he had to say on it, Mr. Crasher, and suggested we get a table with thicker glass, you know like glass blocks and such but old Xavier there fed me some malarkey about price and shipping and all kinds o' other crap. It ain't so bad I 'spose, hell it might just be solid enough for a cowpoke like me to crack their two heads on when they take to acting up," Bernie said.

All three of us ignored the idle threat.

"So what's the good news? Is that a certain object I'd be inclined to desire bulging under your sweater there, Crasher?"

I tossed him the picture. "It is indeed."

Outlaw cradled the photo like he would a lost child. A gaudy ceramic bowl which sat in the center of the table held *Jurassic-Park*-sized walnuts. A pair of iron nut crackers with brass lettering reading TEXAS down one side lay on top of the heap. Outlaw's short arms stretched to the limit as he reached for the nuts on the big table. A smile came to his lips as he succeeded in securing the nut crackers. A frown replaced the smile as a quick tearing sound came from the tight leisure coat he wore after securing the chosen nut. He sat back down heavily and cracked the nut as if it owed him money. He ignored the shells that fell to his tight fitting slacks. As the walnut tumbled around his teeth and gums he spoke in a lower voice.

"Lou, I want to thank you and my staff here for a job well done. I gather the fellas filled you in on everything? I mean with respect to Angela, you, Abbott and so on?"

"They went as far as your paychecks would let em', sure." I grabbed myself a nut with arms longer than Bernie's and sat back. "But they didn't answer the $65,000 question. What's the hub-bub with this picture?"

"My friend that would be $64,000 question."

"Inflation, Bernie."

"Sure," Bernie said. "Mr. Crasher you seem to be a principled man, a man with a keen sense of right and wrong. I mean, who would take the risks you took in stealing that equipment unless you were guided by some sort of moral something-or-other? It is your rigid set of principalities that I'm about to reach out to."

I let Outlaw carry on for the simple fact that I didn't have the slightest idea what he was talking about.

"You stole from a man by the name o' Dave Abbott. He's a man that I allow to operate in Hollywood and West LA for a not-so-small fee, as you know. It's business. We're businessmen."

"Businessmen. Abbott is a maggot and public enemy number one to musicians. This is old news, anyway."

"Old news eh? Well, the new news is that I don't believe that you are all the way Boy Scout. I believe you stole that stuff to impress this here girl, now ain't that the truth?"

I didn't like the way he dragged his index finger across Angela's picture.

"Anyway, Bernie, it has been real."

I got up to leave.

"Sit down, boy, we ain't done yet."

"And that will be the last time you call me boy, short stuff," I said.

I could feel Xavier slide in behind my seat. Nobody spoke. The only sound was testosterone particles bouncing off the walls.

"All right, all right, na' calm down. I ain't lookin' to tussle. I told you I am trying to appeal to your compassionate side."

Outlaw pulled a single sheet of eight and a half by eleven inch paper from a briefcase that sat at his feet and slid it across the table to me. He sucked at his teeth as I read. At the top of the page the word PASSAGE jumped out at me with full stops between each letter. Underneath this was the meaning: People of Ascension Seeking Serenity Attaining Goals and Enlightenment. I stopped there.

"What is this? Venice Beach psychic tarot card crap?"

"You're not so far off, Mr. Crasher. Read on."

"Why? I despise cults."

"Indulge me, would you?"

I read on about a phony religious cult based on a ranch near Bakersfield, California. Over a hundred believers in this 'passage' followed a man by the name of Genesis. The ticket price to join his phony worship was vague but it appeared from the flier that a large percentage of yearly income was required. I'm sure they considered it a tithe. There were prayer sessions, sports activities, arts and crafts, music, counseling and other programs. The real kicker for me were the 'economic advisory meetings.' In other words: 'give me more money on top of your required contribution.'

"Sounds like Club Med for the weak and dim-witted," I said.

"Yup, Louis I'm going to get right to the point on this. I have a child—my precious. She's my heart and she has fallen prey to this Genesis snake and his freak cult. Bottom line: I want her back. I'll stop at nothing to get her back. Why I'd run with the bulls o' Pamplona to get her back, and I'm talking running in the wrong direction."

"Please do not say what I think you are—"

"I want for you to infiltrate this phony baloney operation and get her out. It is time for my little girl to come home." Outlaw's bottom lip quivered ever so slightly.

"No. Nada. Not a chance. Are we done here?"

"Son, she's my Texas tulip. I die a little more each day that she is with...him. She's been brainwashed. You say you hate cults, I hate cults too, now get her back. You do this and we're square."

My blood was getting up. "We are square now, I'm sorry. This is a no can do. Call the cops. Hire the Navy Seals. Hell, hire a ninja turtle but count me out."

"Cops won't touch it. This Genesis character is a lawyer first, con man second. Not that there's much difference. And he's got this scam done up real legal like." I gave him silence that I hoped would make him feel uncomfortable but he just talked on and upped the ante.

"Every man has a price Mr. Crasher, it's just a matter o' finding out what it is. Let me run this by you: I own a few night clubs down there in Hollywood. You do this little deed for me and I'll put one o' yer bands in one of my clubs. I'm talking house band, and I'll give you a one year contract. On top of which, that money Angela gave you, I'll triple it."

"Triple is a good number, but the contract, that in writing?"

"If you like."

"I would like, but I'm still not interested," I lied. Of course I was interested until I stood back and looked at it. This would make Bernie and me in business together to some degree. This was no good. The whole point of breaking into Chet MacBeth's place was to get off the hook not dig it deeper into my mouth. Outlaw remained calm. I wondered how many other suckers before me sat across the big table and played this game...and lost. He got up from the couch and went and pulled a small photograph from the drawer of an antique side table. He handed it to me nonchalantly. It was a picture of a young girl who looked like she lived next door. His daughter, and also his trump card. Her big blue innocent eyes were ripe for any scam, religious or otherwise. Her thick lashes appeared to be phony but were not. She had long brown hair that was the ironed-down 1960's style and the smile, warm and apologetic. I barely noticed myself saying 'not to worry' out loud.

"I beg your pardon, Mr. Crasher, I didn't quite hear ya?"

I sighed, "Bernie, you're a son of a bitch."

"Not exactly the words I was looking for, but I take it you're on board?"

"I am willing to discuss it further, with added libation of course," I said, holding up my empty beer bottle.

"Great. This will get you into the place." Bernie picked up Angela's photo and flipped it over. He pulled the cardboard backing off the frame. Sandwiched between the photo and the cardboard was what appeared to be a credit card. He tossed it to me. The card was aqua colored and simply said PASSAGE on the front. The back had a black magnetic strip like one would find on any credit card.

"It's set up so's you can go any day this week. You gotta go after four though because they want the supper prayer session to be one of the first things you do."

"Wait, let's look at this thing rationally. Why not take the twins and a couple of goons on your payroll, load them into the Hummer, which I'm sure you have stashed in some barn out there, and let them commando the joint, boom, done."

"Mr. Crasher, I am prepared to let that little comment about Oliver and I being goons slide for the simple fact that I recognize the stress of the situation you are currently in. However I do expect an apology."

"My heartfelt apologies to you both, Xavier, however, I referred to you two as twins and the other fellows as goons."

"He got you on that one, Xavier," Oliver smiled.

Nobody rushed to replenish my beer so I made my own way into the kitchen and pulled one from the massive stainless steel fridge. I thought I'd have an escort but I suppose I was no longer a flight risk. I regained my seat.

"Pardon my over sensitive employees, Louis, but they're from England. Now could we please stay focused on my daughter?" Bernie shouted the last word. He removed his Stetson and ran a frustrated hand through his dark hair.

"Oliver, do you have that videotape queued up like I asked?"

"Yes, sir."

"Roll it."

The TV remote looked like a 25 cent piece in Oliver's hand. The five-foot TV came to life. The view from a hand-held camera shot the front of what looked like a dude ranch. A large man in toga-style garb stood motionless at the gate. To his right a topless woman pulled carrots from the earth and put them in a basket. In the bottom right corner of the screen a digital clock ticked away in real time. After 20 seconds of carrot pulling both parties look up at the gate. A black Hummer moved into the shot and stops at the gate.

"Look at that, I knew you owned a Hum-vee," I blurted.

Oliver stepped from the driver's side of the vehicle and walked to the gate. There was no sound but it was obvious that Oliver and the man in the toga were having words. Nearly half a minute goes by before the gate keeper becomes agitated with Oliver and motions for him to leave. The woman pulling carrots stops gardening. Suddenly the man in the toga throws a punch at Oliver who catches it in his left hand like a first baseman would. He then karate chops the gate keeper in the side of the neck. The man hits the ground hard and does not move. Oliver climbs back into the Hummer while the topless woman runs toward the main building, which is twenty-five yards back from the gate.

Oliver crashes through the gate and heads for the main structure, which looks like a giant log cabin. He doesn't stop the vehicle until it has climbed three steps of the building. Xavier appears for the first time, jumping out of the passenger side of the vehicle. They mount the steps in a hurry. Fifty-eight seconds later the camera swings quickly to the right side of the building. Six fit looking guys in army fatigue pants and black t-shirts are running hard toward the front steps. The camera becomes a little shaky and then zips to the left side of the building. The same scene is developing on the left side of the building. The camera jerks back to the front door where Xavier stands on the threshold with the body of a woman slung over his shoulder in a fireman's carry.

Oliver is directly behind him.

Nobody moves for ten seconds and then as if a starter's gun explodes everyone moves at once. The twins must have known in their hearts that they'd never make it to the Hummer with their cargo. They make a dash for it anyway. The fatigued men fix their attention on Xavier and have the girl in their possession in no time. Three men quickly carry her away from the ruckus. The remaining attacked the twins with everything they had. Half of them sport billy clubs.

I glanced at the twins to see their reaction at this ugly memory. They both watched in silence with blank stares on their faces. An overwhelming feeling of guilt grabbed my chest. I felt like the person who slows down at a car crash to see if there are any bodies to regard.

I brought my eyes back to the video. The twins now look like a pair of lions under an army of hyenas. This was a difficult watch. The twins nearly give as good as they get before barely making it into the Hummer. As Oliver guns the vehicle in reverse, he runs over one of Genesis's soldiers. The camera follows the path of the vehicle's departure, but there is a glimpse of something I wanted to see.

"Ollie, could you back the tape up a little?" He did as I asked. "Stop, right there, that guy in the long robe that comes to the door before the truck pulls away, is that the Genesis dude?"

Bernie answered with venom in his voice, "That's him." The man in question stood with his hands behind his back. He was tall and skinny. He had jet black hair and a neatly trimmed goatee to match. Even from that range his eyes looked dark: menacing.

"He looks like the devil himself," I said. "Who in their right mind would trust a guy like that?" I wasn't looking for an answer. "Fellas, that's way too creepy how he just stares at the camera. Who shot this thing?"

"I did," Bernie said.

"He is looking at the camera isn't he? I mean he made you didn't he?"

"I was about 300 yards down the driveway in the Range Rover." Outlaw got up and turned away to hide his tears from me.

"Three hundred yards? The guy either has eyes like a hawk or he's—it must be totally open terrain, is that it? Never mind," I said. "The video doesn't have a date. When was this shot?"

Xavier answered for Bernie. "Roughly three months back."

"I feel for you, Bernie, but what can I do against 50 survivalist type bastard wanna-be Marines?"

"Louis, I believe Mr. Outlaw has a stealthier plan in mind, as the storm-the-Bastille approach failed so miserably."

"So I'm to be the lucky stealth guy?" Xavier didn't answer me. "Why not take this tape to the cops? She's being held against her will."

"Not exactly, you see when we went into the building she screamed like a banshee when she recognized Oliver and me."

"It didn't look like she was exactly kicking and screaming in the video."

"She fainted as soon as I picked her up."

"You big bully," I teased.

"Do you think this is a joke, son? We're talking about my baby girl here, now let's figure out how to work this thing."

"Same question, what about the cops?"

"Forget the cops. I tried that all ready. They know who I am. Told me that they couldn't see any foreseeable future leads unless I came up with some dead presidents."

"Bloody Neanderthals. Not since my introduction to American television have I heard such unbridled abuse of the English language. I put it to you all that if we are to hatch a feasible plan we should plan it using the Queen's English!" Xavier exploded. I promised myself from that point on to keep my usage as bridled as possible.

"You mean the LAPD tried to shake you down? Sounds like they were trying to protect and serve themselves on that one."

"You hit the nail on the head there, Louis. A goddamned shakedown." Outlaw offered me a drink which I accepted, as my beer was running low. He made two gin and tonics and came and sat back down across the table from me.

"I'm not exactly a model citizen by their standards of course, which means that if I want something done I have to do it myself."

"Or have it done," I added.

"Whatever. Look, I've done some checking on this fake. He has all but drained my baby's trust fund, after which he'll just toss her aside. Once you've been under that snake's heel a girl like my precious will come outta there with about as much self-esteem as a hen in a fox convention."

"If he's truly brainwashed her why hasn't he taken all of her money by now? I mean, why keep her around?"

The pain that showed on Outlaw's face was no act. He told me that he would rather not answer that question. It was easy math for me to figure out. Outlaw's daughter was merely a sexual plaything for Genesis. I was sorry I asked the question.

"The FBI must know about this guy."

Outlaw shouted, "Do you think they want another Waco on their hands?" The twins removed imaginary lint from their black jeans and sweaters. I could only imagine Bernie's inner hell. My mother always used to say that if you do bad things, bad things will happen to you. Maybe this predicament that Bernie was in was for all the wrong he's been doing on the wrong side of the law. Too bad the daughter had to take the heat. At any rate, only the man upstairs could know the whys and how this would play out. The one thing that I did know was that I was going to save that girl. As I was making the full commitment in my mind, I wondered yet again how many men and women before me sat where I sat and buckled under the little Texan's pressure to do his bidding.

"Once I'm in there how am I supposed to get her to leave with me? She's not exactly going to wander off the volleyball court with me hand in hand. I mean I know I'm cute, fellas, but sheesh, give me a break. Even if I could get her to come away with me I don't think that we'd fare any better than the two British tankers here against the phony guru's goons."

"Well—"

"Who are those guys, anyway? They've got to be ex-military. Did you see how well they worked...as a team I mean?"

"Oh I assure you we saw, Louis, right down to the end of their nightsticks," Oliver volunteered.

"What kind of injuries did you guys sustain?" I'm not sure why I asked.

Xavier jumped in, "I got three ribs broken, so don't make me laugh or it's curtains for you."

"Brother, I swear when you try so desperately to sound American I truly believe that mother did have an affair with the butcher from Boston who lived off Paddington Road and that you are the miserable result! May she rest in peace."

Xavier's face reddened, "And you, brother, if I may be so bold, have simply got to wake from your grossly extended slumber and realize that we are no longer in England." They were now standing barrel chest to barrel chest.

Outlaw stood up to and started hollering, "If you two don't cut the crap I'm going upstairs and get my 30-30 and send you both to see yer' mother and the goddamned butcher."

"Why you puny little sot, how dare you mention our mother, in any context. Do you honestly believe that the pittance you give us as salary gives you license to slander our mother's good name? On top of which you would threaten us? Hold still you malignant little bastard—"

"Xavier! I forbid you to harm that man." Oliver grabbed his brother by the bicep in an attempt to restrain him. Xavier shook his grip loose. I turned backward and climbed over the back of the couch. It was time to make myself a stiff drink. Xavier was almost at Outlaw who, to my surprise, did not give any ground, showing limited fear as the giant approached him. In fact the grin on his face reminded me of a raptor I had once seen in a Spielberg movie. Oliver caught up to him just before he reached Bernie and put him in some sort of wrestling hold. Xavier shook the hold with a quick spin move to face his brother. Xavier read the move and tried to apply an arm bar of his own. During the tussle Oliver grunted for his brother to stop this madness. After those first quick moves it was all grappling, dodges, parries and thrusts. Outlaw kept yelling, "Let him come! Come on! Let him come!" As I took my second healthy swig of my drink I saw Outlaw shake a blackjack down from his sleeve. Bernie was definitely a braver man than me, for I'd think twice about taking Xavier on with a .45 caliber pistol let alone a sap. The brothers continued with their dance, neither one really trying to seriously hurt the other. They were family after all. Bernie kept calling Xavier out and I was sucking the last of the whiskey when the vision before me caused me to drop my glass.

Bernie saw what I saw at the same time and stopped yelling and stood and stared. Oliver and Xavier lost their footing and hit the floor together hard. They were still locked when they finally looked up and saw what we saw: in the doorway between the kitchen and the living room stood a man. He had one man over his shoulder and another by the scruff the neck dangling by his right leg. Both men he carried were unconscious. Bernie was the first to snap out of our collective shock.

"Who in god's name is that, Ollie? Xavier, get up. You still work for me, don't you?" The twins were on their feet fast and not quite sure what to do.

Through calm cold eyes Jake said, "When these men wake they will have headaches. I suggest extra strength Tylenol and ice." Jake then laid the men down as if he were tucking his own sons into bed.

"That's Dustin and that's, why that's Fox, my best security guards. What the hell did you do to them? And who the hell are you?"

Jake didn't answer. I was glad to see him do that to other people as well as me. I was glad to see Jake even if I didn't know what his play was. I considered making another drink but I wasn't sure how long we were staying or how sober I would need to be for whatever it was that Jake had planned, if he did have anything planned at all. Oliver straightened up his posture and addressed Jake.

"Young man would you by any chance be the mystery man in all of this? The man who not only took a little whelp by the name of Travis from his home and also aided myself and Mr. Crasher by disposing of a certain employee of the Protek company?"

"That would be me, Oliver." Nothing could be read from Jake's eyes.

"Ah, we finally meet. My name is Oliver as you seem to know and this is my brother, Xavier. We have been looking for you." Jake did not say anything so Oliver continued.

"My brother and I were impressed that you took a man from his home in broad daylight with virtually no shall I say, 'activity'—ah, police or otherwise. And leave us not forget that the little fool has a penchant for knives." Oliver paused a moment and sized the man up, seeming genuinely impressed. "Did he have time to pull one on you? I truly am curious."

"He had plenty of time, just not the nerve."

"Our paths nearly crossed a few short years ago. Does the Bellflower Bar and Grill ring a bell?" Jake nodded. "Well, our employer at the time desperately wanted to add this bar to his list of establishments that pay him protection." Oliver's voice was thick with excitement. It was almost as if he were bragging to his school mates about a super hero he met. Bernie was shifting his weight foot to foot and fondling his sap between his fingers. This conversation was not sitting well with him. I knew nothing of this old story and was all ears, as I knew nothing of Jake.

"...so our boss sends Remo, that sadistic S.O.B., as a last warning to Chazz, the owner of the Bellflower. Well, to make a long story short, Remo walked through the barroom doors at 3:15. He came out on a stretcher and by 3:45 was hospitalized for six months. Witnesses say that a man by the name of Jake gave Remo plenty of gentlemanly warnings until he was forced to...well, you know the rest. Our boss considered sending us until he saw the hospital record on Remo."

Bernie snapped, "Why don't you just get down on one goddamn knee and propose to im'? Xavier, is this the guy you been sayin' absconded with my nephew and busted him up?"

"This is him sir. We've been on him for—"

Jake finished Xavier's sentence. "Seventy-two hours."

"You've known all along then."

"Quite, as you would say."

One of the unconscious men at Jake's feet was coming to. Bernie told Xavier to tend to Dustin and the other useless employee on the floor.

The room was becoming a little more relaxed now. Bernie asked Jake what the hell he wanted, to which Jake said what he did depended on me. Xavier came into the room and now all eyes were on me. I took a short pull on my drink.

"What do you mean, Jake?"

"Simple. If you want to leave, we will leave. If you want to stay and help rescue Crystal, then we'll do that. It is your call."

"Crystal is her name? How did you know that?" Jake gave me no response.

"How the hell do you know my baby's name?" Again Jake came up silent.

The security guards came back in the room with ice packs on various places. Outlaw told them to get back outside before he fired them and that they were on probation forthwith.

They sulked out with their tails between their legs, poor saps. On neither visit to Outlaw's place had I noticed outside security guards. I had a lot to learn.

"I know it sounds crazy, Jake, but I want to get this girl away from this tyrant. He looks like the devil, man, have you ever seen him?"

"I saw the video you just saw." The brothers both raised their eyebrows.

"So what do you think, should we do this thing?" I asked.

"I have already explained my end of it. I would advise caution, given what happened the last time you rushed in to save a damsel in distress."

"Well la-di-da, isn't it great to be the smart guy all the time," I snapped.

"Son, my name is Bernie Outlaw, ya hear? Now what makes you think you can come in here and call the shots?" Bernie walked over to Jake and stood underneath him.

"I have lived among cultures where to stand this close to a man would result in your immediate death. This was one of the mores I enjoyed of those cultures; now stand back before I show you how to use that sap." Bernie's jaw muscles twitched as he reluctantly stepped back.

"There are some men in this culture that enjoy getting even closer than that," I pointed out. Nobody laughed. "Oh come on, lighten up fellas. We've all got to mellow out a bit. This stress is bumming me out." Outlaw poured himself three plump fingers of scotch this time, and slammed it.

"Okay Bernie, let's just say that I'm on board for this thing. But, before we do, why did you send me specifically into that house to find out about Angela in this way? Is it your sick sense of humor, or a lesson I'm supposed to learn, what?"

"Louis, my friend, I need you to get my daughter back, but first I had to show you the hard truth about yer girlfriend there. I couldn't have you all starry eyed and unfocused on the upcoming mission."

"I get it, show me that Angela isn't all she seems, then boom, I'd just jump at the chance to breech a phony church. Bit of a long shot wouldn't you say, Bernie?" I asked.

"Yer goin' ain't ya?" Outlaw slammed another three fingers of scotch. "All right. Let's plot this son of a bitch."

Chapter 25

"Now then," Xavier said cheerfully, "why don't we stop and have something to eat before we get down to planning? I realize it is late, but what say you? I've got splendid leftovers."

Bernie rolled his eyes and mumbled something about his monthly food bill. We decided we were hungry with the exception of Jake, who had eaten before coming over. Oliver said that he'd hop to it, and walked into the kitchen. During the fifteen minutes that we waited, Jake, Bernie, Xavier and I exchanged small talk as best we could. The only problem was that Jake never talks; Bernie was in a sulk, no doubt because a stranger beat up his security guards and knew too much about him, and Xavier was suspicious of Jake.

I was then forced to pick a light topic of conversation that everyone could either participate in or not: Jim Rockford. With the exception of Xavier nodding approval, nobody else took part. When Oliver came back into the room he was clad in an apron that read, 'London or Bust.' He rang a little dinner bell that he was in danger of crushing and insisted that we eat at the dining room table, as we were not Neanderthals. A tight hallway to the left of the living room took us into a huge dining area. A large blown-up framed photo of Bernie sitting on a horse with a rifle across his lap hung on a wall over a massive oak credenza. Oliver asked that Jake and I please excuse Bernie's lack of taste where art was concerned. Classical music suddenly seeped in from hidden speakers and then Xavier came into the room. Oliver complimented his choice of Chopin. Xavier told him to 'forget about it' with a lousy Italian mobster's accent.

"Sounds like Perrier music to me," Bernie said, snapping out his napkin and thrusting it into his shirt front at the neck. The twins simultaneously removed the silver lids from the tops of their trays. When the smells hit Jake's nostrils he decided another meal wouldn't hurt and snapped his napkin open as well. Only Jake placed his on his lap like the rest of us. I was the only one at the table who couldn't get his napkin to snap. The dish directly in front of me was a heaping plate of Cornish game hens. I couldn't make out exactly what sort of vegetable dishes were on the table as they were a football field away.

Bernie told me to dig in before the food got cold. He didn't have to tell me twice.

"Hey Ollie, these game hens are stuffed," I said, always the observant one.

"Quite right," he said proudly.

"And you call these leftovers? Man, you guys live large up here." Jake stood up and leaned over the table to pass me a spinach and cheese dish. When I was done with that dish I loaded some baby carrots onto my plate. The carrots were covered with what looked like one hundred different spices.

Jovially I offered, "Ollie, you need to get out of the bone crushing business and start doing the chef thing man."

"Bone crushing?" Xavier asked.

"Hey, at least I didn't say 'goon' business." I guess some guys are just sensitive about what they do. Jake seemed to be ignoring the whole affair until he asked Oliver about the stuffing in the hens.

"That's correct, Jake, I do use organically grown wild rice but also I toss in a full sprig of thyme, which the recipe does not call for."

"I was over in London a few years back on business and let me say that I was hard pressed to find a meal this rich in flavor." Oliver blushed so deeply I thought he was choking on a hen bone. Bernie stared at Jake in disbelief at his use of so many words.

Xavier nodded and said, "We love England and it will always be home but they have a few things to learn about cuisine, which was a large motivating factor in our migration to America."

I could not resist. I had to get in on this. "Well perhaps Jake would like to explain to our fine hosts just what sort of business dealings he was up to in…London was it?"

I know that there is no way of making Jake talk, but I wanted to see what he'd do. He didn't even look up from his food when I set my little trap. Irritation caused Outlaw to come to his rescue.

"Can we cut all this food and travel nonsense and get down to the real problem here? How the hell are we going to get my daughter back?"

The mood got serious again. Xavier went first by pointing out the obvious that we couldn't storm the place as he and his brother did before. Oliver shuddered at the memory.

"An impressive effort. You couldn't know about the private army," Jake said.

"Son, I'm gonna ask a question, to which I expect a straight goddamned answer. Who the hell are you?" Bernie said clutching his knife in an aggressive manner, of which I'm sure he wasn't aware.

"Jake."

"I don't mean your dern' name, I mean, what are you? Some kind of...wait a minute. You ain't a cop are you? Cause if so I know no damn warrant allows you to be all injurious to my security."

"I'm a man willing to help your daughter and Louis. If it helps you out in the process so be it. I don't expect thanks, nor will I tell you any more than my name." He turned to Oliver, "The ginger on these carrots is a nice touch."

"You are too kind," Oliver said.

"Bernie," I said. "Put the knife down. I've seen Jake do some things." Bernie stared at the knife he held in his white knuckled fingers. He dropped the knife and then laughed hysterically. I was about to save a reluctant free-love child so that she could be reunited with her lunatic father. Outlaw pushed himself away from the table and made himself another drink.

"Do you think you can handle this, Louis?" Xavier asked.

"I don't know. I'm going to just go in there, try to not get made for a spy by this Genesis cat, avoid the army, and see if I can charm her into coming out. Hopefully I can page or call you guys on a cell or—"

"No phones or pagers allowed on his ranch." Outlaw said.

"The woods," Jake said.

"Unfortunately, rescue attempts have been made before in the woods my good man. Not of our girl but of others, by others," Oliver said.

"But not by us."

"Fair enough."

"We will use the woods and the same method you boys tried," Jake said.

"A decoy. I love it. I simply love it." Oliver rubbed his meaty hands together in excitement.

"Let's kick some ass!" Xavier beamed.

"Xavier, please!" Oliver shouted. Xavier threw up his hands in innocence.

"Create a commotion out front while y'all sneak out the back of the barn. I like it, but don't y'all think it's been tried as well?"

I took a page out of Jake's book. "Not by us."

Chapter 26

Jake and I left Outlaw's place at around three forty-five a.m. and cruised over to my place. I decided to go to the lovely camp PASSAGE the following afternoon. I wanted to get this whole ordeal over with and get back to my life. Not to mention I had a few questions for Lady Angela as well. It was obvious to all of us that I shouldn't be dropped off in the Hummer or the Range Rover. I told them that I didn't want to take my Mustang up there either. I had visions of trying to make a quick getaway only to find that Genesis or his crew have pulled the battery out or cut the brake line. I suggested that Jake drive me up there and drop me off. He stared at me in silence and left my apartment. He returned forty minutes later with a one-way bus ticket for me.

"Have a taxi take you from the bus depot."

"Do you ever clue the people in whose lives you are controlling as to how you're controlling them?"

"The ticket is on me."

"Oh that makes it all better—but thanks."

"One hundred and ten."

"That's how much the ticket was?"

"No. One hundred and ten pounds is approximately what Crystal weighs. If you can't persuade her to leave with you, you'll have to carry her. How far can you carry that much weight?"

"Let's see, I've been hauling my drums up and down stairs for twenty years without squawkin' about it, not to mention if Mr. Sunshine's militia is on my tail...I'd say pretty darn far and pretty damn fast."

"Good, plan on making a long run to the trees. Head straight south from the back of the main hall you saw in the video. You'll head straight for the big pond and veer left, and then don't stop until you see us."

"Just how did you see that video? And don't tell me you were hiding under the table because I may have been drinking but you weren't under that table. I would have seen you."

"Surveillance equipment pointed through the window. Outlaw's staff found me and forced plan B. You know the rest."

"I may not make it out of this joint alive so why don't you just come clean and tell me who and what the hell you are?"

"Good things come..."

"If I didn't think it'd hurt in the not-so-long run I'd walk over there and give you my best shot."

"Violence, tsk, tsk."

Jake finally left at around five a.m. He revealed absolutely nothing about his identity, which is what I expected. I took a taxi to the bus and mounted her steps at three p.m. I ignored the scenery on the ninety-minute ride. My thoughts bounced back and forth from Angela to the den of insanity I was willingly about to walk into. The closer I got, the crazier I became. What if I couldn't find the guys in the woods? The woods part of the program gave me concern, as did being forbidden a cell phone. Jake told me he'd take care of it. And what if I was made before the extraction? I tried desperately to calm myself by reading a *Road and Track* magazine I found on the seat beside me. I'd get three sentences into an article and then I'd have to start over due to daydreaming. If Jake wasn't in the picture I wouldn't be here. I'd be on a bus to Canada. I could just see it. "Hiya, grandma, I'm home. A crime boss ran me out of LA. Isn't that neato?"

The bus pulled into port safe and sound. The driver had already set my bag on the sidewalk by the time I got off the bus. I only had to take five steps before hopping into a waiting taxi.

"I'm going to the PASSAGE ranch."

"It's your funeral, pal."

"What do you mean?"

The driver, a Caucasian male in his early fifties, reeked of cigarettes. His thick fingers poked through fingerless leather gloves. He shoved the automatic shifter into drive and pulled away from the curb.

"Do you really buy into all that phony religious brouhaha?"

"Yeah, that's why I'm here."

"I heard that leech Genesis cleared six million dollars last year, and that's profit. His pocket."

I didn't know about the charlatan's income but I was on the same page as this driver. However being in undercover P.I. mode I had to play the faithful PASSAGE devotee.

"I see you are another nonbeliever."

"And you are another lamb to the slaughter, no offense. We hear many things in this little town of ours. It may not all be true but did you know that you can't leave that place until the big Kahuna says so?"

"Leave? I can't wait to get there."

I deserved an Oscar...and a barf bag. I was sickening myself.

"A word of advice, pal, don't stray too far into the woods that surround the place."

"Why, are they full of vampires or werewolves? Come on, man, I'm too old for ghost stories."

The cab slowed down like he took his foot off the gas. He turned his head slowly to stare at me. We rolled at least thirty feet without his watching the road.

"Don't say I didn't warn you."

He turned quickly, eyes back on the road, and accelerated. He didn't speak to me until he drove as far as he wanted to.

"This is as far as I go. I don't want to get any of that crap on me at all."

"I've got that heavy bag to carry, man. Can't you get me a little closer?"

"Nope."

He flicked a switch that opened the trunk. I got out and pulled my bag from the trunk. I walked to his window and paid him. In exchange he gave me a card with his name, number and cab company.

"Percy? I like that name. Thanks for the info. I'll see you around."

"Like I said, it's your funeral, pal."

I had a hockey bag filled to the brim. I wanted it to appear like I was staying for a good long while. I hefted it onto my shoulder and made tracks the remaining half-mile to the gates of PASSAGE. I double checked my left back pocket three times to feel my PASSAGE entry card. There was a different sentry at the gate then the one I had seen in the video. Gone was the lady gardener out front.

"May I help you?"

"Here's my card. I'm legal."

The man pulled a miniature card verifying machine from his smock and slid my card. The machine beeped, paused and then beeped one more time. Satisfied with the sounds he unlatched the gate and opened it a foot for me. I was forced to put my bag in first, then follow it through the tiny opening. It was as if he thought an invisible mob of five hundred people stood behind me ready to crash the gate. I exaggerated the difficulty I had getting in. He missed the subtlety.

"If you don't mind, sir, I'd like to have a quick look at the contents of your bag."

It wasn't a question.

"Sure." I unzipped it all the way. He dug around briefly and told me it was fine.

"Proceed in a straight line, go up those stairs into the Great Hall, and Treasure will look after you. Enjoy your stay, and may enlightenment be yours."

"Okay. Thanks. And may enlightenment be with you too, man."

It was odd mounting the steps where Oliver and Xavier received their beating a few short months ago. I took the ten steps two at a time. At the top I stood on the wide wraparound veranda and inhaled the clear air for the first time. I looked back toward the main gate, expecting to see the sentinel staring at my back. He was not. He was back in sentinel form, moving his head side to side. He probably called it a "hi-def visual sweep" or something cool like that.

A soft, confident voice touched my ears. "Welcome to the home of people of ascension seeking serenity, attaining goals and enlightenment."

"Oh hi, I'm Lou. I didn't hear you come up."

"As you move toward enlightenment, you'll *feel* me come up. Hi, I'm Treasure."

A half-dozen somewhat witty responses flooded my head but I left them all dangling. She was the kind of girl my friend Bob loved; 'petite and sweet,' he called them. She also happened to be the topless gardening lass I had seen on the videotape. She was top-full at the moment.

"Come inside, I'll have Adrian take your bag."

Adrian stood inside the door at just over five feet tall. I was about to insist on carrying my bag myself when he hoisted it like it was filled with feathers.

"You are impressed with his strength, yes?"

"Sure. Does that come with enlightenment?"

"Adrian was a ninety-pound weakling when he first came to us. We at PASSAGE bring out what is inside you. What is inside you?"

"I'm here to find out."

She seemed satisfied with that response, which was grand seeing as it was the only one I had. Adrian came trotting back up to us.

"His things are in the Room of Joy, Treasure."

"Thank you, Adrian, that will be all. Lou, would you follow me please?"

We walked twelve feet along thirteen-inch beige rock tile and stopped. Treasure explained that we were in the Great Hall. The tile met with short, tightly woven beige carpet. On top of the carpet was a long wooden table. The tabletop was made from wood five inches thick. A crane must have dropped the twenty-seater in its spot. The twenty straight-back chairs were made from the same thick wood. Their solid base made them look as if they were borrowed from the Flintstone family. Over the center of the table hung a huge, double-sided tapestry of Genesis standing in a field with staff in hand and Border Collie at his foot. It was the most pathetic attempt of a man posing as a shepherd I had ever seen. However, the artist did a fine job of capturing the wickedness of his eyes. Genesis was the perfect example of a wolf in sheep's clothing. Treasure regarded me closely as I looked at the piece. I did my best to appear awestruck. We moved the remaining soccer pitch distance to the back exit.

When I stepped out of the Great Hall and onto the back veranda I could not believe my eyes until I blinked twice.

"Paradise," I whispered.

"Close, but not quite," she grinned.

I was looking at Disneyland, the private religious ranch version. The property had to be five acres. Directly in front of me was a perfectly manicured lawn volleyball court. A group of men and women, six a side, were engaged in a fun match. Half of the women were topless. The others were in sports bras or bikini tops. None of the men wore shirts. To my left was a horse barn. A man and a woman were working on a pinto's shoe. Beyond the barn I noticed the top of another A-shaped building.

"What's that one over there, behind the barn?"

"That's the Room of Outer Beauty, Louis."

"Outer—?"

"The gymnasium. It's got two racquetball courts, a short lap pool, two saunas and a weight room. You look like you work out."

"It has been awhile, but yeah, I work out."

To the left and back twenty yards from the volleyball court were two side-by-side hot tubs.

"Those hot tubs look huge even from here."

"Yup, they each hold thirty people or more, depending on how close people want to get."

She raised her eyebrows twice, Groucho Marx style. I didn't flirt back in the event it was some kind of test that would be reported back to their big boss. My plan was to put the appropriate oohs and aahs in the appropriate spots until I could make contact with Crystal. We walked to the volleyball court where every individual in the game said hello to me. It seemed as though it was part of a script. As we left the court, two animals bounded in front of our path. I jumped back, startled, grabbing Treasure to shelter her from the beasts.

"What the f...I mean heck were those?"

"That is Tom and the one on the left is Jerry. They're llamas. They just run around free, but don't attempt to pet them. They can be quite nasty."

"Are they a food source here at the ranch?"

"That is the coldest thing I have ever heard."

"I was just kidding. I would never eat a—whatever they are, llama thing. You see, sometimes when I'm overwhelmed I head straight for the joke."

"I don't find that funny in the least. Apologize."

"To Tom and Jerry? Sure."

"No to me, I'm upset."

"I am sorry, really I am." I needed to get the hell out of this place as fast as I could. No telling how long it would take for me to start really speaking my mind. I gave her sincere eyes and she bought them. I'd keep my humor to myself after that. Off to the right of the double tubs was a half-court basketball court. I was impressed that Mr. Genesis sprung for a glass backboard. A handful of people tossed a Frisbee beside the court in the open field. The Frisbee landed at our feet. Treasure picked it up and tossed it to a tall skinny man in a blue bandanna.

"Thanks, Treasure."

"You're welcome, Ishmael. Say hi to Louis here."

"Hello Louis, peace and love."

Unsure of the proper protocol, I simply smiled and waved. Treasure gave me a half grin. She had the type of eyes that knew more than they told. They were also the type of eyes that studied you constantly, even during idle chitchat. As cute and petite as she was I knew I could never trust her. The fact that she was giving me this tour meant that she was high-ranking, and anything that ranked high with the menacing looking Genesis was not someone to whisper secrets to.

Just past the open field was a large pond with three ducks on it. They didn't miss a thing, these PASSAGE folks. This was paradise, or at least it was made to look that way. Beyond the pond and down a short hill was another field that wasn't visible from the rear of the Great Hall. We found the majority of the guests of the ranch down here. By the time we reached them it sounded like a packed stadium. People laughed and cheered as they watched and participated in a three-legged race—a game I hadn't played since childhood. I can't say I missed it. Treasure barely introduced me to a Martin and a Michelle before I was pulled to the starting line.

"You're up, handsome, hold still."

A woman in her late thirties who might be considered plus size was down on one knee tying our left legs together. She tied the knot quickly to piano-wire tautness.

"No wait, I haven't done this in years."

"Just stay with my pace and you'll be fine. Remember, we're a team."

As she wrapped an arm around me I could feel her power. The fact that I hadn't done the three-legged gig wasn't going to matter. I checked out the competition. On our left was an Asian couple who looked like a pair of personal trainers. On our right was a couple that appeared to be more our speed; the man was in good shape but his legs were short and the woman was nearly a foot and a half taller than him. I had my sights set on them. A starter's pistol went off. Mr. Tall and Ms. Small got off to a great start. My partner and I got out of the gates at the same time as the fitness trainers but were behind quickly.

"Come on, handsome, put a little leg into it."

She was right. Here I was dogging it so she could keep up and she had all the steam. Big and Small were still out front with the trainers hot on their tail. We were last.

"Okay, handsome, let's show 'em our finishing kick, second gear now!"

The big woman tightened her grip around my waist and heaved. I almost lost my footing but saved it. We both got down lower and really dug in. We were on the trainers. We passed the trainers. Mrs. Trainer said "Oh no!" We left them in our dust. Big and Small had a steady pace and could see the finish line. The screaming fans got louder and louder. This was fun but it was all about winning now. My partner made a clicking sound like a rider does a horse. I thought it odd but it worked, our outside arms were now in perfect sync. We caught up to the leaders. They panicked and faltered. We were in the lead with twenty yards to go when my foot caught on something. I lost it. My partner did her best to hold me up. I actually started to recover but now she was off kilter. I tried to help her and that caused hell to break loose. We took flight as a unit with ten yards to go. We barely had time to get our free hands out in front of us. My partner shouted "Handsome!" a second before our faces hit the dirt. We bounced once, again as a unit then hit a third time and slid on our mugs finally coming to a stop three yards shy of the finish line. The cheers turned to laughter as Big and Small trotted past with the trainers nipping at their heels. People rushed over to untie us and check our health. I felt like a two hundred pound dolt, which I was. My partner was up before me laughing harder than anyone else. The laugh became mixed with a smoker's cough, but she assured everyone she was fine.

"Handsome, I haven't had that much fun since I can remember."

"Are you all right, though? My face is numb."

"Honey, I was a stunt woman for seventeen years, that was child's play. Ready to go again?"

"No thanks, I've never been a stunt anything, ever. I need to just chill out for a minute, you know?"

"Don't feel bad. Most fellows that hitch to my wagon bail out a lot earlier than you did. The name's Alice, what's yours?"

"It's Lou Crasher, nice to meet you."

"You too, but if you don't mind I'll just keep on calling you Handsome."

"I wouldn't have it any other way."

After the tour and race I was taken to the Room of Joy, which turned out to be my lodgings. The room was a combination tent and cabin that housed ten beds. We were to shave, shower and everything else in the gymnasium facility when the need arose. My bag waited for me three beds down on the left side.

"Louis, the Room of Joy, like other sleeping quarters on the ranch, is not co-ed. So if you make a friend, which I'm sure you will, we have private cabins up behind the Room of Outer Beauty."

"I just have to ask. If this is the Room of Joy and it's just a bunch of cots—lovely cots mind you, what is the name of the rendezvous cabins?"

"Pleasure Palaces. And don't worry, they are much more luxurious than these quarters here. You simply come to me and request one, I handle the bookings. Are you horny? Would you like to try one out now?"

"Treasure, I—now?"

"Relax, I was only trying to scare you," she chuckled. "One thing you will find around here is that people will be up front and honest with you. We promote this in our guests. So you can erase all of the desperate person's bar lines that you have learned. If you want something or someone, just ask."

"Great, I'll keep that in mind."

She was one of those people that stood very close when they spoke to you. I generally need two feet of space with strangers. Her being in my personal zone and the subject matter and just the two of us in the Room of Joy had me off balance.

"Great nothing, try me."

"Excuse me?"

"Come on Louis, pretend you want me and invite me to the cabins, the 'rendezvous cabins,' as you call them."

"That's okay. I think I can manage."

"Don't be shy. Louis, I want you, take me to the love cabins. See? Now you try it, only replace your name with mine."

I sighed heavily, shifted from my left foot to my right two times, avoided looking her in the eye and sighed again. It didn't work. She still stood in front of me.

"Okay. here goes. Treasure, I want…do you, can we, will you come, sorry—go to the cabin with ah, well, what are you doing later?"

"No good. You could be inviting me to volleyball. Try again."

I wasn't sure what kind of game she was running on me but I did know that she was referee, head coach and star player. I thought it best to play it out.

"Treasure darling, I want you like I've wanted no other. I want that firm little body of yours, right up close and personal. Can you dig it? I'm a man who possesses a savage soul and baby you're turning this soul on fire. We need to lie down and get this thing together because if we don't I'm going to spontaneously combust right here, right now. What do you say dollface, are you ready to shake, rattle and roll?"

"Fabulous! That was great and I accept!" She leaped forward and gave me a hug. "Come on, let's go."

"What? No. Are you serious? I thought we were just rehearsing."

Her face turned gray and her body tensed. "Are you rejecting me? I can't believe this. Listen, mister, and listen close. We here at PASSAGE mean what we say and say what we mean."

With that she stomped off like a marching band leader. Over her shoulder she told me dinner was at six and I had better not be late. The Asian couple I had seen shooing the horse were now finished and approached wearing nothing but faces of sympathy. The man spoke first.

"Do not feel bad, friend. Treasure is a very sensitive child."

"She's not exactly a child though, Daniel," the woman said.

"By that I mean child of the universe," he explained to both of us. "Did she propose sex to you?"

"Yes, at least I think she did."

"Gawd, I love that girl's spirit. She's so...free, you know?" the woman said. "My name is Beth and this is my good friend and lover, Daniel. It is almost time for supper prayer so we'd better get dressed, honey."

"Of course, Louis, I don't know if anyone told you but you must be clothed for all meals so if you were thinking of stripping down like us you'll have to wait until after."

"Thanks for the tip."

"Strive for ascension," they said in unison.

I walked to the gym to shower off the long bus ride and three-legged race. This and other showers were to be the only times that I'd be going nude in the next seventy-two hours if I had anything to say about it.

After the shower, I dressed in denim shorts, sandals and a light blue button-up short sleeve T-shirt. Two other gentlemen came back from showers as I was about to leave the tent. We did introductions, after which I received two PASSAGE hugs. I was glad they were wearing towels. As I stepped through the door Treasure stood with her hands at her sides waiting for me.

"Treasure, hi."

"I want to apologize for putting you on the spot earlier."

"Oh, don't worry about it. I guess I'm just a little prudish."

"Please, let me finish, I need this. I came at you too soon and too hard. I spoke with Genesis and he said that my desires of the flesh took me to a bad place, a selfish place."

"What? You spoke to the man himself about this? About us?"

"Of course, always."

This was exactly the type of attention I did not need.

"Our Genesis is very wise and extremely accessible. He said that he would pray on this and that I should too. We came up with the apology together."

As she went through the points of the apology she counted them off on fingers. She either had a poor memory or she was so dependent on the big G that she couldn't think for herself at all. It was her problem and it didn't concern me at all, regardless of how concerned I was.

Torches burned on every pillar in the great hall. A half dozen more of the large tables had been added to seat everyone. I estimated between a hundred and a hundred and twenty people were present. The military men from the video were nowhere in sight, which I wasn't sure was all that comforting. People milled around chatting quietly or exchanged hugs. It was obvious that I was the new kid in town. Everyone came up at different times to introduce themselves, half of them commenting on my three-legged race performance. I had to admit to myself that there was no lack of love in the room. Two sets of double doors opened at the far end on the hall and the room went silent. The man known as Genesis stepped through the door in a shocking red Vincent Price-style robe. Treasure stood to his left in a beautiful Japanese kimono. It matched the big Kahuna's robe. There was a woman to his right in an identical kimono. My heart pounded when I recognized the woman as Crystal. Behind them stood four hard-looking men in toga-like attire. I could now account for four of the military guys from the twins' video. Why the big master needed bodyguards at the free love farm was a tad unsettling. We moved as a herd to a matted area I hadn't noticed before and sat cross-legged, heads down at Genesis's sandal-clad feet. Lacking any significant amount of flexibility I hoped we were not going to have to sit this way for long. With my head down I snuck quick glances at various followers. I noticed that everyone kept their eyes open but would not look at their leader. The sound of paper rustling came from where he stood and then he spoke.

"Here is what has transpired on this day to the south, children. A young lad of twelve and his eight-year-old sister were returning home from the corner store in the city of Carson. It seemed that their mother, their birth mother, needed cigarettes and who better to send to the store..." He let the sentence hang a moment before continuing. I was about to sneak a peek during the break when an elderly black woman beside me whispered to me that I must keep my head down. How she knew I was about to look was more than slightly creepy.

"Cigarettes! Does one not need to be eighteen years of age to purchase these sources of cancer?"

"Yes, Genesis," everyone resounded like a church choir.

"Nevertheless, the youths were permitted to make their purchase and on the way home were caught in the middle of a gang firefight. I think you all know what came to pass."

The choir responded the same as before. The leader's voice was very deep and captivating. The subject matter gave him added weight. His act was polished and these people were his.

"Money, greed, hate, machismo, ego, automatic weapons, what does it all mean? Two innocent lives snuffed out like that." He clapped his hands together loudly for emphasis. Many members of the group flinched. Television evangelists had nothing on this cat. Somebody behind me sobbed quietly. I believe it was a man.

"These children were a blessed gift from the universe and now..."

Paper folded and unfolded. He had two more similar stories for us before leading us in a prayer.

"We the people of ascension seeking serenity, attaining goals and enlightenment thank our universe for the gift of this earth plane which we seem so bent on destroying. We are thankful for the gift of another day of life on your beautiful soil. We weep for the children in these headlines and others of similar fate. We are wretched beasts who through gains personal, spiritual and financial and brotherly love look forward to our day of ascension to your heavens."

"All rise and form a circle. That's it, that's it."

We did as we were told and joined hands. The circle broke briefly to let Treasure in and then closed behind her. She marched through the center of the circle with a blank expression. I thought she was going to stop when she reached the center and lead us in some other prayer or maybe even a dance but she just kept on coming... straight at me. I mumbled shit under my breath as if that would help. I tried to look at the person beside me as if that would make Treasure go away. When she got to me my partners let go of my hands so Treasure could take them in hers. She pulled me into the center of the circle. Once in the middle she gave me a hug and walked back to her spot and joined Genesis who had now joined the circle. I felt like a lab rat about to be pushed on a flaming hamster wheel. The room was silent. I looked around smiling nervously and nodding at a few members. By some signal I did not see the members quickly shed their clothing without so much as a peep. I was now surrounded by over a hundred naked people. Again I mumbled 'shit' to myself. They raised their clasped hands over their heads and held them there as Genesis spoke.

"Children of PASSAGE, children of the universe, before you stands Louis, who until today was a frightened percussionist from Los Angeles. Please welcome him to our family."

Everyone bowed three times as a group and said, "Welcome, brother Louis," with each bow. I had hoped to hear people chant my name one day but not quite in a setting such as this. How Genesis knew about my drumming was a slight mystery. My only hope was that Outlaw put it on some sort of application or something. If he had come by this information on his own he may also know why I was there. I decided it was best not to think of such things especially at that moment. Nobody wants to cry in front of a bunch of strangers, especially a grown man like myself.

"Brother Louis, the family has welcomed you into the fold. Remove your clothes so that you are as we."

I did so more slowly than a snail moving up hill in a hailstorm.

Surprisingly it felt all right, seeing as everyone else was in the same boat...or circle.

"Very good, and welcome. You are one of us now. I have also been informed that you are one heck of a three-legged racer."

The room erupted in laughter and cheers.

"Have you anything to say for yourself?"

People quieted down to a mumble, perhaps awaiting some brilliance to spew from me. I had a dirty version of a three-legged joke in mind but decided against it, what with the nudity and all. I don't know if it was a build-up of pressure or a momentary bout of psychosis but from the depth of my inner fool I let out the loudest, longest wolf howl I could. People laughed and cheered as the circle collapsed around me. I received enough hugs and pats on the back to last me a lifetime. With all of this birthday party-like treatment it was difficult to stay focused on the job at hand. I had to remind myself that I could trust no one. Clothes were returned to bodies, then the flock gradually made its way to the tables.

Genesis sat at the head of the centermost table, flanked by Treasure and Crystal. Everyone else sat where they pleased. I noticed right off the bat that everyone wore bright colors, there wasn't a black garment in the room. The bright ones are the happy ones I suppose. But there was something about the clothes. It was as if the entire congregation shopped at the same Ascension clothing outlet. In the back of my mind I thought maybe it was a rule to make it easier to spot any members of the flock who planned an escape.

A group of servants came in with covered plates and laid them on the tables. I thought back to Oliver's delicious stuffed game hens. People talked, cheerfully ignoring the servants. As I checked the servers for possible Genesis henchmen as casually as I could, I came up with a definite zero. What I did notice bothered me. The serving staff consisted of young men and women, which is great for equality, but the average age was fifteen.

Thinking back to my earlier tour, I realized I hadn't seen any kids around, yet there seemed to be some couples the right age for parenting kids from toddlers on up. Maybe they were holed up somewhere else in a place I was not shown on the tour. Or maybe this was an adult type of joint, which would explain all the nudity. I asked myself what in this day and age of MTV, Snoop Dogg, *Guitar Hero*, Facebook, Youtube, sex, drugs and rock-and-roll would possibly keep these teenagers here? I began to feel a knot form in my stomach at the possible answers, which all ended in Genesis. In my heart I didn't just want to get Crystal out of here, I wanted to burn this snake charmer down. However, one must remember that one's—namely, my own—skills are best applied behind a drumset.

When the last plate was laid, the servants removed the lids. I thanked the pimply faced kid who raised mine for me but he just nodded shyly and practically sprinted away. I let it go and turned my attention to the rainbow trout, asparagus tips, mixed cauliflower and broccoli smothered in cheese sauce, accompanied with a biscuit and mashed potatoes steaming in front of me. The knot in my stomach decided to unravel to make room for dinner. Treasure stood and asked us to bow our heads. We held hands and obeyed. She gave a grace which thanked God, earth and the universe. The food was music to my nostrils. At the end of the prayer we sat down to eat. At first I couldn't locate my cutlery and was not sure who or how to ask for it. I had my answer when I noticed that nobody had utensils, everyone ate with their hands. A large man of body builder size across from me spoke in a very soft voice that didn't suit his physique.

"Do not panic, Louis. Society has pulled us away from such wonderful experiences such as actually holding and feeling the food that we eat. We are what we eat, and we eat what we feel. It is best to have a relationship with the nutrients that go into the body. Think of it as an introduction through the pores of the hand prior to the induction into the body, and eventually the soul."

I told him that I would try to look at it in the way he suggested while actually thinking that this was the dumbest thing I had ever heard. I glanced at some of the 'children' and thought that ancient Rome must have been like this. And with a quick pop of my napkin- into my collar I dug in. When in Rome, and all that.

The meal was excellent and there were seconds for those who wanted them. To drink there was apple, cranberry, orange, or carrot juice, water, milk and herbal tea. No booze and no caffeine. The buzz at the table was that most people were off to the hot tubs after dinner. Others were off to do their own thing. I wanted to find a way to contact Crystal so I declined an invitation to the tub party. Before I got up to leave the table a firm hand was on my shoulder. It was Adrian, the gent who took my bags when I first arrived.

"Our Genesis would like to see you."

He wasn't my Genesis, was my inward response. "Oh, okay just let me head back to my room for a second."

"Now would be best, Mr. Crasher. It shouldn't take long."

The knot was back in my stomach. I rose from the table, tossing my napkin down on my plate before trailing Adrian. We left through the entrance from which *their* Genesis entered earlier. I was immediately in a corridor I hadn't been shown on my tour. I wondered just how much of this compound I really had been shown—a fraction, I was sure. We traversed two lefts and a right before I was lost. I cursed myself for not bringing biscuit crumbs for a little Hansel and Gretel act. The walkway was dimly lit. Every so often I could make out closed doorways. We finally emerged from the maze into a foyer nearly the size of the great hall.

"Heh, heh, we'll need a map to get back eh, Adrian?"

He didn't even shrug his shoulders in response. We walked the remainder of the way over a thick rug that I'm sure experts would recognize as Persian. Adrian knocked three times: one short, one long and another short on a large door. The door looked like solid wood but sounded more like steel. I thought we were going to be let into a large room but it was another foyer. A black man close to my size wearing engineer-style coveralls let us into the hall. His name was Cyril and he was a maintenance man just changing out a few light bulbs before going off shift. The out-of-place oversized chandelier he worked on was so huge that we never saw his face clearly, just heard his voice. There was no way he could have opened the door for us manually, let us in and then raced back up the ladder. He must have had some kind of remote control device. Either that or the door was on a clapper system. The ten foot step ladder creaked as we passed. Adrian did the same knock at the next door and Genesis' voice boomed from the other side.

"Come."

Genesis was more intimidating up close. Not the huge bouncer-standing-in-a-night club-doorway intimidating, but rather the con-artist-meets-violent-criminal type. In fact it was more than that he looked sadistic, which is a difficult look for one to possess when they are not in the grips of a sadistic act. His look causes one to wonder how he could attain and maintain a flock of loyal followers. That is until he speaks. Genesis had the calm voice of a gentle yoga instructor. His mannerisms were slightly effeminate which I'm sure put people at ease; however a trained eye such as mine could tell they were manufactured.

His thinning, dyed-black hair came to a low widow's peak not far above eyebrow height. His eyes were a blue-green with what looked like a thin dark ring circling the pupil. One would have to get a closer look to see if the ring was dark brown or black. I'd leave that for his concubines. Up close the tacky bathrobe, although still tacky, appeared to have been hand embroidered. Nice job, very intricate work. Long bony fingers interlocked in front of his face. His manicure didn't look cheap.

The phony prophet sat at a large table made of four-inch thick glass. It would definitely hold him if he had a Bernie Outlaw-style tantrum. On it was a laptop computer, a small antique lamp and two telephones. Behind him, on what appeared to be a credenza, was a fax machine. Opposite and to his left sat a tall man in an expensive business suit. The suit wasn't cut right. Either he'd lost a lot of weight or he borrowed it from his bigger, older brother. A briefcase lay open at his feet. He was pulling documents from it as we entered and looked cautiously at me as he did so. Treasure stood like a pet poodle at Genesis' side. There was no sign of Crystal.

Adrian closed the door behind us, after which he gave me a slight shove toward his boss. I was already in the lion's den, no need to be pushy, I thought. The big boss stood up as I approached his desk and extended a hand with a Sunday Morning Sermon smile. I gave him my First Day in Paradise smile. After all, I was supposed to be a happy new disciple. We shook before he motioned me to the chair beside who I presumed to be his lawyer. I plopped into the ornate antique looking replica and was introduced to Lazlo. He seemed uncomfortable with my presence. Mine, his own, and everyone else's, for that matter. Hm. Nervous lawyer—not good.

"So, Mr. Crasher, I welcome you once again, and a thank you is in order."

"Thank you?"

"Yes, it's rare that my children that come here put down double the required deposit amount. You must really be searching for something that the world outside cannot offer."

You've got to love that Outlaw. In an attempt to secure my admission he'd already drawn suspicion to me. "True, but I also thought that it might be difficult to get in here based on what I heard so

I took some of that money daddy-o has been saving for me to go back to med school, and voila. I mean it's my life, and this sanctuary is going to be more educational to me than any room full of arrogant over privileged students pouring over test tubes and petri dishes. Am I wrong?"

"You couldn't be more right, Louis."

I could tell he didn't buy my line of bull, so in turn I wasn't buying his smile. I had already been made, or at least I was all the way onto the radar screen.

"I'm curious though, how were you able to coerce the money from your father?"

"I'd rather not say." I looked at the lawyer as I said it.

"Come now, Louis, we at PASSAGE have no secrets."

"It is no secret, I would rather just not say."

"Aha, I feel that your father's money would have been wasted on medical school. For I hear the dance of a politician. Perhaps a contribution to your political campaign would have been better suited."

It was not a question so I didn't respond. He got up from the desk and slid open a door on the credenza.

"Drink?"

"I do, but I thought it was against regs."

"I am 'regs' as you say, Mr. Crasher. You look like a rum drinker, yes?"

"That's one of them, but no thanks." I wanted to keep my wits about me. No way was I going to be the easy drunk girl at the prom.

"Are you promiscuous, Louis?"

"No, and not always by choice."

The Suit laughed loudly and quickly stopped himself. I thought back to my episode with Treasure and decided not to look at her.

"I already know you don't smoke." I thought this may have been a trap to see if I filled it out on some application so I tried to cover my tail.

"I don't remember that on the form. Oh well, it's true. I don't smoke."

"Gamble?"

"Not anymore."

"You don't smoke, gamble, sleep around and I can't offer you my finest Jamaican rum. Why are you here?"

"I've always felt that there is more than the daily grind: Gridlock, B-movies, VH-1, bad talk shows, crooked politicians, irresponsible media, shameless club owners and dicey record labels ripping off musicians. Greed, hate, lust—there must be more."

"Very impactful words. Anyway, the reason you are here is the same as the rest of us. You are looking for love. You need to learn how to love thy neighbor. You need to learn to love the earth and let the earth love you, same as the universe and thy neighbor. This is just a one-on-one welcome."

Treasure nodded with every word he spoke. I prayed that my poker face wasn't cracking.

"We also need you to sign a few minor documents that just basically say that you are here of your own free will and so on. You may or may not have heard that every government agency from the IRS on down is trying to destroy the beauty that we have built for ourselves. The world is a suspicious and jealous animal, Mr. Crasher. 'How could a private little commune have so much happiness and not be illegitimate?' they ask. I don't need to go into further details at this juncture, but that is it in a nut shell."

Genesis was one of those guys who used a lot of words to say nothing and give away nothing. His house was in order, no question. Lazlo handed me some papers and spoke as quickly as he could giving short descriptions of each and pointing to the lines I needed to sign or initial. I feigned that I was reading each document with medium concern before signing. I didn't think that any of this would matter in a day or two but just to be safe, I spelled my name wrong and slightly changed my signature style from the usual. I thanked Lazlo calling him 'Lazzie baby.' The excitement on his face told me that this was probably the first nickname he'd ever been given, poor doofus. We stood, we shook and then Adrian held the door for him and me to leave. To his surprise, Genesis asked him to stay.

"Do you know your way back?" Adrian asked in a tone that suggested he doubted I was up for the task.

"Oh yeah sure, I was best seeker in Cub Scouts." I closed the door behind me.

Directly outside Genesis' office I noticed the ten foot ladder under a different chandelier. I looked around for Cyril but couldn't see him. As my eyes did a back sweep of the foyer I noticed that a section of the burgundy wood paneling was ajar like a secret door. Curiosity killed the cat, but it never hurt me. I moved soundlessly to the crack and peered inside. Within was a small janitor's quarters. Cyril was stepping out of his coveralls getting ready to leave. He folded them neatly and placed them on a chair and then exited through a rear door to the room. I entered like a cat in a dog kennel, walked to the far door and pressed my ear against it: nothing. I turned back to the coveralls and quickly put them on. Fifteen seconds later my ear was now pressed against the office door. Genesis and the lawyer were talking money and of an offshore account. This was probably good dialogue for any government agent but those are the breaks. Genesis was agitated with his lawyer's legalese and told him so with words that I am sure were not PASSAGE-approved. After the scolding he changed gears and asked Treasure where Crystal was. He referred to her as his 'baby Crystal' which caused me to involuntarily clench my fist. Treasure responded hotly that she didn't know. Genesis was playing the two against each other, no question there.

"Mind your tone, sweetheart. Just because we are not in front of public eyes does not give you license to snap at me," Genesis said firmly, with a hint of spoiled little boy. At the moment these two women were his trophies. They probably fought over and worshiped him. He'd probably run this game on several women before these two. I was going to steal one of his prizes, thus weakening the beast. Adrian, standing at the door, cleared his throat.

"Oh yes, Adrian, what do you make of our newest member. Did you find anything of interest when you tossed his bag?"

"No, it was clean."

"Something isn't right about him, young man, I want you to watch him."

"I do that with all new—"

"This one is different I'm telling you, so pay close attention. It is what I pay you for." Genesis' voiced ended in a shout. A long silence followed before Adrian answered.

"Will that be all, *sir*?"

I couldn't hear the reply. The doorknob turned so I flew up the stepladder and buried my face and hands in the chandelier as if I was the maintenance man. I heard the door open and close.

"You still here, Cyril?"

"Hm," was all I said, and it worked. I heard the sweet sound of retreating footsteps through the foyer. I got down off the ladder and listened at the door again. They spoke too softly for me to discern. I could tell from her giggle that they were making up—time for me to find the exit. I moved quickly on my toes to the janitor's quarters and returned the coveralls to their home. I considered leaving through the exit at the back of the room but decided against it. It could put me out on the freeway for all I knew. I'd take my chances on the maze back to the Great Hall. I knew my way for the first few turns of the trip but eventually accepted that I was lost. I knew right from left but not east from west.

With every other step I expected to be grabbed by two hundred angry hands from behind. Every step other than that I expected the floor to fall out from beneath me and, just my luck, the bottomless pit would have a solid bottom after two minutes of free fall. If I did get caught, which I was sure to, I decided I wanted to take some secrets with me to the grave. I began trying some door handles. The first two were locked, which was almost a relief. Door number three opened with a creak right out of a Wes Craven movie.

The room was dark and damp smelling. There was no window. A single light bulb dangled from the center of the ceiling. The cheap flowered wallpaper did its best to jump off the wall. The gray carpet was full of holes and a million little stains. In the corner was a tiny sink with a cracked mirror above it. The room, which could be found in any ghetto neighborhood seemed grossly out of place to the rest of the lush log cabin. The young waiter who previously lifted the lid from my plate sat on a dirty mattress that sat on rusty springs. He stared straight ahead at nothing on the wall. A long chain ran from the bed post to his ankle. Beside him on the bed was a thick book with the word PASSAGE on it. I now envisioned murdering Genesis.

" Hey kid, are you all right?" I whispered.

I knew that he wasn't and was not surprised when he didn't answer. He turned his head slowly toward me. With eyes filled with tears he began laughing, slowly at first, and then building to a hysterical pitch. It was a laugh that I knew would stay with me for a long time. I closed the door and moved on, expecting to be nabbed any second. I didn't know where I was in the building but I did know it was much larger than it appeared from the outside. Convinced that I was headed in the right direction I kept trotting, stopping every so often to listen for sounds of a manhunt. My nose told me I was near the kitchen so I headed there. It could not have been far from the dining room. I came through a side door alongside a large double sink. Only a few of the all-Latino staff looked up. I tried to look like I belonged there so they wouldn't repeat that I'd been there to anyone. I slipped on the slick greasy tile and would have gone down if the heavily tattooed dishwasher hadn't caught my arm.

"*Cuidado, amigo*," he said.

I thanked him and left through a door that led to a short hall that took me to the Great Hall. I was home free. I walked through the hall and went outside. I was relieved to find that nobody was waiting for me. I went straight to my room with the intent of catching my breath and thanking my lucky stars. Once in my room I lay on my back on my bed and stared at the ceiling. I whispered twenty times, "What am I doing here?" I rolled over and opened my bag. I decided to put on some trunks and take a hot tub. I thought back to what I heard about Adrian tossing my bag and began to feel angry. I stumbled across my phone book which I knew I hadn't packed. How the hell did it get there? I opened it and on the first page in red letters in hand writing I knew to be Jake's was a note. It read: Bottom of the Bag Gymnasium 555-0007. The number was as real as a three dollar bill. I spent a few minutes trying to figure out what the number code meant when I realized that it was in the phony gym name. I pulled everything out of the bag but there was nothing at the bottom. When I looked closer I noticed that the bag had a false cardboard bottom. When I pulled it out I saw what Jake was telling me. Under the cardboard was one of the tiniest flip phones I'd ever seen. On it was a phone number in the 310 area code. I now knew how to call in the cavalry. Jake is a good guy to have on your side. I breathed a sigh of relief that Adrian never found it.

"Whatcha doin'?"

Treasure stood in the doorway. Thankfully my back was to the door.

"Actually I was wondering if PASSAGE has an iron or something. My stuff got pretty messed up."

I palmed the phone and put it back in the bag with a handful of clothes.

"Oh yeah, don't worry about it. Where have you been? I came by earlier but you weren't here."

"Oh you know, just cruising around."

"Where?" she asked.

"Okay, I confess it took me a while getting back cause I got a little lost in the big cabin."

She giggled a little girl's giggle and came and sat beside me on the bed.

"Isn't our leader great? Were you nervous being in his office? I was, the first time. I still am sometimes."

"No, I think I was okay. Did he say anything?"

"No. What would he say? He loves you, you know. He loves all of us."

Man, she was in deep. I wondered how she got to that depth. Did she have parents who knew where their daughter was? I started to think about the boy chained to the bed and anger replaced the sadness I felt for Treasure.

"What? Why are you looking at me like that Louis?"

"Like what?"

"I don't know, all of a sudden—"

"So why were you looking for me, pretty lady?" When in a corner, play the flattery card.

She blushed. "I always spend the first few days with the new guests. Besides," she paused. "There is something about you. I like you."

"Don't you love me? Genesis loves me."

She looked uncertain and moved away from me slightly. "Yes." Then she asked through big eyes, "Do you love me?"

"No, I'm still learning how." Silence followed. "So that other woman that hangs out with you and the big guy, what's her story?"

She folded her small arms. "Crystal. What about her?"

"I don't know, she doesn't seem to say much, is she—"

"She showed up about six months ago. She's got some rich daddy or uncle who pays her bills. Genesis seems so, I don't know, not himself when she's around, and she's always around. In sixteen days it will be my eighteenth-month anniversary here at PASSAGE. It's taken me this long to build the closeness I have with Genesis. I don't even know if he knows my anniversary is coming up."

With a heavy sigh she looked down at her feet. Shame came over her face.

"Oh my god, I have allowed jealousy to enter my heart and poison my words. I shouldn't have spoken like this. I must pray on this."

"Wait, don't go. Sometimes it's best to let these things out. Tell me more about her."

"Huh?"

"I mean if you tell me positive things about her you will be that much closer to finding a place for her in your heart." I'd seen enough *Dr. Phil* and *The View* to know how to throw this lingo around.

"Hm, that makes sense, you know. Our leader was saying something like that the other day. Let's see, she loves volleyball, plays it all the time. She reads a lot of spiritual books. She is in to Deepak Chopra, who is a wonderful soul, don't you think?"

"The wonderful-est."

"She's very loving, I suppose. When she first got here she used the love cabins frequently. That all changed when she latched onto Genesis."

"Steady now, just the positive," I said, raising my left eyebrow.

Her eyes became slits, "Is that what this is all about? You want an evening with her?"

This was my cue to get off the subject of Crystal.

"Listen, sweetheart I am just here in search of a better way of life and hopefully to find some inner peace in the process. I don't understand the political goings on between you two ladies and the love cabins and all of that. I got out of Hollywood because of that kind of mess. I just want ascension and lollipops like everybody else, doll."

"You are so right. I'm being adolescent. I think I need a good cry."

"Oh come on, no need for tears sister, just be strong."

The tears didn't come. In fact she bounced back so quickly an NBA basketball would envy her. I didn't trust her. Even if this was no act and she was just plain crazy I still wouldn't trust her.

"So what are you going to do now?"

"Well, like I said earlier, I was hoping to press these clothes."

"And like I said, don't worry about it. We have people here that will take care of it. And soon you'll have a different wardrobe."

"Really, what people? Wardrobe, what—?"

I had an idea it was a certain bunch of teens who served up supper earlier that evening who would handle my laundry.

"Don't you worry about such things. You need to focus on learning the PASSAGE way of life and start your pursuit of the great ascension."

"Right, right, of course, how do I start?"

"Just keep your head up and your eyes open and Genesis will be your beginning." She grinned as if she were clever. I wanted to show Genesis the beginning, middle and end of my left hook. Her blind faith pissed me off. I wanted to take her with Crystal and me, who, incidentally, I was no closer to busting out of there.

"Do you still want me to have your clothes taken care of?"

"Well actually, I think I'll be all right if I just hang my stuff up on hangers."

"Okay, I'll have Adrian or one of the others bring you some hangers. What would you like to do now?"

"I think I'm going to hop into one of those hot tubs."

"Excellent, I'll see you over there. Oh, are you going naked?"

"Will you stop that?"

She ran out with a giggle. I felt the cell phone through the bag and exhaled. I quickly threw on some swim trunks and grabbed a towel. I slipped into some sport slippers and walked over to the hot tub area. Both tubs were busy with people having a good time. I said hello to everyone and climbed into the tub farthest from me. There were around twenty people in the tub. Other than me and a woman I guessed to be from the Philippines everyone was naked. I noticed space beside Alice, my three-legged race partner, so I waded over to her.

"Handsome, how's it hangin'? We can't tell with those silly Hawaiian shorts on."

"It's hanging just fine, Alice, and the shorts are Fijian, so there."

"Whatever. Lose 'em."

"Behave yourself, I'm the new kid."

"All right, all right, don't get your Hawaiian's in a knot. So what do you think of the place?"

"I'm blown away."

"Well it starts out that way, and then carries on the same way. Say, where's your cocktail?"

"Cocktail? I thought-"

"Relax, it's carrot juice. There's a juice bar over by the Room of Outer Beauty."

"Really? I hadn't noticed. It seems like a long way to haul a beverage though."

"Get a load of Handsome. He's here one day and already he's moaning about the digs."

"I'm not moaning, I was just saying—forget it, everything's cool."

"I'll show you cool, Mister Malcontent."

She reached behind her and removed a piece of deck which turned out to be a lid to an ice cooler. Out of it she pulled a thermos and cup. With a cheeky grin she poured the juice into the cup and handed it to me."

"How's that for far?'

"Thanks, Alice."

"Don't mention it."

This lesson, although little, reminded me that I would be best to play the silent observer for the remainder of my stay. I sat back with my drink and let the jets send the hot water to my weary muscles. The juice was nice and cold which is the only way to drink carrot juice, if one must. I opened my eyes to see whose leg brushed up against mine. It was the Asian gentleman I'd seen shoeing the horse.

"Hey, I'm sorry, man, I forgot your name."

"Daniel. How are you, Louis?"

"He says his name is Daniel, but around here we call him Horse Whisperer, or Whisper for short."

"Only you call me that, Alice."

"Hey, why so blue, Whisper?"

Staring blankly at the bubbles Daniel spoke in a monotone. "She is with him again, right now, as we speak."

I sat with open ears and closed mouth.

"Oh come on, Whispy we've been through this pal. She doesn't go that much. And remember, nobody owns anybody in this blink of an eye that we're here for. Besides, she hasn't agreed to the advancement right?"

Daniel continued staring at the bubbles in silence.

"Uh-oh. When did she change her mind?"

"Today, at least today is when she told me. I am sorry, Louis, you must be confused."

"Oh no I'm just enjoying the—"

"I know you are listening. It is okay, these are things you should know. The advancement we speak of is a program or process, if you will, here at PASSAGE, which is intended to ensure that this family grows. That it grows with the right stock, if I may."

"What the Whisperer is trying to say, Handsome, is that there are two ways of joining the PASSAGE family: to wander in here like you and me as a lost sheep, or to be born here. In order to secure breeding of good stock Genesis offers an open invitation to all women here to plant his seed free of charge."

"Unfortunately he makes this offer more firmly to some than others."

"That's enough, Daniel."

Daniel shuddered at Alice's command.

"So anyway, Genesis has been putting pressure on Beth—"

"My wife, Beth," Daniel said with little wind in his sail.

"—pressure on Beth to be host to his seed. It is an honorable position to be in and it ensures the desired advancement of the family. The Whisperer just has trouble comprehending the scope of this beautiful picture. I'd jump at the chance, no pun intended."

People slowly moved away from us as if Alice's words were a declaration of plague.

"You be strong, Daniel, and look at this as a gift." She downed her drink and climbed out of the tub. Daniel and I had the tub to ourselves. I stared at him as he continued to stare at the bubbles. I could only imagine his pain. Genesis was a first class son of a bitch, no question.

"There is no perfect religion or church, Louis, I understand that, but a word of advice, my friend. If you find someone here and become taken with her..." he swallowed heavily. "Take her and run, don't walk, away from this place. He owns everything."

And with that he climbed out of the tub. Reaching for his towel he spoke over his shoulder. "We did not have this conversation, Louis."

"What conversation?"

As he walked away I moved to another jet and thought about his words. The way he emphasized, 'he owns everything' gave me a chill, which is not easy in a tub of hot water. I lay back with closed eyes and began planning the next day's attack. I wasn't two steps into my plan when I heard females approach. I opened my lids to see Crystal and Treasure climb into the tub. They moved to either side of me. I didn't have to wonder long about what Treasure was up to.

"Louis, I've had a breakthrough."

"Breakthroughs are good," I replied.

"Yes. I went and meditated on...things, and, pow, it hit me. I was so caught up with myself that I allowed jealousy into my heart. I have no reason to be jealous of Crystal. Do you know why? Because I love her and nothing is more powerful than that in the universe."

They looked at each other and hugged, which made me want that earlier drink Genesis offered me.

"As I said, as I was meditating, the universe sent me a sign. Okay, here goes. How would you like to take beautiful Crystal here to one of the pleasure palaces of love for the night?" She didn't let me answer. "You see, the rooms were full but I've asked a couple if they would mind pushing their appointment to daytime tomorrow. I mean, when I told them it would be your debut they were struck with joy for you and they happily postponed."

"Oh, you shouldn't have done that, Treasure; that kind of thing shouldn't be postponed, they need to get their groove on."

"Groove on? That sounds like city talk. Anyway, it's okay. You see it's my way of saying I'm sorry to you and welcoming you, and giving Crystal a treat. You are quite handsome, Louis."

"Thank you, but I'd really rather learn the lay of the land a few more days before I—maybe lay was not the best word, but you know what I mean. Crystal, you are very beautiful and...and...And I'd love to."

"Fabulous! Isn't that fabulous, Crystal?"

"Yes, I'm so excited! Let's go."

They yanked me so hard out of the tub I thought my sockets would pop. The three of us jogged across the lawn holding hands the entire way. People grinned at us as though happy that I was finally let in on some joke. As we trotted past my barracks I asked if I could grab a few things but was told everything I'd need was there. We got to the cabin and stopped outside the door, which had a man and woman in the act of making love carved into it. "Subtle," I said. We panted and laughed until Treasure finally left us.

I considered carrying Crystal over the threshold but decided it would have been overacting. She flicked on a light. Me and ten other average Joes would have fumbled briefly before finding the switch as it was higher on the wall than most light switches. She'd been here before, which was no big surprise. This was PASSAGE after all; the place Outlaw wanted his daughter out of. Treasure was right. This place was not too shabby at all.

Thirteen long-stemmed roses poked out of a large porcelain vase on an antique table just inside the door. Chinese characters were painted near the base in blue-gray ink. The vase sat on top of an off-white lace cloth which draped over the three legged table. Instead of the vase I pictured a six-ply maple snare drum made by the Gretsh drum company sitting on the table. Instead of roses I pictured two thirteen inch pieces of hickory-drumsticks resting on the drums' skin. I'd pick up the sticks, strap on the drum and play perfect marching cadences. Out the front door I'd march with Crystal at my heels. The boy I'd seen shackled to his bed would come from the right and anyone else who really wanted out would come from the left until I'd be like the pied percussionist and lead everyone away from the 'world according to Genesis', to freedom.

Crystal walked to one side of the queen-sized bed and flicked a switch causing both bedside lamps to come on. "There, you can kill the overhead light now." On the bed lay a pair of silk boxer shorts and a sexy woman's teddy. Two thick bathrobes hung from one of the bed posts.

"I'm going to check out the bathroom." I wasn't interested in the décor so much as I wanted to look for possible exits. Two oval mirrors hung over double sinks with brass fixtures. The bathtub was the old style six foot type which sat on four solid claw feet. It had been modified to fit four Jacuzzi jets. I could only guess at the extravagance of Genesis' personal bathroom.

Aside from an octagonal window above the tub, barely large enough to fit three squirrels through, there were no exits. A bowl of potpourri sat on the back of the toilet. Beside that was a bidet. When I came back into the room Crystal stood up from the bed. She'd slipped into the burgundy teddy and it hung from her like a Versace on a Hollywood starlet. She looked nervous. Gone was the excited giggling girl I'd laughed with ten minutes earlier. We stood staring waiting for the other to say or do something. She bowed her head slightly and moved her hands to clasp them in front of her. I walked around the bed to her and turned her so she faced me. I noticed how thick her lashes were for the first time and how good she smelled. I told her she looked beautiful.

She thanked me and looked away.

"Crystal, we don't have to do this." She dropped her shoulders and then slowly sat down on the bed. I joined her. She tended to her cuticles, which needed no tending as I spoke. "I have a sneaking suspicion you were put up to this by the lady, Treasure, no?"

"Yes. She's always trying to pawn me off on someone so she can have our savior to herself. She can't help her jealous nature. She tries but...the thing is she doesn't have anything to fear from me, I don't own our leader—nobody does. He is beholden to none but himself and the universe. I mean, he's in the middle of trying to impregnate Beth right now."

"Really?" I said feigning surprise.

"Yup, and Daniel is none too pleased. Some people just don't understand what our leader is all about. They can't see tomorrow, you know?"

"So it doesn't bother you that he's, he's—"

"Screwing other women? Of course not, I get what is going on."

Something wasn't right. I played another card. "So, if you are hip to the program, and you dig what this is all about then why the long face? Either you find me so hideous that you have to fix your nails that don't need fixing or there is something else. Am I wrong?"

She moved away and lay back on the pillows with her hand over her forehead. The teddy came up enough to reveal the definition in her thighs. Clearly, reminding myself of my mission was not going to be enough to restrain me. Thinking of what Outlaw would do to me if he ever found out about me and his daughter, although drastically compelling, wasn't going to do it either. I never had any intention of going through with this passionate night from the beginning. However, the added dimension of a beautiful girl lying catlike on a puffy queen got my 'party parts' a- stirrin'. Then it hit me like Johnny B. Goode ringing that bell: Angela. That chapter wasn't going to be completely closed until I spoke to her myself.

"It's not you, Louis, you are very handsome. It is Genesis. I love him, I mean, I love everyone here, I do have that capacity. It's just..." She stopped herself and went back at her nails. With a sniffle she carried on. "He scares me sometimes, okay? He scares me, that's all. Please don't repeat any of this."

"Of course not," I said.

I took her hand in both of mine and looked at her closely. She began sobbing quietly.

"Has he ever hurt you, Crystal? I mean, physically?"

She sobbed harder without saying anything. I had my answer. I pulled her up to sitting position and put an arm around her. She leaned into my chest and let it all out.

"You know how I said I was floating around here looking for something?" I said. She nodded her head up and down once.

"Well, I think I've found it. I know this seems fast, and maybe nothing would become of you and me, but why don't we leave? We can be out of here tomorrow night. Once on the outside we can see the world or hang out in LA or San Francisco, hell, even Canada."

I knew it was too early to make my play but hell, I was new at this game and getting anxious to make the call to Jake and hit the pavement.

"And if the great white north isn't your bag then we can go our separate ways. The point is you would be free to make your own choices, Crystal, the way life should be. A man, a real man would never put hands on a woman. I've got a really strong feeling about you—a good feeling. I haven't been here long but already this place gives me the creeps. What do you say, babe, lets make like a trumpeter and blow."

She came up off my chest and gave me tear filled eyes. For years to come her eyes were going to have men doing crazy things. "Are you serious?"

"Dead serious. We're young and wild, come on!"

She wiped at her tears with a chuckle. "Are you an honest man, Louis?"

"Yes, why?"

"Then answer me one question. Did my father send you to get me?"

Chapter 27

Jake pulled his motorcycle up to the bay door of his warehouse loft apartment. A slender black man in his early fifties in a dark raincoat popped to a standing position with the spryness of an eighteen year old. He tipped his old school black derby at Jake as Jake shut off the bike and killed the headlight.

"Evening, Mr. Jake, evening."

"Meadow. Anything stirring?" Jake asked.

"Nothing aside from the usual ignorance, from dreams dashed, political promises broken and trickle down that don't trickle down. We're right up against Skid Row, my brother, but I don't need to tell you that. That said, not even a mouse has stirred around these parts." Meadow moved his head toward Jake's lodging. It was his way of reassuring Jake that the premises were secured.

"You do good, Mr. Meadow." Jake reached into his pocket and pulled out some bills for his homeless friend. His friend declined, which Jake knew he'd do. Jake put the bills back.

"Cold tonight. Blanket?"

"Now that I'll accept, Mr. Jake, yes sir."

Jake punched the code which opened the bay door. He re-fired the bike up and eased her into the freight elevator. On the ride up, Jake thought about his proud homeless friend Meadow, which was short for Meadowlark. Meadowlark took the name from Harlem Globetrotter great Meadowlark Lemon. Meadow owned a voice as deep as James Earl Jones. He had a facial scar courtesy of the street that ran from his right eye down to the center of his lip. Jake remembered back to the night he met Meadowlark. It was the night his friend received the scar. Two crackheads were rolling Meadow for money, as if a man like Meadow possessed any. Jake was usually one who minded his own business, especially living in this forgotten part of the city. If Meadow had cried for help as regular folk would have Jake may or may not have carried on his way, but he heard the older homeless person quoting Shakespeare, and parts of the Bible while taking his beating. Jake believed you picked your fights with care and that night he was going to help the street scholar.

Jake made short work of the desperate druggies and helped the homeless man to his feet. He was hurt badly, but pride prevented him from showing it. He merely dusted himself off like a man who's dropped biscuit crumbs on his coat. Jake recommended stitches for his face, but the man refused. He did, however, finally accept a few items of clothing, the pockets of which Jake slipped a few dollars into. And that's how it was with the two of them from that day on. Meadow acted as security guard and Jake gave little donations in which he'd smuggle currency.

After maneuvering his bike atop the rubber matting, Jake moved to a tall, dark cabinet made from cherry wood which held towels and blankets. At first he grabbed a colorful blanket he'd picked up in Peru, wanting to give his friend a nice piece. He then decided against it feeling it would attract too much unwanted attention and envy from his street neighbors. A plain gray but thick blanket would do the trick instead. Jake spread the blanket out on his bed, dropped forty dollars in the center and re-rolled the blanket.

"Mr. Meadow, I'm taking off for a couple of days. I'm waiting on a call first so I could be gone tomorrow or in a few days from now. I shouldn't be more than four or five days once I'm out. If you're in the area, keep an eye out." Jake paused. "But that's only if you don't have other plans."

Meadow nodded, "I'll be here and there, but rest assured, your home will be safe."

"Keep warm." Jake turned back to the elevator. Meadow thanked him again for the blanket.

Jake woke at 4:45 a.m. seconds before his alarm went off. The clock radio barely chirped before his hand came down on the button. He stood and did a big stretch, arching his back slightly. With a big exhale he picked up the remote and clicked the stereo on. The warehouse loft came to life with up-beat gospel music. Jake did a handstand and then walked on his hands from his bedroom area the twenty feet or so to the kitchen. He came down slowly in front of the stainless steel Viking refrigerator, folding his body in half like an l-shape, and held it a few seconds. Finally his feet came down to the floor. He pulled a bottle of water and a Tupperware container from the fridge and moved to the large table made from a piece of driftwood he'd found in Alaska in 2005. Water was always the first thing Jake put in his body after a night's sleep. He figured that if the body heals itself during sleep it ought to be thirsty after the fact. A separate container he brought out had cheap chunks of steak marinating in a bitter-sweet sauce he came up with. He smelled it before he transferred it into a thick freezer bag. After that he put on his jogging gear, put the meat into a back pack and headed down in the elevator. The air was as clean as it gets at this time of day. Jake drank it in. It was quiet. Meadowlark was nowhere in sight. The freeway was just beginning her rumble. A distant shopping cart could be heard. He ran a circuitous route for thirty five minutes until he ran under an overpass near the train tracks not far from Seventh Street and Santa Fe. A train sat parked. Jake climbed between two of the cars. He walked a little further and then gave a short loud whistle. He was about to whistle one last time when his friend emerged.

"Good morning, Braveheart. Hungry?"

Braveheart was a wild coyote Jake had found injured a few weeks earlier. Jake gave him the name as he was impressed at the animal's bravery for surviving so far into the city's belly.

"You're barely limping at all. And your coat looks better too."

Jake took a knee and put down a paper plate and emptied the steak onto it. He backed away slowly. The coyote showed his canines briefly. It seemed that this had become their ritual. The animal ate quickly glancing at Jake from time to time. In the beginning Jake had to leave altogether before the coyote would eat.

"This is it, warrior. Your strength is back. We part company here today. Good luck."

The coyote stared at Jake a moment then left quickly, its paws scarcely making a sound.

Chapter 28

Crystal and I woke early, like people do when visiting the country. We were locked in a hug on top of the comforter. I felt awkward; probably more so than she did. I had trouble convincing myself that my plan had actually worked and that Crystal was on board with flying the coop. But if she did believe me then I'd done a great job of deceiving her, which I believe is the story of her life. Pretty, innocent girls were slow moving targets for self-serving men. Now I really was sounding like my grandmother. This wasn't sitting well with me. However, what is a little deception when measured against the greater good? As we got dressed, we decided to go about our day separately and leave after evening prayer. This would give me time to call Jake and give him plenty of time to get his ass up here. Naturally, I'd leave that part out of the dialogue.

"Ah, as to last night, I hope you are not upset that we didn't, you know, do anything. It was just such a long day and you were upset. It didn't seem right to—"

"It's okay, Lou, and thank you for being a gentleman, I'd rather wait and do you the right way." Her coy little smile nearly caused me to knock the porcelain vase full of roses off the small standing table. She giggled.

I walked to her and held her. We looked at each other a moment, both of us feeling nervous and excited. I kissed her lightly on the lips.

"Wow, you must use some kind of fabric softener for lips or something. Okay, that was corny but again, wow." I smiled.

Once outside we went our separate ways, each continually looking back over shoulders at the other. I moved from potential rock star to private investigator to cheesy romance novel character. First order of business was to attend the Morning Prayer session and then go for a run. I noticed the day before that a four foot wide wood chip-covered path snaked its way in and around the entire compound. It attracted lots of joggers and today it would attract me. At various spots around the perimeter the trail bellied up against a thick forest. It was obviously off limits to go into the woods, but a guy could pretend to catch his breath and maybe bend down for a quick phone call.

I barely made it through the prayer session. God was mentioned occasionally but it was the universe that was the big winner. It had always been my understanding that God created the universe, but this wasn't my show so I laid low. A Latina woman with thick black and gray dreadlocks who I hadn't met before led the prayer. She had a soft voice but she knew just how to bring power into it. I drifted in and out of the sermon for a couple of reasons. I kept trying to see my upcoming escape in my mind's eye. Was Crystal really with the program? Probably not. It seemed too easy. However, I'd made my play and I was moving forward. Another reason for my drifting off was that as a rule I loathe, hate and despise fanatical cults of any sort, so when the preaching starts spewing my brain tends to start traveling.

I pictured successfully making my call to Jake and Jake putting together a hot-damn crew of his ex-Navy Seal buddies or maybe Marines and helicopter transporting us all out of here before Genesis' goons arrive. Somebody held my hand, followed by someone grabbing my other hand. Next thing I knew we were bowing our heads and repeating the words the sermon lady spoke. I felt like shouting, "Ascension and beers all around! Be sure to tip your Genesis dude. Hip hip hooray!" But I decided against it. As the prayer subsided and heads came up, there were hugs, kisses, slow smiling nods and handshakes; the type where two people use both hands to do it.

A feeling of conflict managed to creep into my being. On one hand, this whole thing appeared to be a gathering of pathetic needy people. But I also couldn't deny their warmth and general happiness. The exception of course being poor souls like Daniel and others silently opposed to Genesis' seed-spreading program, where their loved ones were concerned.

As I made my way back to my room I thought about the expression 'loved ones' then I was hit like two tons of crap in a shit storm. Where the hell were all of the children? I saw a few teenagers, one of which was suffering a nasty fate, but what of the rest of the kids? Genesis is supposed to be the head sire guy, so where the heck were the sired? A

216

knot was fast forming in my guts. For all I knew they were locked up somewhere or sold or sweating it out in labor camp or god knows what else...not to mention the universe. My blood was boiling but I couldn't let on so I managed a brilliant PASSAGE-worthy smile. A run was definitely going to do this brother some good.

I had all of my running gear on and as luck would have it I brought my shorts that have a small pocket in the front scarcely big enough for a key, or four sticks of gum or a large condom perhaps. I referred to it as my useless pocket until this day when I was barely able to squeeze the cell phone Jake slipped me into it. You'd have to be looking for it to see it. Just the same, I wore a light long sleeved number I'd been given back in the day which read 'Venice Beach' across the back. It hung down nice and low so I was doubly covered. I stepped outside and was about to stretch when I saw my good friend Adrian stretching as if he were about to go for a run. With a scowl on his face he stood up straight, gaining as much height as he could.

"Going for a run, Lou?"

"The universe willing, yes."

"Maybe I should join you."

Chapter 29

"I realize it's a tough assignment, boss. I realize that and more."

"Dare I ask what the more is, Special Agent Forbes?" The FBI supervisor rolled his eyes with the question making sure Agent Forbes saw him.

"Look, I know the history of this one, hell, what agent in this territory doesn't? We've sent in three agents. I know the first to go in was special agent Cribbs. He got made his first week there. Next was agent Cranston, a woman. She ended up quitting the bureau and joining the phony PASSAGE church. I don't need to point out what an embarrassment that was to us, or what a boon it was to their grand leader. The last agent ah, what was his name?" Agent Forbes put her fingers to her forehead trying to recall the name. Her boss wasn't going to help her. He wanted to let her make her entire point.

"Oh yeah, O'Doul, like the non-alcoholic beer—he was the most promising of the three. He was in deep for nearly three months before they pulled his ticket. Sad too, rumors say it took him eight months of therapy to deal with the stuff they put in his cranium. It was such a shame at the trial, good cop like that getting picked apart on the stand. I'm willing to bet Genesis got to that damn judge too."

Forbes slid forward in her chair and leaned her elbows on the desk. "So here's the long and the short of it: it is Genesis versus the Feds and we're down three-zip."

The chief supervisor leaned forward now as well, "That's right, and the President is focused on pending wars and healthcare, two areas under which phony church leaders don't fall. Meaning funding is hanging in the balance."

"Regardless, you're about to send in another woman...a somewhat unpopular one at that, to do this shit job that nobody wants. Why? Because of that shit that went down at Turley Lake."

"Watch it, Agent Forbes. I don't recall giving you permission to speak freely."

"No, but you did dare to ask what the *more* was so I'm spillin' it."

The chief let out a sigh and waved her off. "Look, Forbes, I know what kind of cop you are and I know that what happened at that cabin was bad luck. But now, unfortunately, other agents think you're bad luck." He stood and put his back to her.

"Bottom line is it was your show and two officers got hurt. I know it wasn't your fault but you were the quarterback. Remember, I have to answer to people as well, you know." He ran a hand through his graying hair. "It's no secret that some cops around here don't want you to succeed. Nothing I can do about that."

"Oh come on, boss, that's the way of the world. Don't worry about me. I'm in the kitchen and I can stand the heat, all right."

"Good. Then you're going in."

Special Agent Forbes stood up. "I need two things from you. The first is that I need you on the end of that phone when I'm ready. Second, I need you to make sure no one on our side of the fence, you know, my so-called 'friends,' tips Genesis off and blows my cover. If you cannot deliver on those two fronts then bring body bags because there's no way I'm taking the therapy route."

The chief slammed his fist on the desk. "Damn it, Forbes, this isn't the mafia. We're the law." Forbes headed for the door. Her boss wasn't finished.

"Agent Forbes, do you know what Tennet over at the CIA used to say to agents he sent into the field?"

"Uh uh, do tell."

"Don't fuck up."

"It's not really you, boss, sorry."

"Yeah, you're right. Just don't get shot. How's that?"

"Closer, definitely closer to you, chief. Stay by that phone, will ya?"

Agent Rebecca Forbes was LAPD for close to sixteen months before she quit and moved over to the Bureau. Not many cops make the move she made, especially when set up in a posh community like the Pacific Palisades. Big homes with manicured lawns, sunny Sundays so quiet it feels as though the city is abandoned and violent crimes are just unconfirmed rumors. A cop in the Palisades can look forward to peace, quiet and handing out traffic violations if they're that kind of cop, which Forbes was not. However when it came time to write that traffic ticket it was a chore to make it stick because everybody and their dog and cat was lawyered up to the hilt.

That wasn't so bad in Forbes' mind. It was when it became clear, although not spelled out in any manual, that the predominantly wealthy white community liked seeing faces similar to theirs. So if a Latino wasn't cutting grass or an African-American wasn't in a uniform and dropping off a package, the Palisadians wanted to know what their business was, and who better to put the question than LA's finest. Forbes always judged people by their actions, period, and she didn't take to being an overpaid rich neighborhood's security guard. She considered transfer but then chose the Bureau. The pay may have been less, but Forbes liked the idea of the Bureau's larger jurisdiction. Friends thought she was crazy to walk away from the coveted cop job with good pay to join the FBI. Closer friends knew Rebecca wasn't the type of person to take the cushy job just because it was cushy. She needed purpose.

The FBI was only too happy to have her. She already knew how to handle herself physically and she scored off the charts on the psych tests. Although she followed orders well, she was also exceptional at thinking out of the box when up against it. On top of these credits she was a patriot to boot. Politically she was country first, talking politico second. Her background check, which the Bureau always claimed to do more thoroughly than the LA cops, turned up only one incident. One evening during her college days Rebecca attempted to break up a domestic brawl around the pool table in one of the campus watering holes. She nearly had everything under control when the drunken couple turned on her, as pairs do in a tumultuous relationship. Suddenly Rebecca was forced to defend herself. Rumor had it that the man had desires of becoming a no-holds-barred cage fighter. His dream would later change. Witnesses say Forbes knocked the girl out and had the man in a submission hold in three quick moves. That was over fifteen years ago.

Jump ahead to August of last year. Rebecca Forbes' office knew all too well, as did other offices that one of its most brutal special agents had gone rogue. They weren't quite at the nationwide manhunt stage but they were close. Until then Forbes' office wanted the press kept out and the mess tidied up pronto. Embarrassments cut deep and were long remembered. Word had it that now rogue agent Doug Chaney was holed up in a small cabin near a tiny community called Turley Lake, not far from Bakersfield.

Rebecca rode in on her own. The other agents, Smith and Dickens, followed closely down the dirt road. The sun had just gone to sleep. Nobody used lights. A half mile before the cabin they shut the motors down and hoofed it. Former agent Chaney had been fast making connections and a name for himself in the drug community. He could almost be considered a player. His problem was he needed a little cross country travel money. He'd briefly kidnapped a newlywed couple, forced them to withdraw their ATM limits and stolen their car. Ninety miles down the road he ditched the car and stole another one. He was sloppy, to say the least. This was a good and bad sign to the boys at the Bureau. It was good because it meant Chaney was using his own supply and his luck would soon run out. The bad news was that a fully trained former agent on cocaine was capable of doing some supreme damage to himself and others.

"He's here, fellas, I say we take him now, right here." Forbes wasn't putting it to committee. "Smith, take the back, Dickens, looks like there's a side window or maybe a door; that's you. I've got front."

"Negative, Rebecca. He's pacing like a madman, getting antsy. Why not let him leave and pin him in the car?" Smith suggested.

"No way, he's headin' to Los Angeles and he ain't drivin' a slow white bronco if you get my meaning. It ends here. It's my call."

From her look the agents knew Rebecca was done talking. The two men separated and crept toward the small cabin. Forbes waited thirty counts then began creeping herself. She'd barely moved fifteen feet when she heard two quick pops and shattering glass.

"Shit," she said taking off at a run. Her radio crackled. "Forbes, I think Dickens is hit, get the fuck down here, I'm going—" The transmission cut.

Forbes reached the cabin, leaped up the two steps and threw her shoulder into the front door. It budged slightly but held. She heard another three shots—different gun. She tossed the radio aside and jerked her Colt from the shoulder holster. Taking a step back she hopped in the air and did a front jump kick to the door near the handle. The door gave. Another quick step back and again she let door have her shoulder. The door flew open with Forbes on top of it. She and the door crashed inward and landed on top of former agent Chaney. The door caught him off guard, as he was forced to turn and fire into the back bedroom. He'd already dropped the loser at the side window. Now there was another soon-to-be-victim trying to pick him off from the back.

Chaney wondered what the fuck the heavyweight on top of him was. One second he's about to waste the Boy Scout at the back of the cabin, next he's pinned under the door; it must be the door.

Forbes cursed herself for not keeping her feet. She spread her body out, hoping to keep him down. Neither one of her two companions were in the main part of the cabin with her. She cringed at the sinking feeling in her gut. Two agents may be dead. No time for such thoughts. She pushed them out of her mind.

Chaney, pinned flat on his face, was slowly able to roll onto his right side. Leaning the gun next to his left shoulder he pressed the muzzle against the heavy door and began firing. He heard a woman utter the f-word then the door tilted to one side. She must be rolling off, he thought. He squeezed out from the opposite side of the door and struggled to his feet. He could see that the woman huddled behind the black cast iron stove. A piece of her foot was exposed.

"I'm gonna blow the bitch's toes off," he whispered. He took aim with a two handed grip. Another pop came from the back bedroom. Chaney felt a stinging in his shoulder. He kept his feet. Wheeling to his left he fired two times into the dark bedroom.

Forbes saw her chance. She leaned out on one knee, the other foot planted solidly on the wood floor. Closing her right eye she fired three times. Two bullets caught Chaney—one in each knee cap. He went down like a ton of bricks, screaming like a schoolgirl. His gun slid across the floor under the window, where Forbes knew Chaney had fired at Dickens.

"Agent Dickens! Agent Smith! Hold your fire! Subject is down. I repeat, hold your fire." Rebecca Forbes sprinted ahead and put her gun to Chaney's temple.

"You're under arrest, asshole," she yelled.

"You bitch! Do you know how much this fucking hurts?"

"Can it, druggie! You're a damn disgrace to the badge. Smith, Dickens—are you guys all right? Holler out." They both answered, although Dickens' voice was weak. Smith was apparently hit too.

"Suckers," Chaney said. "It took three of you to take me." He chuckled briefly before throwing up to his side. "Hey lady cop, do a brother of the badge a favor and let me get a hit o' coke out of that bag over there, would ya?"

The former agent was bleeding and sweating hard. Forbes handcuffed him behind his back. She then ripped his shirt and tied off his legs above the knees. Chaney screamed again. She picked up the bag and walked it back to Chaney.

"This what you want?" Chaney could only nod before Forbes put a fast moving boot into his face. She picked him up and dragged him the short distance and dropped his sleeping face in his vomit. She then went and checked on her agents.

"Who's the sucker now, Chaney?" Agent Rebecca Forbes sneered.

Chapter 30

If it were up to me, which it was, spending five seconds with Adrian— let alone jogging side by side with him, was never going to happen.

"You can't be serious, Adrian. You're a fit guy and I'm not. I'll just slow you down."

"Are you afraid, Lou?" Adrian dropped low into a stretch, never taking his eyes off me. I felt like I was involved in some kind of bizarre gun fight...or run fight.

"Adrian, my brother, my focus, or my dream, if you will, is to attain and then maintain ascension. Is that a crime?" Spread it on thick and hopefully this too shall pass.

"I'm on to you, Crasher!" And with that Adrian was off at a pace I definitely couldn't have maintained longer than forty seconds. That is not jogging, you idiot, I thought aloud.

I took off at a much easier pace along the soft chip-covered path. It had been awhile since I'd stretched these drumming legs out. As I was passing the hot tubs I was joined by yet another stranger. She was a tall brunette with a ponytail popping out of the back of a baseball hat. Her running gear was Nike from top to bottom. She had the type of abdominal muscles that many southern California girls throw up for or pop mass amounts of diet pills over. Her blue eyes were flecked with bits of turquoise.

"Welcome, welcome, new guy. Mind if I join you?"

"Not at all. Name's Lou."

"Lucy. I met you at your first dinner. I looked different. My mom use to call me the chameleon for all the different looks I could sport." We managed to shake on the run. Although her hands were slender she had the grip of an auto mechanic. I liked her smile and told her so. She smiled a little more. I asked what brought her to PASSAGE and other similar small talk questions.

"Are you a detective, Mr. Louis?"

"No, I'm just a starry eyed Canadian with an inquisitive mind."

"Canadian eh?"

"Ha, ha, ha."

"Race you to the fountain." She was off like a shot. If I hadn't been a 400-meter runner as a teen I wouldn't have made up the stagger. Once I did I held it there and then let her beat me by a nose. We stood at the fountain with our hands on our knees catching our breath. I let her drink first.

"You're full of spunk, but it's more than that. You're kind of kooky aren't you?"

"Kooky, that's a new one. Is it Canadian?"

"Cheeky, too," I said.

"I'm going to head back. I've been out here a while. I just wanted a last sprint before I hit the pool. If you need anything I've got your back." We shook again.

"Do I need my back covered?"

"Who was it that said things aren't always what they seem?" She crinkled her model-esque nose.

I had a wisecrack response but she took off before I could get it out. I went in the opposite direction and tried to decide what she meant by her comment. If she was telling me this place wasn't on the level that was obvious. But it was the 'got your back' comment that got my antennae up. I jogged on until I was near the duck pond. The llamas fled as I approached; funny looking animals. I walked to the edge of the woods and got down on the ground to do some stretching. When I was satisfied that I was completely alone I rolled into the forest. I got up and walked for two minutes and stood beside a large evergreen and listened to the birds, rustling squirrels and wind through the trees. I concentrated but heard no human sounds. I pulled the tiny cell phone from its hiding place.

"Please, lord, let there be a signal, please, please, please." I was in business. I dialed the number Jake gave me. He picked up before I even heard it ring: Creepy.

"Yes."

"Jake, nice touch with the phone. Anyway I've made contact, she's on board, pal. She wants out."

"Are you sure?"

"Oh yeah. Midnight tonight we meet in the woods, west side by the basketball court."

"I know the spot."

"Naturally. You'll be there?"

"Dumb question." I had to agree. "Watch your back, Lou."

"You're the second person today that's—" The line was dead. I flipped the phone closed and returned it to my shorts. I listened for a moment before marching through the noisy ground cover toward the track. I stopped thinking I heard another set of footfalls but only heard the usual forest sounds. I was nearly out of the woods, literally, when a voiced from behind stopped me.

"Hold it!" I held without turning around. You never know when the voice from behind belongs to a trigger happy gunman who may not take to sudden moves.

"Hands where I can see 'em. That's it, now turn around like you're in a slow motion movie."

I turned to see a short stocky lad in a dark green t-shirt and army fatigue pants moving toward me with careful steps. He had no gun as far as I could see but a leather handled Bowie knife with a five inch blade hung upside down from its scabbard near his left shoulder. Cold blue eyes jumped from behind the green and black face paint. The front of his brown brush cut had a blond wisp in it, giving him a skunk-like appearance. Black nylon climber's rope hung diagonally across his chest. From a side pocket of his pants he pulled one of those combination cell phone-walkie talkie numbers.

"Got 'im, third quadrant." He clicked off the talkie. "Who are you?"

"I am a member of this peaceful church, PASSAGE. Who are you?"

"I'm the guy asking the questions. Again, who are you?"

"My name is Lou."

"Got a last name?"

"Yes I do."

"Well, spill it."

"Not until I know who you are and what this is all about. Who were you saying, 'got him' to on that thing?" From another pocket he produced his identification and flashed it.

"Nathan Briggs, head of security, section C. That is the last question I will answer. Now give me a last name or we're going to take this little interview in a violent direction."

"Louis Crasher."

"State your purpose here."

"I was jogging and had to take a piss. The woods seemed like the right place to do it. I mean, I've always thought of the woods as one giant bathroom, you know?"

"Shorten your answers, Crasher, we ain't friends." He clicked his talkie once more. "Harley, you there? Harley?"

"Yeah, I'm here."

"Come on up, third quad edge of the woods. We've got a wiseguy that needs transporting." He never took the ice blue eyes off me as he said it. If I had a gun I would have shot him in the knee. He blinked both eyes at me. He did this two more times. His breathing became labored. He pinched the bridge of his nose and said, "Not now, please not now." He was having some kind of major headache, maybe a migraine or something. The pain forced him to one knee—the one I would have shot. From yet another pocket he pulled a small jar of prescription pills. His hands shook causing him to drop a few pills to the ground. "Shit."

"What's wrong with you, man?"

"Shut up! Just shut—" He got one in his palm and threw it in his mouth. He rocked his head way back in order to swallow the large capsule, but he was having difficulty. This was my cue to fly. Whatever was going on and where ever they were planning to take me, I had to assume they knew everything. The jig was up, in other words and I was in no mood for cement shoes. I kicked him hard in his chest, sending him sprawling on his back. I kicked him again in the ribs, which caused the pill to come flying out and hit me in the shin. He grabbed his head in both hands and screamed. I took off like an Olympic sprinter, exit stage left.

There was a barely determinable trail that didn't head toward the compound nor in the direction the stocky soldier came from. Here I was again in a life situation that found me running to the beat of my own drum. I could see my mother shaking her head as I ducked and bobbed away from thick, overhanging vegetation. The path was rocky with many twists, not unlike running the tires in football practice...or so I told myself. I was just over fifty per cent positive that I was moving south-easterly in direction. My short term plan was to make a wide arc around the compound and wind up a half mile or so down the road from the entrance.

Bernie Outlaw was going to have to be satisfied with my old college try. I wasn't dying for this damsel in distress. I'd crash through the brush onto the freeway then hitch a ride from a pleasant elderly couple who would hand me an M16 and tell me to feel free to fire out the back window at any followers. The alternative would be to hide out John Rambo style and use the woods as my weapon, picking these guys off one by one. Unfortunately, I'm not built for that kind of mission. After running close to top speed for nearly a quarter mile I slowed slightly so I could run farther. I listened as best I could without looking back. Never look back. It is when the damsel in distress in movies looks back that she inevitably trips over the unseen tree branch, and I am no damsel. I came upon a sharp right turn in the path. I slowed so as not to twist an ankle when in front of me popped up a man dressed similarly to the stocky soldier Nathan. Harley, no doubt. Without warning he raised a shotgun to firing position and pulled the trigger. "No!" I said with my flailing drummer's hands in front of me. I remember a pop sound and then a massive pain in my guts. Was this it? If I lived, my mother was going to kill me. I felt my legs go shooting out from behind me. I gasped for air but it wouldn't come. I waited to see yards and yards of entrails spilling from my body. I could see one side of the shooter's face above me.

"Try to relax, sir, you've just been shot by a police riot bean bag and you're winded. Now, say goodnight." The last image my left eye saw was a gun butt moving fast toward it. I managed to close the eye just before impact. At least I didn't have to see my innards spread everywhere...at least there was that.

Chapter 31

Bernie Outlaw wore black and red leather cowboy boots. His polyester slacks were dark black with a red cuff the same color as the boots. The blazer was jet black with dark red seam stitching to match the boots. Beneath he wore a white shirt with tiny pale blue banjos on it. The tips of the collar had banjos as well, of raised red velvet. A black leather belt with a large silver belt buckle held the pants up. A large-mouth bass with a fish hook in its mouth was raised in the center of the buckle. For his earrings he decided to go with the fake diamonds his cousin gave him two Christmases ago.

He sat outside in the courtyard with Oliver and Xavier, all three of them waiting for things to happen. Bernie focused on clipping the end of his cigar just right when the phone rang. Oliver, who under normal circumstances would have answered the phone, handed it to Bernie. An excited Bernie jumped every time the phone rang since their little meeting, hoping his daughter was calling to say, 'I want to come home.'

"Yes? This is Outlaw. Yeah, what do you got? Uh huh, huh. Nuts. All right, let me know when you do know something for chrissake. Over and out." Outlaw tossed the phone over his shoulder in disgust.

It landed well behind him at the edge of the garden. An empathetic Oliver leaned forward in his chair. "Be strong, Mr. Outlaw, we'll hear something soon."

"You know something, fellas? I just wonder why I pay for information when the fella who's supposed to give me information has none. I mean what am I paying for, air? I mean at least with a goddamn cell phone air time means minutes—a fella can talk to a fella, but shoot, I pay for information, get none and what does it mean? It means I'm payin' top dollar for squat, boys, squat!"

Jake approached soundlessly, picked up the telephone and tossed it onto the patio table. All three men jumped at the intrusion. Xavier had his nine millimeter three quarters of the way out of his side holster before he clued in that it was Jake.

"Jesus H. Christ, son, I wish you wouldn't do that sneaky shit. I damn near spilled this here mint julep all over m' duds," an angry Bernie growled.

Jake smiled to himself. It amazed him how some men could dress. Dustin and Fox, the two security staff that Jake immobilized from the other evening came tumbling out of the house to the courtyard, guns drawn. Their boss was not impressed.

"Put 'em away, ladies, before you get hurt. Hell, a fella could be dead twice before the likes o' you did what you was paid for. Now get out of my sight before I fire yuz again." Bernie put his Stetson on, then quickly put it back on the frosted glass table.

"Mr. Jake, you are looking at one tired hombre. Tell me you've got some news."

"I have."

"Spill it."

"I spoke with Louis this morning. He has made contact with your daughter and plans to pull her out at midnight tonight."

"Midnight, how original."

"Xavier, please!" Oliver snapped.

Bernie got out of his chair. "Well, this is great; I'm going to get my baby back. Is everything set at our end? Er, I mean your end?"

"No."

"What's the problem?"

"Sixteen minutes after the call from Louis I got another call. When I answered, a man's voice I didn't recognize demanded to know who I was three times before I hung up."

"So, maybe it was a prank call."

"No Bernie, this guy hit the re-dial feature on the phone I gave Louis. The decoy plan is now scrapped. It is a straight-up rescue in through the front door. We have to assume the worst, and that is that they have Louis and the girl."

Outlaw slumped back into his chair. Again the Stetson went back on his head and then off. "What did I ever do to deserve this?"

"Karma. The result of many years of criminal activity," Jake said.

"Horse hooey, I don't go in for that new age sissy crap."

"What you go in for is irrelevant."

Bernie hoped that when this was all over he'd be able to find a way to hurt this man with the audacity to beat up his men and come and go as he pleased, mocking Bernie's security system. Which reminded him; he definitely had to do something about Fox and Dustin.

"Mr. Outlaw, if I may?" Oliver inquired of Outlaw, then getting his permission, turned to Jake. "Jake, what is to be our immediate move, old boy?"

"Xavier, Oliver, saddle up. We're heading north."

Chapter 32

The room where I woke up could easily have been the room where I'd seen the youth cuffed to the bed the day before. Half of the drums of Africa pounded inside my head. I was back in the gear I wore the day I showed up. This meant that somebody dressed me, what the hell? Swinging my legs over the side of the bed, I reached for the bruise I knew to be near my left temple. I could not touch it, as I was now the one handcuffed to the bed.

"Welcome back, loser."

"Adrian? Adrian, old buddy old pal, how about popping these cuffs off for a brother. I'm sure I'm missing a prayer session or something."

"Ha! I pegged you for a phony the second I saw you. Who did you call on that cell phone of yours?"

"Your mother," I replied.

Adrian crossed the floor before I could thoroughly enjoy my joke. His backhanded slap to my cheek caused my skull to hit the headboard.

"That's what you get for wisecrackin' so why don't you keep it up? I'm going to get the boss. He has questions for you. After that your ass is mine." He headed for the door and stopped, "Hey Lou, if you want to cry about the slap, go ahead, I won't laugh."

"Yo Adrian?"

"What?"

"Your mother slaps harder than you do."

He came at me again but I was ready with two feet and one free hand. I was spared the engagement as Genesis's voice boomed from the doorway. "Adrian, stand down!"

Like a well-trained seal, Adrian stopped on a dime. Genesis entered the room with two large men, no doubt from C-unit. He came and stood over me. He looked even bigger than I remembered in his dark blue and gold frock. The mouthwash he used struggled to keep the hard liquor fumes down. His eyes looked particularly beady in this dim light. He'd received a trim since I'd last seen his goatee. He clasped his hands in front of him and took a deep breath before he spoke. Lawyers in courtroom dramas use the same trick on difficult witnesses. This is not to say that I wasn't afraid, I just knew the game, is all.

"It is not nice to provoke my staff, Mr. Crasher. Do apologize."

"At my earliest convenience I'll be sure to," I promised.

"The machismo act is an odd choice of behaviors given your situation. I'd think you'd be singing like a canary in exchange for your life."

"A guy has got to know the tune in order to sing for that to happen."

"I knew he was a phony, boss, from the—"

"And you have stated such many times over, thank you, Adrian. Now then, Louis Jackson Crasher, I do not know how you answered our questionnaire so well, or how you acquired your ticket into my peaceful home, nor do I care too deeply. What I would like to know is which exact government agency you are working for. The Bureau? ATF? LAPD? Which? This is the part where you sing and then we let you go."

"But boss—"

"Oh yes, that's right, I did promise Adrian ten minutes alone with you."

"I'm not that kind of man, Adrian. However, if your mother is on the premises..."

Adrian took a quick step toward me again but was stopped by one of Genesis' body guards.

"Tsk, tsk, Mr. Crasher. I am a busy man. Here is how it is going to work. I am going to ask one more time who sent you and then one of two things is going to happen. You tell the truth and we let you go after

Adrian tosses you around the room awhile. You lie to me and you get a shot of a nasty little cocktail that the government used once upon a time."

"What are you talking about G-man?"

"Mr. Darkness, if you would be so kind." One of the two guards walked over to a table where a leather doctor's bag sat and opened it. From it he withdrew a syringe and a vial with a clear liquid in it.

"What I have here is CBX90. This little gem was used during Gulf One as a truth serum. It worked wonders, however, there was a side effect." He paused to build tension, which was hardly necessary. I was terrified.

"Many prisoners were driven insane by the drug often before the truth was discovered. The drug causes madness and then the drug attacks the spinal cord, so what you're left with is a paralyzed madman, if you will. As you can imagine, the drug was eventually scrapped. However, I'm willing to bet that the Homeland Security boys are still using the drug, unofficially of course. Why, I think our Mr. Crasher is turning white. Don't you think so Darkness?"

"Yeah I do, boss."

"Hysterical. Vegas needs you two. Tell me something, Genny boy, if this big fool's name is Darkness, what's that make the other guy, Light, or Mr. Illumination perhaps?"

"His name is Fred."

"Fred?"

"Yes, Fred."

"Fair enough. Continue with your dime store loose leaf Count Dracula routine. It's a riot."

Adrian stood with shaking clenched fists, "Let me shut him up boss; just let me do that."

Mr. Darkness poked the needle into the vial and loaded the shot. I threw up at the sight of my fate in front of me. Adrian laughed like a kid on a merry-go-round.

"There, there, Louis, it is okay to be scared. Now I ask you for the second and last time, who do you work for?"

"I am a paleontologist. I believe this compound is sitting on a Brontosaurus grave yard. Let me go now and I promise to mention your kindness when I accept my Pulitzer. And that includes the little girl Adrian there too."

"I'm incredibly wealthy, Mr. Crasher, I have little time for humor."

Crystal walked into the room with a dangerous grin on her face. "So, what do we have here, a mouse in a trap?" She walked over to Genesis, stood on her toes and kissed him gently on the lips.

"Your surprised look is ruining your tough guy act, Louis," Genesis smirked.

The writing was on the wall, Lou had fallen for one of the oldest gags in the book— the damsel not really in distress act. I still needed to stall for time, however.

"What's going on here, Crystal?"

"Are you always a sucker for tears, Louis?"

"It would seem so."

"Men never cease to amaze me. You spend your whole lives thinking that saving women is the answer of all answers. Answer me this: has a woman ever actually said, 'Oh Louis, please save me before I go over the deep end?' Men like you think we can't survive without you. It's pathetic."

"Ouch."

"You see? When we don't need you, you get all pouty on us."

"If I'm 'pouty' it's because I'm handcuffed to a bed by a phony evangelical psychopath." All eyes were on me, as if waiting for me to finish so I filled the gap. "Tell me, Crystal, what's your angle? I mean if we're all saps, including the big Kahuna there, you must be getting something out of the deal, right? Because if you're not then it means you came to this place looking for some kind of sanctuary from

Genesis' church. This of course can't be the case because you don't need a man and this church is a scam. So, what is it? You getting a percentage? A cut? Don't tell me you're just sleeping in the fancy quarters with the fancy Poobah because even a two dollar whore would squeeze more than that out of old Genesis."

"You're a strange animal, Mr. Crasher."

"Are you kidding me? The guys down at the Lodge think I'm a riot. By the way, you owe me twenty bucks; I know you copped a feel last night. Say, do you have any idea how much dough lover boy here actually has? Ha, and you ask why we try to save dames like you. It's because you are ripe for the picking, like a golden delicious apple from a Bakersfield farmer's market."

Genesis now noticed Crystal's balloon was losing air. "There, there, my precious, don't pay him any mind. He's just trying to cause trouble in the ranks so that he might crawl under a door sill. A moderate effort at best, Mr. Crasher."

"I don't think he's funny, boss. Give me five minutes with him."

"Hush, Adrian!"

"Yeah, be a good little doggie and hush, Adrian. In fact, go pee on a fire hydrant, why don't ya."

Adrian snapped. Ignoring his master's voice, he charged. He stopped in front of me to deliver another back hand. I pulled a move I'd seen in a movie once. Just before contact I lowered my head causing him to connect with the top part of my skull. It stung like hell, which did not happen to the actor in the film, but Adrian screamed like a British tea kettle. He stared at his hand in horror. The middle knuckle of his right hand moved an inch up the back of his hand while his middle finger looked like it was made from silly putty. The more he screamed the paler he became.

He staggered backward toward the door. Genesis sent Mr. Darkness out with him. The numbers were moving in my favor. Crystal still hadn't said a word.

"Quite the finale, Mr. Crasher but I'm afraid its time—"

"I know, I know, insanity, frothing at the mouth, madness blah, blah, blah. One last question so that I have something to roll around in my soon to be mushy half brain."

"Shoot."

"I found a boy in this room, or one just like it, handcuffed like me. I recognized him from serving my first supper. What's the deal with him?"

"You have been busy. He is still in training."

"It was called slavery when they did it to my ancestors." He let that one hang. "Why are there no children here? No young teens? The way everyone runs around naked at this place I thought I'd see lots of babies nursing at exposed breasts."

"I can appreciate that you are trying to buy time, but very well. The boy you saw is sixteen years old and he is not yet eligible for this sanctuary until his twenty-first birthday. The youths of this lovely church are trained, or rather, schooled, at our other facility outside of Sacramento. Dwayne, whom you met, is a somewhat difficult child, which is why I have him here, where I can give him the utmost care and attention he needs."

"Care? Do you really buy the crap you're shoveling, G-man?"

"I don't much care for interruptions, Louis." He ran a hand over his goatee before continuing. "There are two other places of serenity like this one under construction. Someday we hope to have more money and power than the Scientologists."

"Good luck. So how do you pay for this burg? You can't be getting by on the fees from the flock."

He gave me a long, level stare. I could tell he wanted to tell me. He was proud of himself. He had succeeded in this phony church where he failed as a Hollywood movie producer, according to Bernie Outlaw. His ego was so large he completely forgot about Crystal. I didn't dare move my eyes to her. The longer he talked the greater chance she had of fainting, fleeing or attacking him in a rage. Any form of distraction would benefit me.

"Business ventures, investments, goods and services."

"I'm sure the business venture stuff would be over my head but what about this goods and services jazz?"

"Ah yes, I see where you are going with this. What did you think you saw on your little jaunt into the forest?"

"Stop playing games, Genesis. It's not about what I saw, but what I know. You lay down with half the dames around here and knock em' up. Add to that you've got the woods troughed off like Fort Knox. You see, if you didn't want anyone in the woods you'd put your guards at the perimeter or just inside the woods. But I ran nearly three quarters of a mile and then got popped." I leaned forward, elbows on my knees. "You've got those kids stashed out there in those woods somewhere and we both know I'm right."

He produced a toothpick from his sleeve and slowly picked at his teeth. He was a man trying too hard to appear casual.

"Cut the melodrama, Genesis. If your little congregation knew about your kiddie sweat shop or whatever the fuck you're doing, your days would be numbered."

"It is amazing how people see things with the correct packaging. Our children are merely performing chores for the church so that they may one day become one with the church and then ascend the moment following their last breath on this beautiful earth plane. For nothing comes easy in this world, Mr. Crasher. Surely even you can appreciate this. Children must learn the value of hard work. In the world outside, a child loses innocence by their fourth birthday, what with mindless video games, violent movies, bad parenting, and molestation from within their own churches, at times.

I couldn't believe I was right and that he had admitted as much. "Valid, valid, but the world you describe is for the minority of kids out there. And if you mean to tell me that having a whip dragged across their backs by some dimwit in army fatigues is a better way of life you must be crazy. It's slavery no matter how you slice it, bubba."

Genesis held up his hand like a crossing guard and rolled his eyes. "Please don't tell me that I'll never get away with this, Mr. Crasher, I detest clichés."

"You're not an evangelist, you're an evange---loser... and you'll never get away with this." I couldn't resist.

Heavy breathing caught our attention. We had both forgotten about Crystal, who was crimson. Arms at her side with clenched fists and trembling slightly she exploded just as Genesis turned to comfort her.

"Don't touch me. A child labor camp? You said they went for a stay at your beautiful Switzerland sanctuary." I laughed out loud and was ignored.

"Is that why you want to impregnate everybody around here? You would make your own children slaves? What is he talking about? No, don't! Don't!"

"Darling, please, you must understand this sanctuary—"

"What now, are you going to package it for me? I'm not an idiot, Genesis. Now it's all clear as to why you've never taken me to Switzerland. How could you? I believed in you. I have deceived for you."

I could vouch for that one. I finally had the diversion I was looking for, but how I was going to use it now was a mystery to me. Fred the goon remained perfectly still as if nothing was going on. He had probably seen a handful of similar outbursts from his master's various women in the past.

"Hush, hush, my pet and come to me now." He repeated himself with more juice. "Come here, child."

"No! Don't hush me like I'm Adrian."

"Maybe she needs a lesson out at kiddie camp, Genesis, big Pooh-Bah."

"Silence Louis, you've done enough damage here." Genesis stepped to his 'pet' with open arms only to receive a slap across his face. He closed his eyes and exhaled deeply. Then slowly he raised his lids.

"Very good, G-man, now turn the other cheek, or doesn't it say that in your good book?"

Ignoring me, he rubbed his hand slowly over the area where she'd slapped him.

"You ignorant little slut, you would strike me? After all I've done for you, you ungrateful little trollop. How soon we forget the state you were in the day you showed up penniless, homeless, whining about your overbearing daddy. Do you know how much it costs to get into this place? No, you do not because I haven't charged you penny one. And you would listen to this half-wit musician over me?"

"Tell me about the children, Genesis, tell me! Are they slaves?" Crystal screamed her last question. Genesis raised his hand to slap her face.

"Hey!" I shouted, "Doesn't she have a trust fund or something you're draining?" It was enough to stop him from striking her. I had to give it to her, though, for she was ready to take the hit full on. She didn't flinch an inch.

Genesis glared at me as he gave Fred instructions. "It's time we crushed the Crasher. Give him the goddamn shot, Fred, and give it to him slowly. And make sure to look into his eyes when you do it and describe the fear you see to me later. I'll be in my office. Come with me you insolent little bitch."

"No!" Crystal screamed, but she was overpowered by Genesis' strength.

Fred seemed oblivious to the two as they struggled out the door. With eyes fixed on me he revealed bad teeth in a sadistic grin. He pointed at me then ran his finger across his neck, signifying my demise. He walked casually over to the table where the shot was. He picked it up like a heroin addict and came at me cautiously, down low. He merely had to knock me into tomorrow then just step up and sink the needle home. However, with Genesis' instructions he'd have to have me conscious. He could tell by my stance that this was going to take some doing. I had enough slack in the chain to get up on the bed in a low back-catcher's squat.

"Come on then, you big dumb son of a bitch, I can't wait to leave you something to remember me by!" My threat seemed to give him pleasure. He probably spent most of his days following his master around with nothing better to do than restrain the odd hysterical damsel. This was no doubt the type of action he was looking for. So glad I could be of help.

I focused on the needle. I had to make him drop it or better yet stick himself. His eyes betrayed that he was going to try for a leg entry. He took a few swipes at me in an attempt to move me into the wall. I jabbed a straight right at his nose, so if I landed, it would make his eyes water at the very least. He was way ahead of me. He pulled his head back and then came in fast and grabbed my ankle with his free hand. He jerked it, causing me to sit down hard on my tailbone. He chuckled. I kicked his arm at the elbow. His arm flew up but he didn't drop the needle. I managed to get back into my squat. Fred felt that the game had gone on too long. Out of frustration he jabbed the needle at my face. Startled, I was back on my haunches. He came down hard with an overhand strike. I was able to deflect the shot away from my face, but it did sink into my shoulder. With all his weight on me he brought his face close to mine to taunt me before pushing the plunger down.

Somewhere he had a liquor supply of his own and had tipped some earlier in the day. I spat in his face. As a reflex he moved the arm he had across my neck to clear away the mess. I reached over with my free hand and in an attempt to pull the needle from my shoulder accidentally broke it off leaving part of the metal inside my flesh. Chest to chest now, he put a vise-like fist around my throat and tried to get the broken needle from me with his other hand. I thrust my head full force into the side of his jaw. He leapt off me, shaking his head to clear it. His chest heaved from fatigue and anger. A lot of big guys don't bother with cardio in their workouts. His expression told me that he was shocked that this scrawny, wisecracking punk was giving him this much trouble. Gone was the cautious approach from before. He charged me like a rhino, lowering his shoulder just before contact. All I could do was brace for impact. As we sailed backward I plunged what was left of the needle in between his shoulder blades and sank it home. He was on top of me again only we were further across the bed.

I felt as though my shoulder had been ripped from the socket as my wrist was still handcuffed to the bed. When my eyes cleared I could see the shot protruding from his back. He managed to get one foot on the floor for leverage and with both hands this time began choking the life out of me. I'm not sure what scared me more, the rapid loss of air or the sound of neck bones crunching under the pressure. I could hear my heart pounding in my ears as if I were underwater. I had just enough strength left in me for my brain to register that I was soon to be checking out...for keeps. Faintly from the shore, I heard two quick 'pops' before Fred's grip released. As I coughed uncontrollably somebody worked on my hand cuffs. Fred was then rolled off of me; this I greatly appreciated. Out of my blurry vision I saw Alice, my three-legged race partner.

"Alice, what the hell? Thank you, but what the hell?"

"Hiya, Handsome, here, sit up. That's it. Mr. Crasher, I'm special agent Rebecca Forbes." She flashed me her badge revealing the three most beautiful letters she could have shown this brother at that time: FBI. "Sorry about all that Alice stuff earlier. It's my cover name. Was anyway. We're blowin' this pop stand."

"You don't need to tell me twice. So why Alice?"

"My mother's name, now let's move out before somebody shows up wondering about those shots."

I looked down at Fred. He was dead. Fred was dead and I liked him that way. As I leaned forward to get up, Agent Forbes stopped me. "What's this?'

"The other end of that," I said pointing to the needle in Fred's back. She pulled it out and tossed it on the floor.

"What were you injected with?"

"It's okay; I managed to nail his ass with the juice. It was probably going to drive him crazy if you hadn't put two slugs in him. Thanks very much, by the way."

"It ain't over yet, Handsome Lou. Now let's roll."

A fresh dose of adrenaline coursed through my veins, numbing all my pains and some of the aches. We moved quickly through the hallways with me close at her heels as instructed. The hallways were cold and narrow and had a flooded-basement odor. I was certain we were treading through several rat's homes. Rarely did we see any doorways. After a half dozen lefts and as many right turns, she stopped, shined her tiny flashlight on the floor baseboard, revealing an X inside a circle drawn in black felt marker.

"You?" I asked.

"Like Hansel and Gretel, baby."

"Very nice. No doubt you have agents surrounding this place, Agent Forbes?"

"It's just you and me, kid. That little upstart Adrian was getting close. In short—no cavalry. How's the shoulder?"

"If I live to see tomorrow it won't hurt as much as where they got me with that damn bean bag."

"Right, stay close."

"Hold it. I have a small but formidable posse waiting for me at the basketball courts if it is anywhere near midnight. Can you get us there?"

"It's barely four. If I can manage to put us behind the pool, is that good enough for you?"

"That'll be just grand. I came here to rescue a girl, or did you know that?"

"I figured it was something like that. Why, tell me?"

"Genesis has her against her will. That's a kidnapping beef, right?"

"Kidnapping beef? Lay off the television, Louis. And don't tell me you want to go back and play hero."

"Not if when we blow this pop stand you'll come back with a whack of agents and get her out."

"Done. Let's keep moving."

We quickened our pace, Rebecca shining her light less and less on the baseboard as if she were beginning to remember her way.

We carried on for a stretch close to a par five fairway in length before she needed to return to the light trick. Shining left, right and left again she accepted that we were lost.

"We're riding on wits at this point, kid," she said.

"Yours, I hope."

A few quick turns brought us to a corridor which gave no light at all. We clasped hands and moved a tad faster than a snail's pace. I could hear her little footsteps. I could feel her warm palm and I was close enough to smell her hair. That was it for the senses. If she fell into a bottomless pit I'd be going in with her. Somehow she found a door with light escaping beneath it.

"Cross your fingers," she whispered.

It was unlocked. I heard her service revolver slowly leave its holster. She counted backward from the number three and we were into Genesis's office, behind his desk. We had just traversed the big Kahuna's escape route in reverse. Genesis stood on the other side of the desk with his hands on Crystal's shoulders shaking her gently to make some kind of point. She had been crying but was holding back the tears for now. Her face showed no cuts or bruises which helped me keep my temper in check. None of Genesis' bodyguards were present. The boss obviously needed some private time with his troubled subject.

"Federal agent! Let her go, Genesis!" Rebecca's voice was authoritative Bureau all the way.

"You! Well I never would have figured you, Miss Alice."

"Nevermind that, let the girl go."

"Hello again, Mr. Crasher, please be kind enough and tell me what you have done with the good Mr. Fred?"

"I believe he's trying to cut an ascension deal with his maker."

"Shame, but you see it is you people who have brought violence to my peaceful home. Why can't you just keep to your cesspool of a world, huh?"

Crystal made an effort to get away but he wrapped an arm around her neck and threatened to break it.

"Pardon me, G-boy," I said, "but isn't that violence?"

He hissed at me like a cat and then said that he should have stuck me with the needle himself. Rebecca Forbes took slow steps and moved toward her target, ignoring his threats of violence to his once-beloved Crystal. Genesis, now backed against the liquor cabinet, felt a cold gun muzzle against his temple.

"You're a scum bag, Genesis, but you're no killer. For the last time, let her go."

Sweat raced from his widow's peak at two places.

"You're getting my gun barrel wet and I don't like it." He released

Crystal who came running into my arms. With a short sharp yell Forbes rammed the butt of the gun into Genesis' temple. He slid down the cabinet and was out before he hit the floor. Wiping the gun off with a towel from the bar she looked at Genesis with indignant eyes.

"Handsome, check the closet by the door and pull the sashes from a couple of his robes. Then tie the maggot up." Re-holstering her gun, she gave Crystal orders to make sure the front door was locked. Crystal stared at her former 'savior' and didn't move. "Crystal, hop to it, sister!" Rebecca ordered with a snap of the bar towel.

The sashes were softer than the down in my pillows. I bound and gagged him as best as I knew how. "Ms. Forbes, you better check on my knotsmanship. I never was a Boy Scout."

"I don't believe that's a word, Louis," Crystal piped up, having returned from her trance.

"Which proves my point about...knot tying."

Agent Forbes worked frantically at Genesis' desk. The phone atop the desk needed a dial out code, which Agent Forbes couldn't figure out. A flash drive was downloading some documents while she rummaged through his drawers. When the bottom drawer wouldn't open she began working at it with a medium-sized knife she produced from her boot.

"You'll probably just find the expensive whiskey Genesis drops on his heavyweight clients with the offshore cheddar."

"Cheddar, Lou?" Crystal asked wiping an eye with the sleeve of her shirt.

"Scratch, moolah, bullion, green, ducats, salad, lottery dust. Sorry. I'm talking about money, darling."

Forbes nearly snapped her knife blade getting the drawer open. "Huh? You were right, Handsome. Booze. Only it's tequila; Sauza Conmemorativo, to be exact. Smooth stuff. Crystal, do you need a belt of stability or are you up for this?"

"I'm fine, really."

"Good. Here's the deal, lady and gentleman. We walk out that door through the Great Hall into the compound and head for your friends like nothing's going on. I know they won't be there yet but we'll just lay low in the woods awhile, or slip through the dragnet or I don't know—we'll cross that bridge. Who knows when they'll discover the fearless leader, so I need brisk walking, smiles and, you know, small-talk. Are we ready?"

"I've been ready for a while, lady," Crystal answered. Even though I'd heard this line before, I believed her this time. Although I believed her last time too...shit.

Rebecca grabbed her USB stick and came around to check my knots. "I'm impressed. You are a knotsman after all." Her sarcastic grin relaxed me until she unlocked the door and it was time to go. Crystal took one last look at Genesis with vacant eyes. Once outside the door agent Forbes jammed the tip of her blade into the keyhole and broke it off inside the lock. For small talk, Rebecca introduced herself by her real name to Crystal. Crystal wanted to hear all about the agent's profession and her current assignment but was told that this was not suitable small talk. "Too many ears," she said.

I was glad the agent took Crystal's mind off Genesis. Her excited curiosity aided us in looking like happy campers heading for the basketball court. Fortunately, my disheveled look and the fact that we didn't have a basketball didn't seem to raise any suspicions.

"Keep moving, almost there, that's it, nice and easy." Rebecca's soothing words were meant more for Crystal than me. I glanced at Crystal as we neared the court. She had a half-smile on her lips and a distant look in her eyes, like she was planning to ask another 'assignment' question of the agent. She opened her mouth briefly then decided against it.

Chapter 33

When Katherine and Tamika received the call from Jake that he needed their help, all he had to do was name the job. When he told them about Lou's mission and that they were needed for Lou's extraction the 'derby twins' cussed Jake for not bringing them into the fold earlier. Jake and his crew of Oliver, Xavier, Kat and Tami spent the drive up to the ranch getting to know one another. Everyone was giving excerpts of their various pasts in turn. But the way these people, people of action, familiarize is not like the average Jane and Joe going to a cocktail party. The Derby twins had worked a variety of adventurous jobs regularly suited for thrill-seeking men. Tami formerly taught skydiving while Katherine had given rock climbing lessons. With their weightlifting and martial arts backgrounds they briefly had a private security company business on the side. The twin towers were visibly impressed and asked what had become of that business. The money was good, jobs interesting but the clientele was difficult to wash off at the end of the day. Oliver and Xavier exchanged a raised eyebrow look as if making a mental note.

Jake kept his eyes on the freeway without comment. He knew more about the ladies' backgrounds than they knew he knew. He found it odd that people found him so mysterious. He found that people often tell you things about themselves, and not always through dialogue. Jake was an open book in his mind, but people were either too busy handing out their own resumes or they were put off by his look. He cracked a faint smile at the thought.

Bernie Outlaw was the second employer that Oliver and Xavier had since their landing on U.S. soil in 2005. Their first boss was small time drug dealer and extortionist Vinnie. The brothers did not entirely approve of the criminal businesses, but Vinnie had enough legit operations to supply U.S. sponsorship. Three assassination attempts were made on their boss until the rival gang achieved their goal. Xavier took a bullet high in the shoulder, which to them was amazing seeing that over a hundred rounds were fired in the fight. At least that was the Fox News statistic. The twins counted their blessings, one of which was they got their green cards. They then swore off drug dealers for employers. Outlaw may be a small time crook but they are certain he has nothing to do with the drug trade. Their goal was to save enough money of their own and go into business for themselves.

"Pardon the interruption, Oliver, but when our paths nearly crossed I understood that your boss wanted to squeeze protection money out of Chazz, not run drugs.

"Actually, Mr. Jake, at the time we believe Vinnie was seeking out a money laundering facility."

Jake nodded. That made sense.

"What kind of business?" Tami asked. "Sorry, what kind of business do you guys want to start up, Oliver?"

"Basically what we are doing now, with a few changes. But the point here is that we shall be our own bosses. Once it is up and running smoothly I hope to pay closer heed to my passion."

"Ooh, passion? Do tell." Tami leaned forward in her seat.

Oliver glanced at his brother. "That would be acting. I'd like to teach youths the finer points of becoming a true thespian."

"Okay, well you go ahead now Oliver, good for you. What about you Xavier, are you a man of the theater?"

"I am dabbling with writing. I would like to bring back the Western, on film, mind you. I am a huge John Wayne fan."

"Too huge I'm afraid," Oliver piped in.

Kat gave Jake a light punch on the shoulder. "What about you, Mr. Quiet? If we're going into battle together we need to know a little about each other."

"All is well in the land of Jake," Jake said.

Oliver got in of the act. "Oh, be a good sport Jake and reveal the man behind the mask."

Jake didn't respond. Oliver looked back at the others in the back seat and raised his eyebrows. Jake knew that the less they knew the better; however, he didn't want them to think he was some crazy, danger-seeking psycho. He decided to throw them a bone; they were in this together, after all.

"Did I ever tell you how Louis and I met?" No's all around.

"Jake, my good man, being a man of few words such as yourself you have the distinct advantage of remembering your words and to whom you spoke them. I'd wager that you know bloody well that you haven't told anyone in this vehicle how you came to meet Louis. Now for the love of her majesty the Queen, toss us a bloody biscuit, man, hell!"

A brief silence passed before everyone started laughing. The left side of Jake's face arched up ever so slightly.

"Nicely put. A little over a year ago a friend of mine who ran an all-night gas and food stop was having break-in trouble. He had been hit three times in four months and he was certain that the man in the stocking was the same thief. His mode was the same every time. He'd enter the premises, spray shaving cream on the camera lens over the door, walk to the counter, pull a knife on my friend and demand cash register loot only. He either knew the safe was too much hassle or was too time consuming. This friend of mine found that the police did their best but would arrive only after the perpetrator had fled. I agreed to stand in his stead and see what I could do."

Kat leaned forward in her seat and smiled at her friend Tami, who was equally excited at hearing the story.

"I worked the late shift for ages it seemed until the perp showed himself. I was the only one in the store. He blacked out the camera as usual. He stepped to the counter and to my surprise he pulled a silver plated Colt .45 from the small of his back and shoved it in my face. I stood perfectly still. I could have killed myself for not being heeled; it was careless.

"A moment my good man," Oliver said. "Ah, heeled?"

"Sorry, Oliver, it means to be carrying a gun."

"Cheers."

"He screamed for me to empty the register. His gun hand shook, which meant he didn't want to shoot. That and the fact that he was a knife man confirmed it. However, guns in shaky hands have killed many Americans—too many in fact. At that point Lou shows up. He yells at Lou but I manage to get Lou out of there. Becoming frustrated with my defiance, the gunman fires a round twelve inches to my left, sending nine volt Duracells all over the place. I moved to the register slowly. Next thing I know a vintage Mustang comes barreling in reverse, smashing garbage cans into the store. The cans come sliding across the floor toward the gunman. He manages to jump over the first one, and while he negotiates the second can I hop the counter and manage to disarm him. During the tussle Lou backed his '65 Mustang on top of the miscreant. Lou poked his head out his window and said, 'You all right, man?' There are a few more minor details but that's the gist."

Tami piped up excitedly, "I bet you kicked his little chump ass, didn't you, Jake?"

Jake did not answer. Instead he slowed the vehicle down and maneuvered it onto a narrow pullout. He ordered everyone out then moved the truck onto an old trail and into the brush until only the bumper could be seen from the road. He climbed out and met the others at the rear of the vehicle.

"We go in here. Bring everything you'll need, but pack light."

Xavier nudged his brother aside and then pulled everyone's things out of the back, starting with the ladies' bags. As everyone checked, re-checked and fitted things into place Jake got back into the SUV and pulled it another three feet into the dense growth. One would have to be on foot and looking for the vehicle to see it. After a brief moment he emerged in full gear. The women smiled in surprise at how quickly Jake suited up. It inspired confidence in them.

"Come," Jake instructed the group.

He stopped at the front of the car and spread a map on the hood. "Have a look at that. I apologize for its crudeness. I'm no map maker."

The group studied the map carefully. Jake's apology was not necessary, for it was as good a map as any they'd seen before. They were going to be moving in a straight line to the northeast for just under three miles, then jogging northwest for a half mile. This would put them at the compound's basketball court. In different areas Jake had marked out the type of terrain they were to expect. The twins were impressed. They whispered as much as they tied and cinched final straps and buckles. Jake folded the map up and quickly applied face paint. The group turned back to see Jake in full green and black face camouflage. Oliver nearly went for his knife hilt, not recognizing Jake immediately, as he held tiny paint containers out in front of him for the others. They each declined, not out of a belief it wasn't necessary, but more out of the knowledge that it would take any of them three times the amount of time applying it than Jake and they didn't want to hold their leader up any longer than necessary.

"Ready? Good. No dialogue unless absolutely necessary. We can assume that our enemy is well-trained, so look to the trees for aerial assaults as much as the ground cover. Stealth is the key. We're coming out the same way we're going in. Questions? Good. Kat, you're our navigator here," he said, handing her the map. She welcomed Jake's confidence.

"Wait," Xavier said, stopping everyone. "Let's have fun out there, people," he said in his best John Wayne impression.

"Brother, you truly, truly, truly are a twit. If we survive this I shall inflict a devil's beating on you, I swear!" Oliver growled. Tami barely managed to stifle a snicker. Jake stared at Xavier with empty eyes briefly before moving into the thick brush.

Jake's last comment on the trees was a wakeup call to Kat. She was knee deep in it now, the point of no return. But she would do just about anything for Jake, the man who made that awful stalker go away three years back. Jake succeeded where the law fell short and Kat was forever in his debt. And she would almost do as much for Louis as well. He was a good, honest man who treated her with respect. When they met, Lou had a sort of grade school crush on her which she found cute. However, timing is everything, and when Lou made his bumbling play, the time was not right for her. Lou took it like a man and acted the perfect gentleman and they remained good friends. As time marched on and the time was right for her Lou was still in 'friend' mode and never took the true meaning of her flirtatious gestures, the knucklehead.

When Jake called her and asked for her help she was beside herself with excitement at finally getting an opportunity to repay him. When he laid out the details of the fix Lou was in, her excitement turned to worry. She knew Lou to be a fairly resourceful guy, but cults always scared the hell out of her.

The troupe moved ahead with relative ease, the terrain giving them little problem. After a short section of knee-high foliage which made far more noise than they would have liked, they came upon a clearing—man-made by forest fire. The group crouched low and peered out for signs of life.

"We'll be sitting ducks out there. Is there another way?" Oliver asked.

Jake ignored the comment and stared out at the blackened clearing. A hawk circled overhead and let out a cry as if to blame the travelers for ruining her favorite hunting ground. Nobody spoke. Nobody moved. Finally Jake rose soundlessly to his feet and darted in a low crouch over the charred ground. The others followed quickly but carefully. From the hawk's view, they looked similar to a small flock of birds traveling in their V-shape formation.

Once across the clearing, Jake hit the ground and remained motionless in the down position of a push-up. The others hit the ground also holding their positions. Jake peeled his ears; nothing. As he was about to slowly get up he heard that something had discovered their arrival. The unmistakable call of a rattlesnake sounded far too close for Jake to move. He shifted his eyes around until he saw the forked tongue of the reptile poke out as if to say 'Over here, pal'—a foot to his left.

Jake slowly moved his left hand to a position that would better suit him to push up and away quickly. The snake, unsettled by the movement, pulled its head back to strike. Jake sprung knowing he would have slim chance of avoiding the snake's wrath. As it struck however, it was lifted in the air and pulled backward.

At the end of a five-foot stick stood a smiling Oliver, carefully hoisting the snake away from the scene.

"There, there, sweetheart, off you go then, love."

Satisfied with the snake's safety, Oliver turned back to the group. "I should say, that was a close one, eh laddie?"

"Thanks," Jake responded

"Cheers."

Jake was about to lead the way out of there when Tami stopped him. "Hang on a second, Jake. It looks like the little bastard got you with at least one fang after all."

Jake looked down at his shoulder to see a small puncture mark with a little bit of blood trickling from it. "That's unfortunate."

"It is unfortunate that my animal-loving brother was too slow," Xavier said.

"I got it," Tami said stepping to Jake and sucking the venom out of the wound, spitting it out. "I think that's it. You have your snake bite kit with you right?"

"Yes," Jake said.

"If you start feeling a little weak then you take the shot, all right?"

"Fine."

They moved forward, returning to 'no dialogue' status. Forty-five minutes later they came up to a small pond. A young deer drinking at the pond took flight as they approached. It startled all but Jake, who had spotted the deer long before the others. Before going around the pond Kat pointed out several boot prints in the mud.

After taking a small drink from his canteen Jake whispered, "It is too difficult to tell which way they went or how many there are or when these were made, although I'd guess some of these were made this morning, perhaps by a patrol. We'll creep around on the left side of the pond. Stay alert."

On the other side of the pond, a path had been beaten. They moved down it single file, staying low. Half way down a fifty-yard slope they heard a quiet sound like someone was zipping up a large sleeping bag. Jake knew the sound right away.

"The trees," he shouted.

The others looked up. In front and behind the line men were rappelling from the trees on long nylon ropes. There were three in total. Jake barely let the man in front of him let his feet touch the path before Jake kicked his legs from under him. The soldier, in solid green face paint tried to un-hook himself from the rope to take on the stocky black man in menacing war paint. He never got the chance. A solid arm hooked under his chin and choked him unconscious. Had he un-hooked before hitting the ground as Jake would have, he may have stood a chance, Jake thought to himself. Jake looked behind him to see Tamika deliver a straight palm under the jaw of the soldier in front of her. The man staggered back toward Kat, who placed a perfectly aimed kick to the man's groin from behind. Jake wondered if it hurt more to be kicked there when you didn't see it coming. He shuddered slightly at the thought.

Xavier had the third man in a bear hug. The soldier attempted a head butt, but Xavier's grip was so tight that the man passed out before he could bring his head forward. Xavier let the man drop to the muddy floor and whispered, "Say goodnight, Gracie" once again, in his best John Wayne accent.

"Promise me that will be the last of that pathetic accent during this bloody mission, Xavier," Oliver pleaded. All he got was a snicker in response.

They used the ropes the men had rappelled with to tie them up. Kat duct taped their mouths shut. Their watches told them that Swiss time was running out. They would have to jog the rest of the way if they were going to be of any use to Lou and Crystal.

Jake and his unit had no more surprise guests en route to the basketball court. Jake held the group forty yards from the compound where the court was visible. Gathered in a tight group, Jake held court.

"We'll take cover just inside the bush line adjacent to center court. Remain low at all times, because we are also going to be near the running track. You never know when a jogger..." He let the sentence hang as he glanced over Kat's shoulder at the destination. "Find yourself a position that is comfortable that you can hold for a while until we see what's up."

"Why do I feel that this is the calm before the storm?" Tami asked.

"Because it is," Jake replied, rising to lead them through the last little stretch of wood.

Nestled beside a fallen redwood, Jake had a clear view of the court and of the path they came in on. They'd tucked the bound soldiers off the beaten path, but he knew this would only buy so much time before a patrol party would discover them. After that, any number of men would come barreling down the very path he'd just taken.

Ideally, Louis would arrive within the next five minutes, enabling them to leave right away, but that was obviously out. He hoped something in the behavior of the flock or staff would indicate Lou's current situation. Jake wished that plan A would have been possible, but as with many extractions Murphy often shows up and rears his ugly law. Whatever was in store, Jake was content with his crew and their abilities. Coming out with a civilian, Crystal, was a bit of a wild card, but no telling whether Lou and the girl were together. Jake's thoughts were answered not a minute later as he heard Lou's voice accompanied by two females, which of course was one too many. It was never simple with Louis.

Chapter 34

As Crystal, Agent Forbes and I made our way off and down to our left, a half dozen people were playing topless volleyball. Their laughter carried as voices do over a calm sea. We could even hear what they thought they were whispering. For a minute I envied them. They bought into the whole PASSAGE deal. It was what they believed. Some day they were going to ascend to the big show in the sky and until then it was all hot tub parties, prayer sessions and nude volleyball games. Nothing else mattered. Maybe ignorance was bliss. We were risking life, limb and sanity to rescue the confused daughter of a small time hood. Ignorance is bliss, I suppose, but we were doing right, and right is always right. I was ready for it now.

Where the court met the running path I stood with my back to the woods. The women faced me and carried on our mock conversation. In a loud whisper I called out Jake's name. Not a chance in hell did I expect him to be there. I just did it to give false hope to Crystal that this escape was without flaw. Pretending to point out beautiful cloud formations we'd one day ascend to I moved us along the paved surface. At center court, Jake responded. I nearly had an accident.

"Directly in front of you, Lou, hold hands and walk straight ahead."

We did as instructed.

"I'm right under you. Keep moving down the path and wait for us at the hollowed out fir tree. You'll see it. Don't look back."

We moved single file. The hand holding element was meant to make it appear that three of us were up to some sort of naughty rendezvous. I kept my head up but dropped my eyes to spy Jake. I saw nothing. We held up at the downed tree.

Gradually bodies materialized out of the forest. When Jake said 'we'

I was sure he meant him and the twins, Oliver and Xavier. I was pleasantly surprised to see Kat and Tami emerge. I hugged them both hard. Jake was the last one to arrive. He seemed to float, he was so quiet. I was reminded of the legends of Native Americans. In his face paint Jake looked like a man who kills for a living and enjoys it. Crystal clung to me when she caught sight of him.

I thanked everyone for coming and introduced Crystal, after I managed to peel her off me.

Agent Forbes was visibly impressed by Jake in a way that seemed professional. She stepped to him, back tight and thrust out her hand.

"Pleased to meet you, Jake, I'm special agent Rebecca—"

"Forbes, I know, and the pleasure is mine."

"Oh, you know me?"

"I've read about you."

"Huh, well, don't believe everything you read."

"Precisely why I read between the lines, agent Forbes."

Forbes was glad to hear it. She liked Jake immediately. Forbes opened her mouth to ask a question but Jake turned his back to her and addressed the group.

"We've got to get moving—yesterday. Agent Forbes, I take it you know the way to the freeway. Rocky's bluff?"

"Yup."

"Good. Do you mind taking the lead?"

"Ah, hang on a second Jake, everybody. There's more to this twisted play. I believe Genesis has a bunch of kids held against their will somewhere in these woods. Agent Forbes said she'll come back for them with the cavalry, but what if Genesis moves them?" All were quiet as I knew they were seriously considering my words.

"It's not a question of bravery with this group, and we've all got heart strings, Lou, but you know as well as I do we're outgunned. And outside of me and possibly Jake, you're all civilians."

Kat stepped forward, "We can hold our own, Ms. Agent Lady."

Rebecca held up a peaceful hand. "I'm speaking from a FBI procedural standpoint. I don't question anyone's ability here, I assure you." Kat was satisfied with the response.

Oliver cleared his throat, "Pardon me, lads and ladies, but I agree with Ms. Forbes. Remember the video you saw young Louis. They may have even more men than we tussled with."

Oliver was right and we all knew it. The kids were officially in the Bureau's hands. We moved single file at a pace just under jogging speed. Forbes took the lead in front of Crystal and me, with Kat behind us. The twins followed Kat. Tami was behind them with Jake bringing up the rear. Breathing and footfalls were the only sounds. No dialogue. Every now and then I could hear Crystal's breathing increase as if she were sprinting a hundred meter dash. I'd pat her on the shoulder for reassurance. A sudden wind rushed past me. It was Jake.

"Get down!" he ordered and continued up the line. We hit the deck. Crystal trembled. A type of silence that could only mean trouble was coming enveloped us. Next, small little explosions of yellow colored smoke surrounded us. We were sitting ducks.

"Sod it! " Xavier grumbled.

"This way!" Jake yelled.

We were back on our feet and on Jake's tail like Alaskan Huskies chasing the lead dog. Crystal was terrified, or maybe she was just fast. The explosions forced us off the path that would apparently have taken us to the freeway. It felt like an entire minute passed before the sounds of pursuit hit our ears.

"What took them so long?" Kat asked.

"I may have erred," Jake replied.

"Meaning what, brother?"

"They want us to go this way."

"A trap? Bastards," Kat said.

"Jesus bloody wept!" Xavier cursed.

We went up a steep rise. Jake crested it and disappeared. I half expected to see him in one of those net traps you'd always see on *Gilligan's Island* as we came over the crest. A steep drop waited for us on the other side. At the bottom was a sharp left turn and then the path straightened out. I caught up to Jake and ran beside him.

"I know where we're going," I shouted. "I think we'll see those kids after all."

"I sincerely hope somebody's got a plan B, lads and ladies," Oliver called.

Forbes decided to get into the mix. "Well, you're really advancing my career for me Louis—kidnapping, child labor, fraud… I'm going to owe you big time for this. Assuming we come out in one piece. "

She seemed to be over the fact that she'd had to pop a guy. I suppose it was her job and she was trained for it. Being foolish and old fashioned I've always felt killing was something men did. The reality was that agent Forbes was a cop and a damned good one, as far as I'm concerned.

It was great to see Kat and Tami again. With their martial arts and weight training backgrounds they too were suited for this adventure. The twins obviously lacked nothing in the power department, but I was particularly impressed at the agility they possessed in negotiating this trail's tight turns. It seemed that Crystal and I were the only novices in the art of engagement.

As a kid I skinned my knuckles on as many kids who skinned theirs on me. I had a sadistic uncle who was a great boxer, or so he claimed. My dad often sent me to his place where he had a makeshift ring and we'd study the art of pugilism. At the end of adolescence I put the fist aside for the football helmet, and it was there that I learned of toughness combined with teamwork. After leaving the helmet on the sidelines, music became my *thang*. The only battles I've seen since the sticks have been in my hands are battles between bands; the type of battle where the only casualties are the losers who can do no more than gaze at the trophy from a distance and add nothing to their band fund for prize money. As a seasoned percussionist, I did not exactly feel one hundred percent up to this task.

"Heaven take me!" Oliver cursed. I looked back and saw Xavier helping his brother to his feet. "Come along, old man."

"I'm only older by two minutes, you cur!"

We burst from the trail into a clearing. I pulled Crystal to the front of the pack. "Follow me. We'll head around the back of the building and see what's doin.'"

"Is this the labor camp?" Tami called.

"Most likely, make a mental note." I answered. "Look. Trail!"

We took it full tilt. Every eight to ten feet or so we could see shapes of people—small people—through frosted windows. I began to slow my pace, but Jake shouted at us to keep moving, now was not the time.

Once we'd breezed by the building we found ourselves on a tight trail. I couldn't help but expect my buddy with the riot bean bags to leap in front of me. Choices being few I plunged headlong. The trail curved to the right for a long time. A sinking feeling told me that we were going to travel 360 degrees. A ledge that seemed to spring from nowhere brought us to an abrupt stop. It took everything not to do the keystone cop routine. Forty feet below us stood a log cabin. Smooth rock led to thick brush and then a gravel slope. Handfuls of men poured out of the cabin and began their ascent toward us. We'd nearly tumbled on top of barracks that housed Genesis' private army. It would appear that they had been expecting us.

"Back it up, people; the bees are coming out of the hive!" I commanded as I ran.

"Haul it back to the labor camp then!" Jake agreed. "We'll make our stand there."

"I suggest we bloody hurry," Oliver said. "The first unit is sure to be there waiting for us." He confirmed what the other six of us were all thinking. Taking to the trail at breakneck speed agent Forbes led the way back. No sign of Genesis' men at the back of the building or the side. We crept along the building until coming to a stop at the front.

The large dirt courtyard was so quiet even the wildlife held its breath. As answer to our collective unspoken fear of this quiet an arrow dove into the wood beside Rebecca's head.

"Shit," she said backing us up. Two-thirds of the way down the side of building Jake found a door that was meant to appear like the side of the structure. Gently shoving Tamika aside he raised his foot and kicked the door open. We piled in like sand grains at the thin portion of an hour glass. We were greeted by close to thirty silent, dirty faces. They were all small children — no teens. Jake ignored them and began surveying the lay of the land.

The place, although small, was set up like a cramped factory. There were tables with sewing machines, over-sized bins, and fabric all over the place. The center of the room was kept clear with most of the machinery set to the perimeter of the joint. The ceiling seemed far too high for the square footage of the place.

The kids were all dressed in the same pajama-style frock. The material seemed thin, which was probably a good thing seeing as the room was very hot.

"My God, look at the poor souls," Forbes exclaimed. We approached carefully so as not to frighten them but they took a collective step back once we got close. They all had fingernails worked down to the nubs; some of which had dried blood. I also noticed that they were all very dirty even though the building seemed clean.

"It's okay," I said. "We're the good guys."

A pimply faced boy with thick-lensed glasses squeezed past a taller boy and eagerly asked if 'the master' was coming to visit them tonight. The depth of his hopefulness angered me.

"Shocking," Oliver uttered.

The pimply faced kid received a few mean stares from his comrades for his question, which meant that not all of the kids here were hip to the PASSAGE leader's visits.

"Children," Xavier said squatting down, "It would seem you are put to work here. Are there no guards in the building at the moment?"

A tall freckle-faced girl stepped forward to answer him. One of her pigtails had come undone. "About five minutes ago that bastard Toby, he's the boss of the guards, got a call on his stupid little hand radio. He got all excited, ordered the other jerks out and locked us in. They didn't tell us to keep working so we're not. Now you guys come barging in."

"How old are you, little lady?" Oliver asked.

"None of your business." Clearly we were talking to the ring leader. I liked her spunk.

"I'm going to guess eleven."

"Twelve, if you must know."

"And your name?"

"They call me Red."

"Because of the hair."

"That's what people think at first, but it's because when I get pissed off I see red. Someday I'm going to see red and I'm going to kill Toby and some of the others maybe...definitely that bastard Genesis."

The faraway look told me that she had already committed the act many times in her mind and couldn't wait for that day.

"Well, let's hope that we can just get you out of here and the authorities can take care of these awful characters," Xavier said, moving his voice up a half octave.

"What's your name, Mister Inquisitive?" she asked, folding her arms in front of her.

"My name is Xavier and this is—"

"Well, Xavier, I am going to kill *before* the authorities get here and there's not a court in the land that will convict me when I show them these."

Without warning she turned her back to us and pulled up her raggedy top revealing whip marks old and new. "Besides, I'm a minor anyway."

Tami rushed to her and pulled her shirt down. A tear had formed in the corner of her eye when she turned back to us.

She tried her best to console Red and reluctantly Red allowed it—tough act gone. Kat called from the door we'd entered and asked the twins to help her barricade Jake's handiwork. Jake re-emerged.

"Do you get the feeling they wanted us to end up here?" I asked.

"Mice in a trap," was the helpful reply he gave me. Forbes walked up to Jake.

"Whatever they plan to do with us, they plan on doing to the kids as well, otherwise why lock them in here too?"

Jake nodded in agreement.

"Listen, children, please," Kat announced, adding a nice tone to her voice. "We need to find a safe place for you all until this thing blows over. Do any of you have any suggestions?"

She got blank stares with the exception of Red. "What is this 'thing' you're talking about? What the hell do you mean?"

"I'm not sure what is going to happen, but we are here to help. And sister, you'd better mind your tone with me..." It was the kind of discipline Red needed. She looked down at her shoes and mumbled that they could all fit into the office but not for long as it 'gets hot in there.'

The children moved toward the office as a group that has grown accustomed to following the orders of elders. Their spirits near broken they did not appear enthused about their new saviors. For all they knew, we were the new group of adults who would carry the whip to raise welts on their weary backs.

Jake gave another stoic nod like a judge allowing a piece of evidence. Red, trailing at the back of the line, stopped at Jake and looked fixedly at him. The warrior in the face paint scowled down at her. Slowly she raised her index finger and ran it gently down an old scar on Jake's forearm. He looked at the tiny pale hand and then looked at her face.

"You're the leader, aren't you, sir?"

Jake said nothing.

"That door is almost four inches thick, trust me I know. And you come along and just kick it in." She paused to gaze at other scars.

"You're very strong," she said finally.

Jake remained statue-still and silent. Red was transfixed by the power she saw. Standing on her toes she cupped a hand to her mouth to tell Jake a secret. Jake stooped, lending his ear.

"Kill them, Mister Leader. Kill them all and set us free."

Jake clenched and un-clenched a fist. She'd struck a nerve. The nod he gave to Red looked more like a promise than a patronizing reassurance. The goose bumps on my arms confirmed my thought. Red slowly walked to the office and closed the door behind her without looking back at us.

Xavier stepped up to tower over me. "Louis, you've met this charlatan Genesis. What kind of man is he? Beyond what we've seen here, I mean?"

"He's a son of a bitch motivated by greed."

"But what is he likely to do next? That is what I'm after?"

"I'd like to think that he wouldn't kill, I mean, he just loves money and his flock's attention. However, he was going to shoot me up with some crazy cocktail and dump me in an asylum. And that was before I broke the left hand of his right hand man. Not to mention that Agent Forbes killed his number one bodyguard and knocked the grand pooh-bah himself silly with her pistol."

"So what exactly am I to glean from that, young Louis?"

"In short, we're fucked, pardon my Canadian."

As if on cue, smoke canisters crashed through three different windows. Jake sprinted to the nearest one, picked it up and tossed it back out the window. Tami and Oliver quickly followed Jake's example.

"It'll probably start with smoke canisters," I cracked.

"Gee, do ya think?" Kat piped, "I'm going to check on the kids."

Slightly panting, Tami came back to the group. "Well, we can't do that all night. They'll probably send more next time."

"What I fail to understand," said Oliver clearing his throat, "is why pin us down here only to smoke us out?"

"Perhaps they were awaiting the full regiment, you know, so they can surround us at full strength," answered his brother.

"That and they were probably waiting for the big boss to get here. I bet they were instructed to keep us alive until he could bear witness. Otherwise they could have picked us off when they had us on the trail," added Agent Forbes.

"Your words have merit, Miss Forbes," Oliver maintained.

"Most likely they decided to leave the kids here because hey, who wants to babysit a kid when you're trying to pin an enemy down?" Tami offered.

Chapter 35

Genesis woke like a man coming out of a nightmare. It seemed to take forever for him to get out of his very own sashes. He swore that after all was said and done he was going to change his wardrobe slightly; in short, no more goddam sashes.

Gasping for air he scrambled to his feet. He quickly played the events through his head that led to his struggling to his feet with a pounding head. The FBI is here, has been here. This was not good. How many agents is that now? Ah, forget it, he thought. It didn't matter. He needed to find the agent and that upstart musician and ensure they didn't leave the compound.

But what about the rest of the flock? Fuck 'em! If they panic over the upcoming manhunt so be it. He could always put some kind of spin on it later. That was his specialty. Spin is practically how he built this place. 'Bill O'Reilly ain't got nothin' on me,' he thought. Still, he couldn't help feeling that his creation may be close to meeting its demise. No way, no *way* could a two-bit drummer and one female agent bring him down. His soldiers better be doing what he paid them for or heads would roll. *Damn, how long have I been out? I need a drink.*

He stumbled behind the desk and yanked the bottle from the drawer. He drank deeply. Immediately he choked. He fumbled for his intercom. "Darkness, Fred get the hell over here, there's been a breach, a breach goddamnit, did you hear me?" He let go of the button and took another big drink. His head seemed to hurt more from the booze, but he didn't care. He drank again. He winced at the pain and hit the talk button again. "Dammit boys, get in here and let me know how Adrian is doing."

Mr. Darkness called from outside the door, "Boss, open the door, it's me."

"Then let yourself in, you docile son of a—" Genesis shouted.

"Boss, the door's locked."

Irritated, Genesis walked to the door with the bottle in hand. He tried the knob but all it did was turn round and round. "Shit, she must have done something. Kick it in."

"She who, boss?" came the muffled reply.

"Just kick the damn—"

Mr. Darkness was way ahead of him. Splinters from the door hit Genesis in the face. He staggered back.

"You imbecile, why didn't you warn me? Damn, that stings."

Genesis handed his soldier the tequila bottle. Mr. Darkness took a big pull.

"No, you idiot, you need to stay sober. I just wanted you to put it down while I check my eyes for splinters. Listen, Crasher and some fed are running around this place. We need to find them, and I mean twenty minutes ago."

Just then Mr. Darkness' walkie talkie chirped. "Go ahead. Uh- huh. No don't engage them there. How many did you say? Mm-hm. Force them to the other compound. What do you mean which compound? Compound B, dummy; we don't want them back here with the suckers." Genesis shot his employee a look. He knew his hired muscle referred to the congregation as suckers, but sometimes the help were too loose with the term.

"Copy that, out. I said copy that comma over and out... fuck off, Gibbons, you're such a tool." Mr. Darkness raised his eyes to Genesis, who was shaking his head.

"Give me the details. All of them, Mr. Darkness."

"Crasher, that Crystal broad that you...and some other broad, the agent, I guess, entered the woods off the basketball court. They were met by friendlies, theirs of course, and are about to be forced to the kiddie compound."

"I wish you wouldn't call it that, it sounds so... Michael Jackson Neverland Ranch-ish," Genesis said stroking his goatee. "How many friendlies? Theirs of course," he mocked.

"Five. Two women, three men, and sir, they are pretty good too. Bravo team jumped them and found themselves tied up in cute little packages."

"Dock Bravo team's pay. And ration their booze as well...heavily."

"Yes, sir."

"Let's get moving," Genesis said with ruffled frock trailing behind him.

"Ah, through the woods sir?"

Genesis slowed and gently picked up the tequila bottle. Three big gulps raced down his gullet. "Look at me, Mr. Darkness. Do I look like I go traipsing through freaking forests? We'll take the Hummer and the pickup truck down the old logging road. Now put this bottle back to bed."

Mr. Darkness walked around the desk and was about to drop the bottle in the drawer when he decided to take a long pull of his own.

"For courage, sir," he said in answer to Genesis' scowl.

Genesis then asked, "Why hasn't Fred shown his sorry ass?"

"Because Fred's sorry ass is a dead sorry ass...sir."

"So then it's true. They weren't bullshitting, tragic. Let's go."

Chapter 36

Satisfied that we had all the necessary answers, we set ourselves to making a plan. The brief confab was interrupted by Genesis' voice blaring through what sounded like a Dolby sound system.

"Ho there, interlopers, are you comfortable?" His voice was two-thirds taunt and one- third arrogance. Everyone drew pistols but Crystal and me. She clung to my arm at the sight of the imposing hardware.

"Mr. Crasher, I see you've brought guests to my home. Perhaps we should call you, Party Crasher. Did your mother not tell you it is rude to have a party and not inform the host who is coming?"

"How's the head, G-man, a little sore maybe?" I had to really shout.

Jake rolled his eyes at my wisecrack.

Genesis chuckled briefly but didn't rise to the bait. "Crystal? Crystal honey, are you happy with your new friends? You see, Sunshine, you have made your choice, or your bed, if you will, and now you are going to have to lie in it. Ah but what a shame. *C'est la vie*, you ungrateful whore."

Another voice boomed without the full assistance of the PA system. "You're finally going to die, punk!"

"Thank you, Adrian, I can manage," Genesis shouted off microphone.

"Adrian, is that you buddy? Say, I was just telling my friends about your girlie scream. Do it for us one time, would ya pal?" I really had to pump my voice up to be heard. Genesis came back over the speakers composed.

"Mr. Crasher, ladies and gentlemen, you are trespassing and have committed murder. It will be considered self-defense when I kill you interlopers."

The girls, twins and Jake loaded clips, cocked hammers and checked sights. More windows broke with the next wave of smoke canisters. Jake handed me a gun as he passed me en route to a smoker. I'd held a gun only one time before. My uncle the boxer took me to a range for my sixteenth birthday. My mom later kicked his butt for it.

The combination of scary yet powerful feelings returned immediately. Tami had been right. The smokers seemed to just keep coming. A T-shirt over the face did little to combat the noxious fumes. Fluid gushed from my eyes and nose like Niagara Falls. Through our coughs, we all tossed canisters as fast as we could. Yellow smoke filled the room. The little wannabe assassin named Red came flashing through a cloud of smoke to latch onto Jake.

She ignored his orders to return to the office. As he shook her arm and shouted, her body suddenly twisted toward him. Horror registered on her face.

She'd been hit by a bullet on the outside of her shoulder. Jake threw himself on top of her, returning fire as they went down. Two of Genesis' soldiers had penetrated the barricaded door. Jake managed to put one down, with Oliver pumping three rounds into his partner. The women ran to the door firing as they went and this time used everything they could find to block the door, beginning with the kitchen sink— literally.

"How is she, Jake?" I inquired.

"We're fine."

"We?" I asked.

The bullet had gone through part of Red's shoulder and nicked Jake's tricep. 'Cheese and crackers, man,' was all I could think of saying.

"She took most of the heat, stubborn kid."

Crystal bent down to help Jake with the girl.

"Can you handle this?" I asked.

"What do you have in mind, Lou?"

"You guys came all this way to get me. It's time I gave back. I'm going to set things right."

"Do you know how to use the Roscoe?" he asked without looking at me.

"Don't worry about me. Okay, worry, but rest assured it's not this gun that'll kill me. Can you handle—?" I motioned with my eyes to Crystal and the little girl, a glance to which Jake responded with a glare. Stupid question.

Kat trotted up to me and tried to use anger to hide her worry. "What the hell do you think you're doing?"

Kissing her forehead, I promised I'd be right back, and made tracks for the back of the building. At the far end of the building an old emergency ladder leaned against the wall.

Tucking the gun in the back of my pants the way Magnum PI used to, I took the ladder two rungs at a time to the ceiling. Seeing there was no back door to the building, I figured the soldiers wouldn't bother patrolling that area outside. I crawled and clawed through dirty rafters to a high window, unbroken by canister.

Jake and Crystal finished tending to the wounded child. Jake fought to keep the one thousand unthinkable things he'd like to do to Genesis out of his head. Bilking the weak was one thing, but a man who gives the order to go in blazing where children are present is a man with numbered days, as far as Jake was concerned. Keep a cool head and win, Jake. It was that simple. Violence, intensity and precision were things that always came easily to Jake. It was him or the other guy. In the early days he was often left with a feeling of guilt afterward, but he learned that people put themselves into situations where the solution necessitated the use of force. He knew that one day he would probably come to a violent end but if he were 'setting things right' at the time, as Lou put it, then so be it.

Jake looked at the youth and knew that she felt some sort of pride at being struck by the same bullet as 'Mister Leader.' Maybe it made the whole ordeal easier for her but something told Jake that she was just plain tough and she wouldn't squawk about being clipped whether Jake had been hit or not.

"Why did you come out here?" Jake demanded.

"I felt safer being near you." She seemed embarrassed by her tears.

"Had you stayed put you wouldn't have been hit," he responded looking at the bandage for leaks.

"It's just a scratch, besides I have to see you take them down. That's right, I've been praying lately for help and God has sent you. You're the avenging angel with the painted face. I'm not afraid."

"I'm no angel and violence should be avoided at all cost." He helped her to her feet.

"The chosen ones are always the last to know that they are the chosen ones." She attempted to straighten out her clothes. Jake admired her pride.

"Mr. Leader, Genesis is the key to PASSAGE. Waste him and the others have nothing. Fu...I mean dang my arm hurts."

She was wise for her age. Jake was the same way at that age. She was also right on the money with her theory about Genesis' importance. His men were nothing more than hired goons. Remove the employer—no more employees.

Oliver joined them. "Pardon me if the question seems absurd Jake, but do you not have a cell phone?"

"No signal this far out."

"Jake, that your name?" Red asked.

Jake didn't respond so she said she'd continue calling him Mister Leader. Pointing at the ceiling, she asked where Lou was going.

"He's going to set things right, now get back to the office."

They watched Lou crawl over and under rafters until he got to a window. Two short shotgun blasts hammered through the front door. Men came in blazing once they found their target. Jake's crew took cover. Tami reluctantly jumped into a large blue dumpster, popping up frequently she fired rounds at the incoming mass. They were dropping at a rate that told her she was in the company of good shooters. Unfortunately some men were regaining their feet. "Kevlar!" Tami shouted over the racket, unsure if her comrades heard her. The twins shared a common thought—it was shocking that these Neanderthals would barge in blazing knowing children were present. It angered them both. For the first time, Tami glanced around at the contents of the dumpster. Expecting the usual filth she was surprised to find name expensive brand running shoes. Only the product had flaws; odd stitching, misspelled names, tongues too long and the like. "Knock-offs," she muttered. "Knock-off rejects in fact. Genesis, you sneaky little bastard." She now knew how her adversary paid for his make believe world.

Meanwhile, Kat high-tailed it to the office and locked the door behind her. Anybody that came through that door that wasn't on her team was going to get the business. Some of the kids sobbed quietly while others covered their ears to block out the scary world of the big people. Every so often Kat would crack the door and fire at clueless soldiers and then rejoin the children. She kept up this routine until the third time she checked the door a dark face with a close cropped beard met her stare at point blank range. The last thing the smirking soldier saw was Kat's soft brown eyes beneath a furrowed brow before a slug from a nine millimeter Berretta blew his face apart to exit out the back of his skull.

"Curiosity killed the cat, motherfucker," she whispered as the body folded into a heap at her feet. She stepped out the door and dragged the carcass to the side. She saw Crystal and Red huddled where Jake had stashed them. She quickly got their attention and signaled them to run to her. After such a spectacle, and with the new additions safely in the office, Kat found it absurd to tell the kids that everything 'was going to be all right.

The twins, Jake, agent Forbes and Tami were doing a stellar job at racking up casualties, but this was no video game and the enemy kept coming. Time was running out, as was ammunition.

Red was beginning to have doubts about the man God sent her. Surely there were too many guards for her newfound hero. However, she found some comfort in the knowledge that Mister Leader was wasting tons of bad guys. She squeezed her eyes tightly and imagined every shot she heard was the one that would end Toby's life.

The office was small and sparsely decorated. A nondescript desk held a three-layer tray to the right with minimal papers. A gray four-drawer filing cabinet was to the right of the door. On top of it were three phone books. The concrete floor needed sweeping. No way did Genesis use this office, Kat thought, not lavish enough. This room belonged to a foreman, probably the one charged with corralling the kids. The kids huddled closely, most were crying. Red pulled off a corner of her bandage for a sneak peek. She winced and then fought that away with a nasty snarl. Her face was nothing short of ferocious, Kat thought. It was unfair that a child was forced to develop such a thick defense mechanism. This kid should be texting friends, chatting on Facebook and heading for the mall with her friends. The hairs on the back of her neck raised a millisecond before three pairs of children's eyes grew to saucer size. An enemy was behind her.

Kids screamed. Kat whirled around as fast she possibly could, gun coming up. She was face to face with a man a foot taller than her and a hundred pounds heavier. His first move was to knock her gun away. He succeeded and even had enough time to fire his own gun, but he didn't. Kat took this as a gift and grabbed the gun in both her hands and spun around. Her back now to his stomach she regretted the move, for the gun was now trained on the kids. Shit. The intruder's arm was wedged under her armpit and elbow. The gunman called her a bitch. No imagination, Kat thought. The kids scattered left and right like cockroaches do when the lights come on. Good kids. Instead of breaking his arm over her knee as is often seen in the movies, she managed to grab hold of two of his fingers which were low on the gun grip. She snapped them backward without a second thought. This time when he called her a bitch he sang an octave higher. Kat couldn't believe her luck—she now had the gun in her hand.

Victory was short lived. The soldier grabbed her by the shoulders and threw her like a laundry bag filled with baby socks into a steel workman's tool shelf. Kat barely had enough time to raise and hand in front of her face before impact. Her elbow screamed with pain. She also lost the gun. Bouncing off the shelf, she hit the concrete floor hard but managed to break her fall just like her martial art taught her. Immediately she covered her head as the shelf crashed down on top of her. She began to panic, as she was now useless to the kids. As suddenly as it happened the shelf was lifted off of her and she was being dragged to her feet by her hair. She briefly feigned struggling to gain balance then without warning flexed her quad and calf muscles and sprung up bringing her palm under her attacker's chin. He partially read the move and was able to shift his head back slightly. This softened the blow. She noticed his right hand ball into a fist. Without wasting any time she grabbed the hand that held her hair knowing it was the one with crippled fingers. This time the gunman flat out screamed as Kat heard several cracks. Red came out of nowhere and kicked at his calf. It had no effect.

"Get back, Red," Kat thought. If he so much as swung a backhand at the child she'd be done. The combatants circled, each being careful not to trip over any shelf debris. There wasn't nearly enough room for Kat to throw any of the Tai Kwon Do kicks that she wanted to.

"You're all out of tricks now you little bitch."

"Well aren't you just a one-note, dickless pony."

His face flushed momentarily and he charged. Kat was pinned too close to the desk. All she could do was brace for impact. Their combined weight took both bodies over the desk and through a flimsy wall. It had to be a false wall, Kat thought, because although the collision hurt, the wall did not. Now she was pinned under the soldier on a cement ledge. Directly above was a metal railing. In front was a staircase. He pushed his torso up and was planning a downward punch at her face. She came up in a fast half sit-up and wrapped her arm around his head. She then sunk her teeth into his ear and with all her hip strength and the element of surprise rolled the two of them off the ledge. They fell eight feet to the floor below. Kat also managed to land on top of the gunman. He was dazed as he hit his head. Kat couldn't breathe. She didn't think she should be this winded seeing as she landed on top. She was wheezing now and felt like she was drowning. Then a thought occurred to her. She crawled to a nearby chair and got to her feet. Throwing her stomach harshly over chair back enabled her to cough up the bottom portion of the attacker's ear. It was the classic Heimlich maneuver. She continued to spit and cough as she gulped in new air. The gunman struggled to get up. Kat calmly walked behind him, took a knee, set her lock in and snapped his neck.

When the shooting started, Agent Forbes overturned two tables with sewing machines attached to them and lay as low as she could. Flipping onto her belly, she fired around the side of the table. In an ideal situation, an accurate shot from the ground is best achieved when one can have both elbows on the floor, one hand supports the gun hand. The sewing tables didn't afford this type of luxury. She was able to hit most of her targets but was not always able to nail the fatal points, heart and head. Secretly, she had a private favorite of her own and that was the neck. Something about a pulsating neck wound which ended in death moments later…well hey, it's not as if she ever had nightmares about it or shot a loved one in that way. It was private; a private edge, she told herself.

On a few occasions, she managed to drop the enemy with a shin or knee shot and then finish with a torso shot. She thought the way she always did in fire fights, remain calm and shoot to kill (even if that meant maim first) because given the chance the other guy will kill you. Rebecca Forbes had always been an exceptional shot. From her early days in the academy, she was groomed as a sniper, and although she had respect for snipers, it wasn't for her. She was built for the field, and had believed so since she was a child. When her childhood friends were matching outfits for Barbie, she was playing cops and robbers. Growing up as a tomboy in the small town of Kenosha, Wisconsin her parents suspected she might be gay and told her that if she ever came out of the closet they would still love her. She told them the same went for them. Her father failed to see the humor in her joke.

When too much fire rained at her prone position she would pop up to her knees and fire with both guns. On the day of her arrival at PASSAGE she had used a tiny little nail puller and popped the floor board under her bed. Removing a plank, she wrapped her guns in cloth and placed them in the ground. After her first supper she returned to find that her belongings had been rifled: Adrian, no question, the pathetic little big man. Even if she weren't an agent she'd have discovered the sophomoric attempt the invader made at replacing her items to their original state. She purposely packed her sexiest lingerie from Victoria's Secret. To augment her plan she stopped by a sex shop, purchased a few toys and feigned an attempt at concealing them in hidden compartments of her bag. The moment a snoop spied the sexy lace outfits, skimpy panties and sex paraphernalia she'd be labeled kinky or even freaky, but not an FBI agent. It had worked before.

Agent Forbes had successfully infiltrated the camps of crack-smoking drug dealers and in her experience a more paranoid animal does not exist. Tailing Genesis was easy. He was greedy but not paranoid...enough. As she was lining up a stout, bearded target she saw a soldier to his left with a shotgun and a bead on her. "Shit," she uttered as she rolled as far out of the way as she could. The desk was blown apart, leaving behind half of the sewing machine where she'd just been lying. She now had one sewing table for cover.

The twins took cover as best they could behind three barrels. The bullets that peppered the barrels sounded like hundreds of hailstones on a tin roof.

"I fear these barrels are going to be of precious little use to us before long, Xavier."

"I quite agree, brother."

"Ah, but what I wouldn't give to be on stage at this very moment— Hamlet perhaps, or MacBeth."

"You shock me, Oliver. I thought it certain that you would rather be conducting an acting class with Mr. Outlaw."

"I see a hail of bullets hasn't removed that bizarre sense of humor of yours."

"Say, old chum, give us a few bullets then?"

"Blast you! I was about to make the same request of you, Xavier. Well, I'd say the pooch is screwed on this one, old boy."

"Quite—buggered to the fullest."

Xavier cast his glance around the room in desperation. His gaze came to rest on the dumpster Tami was in. She was doing a fine job at keeping the wolves at bay, but they were slowly closing on her, no doubt about it. The nearer they got, the less frequently she was able to pop up and return fire.

"Oliver, look yonder! Our Tami's a bloody rabbit in a pot!"

"Oh Christmas! Get over there man, I'll cover you."

Oliver laid down the cover fire, but was forced to do it sparingly, which almost defeated the purpose of cover fire. As a result, the going was slow for Xavier. Each cursed to themselves repeatedly. Xavier found minimal coverage behind a machine that looked like a big printing press, and fired around the sides. A bullet whistled past him so closely that he swore it took an eighth of an inch off his already buzzed cut. "Saint Christopher's ghost!"

As he loaded the final rounds into his gun, he spied the dumpster and saw a shoe fly out of it. 'A hallucination,' he told himself. He fired off a round and turned to see another shoe fly out. "Good god, the poor girl must be out of ammo."

Oliver saw the same thing his brother saw and began firing at the men approaching the dumpster. This made him particularly uncomfortable as he was forced to fire over his brother's head. He had no choice. Tami was now jumping up and throwing shoes instead of bullets.

"Give up girl, surrender," Oliver yelled but was not heard. Confident that they were covered, four men charged the dumpster with guns hanging low. Oliver dropped one of the men before being forced back down by fire from his left.

The three remaining men held their path but slowed as they got closer. One shouted, "Let's take her boys, she's out." Ten yards from the bin, blood exploded from the neck of one of the men. He staggered sideways for three steps before falling face first on the floor. It didn't matter to him that the fall broke his nose. A pool of blood flowed between the fingers he vainly put over the wound. He was dead ten seconds later.

"Jake," Oliver muttered to himself happily. He wasn't exactly sure where the man was, but he appreciated his handiwork. His celebration was cut short as he noticed the two remaining men nearing the dumpster. His hideaway continuously riddled with bullets, he dared not risk a shot to help the poor lass. He tilted his head enough to see that his brother was in no better shape. It was all on Jake now.

"Come on Jake, have another go lad, have another go," he growled. The men slowed their approach but still held their guns low. It was as if they knew that the enemy had no clear shot. Xavier cursed them their confident air. Tami's hand crept slowly over the lip of the bin. In it was a large men's hi-top basketball sneaker.

"Let's see the other hand lady, and I mean slow, like a retard." The lead soldier's voice was all snicker. One of the other soldiers laughed at his comment. She began to do what he asked then threw the shoe high into the air. One of the men followed the shoe with his eyes. The lead soldier knew the ploy but wasn't quick enough. Tami came up with her pistol in her other hand and shot the leader two times; once in the trapezoid muscle and once in the collar bone. She had more time with the other one and placed a bullet in the center of the second man's forehead. "I don't like the term retard, asshole!"

Pulling up her second gun she began popping off rounds at the five men who were spread around the room. They returned fire from their shelter. Xavier, able to reach her now, yanked her out of the bin as if she were a five-foot-six inch piece of tissue paper.

"Possum? You played possum with those brutes? Bloody good, my lady, bloody good show." Without another thought he kissed her on the lips and followed this with an immediate apology after realizing what he'd done. She said it was 'all right' with a laugh. Oliver, now feeling the effects of a neck cramp shook his head in disgust at his brother's audacity. Imagine forcing a kiss on the poor creature at such a time, the brazenness! He'd scold him later.

Chapter 37

I was covered in dust and cobwebs, but naturally I didn't care. I had work to do. As the window slid back I thanked the universe for it not being painted shut. I lumbered out onto the roof without grace and lay on my back. I drank in the clean air like a desert traveler who finds water. The sun slumbered, the sky now littered with stars. Beauty above me, carnage below. I got into a low crouch on the pitched roof and made my way to the peak. Peering over the top, I saw a large black Ford truck. It was the F-350 model with the extended cab. It sat on expensive rims and had black tinted windows. Beside it was a bright yellow Hummer, jacked up high on huge tires. This guy possessed no subtlety. Genesis stepped from the back seat, and even from this distance I could see an oversized bandage on the side of his head. He probably insisted on the extra big bandage in an attempt to show his men that he was in the trenches with them. A side of beef to the bruised area for ten minutes with a couple belts of his high priced tequila would have done the trick on his boo-boo.

One of Genesis' lieutenants handed the microphone to him. Genesis was about speak, decided against it, and leaned back in the truck. When he popped back out he threw his head back, pinched his nose then gave his head a shake. He'd just done a quick line of cocaine. I'd been around enough wanna-be lead singers to know the dance.

To my surprise the warehouse was not as tightly surrounded as I thought. In fact, some of the men leaned against trucks or smoked amongst themselves as if they were at a tough guy cocktail party. They must not have been aware of the casualty rate my team was piling up. Truly, they were paying for this arrogance. One of the doors on the far side of the truck opened and a man got out carrying a cup and saucer. Genesis took the cup as the man held the saucer and sipped the drink. The small cup suggested espresso. That was enough for me. If he thought that he could stand there doing blow, drinking exotic coffee like it was tea time in England then he had another thing coming. I felt slapped in the face. This was war!

I recognized Adrian. His movements were those of a fly in a spider's web. To his left with his gun across his chest was the man who first discovered me talking on the cell phone. He was 110% business, with head on a swivel, eyes searching. I took this to be my cue.

Careful to keep my head low I inched down the back side of the roof until I was far enough down to stand up. The pitch was steep. Growing next to the building at the rear was a fifty-foot baby sequoia. My plan was simple; I'd jump to the tree, climb down, sneak around the front and take out the bad guys. Brilliant.

I steeled my nerves, got down to near football player's three-point stance and took off at a run. I had to run before I had a chance to think about how dumb my plan was. As I passed the window I'd crept out of I began to veer to the left. Soon I was running straight down the pitch toward the tree, which stood heaven only knew how far from the building. I began to wonder if I was running fast or falling down.

Three, two, one—I pushed off the roof inches or centimeters, take your pick, from the gutter with my right foot. My arms and legs cycling like a pro long jumper I reached, stretched, visualized and prayed for the tree. Half way to the target I knew I was going to make it. Two-thirds of the way there I realized I was coming in too hot and only cartoon characters have mid-air brakes. I back pedaled on an imaginary elliptical trainer—useless. Gravity and inertia have rules and they stick by them. I suppose I had to respect that. I crossed one of my arms in front of my face and the other in front of my wedding tackle, as the Brits would say, just before impact. I collided with a thick branch under my arms, which was far better than the trunk itself. Tree and ribs cracked simultaneously. My legs swung underneath the branch with such force that I nearly went all the way around like a gymnast on uneven bars. The pain in my ribs made it nearly impossible to hang on. It was the branch that quit. I was heading south, no question. Several branches slowed my fall every few feet. At one point a limb connected with my head causing the night stars to multiply. I finally came to rest on my back. I rolled over to get to my feet only to find that I was still six or seven feet from the ground. Miraculously I landed on my feet, fell to my knees and threw up. I am so sick of puking, I thought.

As I wiped at my mouth I saw the gun Jake gave me a few steps away. I checked my belt to make sure it was mine. Nothing but belt and loops. Returning the gun home I crept to the building and moved toward the back. At the corner of the building I peeked around. Nobody seemed to have heard my great fall. The drive was gravel butting up against short grass turned brown by the sun. After five or six feet, the dead lawn grew into tall grass, like wheat. The wheat surrounded the perimeter until thick woods took over. Every breath was a needle in my side. Genesis was still in the same spot flanked by eight men. He appeared to be agitated now, as his men hadn't completed the job yet. He barked orders, one of which included, "take this bloody coffee away, it's cold." Poor baby, I thought.

I rolled into the tall grass and lay there feeling the pain in my ribs pound with the beat of my heart. Accepting that the pain wasn't going anywhere I began belly crawling through the grass as quietly as I could, stopping every so often to listen for my discovery. A blow horn sounded. I looked up to see Genesis with an air horn in his hand blowing it off in short bursts. It was meant for the soldiers inside, but they couldn't hear it from where they were. Perseverance and fear got me parallel with the truck. Two men with M-16 machine guns over their shoulders stood between me and the truck. I was practically underneath them. The taller of the two smoked a cigar while the shorter man complained.

"I don't like this, Toby, our guys should have dragged the wounded out by now. And listen to all that shooting."

"Hm," replied Toby.

"Geez, that's a lot of gunfire. The boss wanted em' alive." Another thought came to the soldier's mind "Say, you don't think they're wasting our guys do you?"

Toby turned his head to the little man without answering.

"Fuck it, T. I'm goin' in."

A big hand landed on the smaller man's shoulder, preventing him from moving. "Stop worrying, half of them are broads. We stay here as ordered."

"Why? All the shootin's in there. Genesis ain't no tactical man. He doesn't know how to handle something like this. You see the smokers did squat. I'm outta here."

The smaller soldier twisted free and moved toward the building. Toby was on his tail. The smaller man broke into a trot and I followed on their heels, gun out unnoticed. Genesis, about to speak from the bed of pickup, stopped as the two soldiers ran by. He never got the chance to reprimand them for going in without an order. When the men passed the truck I leapt onto the bumper, climbed into the box, jumped and landed on top of Genesis. The soldier to his left heard my footfall on the truck bed and turned, but was too slow. I had Genesis on the bed liner straddling him with my gun at his bandaged head. All guns were on me with everybody shouting.

I shouted also. "Get back or I blow your gravy train away!"

"He's bluffing," somebody yelled.

"Get back, I ain't fuckin' around! No heroes either, fellas. If you pop me my finger goes too and no more paychecks for you ladies." Nobody moved back. In fact they crept forward inch by inch. Genesis snapped out of his initial shock.

"You're going to die by torture, Party Crasher. Somebody take aim and shoot this piece of shit," Genesis barked.

"Weren't you listening, you dizzy bastard?" I said.

Before any of the soldiers got the notion of playing hero for the boss I yanked my hostage to his knees and fired a shot point blank beside his right ear. Genesis went down again kicking and writhing around screaming in short little high-pitched yelps. Adrian charged me, yelling something about his daddy. I ignored the disturbing revelation, which explained a lot, took aim at his thigh and pulled the trigger. Missing my intended target I got him in the shin, which still counted, as far as I was concerned. Adrian joined Genesis in the screaming. I had the gun back to Genesis' head and hoisted him back to his feet.

"Let me get this straight, Genesis, Adrian is your son?" He didn't answer me but I knew what I heard. "Well, that would explain the asshole gene he possesses."

Next, I forced the soldiers to put their weapons in a pile and line up single file on their knees, with their hands behind their heads. I was running the show purely from adrenaline, fear, and what I'd seen in films. I noticed for the first time the shooting inside had stopped. I reached for the microphone and stuck it Genesis's face.

"Tell your men to toss their weapons out the door and come out hands over their heads." Genesis clutched the microphone in trembling hands. He went to speak but cried instead. "Do it!" I shouted.

His voice had a quiver in it but the speakers on the five poles carried the message clearly. No doubt the sound system was usually used for some kind of training or brainwashing detail. I waited but there was no response. Nor were there bucket loads of guns and ammo spilling out the door. This time I grabbed the microphone. "You heard him, it's over. I've got the asshole who writes your checks, ladies. Come on out nice and easy or G-man here sleeps the long one!"

I was behind the line of soldiers all on their knees. Some of them turned their heads to me as yet again my command was met with...silence.

Chapter 38

A soldier with a higher vantage point than Jake kept him pinned within the little dip he'd found in the wall. He was lucky to tag the soldier as he did that approached Tami at the dumpster. What he wouldn't give for a grenade launcher to rock that little crow out of his nest. He felt relief at the sight of Tami's trick and vowed to chastise her later for pulling such a nonsensical stunt. Between gun blasts Jake heard an air horn. He shrugged it off and kept firing when he could. Why not, he was almost out of ammo anyway. Time to let the gun speak and have the coroner sort it out. It was obvious that his colleagues were in the same leaky boat as he.

Eventually all were forced from their shelters with hands high. Agent Forbes had the hardest time parting with her weapon, and wouldn't until hearing Oliver's gentle urgings. The twins and Tami were the first to be frisked and then forced to their knees with hands behind their backs. Kat came out of the office and closed the door behind her leaving the children within. If she was walking to her execution the least she could do was shield the kids from witnessing it. Finally Jake emerged and joined the group. Ignoring the "drop your weapons" command, Jake walked to the heavy set man sporting a thick handlebar mustache who seemed to be in charge and handed him his guns, butts first. Another man frisked Jake before he joined the others on his knees. The group looked to one another as a sort of "Chin up," except for Jake, who seemed to stare at nothing.

"Where's the troublemaker, Larry or Lou, or whatever his name is?" Handlebar said to the group.

"Never made it to the warehouse," Agent Forbes chimed in.

"Bullshit," the stocky soldier Rebecca had had in her sights growled. He had no idea how close he came, she thought. She heard his footsteps behind her. He drew back his weapon to strike her in the back of the head, but Jake pushed her to the side with little effort. Missing, the soldier's momentum carried him prone to the floor. Jake was on him like a lion on a gazelle with a hand under his chin ready to break his neck. Spectators both friend and foe were awed by Jake's quickness. It was a warning more than an intention.

"Kill him, Mister Leader!" Red screamed. Crystal put a hand over her mouth.

"Don't even tink about it," a soft spoken soldier with an Irish accent said with his gun to the back of Jake's head. The stocky man panted heavily. Jake could feel the sweat off his chin. He let him up. The man came at Jake and stuck his gun in Jake's face. Jake stared the man in the eye as if unaware of the gun that dug into his cheek bone.

Handlebar shouted, "Buckey, stand down! You heard Genesis, we march the survivors outside and then the boss decides their fate. And if I know the boss, which I do," he paused, "He'll have something slow and painful in store for our guests here. Now stow that weapon, soldier!"

Buckey reluctantly did as told but not before spitting in Jake's face. In a low voice, Jake told him he would die for that. Only Buckey heard the threat, and was glad no one could see the goose bumps on his arms or the fear that was sure to show in his eyes.

"On your feet, prisoners, and you, Mister Hero," he said to Jake, "one more stunt like that and a second later you'll be a martyr in a hole." He racked his double shotgun for impact.

Rebecca muttered a thank you to Jake as they were marched single file toward the main entrance. Buckey heard the dialogue and slapped her hard on the back of the neck, causing her baseball cap to hit the floor. As she bent to retrieve it Buckey kicked her, sending her to the floor. He smiled as some of the other men laughed. From a sitting position, she placed the hat back on her head.

"Try that again, junior, please," she taunted almost seductively.

The procession stopped. Buckey had to save face and she knew it. Cocky strides took Buckey to Agent Forbes. Jake and the others stayed put, knowing that they were about to witness some FBI training in action. Buckey drew his leg back to kick her again. She flipped onto her hip and kicked Buckey in the leg he stood on, catching him in the knee and forcing it backward. Red grinned as she heard bone and cartilage crumble. Buckey fell to the fetal position, clutching his knee. She then rolled to her back, pushed with her hands, thrust her legs up and forward and was on her feet in one move. Three soldiers brought up the rear behind Kat and Tami. When they saw their comrade go down a lean soldier with high cheek bones and thick brows left the others to help Buckey. Agent Forbes threw a right hand at the soldier's jaw. He blocked it briefly with his left before turning it into a left cross. Forbes staggered back but kept her feet.

Handlebar leveled both barrels of shotgun at Jake's chest. "Think you're fast enough, Spitfire? Try it."

Another soldier from the back of the line instructed the last soldier to watch the girls and moved toward the fracas. Tami tripped him as he marched past, slid to his left and brought her knee into his abdomen three times quickly. As he went down he wrapped an arm around her legs. They grappled like evenly matched Olympic wrestlers going for the gold. Kat and the last soldier exchanged that brief look like dogs do just before they fight for territory. The soldier cursed himself for having holstered his gun to light his smoke. He threw a flat backhand at Kat's face. She ducked it easily, stepped in close and in one hand grabbed the back of his hair while throwing straight palms into his chin with the other hand. He eventually managed to block the palm shots and went for a wrist lock. She pulled free before he could gain purchase, jumped up high and kicked him in the chest. He stayed up for three steps before falling on his back, winded.

Oliver had his opponent in a standard police issue choke hold and asleep before he could gurgle, 'No, wait.' The soldier guarding Crystal immediately took his ally's spot to lunge at Oliver with a six-inch hunting knife. Oliver backed up but not far enough as he bumped into his brother who was busy avoiding a roundhouse kick from his own adversary. Blood trickled from the three inch slash to Oliver's sweater.

"Hells Bells, Xavier, would you move your bloody tail, man!"

Xavier apologized, never taking his eyes off his opponent with the lightning fast kicks. The blows didn't harm Xavier too much so long as he took them on the shoulders and outside of his arms. Should one of these kicks connect with his head it would be all over, he feared. He just had to hold his own a little longer; surely the man had to tire soon.

Xavier had dealt with this kind before. Many men don't like to get close to Xavier due to his size, so the ones that can kick opt for the feet. Patience in this situation was the key. Oliver schooled him many times in their youth about that concept. Xavier cannot remember how many times he looked up from the canvas to hear his brother boast, "Good things come to those who wait, young man. On your feet then..."

Agent Forbes surveyed her enemy's limping footwork and decided to switch from a martial arts stance to bounce on the balls of her feet like a boxer. Her challenger grinned through blood-covered teeth. "Are you sure about that, lady? Big girl like you can't bounce around for long," he sneered.

"Speak for yourself, Hopalong," she replied. Her right eye was beginning to close.

"Game over, bitch," he said, charging in. Rebecca tagged him with three right handed jabs, further bloodying his mouth. He threw a kick at her midsection which she easily sidestepped. Concern registered on his face. He tried another front kick but caught nothing but air. She shifted her feet so that she was now boxing regular instead of south paw.

Fear screamed from his eyes but there was little he could do. Her overhand right came in at high gear to nail him just behind the ear. Jake heard the perfectly executed punch from where he stood and let the right side of his mouth rise.

"Dropping like flies," Jake said.

Handlebar did not like the way the brawl was going but dared not risk taking the gun off 'Spitfire'—he moved too damn quickly. He decided to put the gun to his head and use him as a hostage and march them out that way. At least Genesis would see who held the cards in the end.

As Handlebar took a slow step backward so as not to alarm Jake, Jake grabbed the gun with both hands. The gun now faced the ceiling, sandwiched in between the two brutes fighting viciously over it. Handlebar got close and head butted Jake. This stunned Jake, but he did not let go of the gun. Regaining his senses Jake returned the head butt. Handlebar went down on one knee. Jake got around behind him and tried to use the gun to choke Handlebar, who saw the maneuver coming and got his hands between the gun and his neck, preventing the choke. Handlebar pushed with all of his strength as Jake pulled on the gun until Jake suddenly let go. This caused Handlebar to involuntarily throw the gun a good distance in front of him. Jake went for a choke without the gun this time, but Handlebar was able to shrug him off. The two of them squared off hand to hand, Handlebar breathing heavily while Jake breathed as though out for a stroll. Jake's opponent came at him like a sumo wrestler. Jake set his feet, twisted his body 360 degrees and caught him on the jaw with a spinning back punch followed immediately with another. Oliver, who was moving toward the fight, scarcely believed his eyes. Jake dropped his opponent with incredible speed and accuracy with a look in his eye like he'd just received news that his restaurant table was ready.

Kat sat straddling her victim and delivered a flurry of rights and lefts to his face and would have continued had Crystal not convinced her that "he's done."

Xavier's patience paid off. The kickboxer's kicks began to slow to the point that Xavier managed to catch his foot under his arm. "Shit," the kickboxer mumbled as Xavier slammed his other fist into the man's groin. That was the only shot he needed to deliver.

Agent Forbes now stood over Buckey, who still clutched at his knee and his ear. Sweat poured from his forehead as he called her every derogatory name he could think of. "You kicked me from behind. I don't like that," she said as she stepped on his knee. Buckey wailed briefly before passing out from the pain.

"Right on, sister!" Tami roared with a fist in the air. As the group huddled together they heard Lou's voice ordering the occupants to come out. Tami, Crystal and Red grabbed all of the soldier's weapons and rejoined the group as they headed outside.

Jake's trot turned into a run as he heard Lou's call once again. It could have been a trap but Jake took the chance that it wasn't as he barged out the door without caution. The clean air felt good. He found Lou with the gun he'd given him at the play-Priest's head.

Ten men were on their knees in a row, each with their hands behind their heads. Genesis held his ear and sobbed. His cries were the final nail in the coffin, telling his men that it was all over. Adrian repeatedly called to his dad, "It can't be over, Daddy, it can't be over."

Jake could see defeat in the few faces he looked at. Having been in their shoes before, he knew that in the minds of most of these men were two questions: will I see the inside of a jail cell and if not, where is my next paycheck coming from? He was genuinely impressed with Lou's handiwork and maybe even a little proud of the smart-talking fool.

"Bloody good show young Louis, bravo!" Oliver blurted as he took Genesis from Louis, which was just dandy, as his arm was beginning to cramp from holding Genesis steady.

Chapter 39

Our group consisted of my crew, Genesis and his goons, and twenty kids. The teens that did most of the cooking were stashed in another part of the property, and it was agreed that Forbes would collect them later with the full Bureau cavalry. We used handcuffs reluctantly provided by the PASSAGE security guys and cuffed the goons behind their backs. We moved as a giant, slow serpent through the woods. Jake eventually got a cell signal and raised both local law enforcement and the feds giving them agent Forbes' information.

Genesis moaned and complained most of the way. He even stooped to bribery, and finally more tears. For the second time in twenty four hours I was ecstatic about seeing the three letters FBI as they waited with local cops at Jake's truck. Guns were trained on us in the event that Jake's call was made under duress. Agent Forbes' badge kept everything calm. Being that we were in southern California, I half expected news crews waiting with bated cameras and mikes. Apparently, the law had managed to keep a lid on it for now. Paramedics scampered all over the place, tending to children first, adults second. Tami told a paramedic to box Genesis' good ear to balance out the ringing in the other. Oliver tsk-tsked her.

A couple of bureau agents were getting into it with a pair of child service workers over the kids. I didn't envy them the mess they had to work out. A second team of agents was moments away from advancing on the main sanctuary to sort out that mess. Their orders were to handle with extreme care. Nobody wanted another Waco. The knock-off shoe operation, child labor camp, offshore accounts, 'sucker' clientele and so on was all about to come crashing down. Genesis and son began wailing at the reality.

My heart nearly split as we witnessed some of the kids run to the cruiser that Genesis was loaded into. He was the only father figure they knew. On the other end of the spectrum, you had Red who wanted to kill, kill, and kill. Neither scenario was pleasant.

"A truly fitting punishment has not yet been written for a man such as Genesis," Oliver said softly.

Agent Rebecca Forbes was in her element. This was her show. She even had enough pull to get our group a helicopter ride back to LA, which was dynamite with me. She wasn't coming with us, as she was joining the second team at the ranch. Better her than me. Before getting in the Suburban she turned and jogged back to me.

I spoke first. "Thanks for saving my life and everything else, Rebecca, you're aces, doll."

"Never mind all that, Handsome Lou, just give me a call if things don't work out with you and Kat." She winked.

"What?"

"Open those pretty little eyes of yours, Louis Crasher, you have an admirer." She kissed me on the cheek and moved off to the suburban.

I looked over at Kat, who was comforting Red. Even though it was over, I still didn't know what was going on. Jake needed to return the rental SUV, so he was unable to join us for the helicopter ride. It was the perfect out for him. He'd prefer riding back alone. He barely allowed me to thank him before he split.

"Be smart," were his last words.

Crystal and I leaned against a sheriff's car awaiting the ride to the helicopter. I gave her the short version of how I came to attempt her rescue. She was happy that her father loved her but she had no intention of living with him. It came out as a warning. I'm sure she thought I was going to try and force a happy reunion.

"Crystal, your father is your father and you should at least have a sit-down with him. But hey, you're a grown woman and you can flop anywhere you want."

Her eyes welled up. She leaned into me the same way she did when we shared the sexy room.

"Crystal, your old man runs with some shady dudes, so I for one would be happy to hear that you moved on. Just let him know that you're safe and do not run into the arms of another Genesis. Keep your head up, shoulders back, and walk your own path, baby doll. Now that's it. I'm all talked out."

She sobbed a little harder and hugged me a little tighter. Dames...they confuse me. Finally she said, "You're right. I don't need a man to validate me."

"Right on!"

"In fact, I hate men."

"Now, now wait a minute. What about me and the twins and Jake?" I asked.

She pretended she had to think about it.

"We should have left your ass up there," I teased.

She poked me in the sore ribs for my statement. "Oops, sorry Lou," she laughed. "But seriously, Louis, I want to—"

"No need to thank me, I mean us," I said.

She moved the gravel in a circle with her foot. "So why did you come for me? I know daddy had you over a barrel but you could have skipped town. Why take the risk."

"I saw a picture of you. Your face had the same expression you have on right now. How could I not play hero?"

"But, you kind of messed up and your friends had to come and get you."

"Easy sister, I never said this was a Hollywood movie. My intentions were good."

"The road to hell is paved with good intentions, Lou."

"We really should have left your ass up there," I teased.

Chapter 40

I can happily say that my first helicopter ride was a success. We didn't crash into any mountains, oceans or flying saucers. Jake had apparently called Bernie Outlaw and told him we were coming in—something I hadn't thought of doing. A stretch white limousine sat idling for us at the curb. The driver loaded our gear into the trunk. By the time he climbed into the driver's seat the twins were snoring. Kat and Tami each took a shoulder of mine for pillows and were out soon after the twins. Crystal found a little corner and curled up like a little kitten. That left me. I was wired. How could I sleep? I kept thinking that if I slept I'd wake to find that the last week was a dream, and I'd worked too damn hard for that kind of finale. I ran through the events with my brain operating in fast motion. In between frames, my thoughts would travel to Angela. I had to talk to her and hear her end of it but I could already feel myself pulling away from her. She was way too deep into the world of Outlaw and his brother and I couldn't help thinking she volunteered for it, at least in part anyway. I desperately needed to get back to my life of drumming. At least in that life I'm not a sap.

I have no recollection of the route we took to Bernie's or how long it took to get there. The limo stopped and the door was opened by the driver. I woke the sleeping beauties Kat and Tami with a soft whisper. To the twins I shouted, "Next stop Piccadilly Square!" Oliver called me a twit. I got out and helped the driver with the gear. It turns out he's from the same place in Jamaica as my mother. His friends call him Byron.

Bernie Outlaw bounded down the steps three at a time in snakeskin cowboy boots and pale blue silk boxers. An oversized navy blue and burgundy velour bath robe with gold embroidered lettering on the left lapel billowed out behind him. His thinning hair was out of the usual pony tail. Disgruntled bookends Dustin and Fox burst through the door fifteen seconds later with guns drawn, wiping sleep from their eyes. Bernie ran up to his daughter, who held my hand tightly, and stopped on a snakeskin dime. He didn't know what to do or say. While spending all those hours by the phone waiting for it to chirp, no doubt Bernie hoped for a huge 'run into each others' arms' type of reunion. His little chest heaved up and down. Her bottom lip began to quiver.

"Hi, Precious," Bernie squeaked.

"Daddy," she finally said faintly, moving in for a slow hug.

"Oh my God, are you okay, pumpkin? Are you? Damn it Lou, is she all right?"

"She's grand, Bern' can't ya tell?" We left them like that and headed toward the house. Dustin and Fox scowled at us.

"Evening, fellas," I said cheerily. Fox nodded in spite of himself. Oliver and Xavier led us into the very same living room where we'd planned the whole episode. Making sure we were comfortable they excused themselves. They each returned through different doors but now wore identical tracksuits. They both sighed and rolled their eyes at the sight of each other. The girls and I were amused.

While Oliver went to the kitchen to fetch us some treats, Xavier set up drinks. The girls asked for water but then changed their minds when they heard me order beer. I gently held the chilled bottle of Molson's in both hands and spoke softly to her.

"Baby, you have been dearly missed. Here's to you and many more as I live a peaceful rock-and-roll life without cults and guns and things." Without hesitation I knocked back half the contents. The girls shamed me for not cheering our bottles. "Oops, sorry," I mumbled.

Bernie and Crystal came into the room, Bernie's boots clip-clopping all the way. They'd had a good cry and now wore sheepish smiles on their mugs.

"Mr. Crasher, I owe you my life. This here what you done more than squares ever' thing between you and me, dya hear? Me and my heart here Crystal got some work to do but we're gonna make it, I swear." Outlaw made me get up and give him a hug. Kat winked at me over Bernie's shoulder. She found my discomfort amusing. When I pulled away Bernie's eyes were full of water again. He ran to write me check but I refused it. Just as long as we were square, I told him. Oliver came back into the room to announce what he'd prepared but Outlaw cut him off and pulled the two big 'tankers' into a bear hug. Crystal laughed. She looked twelve years old again.

"You big sons o' bitches really done come through fer me. Oh bull's balls, where the hell are my manners? Damn it, Olly! Ladies I apologize, I have y'all to thank as well." They were now pulled into the little Texas hug machine. It was my turn to wink at Kat.

After we ate Oliver's barbecue chicken drumettes, smoked oysters on Triscuits, sour cream rolled in prosciutto meat, assorted fruits and veggies, nuts and some homemade banana bread, and, naturally, tea (which I passed on), we shared light conversation. Bernie told Dustin and Fox to take a plate of food out to Byron the driver and make sure he was awake, and why the hell weren't they patrolling the grounds?

The hugging started again as we said our goodbyes. The limo took us to the derby twins' place first. The girls decided in light of everything, they'd take the day off tomorrow from the gym. Tamika gave me a big hug and a kiss on the cheek and then hurried up the walk. Kat stayed behind a minute.

"So what are you going to do?" she asked me.

"I've got it all planned out. I'm going to have a beer or two while I soak these weary bones in the tub. And do you know who I'm going to listen to?"

"Buddy Rich?"

"No, good guess though. No, this cat is going to listen to the sweet sounds of Wes Montgomery, and then tomorrow I'm going to be a drummer again, yeehaw!"

"You're a nut. Call me when you get up...on my line." She scooted across the seat and we hugged. As I went to give her a kiss on her cheek she grabbed my face and twisted it toward her. Her lids came down slowly and then she kissed me full on the lips like she meant it. I was still kissing air as she slid back across the seat and out the door with a giggle.

"Thanks for ride, Byron, sorry I've got nothing for a tip," I said shaking his hand.

"No problem, mon, and congratulations on dat girl. She's tough, y'know."

"Who ya tellin'?"

Jake drove down toward Los Angeles in silence for a while. He wanted to digest the previous events in peace before turning on some music. The whole episode came off without too many hitches, but Jake could not deny that his group had a huge amount of luck on its side. And Jake was not a man who believed in luck. After playing out the events like a quick slideshow with the boring slides missing he thought that it was time. This recent adventure of Lou's confirmed it. It was time Jake let Lou know who he was.

Chapter 41

The sun had been up for a few hours by the time I woke. I felt much better than expected, thanks to Wes Montgomery, I suppose. I gathered all the healthy food I could find in my fridge and tossed it in a blender—breakfast of champion drummers. After a quick shower, I stepped out to a ringing phone and caught it before voicemail picked up.

"Hello."

"Hi Lou, it's me, Angela."

"I know your voice Ang," I said, more coolly than I intended.

"How are you?"

"Happy to be alive. And you?"

"Fine." I could tell she was nervous. "I need to explain a few things."

I gave her silence so she could do her thing.

"Bernie told me about how you saved his daughter. He also told me how he had you get the photo from his brother and all of that too." She paused. "I'm sorry, this is hard."

"Look, forget it. You and Bernie and his brother, it is none of my business…happily so."

"Don't do that. I want it to be your business—our business."

"Fine, let me take a crack at this. You see, Angela, I've heard, seen and been through a lot so I've got it all figured out except one thing.

And that is, are you seeing Bernie or his brother with the different last name?"

"Bernie," she said quietly.

"Well then it's definitely none of my business, because I don't want to go near Outlaw, MacBeth or any names that friggin' rhyme with those names for the rest of my days."

"Will you just hear me out? Now you of all people know how hard it is to get anywhere in this business, especially in this town. I have worked my butt off to get where I am. Do you know whose name is on the contract of my deal? Mine, no one else's in the band, just mine. I front the band; I manage the band, working full time. Hell, gimme a break." She paused. I could tell she was getting emotional. "In the beginning it was all backup vocal gigs for no cash, then Bernie came along. His label is small but they take care of their people. As time passed we, I guess—"

"I get it Angela, you don't need to lay out the Meg Ryan movie part for me."

"Anyway, my last album didn't do so well and Bernie tells me investors are getting restless. It's how it works, Lou. One afternoon he tells me all about his daughter, I mean he just broke down and told me everything. We talked a long time until we decided I should get close to his brother and get a pass to that PASSAGE place from him."

"So you didn't know I was going to go there?"

"Not at first. In fact I thought he'd hire a private investigator or something."

A picture was taking shape in my head. "Go on."

"I didn't want to do what he was suggesting at all but he made it clear that my help would lengthen the life of my deal. So I agreed. I dated MacBeth for a while and eventually learned about the tickets."

"Tickets? Tickets plural?"

"Yeah, he had a few. He and Genesis had some kind of business connection or something. He had tickets in his car and wallet. He may have had more, I don't know."

"I wondered about that. Back up a second. What kind of business connection did MacBeth and the lovely charlatan have going?" I asked, half knowing.

"I don't know, some king of goods, garments, something, I don't know."

"Well let me tell you, because I'm kind of getting good at this. The aforementioned bastards of which we speak were into knock-offs, shoes mainly, probably clothes and so on—"

"I knew nothing about that, and why would I care who buys their phony crap?" She was defensive but I could hear the guilt in her voice.

"You might care, Angela, because children in a sweatshop under shit conditions and the lash were making the knock-offs. I bet if you weren't so fixated on your deal you might have opened your pretty little eyes and seen it."

My voice was raised by the end of the sentence. I just succeeded in bullying a woman. Was I a righteous dude or just a frustrated cat...or both? The pause went on for eons. Finally after way too long for anybody to stay on a phone in silence, I spoke.

"So why not grab a PASSAGE ticket yourself? Why tell Bernie where the toughest one to snag was?" I already knew but I wanted her to say it.

She started to cry. "I thought that if he got his daughter back he'd no longer need my help and then—"

"Bye-bye recording contract. So you led him to what you thought was an impossible ticket to snatch." I finished for her. The crying heated up.

"I don't know if you know this part, but I was held prisoner there, and you know I couldn't help feeling that they were suspicious of me from the get go. Especially Genesis' little pissant son Adrian. You tipped him off that I or somebody was coming, didn't you?"

She cried harder. I kept going. "One last thing: I saw a video of Outlaw's lads attempting to snatch Crystal. Genesis' thugs were waiting for them under and around the Great Hall. Funny thing is that their headquarters, if you will, is nowhere near the Great Hall. Did you tip the G-man on that occasion as well?"

Again more tears followed by, "I'm sorry."

"They could have been killed, Angela. I could have been killed— not to mention my friends who came to—" I let it drift. "How does my hunting for your gear tie into all this?"

"That was real. I was just trying to be a good sister helping a brother out."

"That's right, paying a guy out of a record label, 'Out and Out Records,' to be exact." She gave me silence. "I probably would have figured this thing out earlier if you'd mentioned the label name, Angela. Anyway, the point here is that you didn't expect a fumbling, bumbling brother with a high school crush on you to find your stuff."

"Yes," she sobbed.

"I should have warned you that I'm a genius."

She laughed. A laugh I wasn't likely to hear again. She asked me in a soft little voice if we were done.

"Angela, you're dating the little Texas twister, what do you think?"

"I'll leave him."

"Look, baby, it's like Tupac said: 'I ain't mad at you...' You did what you felt you had to do, and now I gotta do what a man's gotta do. Dig? Besides, you kinda scare the hell out of me."

"Good bye, then Louis."

"So long, sister."

My phone rang as soon as I hung it up. I figured it was Angela calling back but it wasn't.

"Hey."

"Jake, Hey thanks again for all your help."

"You said that already."

Same old Jake. "So what's going on?" I ask.

"Just thought you'd like to know Genesis is trying to play the insanity card."

"I thought you could only do that on murder charges," I replied.

"He's a desperate man."

"I just talked to Angela." I gave Jake the shortest possible version of our call.

"On to the next episode," he said. Direct. Simple. And he was right.

"Exactly, I'm off to play my drums and that's the only episode I need."

"Aren't you supposed to call somebody?"

"Huh?" Then I remembered the kiss with Kat and that she told me to call her.

"How the hell do you know about that, man?"

"Does that matter?"

"One last time Jake, who the hell are you?"

He ignored the question. "Speaking of episodes, look outside your door." The line went dead. I opened the front door and found a brown paper bag sitting on the floor. Inside was a three-DVD set of James Garner's *Rockford Files*. A note was attached.

Hopefully this is as close as you get to the P.I. business.

Nice work at the ranch.

J

P.S. You owe me a cell phone

I looked up from the note to see Byron the limo·driver walking down my hallway.

"Byron, dude, what are you doing here?"

"Hey mon, a little somet'ing from Bernie. Him say it non-negotiable. Say hi to yo girl fo' me."

He'd handed me an envelope and inside was a check made out to me for two thousand dollars. The note told me thanks, and to not try rejecting his thanks or he'd send the twins by and it would start all over again. Well, a guy couldn't argue with that, I suppose. Besides, Jim Rockford hardly ever got paid. It only made sense to keep the money. I chuckled at how Bernie had signed his note: The Outlaw.

I sat down and looked at the check for five minutes. My phone rang as I was about to call Kat.

"This is Lou."

"Louis, my good man, it's Xavier."

"And Oliver on the extension old boy. I gather you are well this morning?"

"Fine lads, fine. Hell of thing wasn't it?"

"Quite," in unison.

"Has Byron popped 'round yet?" Oliver asked.

"Yup, what a pleasant surprise. The kind I can dig you know."

"Naturally, ah Louis, we've done it, we've left Bernie's employ and not five minutes ago."

"Blast you Xavier, always rushing in," Oliver scolded.

"Don't start with me, brother, I warn you."

"Hey hey fellas, let us chill shall we?"

"Sorry, Louis. Anyway, if I may without interruption, we have quit Bernie and are all set to go into business for ourselves." He paused.

"That's great, lads. What are you going to do?"

"The plan is to do similar work to what we're doing now with the addition of private investigation."

Oliver sounded very excited. A little too excited.

"Oh, do get to the point, brother," Xavier blurted.

"We need a third man, Louis, and you are a man of substance, good character and you possess a sharp ability to think outside of the box. What say you, will you join us? We have the startup money so you won't need to buy in. Well?"

"Either you're in or out, padre," said Xavier in his awful John Wayne impression.

"Cheese and crackers, lads, I'm flattered. But I'm a drummer. I don't know...and I'm still working at the space and...can I sleep on it?"

"By all means, young Louis," they said, again in unison.

We hung up after brief small talk. I was definitely tempted by the crazy offer. I pondered a moment, then remembered what it was I'd set out to do.

I called Kat. She was old school and had a vintage answering machine. "Hiya doll, it's Lou Crasher. Again thank you and Tami so much for sticking your necks out. I'm taking you guys out for dinner...for starters. Oh, and count me in on a gym membership once you guys are live. But I just want weights, so don't put me down for any spas or spin class crap. Oh yeah, and no pilate-yogi stuff where I have to bend backwards to find my inner intestine. And the best for last, drum roll please; about that kiss—"

"Lou, Lou don't hang up, it's me, Kat."

Chapter 42

Even with all of this good fortune, something still bothered me. When one can't put his finger on exactly what bothers him it's even more bothersome. So, I thought, mused and pondered as best I could.

When I pulled into the Practice Joint lot, my boss's dirty black Jeep Cherokee sat in its usual spot; the handicap spot. He wasn't handicapped, but being that it was the closest spot to the building, he, being the boss, felt entitled. The dent in the front passenger door appeared to be getting larger. No doubt he smacked it on the yellow pole at the side of the building again on the way out. The price of parking in the handicap spot, often while stoned. A car that was all too familiar to me was parked on the Cherokee's right side. The recognition raised my heart rate a dozen BPM.

I let the ol' gal idle as I thoroughly scanned the lot. I parked as far as I could from the two rides. I slammed the shift into park, shut her down and hoisted my trusty steering wheel club with me adding a quiet, 'fuck it' to myself. Michael's new security door was open and latched to the back wall. Daytime. The inner door owned a nasty squeak that would irritate a randy alley cat so I opened it slower than a slug with a hangover moves uphill. It felt like two minutes had passed before I was in the main hall. Creeping into my own place of employ seemed odd to say the least, but there I was. On the balls of my feet I eased room to room. All rooms empty. No un-friendlys laid in wait. Low voices seeped under the office door. I briefly pressed my ear to it before repeating my earlier phrase, 'fuck it.' I burst into the room. Both Michael and Travis jumped in their seats. I didn't wait for them to recover.

"What the fuck is he doing here Michael?" The room smelled of pot. My boss clutched at his heart in full melodrama. I pointed my club at Travis's head. He gathered himself just enough to smirk at me while sitting behind the desk as if he owned the place.

"Jee-zus Lou, you scared the hell out of—"

"Never mind that. Answer the damn question, boss. What's this prick doing here? Talk before I let this club do the talkin.'" Worry spread over Travis's face, which he did a poor job of masking.

"Okay, Lou, okay. Calm down, no point bullshitting anymore. Travis and I are tight, okay? There it is, please put the club down."

I laughed and then laughed some more. And then my laughter worried me. It was as if the events of the last few days finally bubbled over, like a pot of stress porridge. The harder I laughed, the more they stared, dumbfounded. I finally stopped by bringing the club down with serious heat onto the desk. They both jumped again, but his time Travis made a move for the club. Instead of using the club I gave him a straight right to his jaw. I pushed off my back foot, turned my hips then dropped my shoulder; textbook boxing. It was the hardest I'd ever hit anybody in my life. His legs folded under him. He didn't even manage to collapse in the chair. He just crumbled like a dry biscuit and slumped half under the desk half on the floor. My hand didn't even throb like I thought it would.

"Holy shit Lou, take it easy, ya nearly killed him." Michael rushed to him and cared for him in way that seemed...excessive.

"Okay, boss, spill it," I said. "What's your connection?"

"You don''t want to know." My look told him I did.

"All right," he said with a sigh, getting up. "Travis and his buddies jumped you that day for the phone. And well, there was a reason for that. I needed to erase a photo, or rather photos, on the phone and I didn't know how."

He walked over to our cheap little fridge and grabbed himself a

Coke. I declined the one he offered me. He went back and propped Travis up against our filing cabinet. He then picked up the phone, scrolled through and handed it to me. I was looking at a picture of him, Travis and two girls partying in a cheap looking motel room.

"So?" I said.

"Just keep flipping to your left and you'll see". A half-dozen pictures showed the party escalating. Just as I was getting bored there it was. A picture of Travis and my boss getting close in a way that one would expect he and his wife to.

" Well, whaddyaknow?"

"I've got a wife and kid, Lou, and I want to keep 'em. It's not like we're—look, we did a lot of ecstasy that night, among other things. But..." he paused. "I know how it looks."

"If ecstasy makes you play kissy-kiss with losers like Travis, remind me never to do ecstasy!" I said. "Why not just delete the pics yourself? What do you mean you didn't know how?"

"Travis kept them on there with some kinda application or virus, I don't know. He promised that if he had the phone he'd enter some kinda code and erase 'em."

"So you told them where I'd be and they put the screws to me," I said, pissed.

"Well, they were supposed to come here pretending to be a band, distract you and work the phone. But, the little guy just happened upon you on the street with your window open and...well, you know the rest."

"You're an asshole. Keep going." He gave me the world's worst innocent look. "Tell me about the robbery. And don't hold back or I'll do mean things to sleeping beauty there." He didn't say or do anything so I took a step toward Travis and held the club in a baseball batter's grip.

"Okay, okay. I got a little something from Abbott for tipping him off about the ah, fullness of merchandise in this place."

"Man, I've been played so many times this week I feel like a vinyl record from the 70's." I put the club on the desk then briefly rubbed my temples with my palms. A dumb idea flashed across my boss's face. I picked up Michael's can of Coke, shook it up and sprayed him in the face.

"What the fuck! Why d'you do that?" he said sputtering.

"Because I saw you eyeballing the club. Don't get any bright ideas, Mikey! Now then, open your wallet and give me all the money you have."

"Why?

"Severance, asshole. You and me, we're done."

A voice boomed from behind me. "That won't be necessary, Lou."

I turned quickly with club in hand to see big Eddie Carruthers, Michael's dad, standing on the threshold. He was in a long trench coat even though it was hot outside. He had on shiny black military issue boots and leaned on a well weathered, thick bone handle, mahogany cane. To say he looked imposing would be an understatement. He looked huge, ten years younger than the day I'd met him, and ready for business. I nodded and stood aside. He didn't come into the room. It was if he didn't want to get any of Michael's life on him.

"You're a god dammed disgrace son. How many times is this? Don't speak! You don't deserve that woman. You don't deserve your family! And you thought you'd get a little insurance money, and kick back from a two bit robbery? Ha!" He paused glaring at his son, who suddenly looked five years old.

"Take a good look. Here's the insurance money. I'm giving it to Lou."

"What?" Michael yelled. "You can't, he's not family."

"Lou, did you know he was skimming two bucks an hour from you out of your pay?"

"Motherfu—"

"Steady, son. I don't take to that kind of language," Eddie cautioned me.

"Yes sir," I responded, wondering if I also looked like a five-year-old.

He put eyes back on Michael. "I've covered for you, bailed you out and had your back for the last time, boy. This is quits. You've made your bed, so lie in it." He shouted the last part then handed me an envelope with hundreds in it. "For the skimming, the beating Lou took and the enjoyment he gave me watching America's great game of football. I'm giving him the insurance money."

"I can't take this, Mr. Carruthers."

"You'll take it, and I'm not going to ask you twice. Leave your pride out of it, Lou." His bloodshot eyes burned right through me. It was at this juncture that I left pride, morals and decorum out of it and took the dough.

"Thanks Eddie, and please give my best to the missus."

"Do it yourself next time you come by for football. I hope you'll do that."

"Absolutely," I said.

"Oh, and bring some beer. The old battleaxe only lets me buy six at a time."

"Consider it done."

Epilogue

I heard a weird knocking sound coming from under the old gal's hood. I shouldn't say weird, as it was one of the only unhealthy car sounds I did recognize. It's a clicking sound, similar to when a kid puts a playing card in the spoke of his bicycle tire, only a touch deeper. My lady needed oil. I always kept a couple extra quarts in the trunk or under my seat as many of us cats do who own classic rides.

"Are you thirsty, girl? Huh? That's right, drink up. Hey, hey slow down." I checked the level again with the dipstick and she told me she was good. It had been three weeks since the Outlaw/Crystal rollercoaster. Kat and I were hot and heavy. I had subbed on a few gigs including a punk rock gig which was…interesting to say the least, especially when someone threw a bloody chicken heart at me. As it turned out the act was done in approval of my performance. So, the drumming was in order but I needed a day gig so when the twins Oliver and Xavier called me for the umpteenth time asking advice on their very first case I finally decided to join them.

When I put the hood down, Jake was standing beside the car. This time I was ready for him. Well not really, but I managed not to flinch. However, when I exaggerated my 'I knew you were there the whole time' vibe I think he grinned. Truth be told, I was more relaxed these days. I didn't ask Jake what he wanted, as I am cut from a cloth that would consider that rude. Plus, he was the type to get to the point pretty darn quick…or whenever he saw fit.

"She needed oil?"

"Yup. You know, she's not getting any younger."

"You're going to need to rebuild that engine before long," Jake said. "Got any beers upstairs?"

"Ha, you know me," I said. "Oh, hey thanks again for the *Rockford*."

We took the stairs in silence. Something was up with Jake and he knew I knew. Scary, we were becoming more like Abbott and Costello every minute.

"Miller High Life or the good stuff?" I offered.

"What's the good—"

"Miller Genuine Draft, of course." Jake took me up on the good stuff and sat at my tiny Ikea kitchen table. He raised the beer briefly at me as I pulled one out of the fridge for myself. Just then he lifted his right ankle to rest it on his left knee. No big deal, guys sit that way all the time. But it was what he did next that nearly had me drop my beer. He creased his brow then picked two times at some lint on his right knee pant leg and then sort of brush patted the lint away once, twice, then paused, and then a third time. I had seen this before.

"Holy sh—"

He looked up at me with a 'what?' expression on his face. I had to sit down. I took a long hard pull from my beer and then placed it on the table gently. I'm sure to Jake I had a faraway look in my eyes. He waited, as was his method. Then I spoke.

"Whew, it all makes sense now. Man, you see, I was always trying to figure out what the hell it was or is you do for a living when I should have been looking at *who* you are. I helped you out that night way back in the day when you were at that liquor store and you said you owed me. Well as thankful as I was…sorry, as I am, it was way beyond the call of duty as far as payback goes. It just didn't make sense you always having my back the way you do. I knew you weren't gay, thank God. Not that there's anything wrong with being gay, but me being uncomfortable…now that would have been wrong. Anyway, oh yeah, there were a couple of phone calls I had with my parents…the few times I'd mention your name, my old man always got a little squirrelly. He'd either change the subject or warn me to be careful of anyone from California. I just chalked it up to basic parental peculiarity."

I stopped talking to see if Jake's mug would reveal anything. Nothing. "I got an uncle who said if you've got three points to back up a hunch or, or a suspicion then 'boom'—that's three times the proof you need. I know you're wondering what the third piece is or just generally what the hell I'm talking about."

I killed the rest of my beer. He sipped casually. "Jake, just now the way you half crossed your leg and removed that lint with the pluck,

pluck, and pat, pat, I've seen that ritual for over twenty-five years. Now look me in the eye and spill it because I know you don't lie."

I leaned forward nervously, slowly. "We're related somehow and you've known it for a long-ass time."

Jake just stared at me. He took another sip, never moving his eyes from mine. "Don't play games, Jake, my dad's been doing that pant leg thing forever. And he's always skittish at the mention of your name, like he doesn't want—" I got up from the table. "It's as if he doesn't want my mom to know. No, but that doesn't make sense, unless..."

My pea brain struggled so Jake helped. "We're half-brothers, Lou. Same dad, different mothers. I don't believe your mother knows about me."

Jake slowly twisted his empty beer bottle in his hands. It appeared as if the bottle carried considerable weight, but that wasn't the case. It was just that his rope-like veins moved over his thick forearm muscles like seaweed over rolling waves. I pulled open my freezer door and was hit in the foot by a bag of frozen corn. With an expletive I picked it up and put it in the place of the Jamaican rum bottle I retrieved. Jake declined the offer as I grabbed two tumblers so I gave him another beer instead. He rarely accepted a second in the past. I poured myself three obese fingers of the sauce over rocks and added a splash of Coca Cola for décor, or decorum perhaps.

Over the next twenty minutes or so Jake spread out a brief history for me of how I came to be related to a brooding, gravely-voiced SOB. My parents met in college, and in fact got married while still undergrads. This much I already knew. During those days money was tight and the scholarship my old man was on wasn't quite cutting the mustard. So being a responsible dude, the old man took on all kinds of different odd jobs—some on campus, some off. One off campus job was delivering pizzas. This was ironic in that I had done the same thing in the eleventh grade. Strangely, my dad never told me then or since that we shared that profession. During one of his runs, he met Jake's mom Vera. They flirted, they talked, they teased, and after a while my old man started visiting without the pizzas. This was strange for me to hear, but I had to. Details not being important, obviously one thing lead to another and voila, Jake. My parents dated about two years and shacked up for one and were engaged for another which meant Jake had just over four years on me.

I poured myself another two fingers and Jake told me to slow down. He made a good point so I downed a finger and a half before dumping the rest down the sink. Then I switched back to beer, naturally. My dad and Vera's relationship eventually fizzled and they went their separate ways. Apparently Jake's mom didn't tell my old man, but he found out about Jake when Jake was around six months old. Jake didn't find out who his dad was until he was eleven.

"My mother had some vague story about who my old man was but it was full of holes. A card came in the mail one day, the Hallmark kind. It wasn't the first of its kind either. Mom always threw them away after reading them, so this one afternoon I fished it out of the trash and there it was…'Sorry about how this turned out. Hope this helps,' end quote. The help was obviously cash. The letter was postmarked Canada." Jake never took his eyes off me when he spoke. His expression gave away nothing. He could have been reading a list of names in the phone book. This was a story Jake had lived a long time. Maybe that explained the indifference.

"Why didn't your mom just BS you?" I asked.

"She'd tried that, weren't you listening?"

I could clearly see how his mom would have cracked under Jake's penetrating eye, even if the eye only had eleven years to it at the time. I had a mix of emotions, the foremost of which was anger. Jake spoke to my dad a half-dozen times between ages fifteen to eighteen, and then cut it off. He claimed my dad wasn't too busted up about the separation either. The tangled web we weave.

For the moment, I decided not to call my parents or anything, and I'd probably never tell my mother. As far as Jake and myself, he'd been keeping tabs on me on and off for close to ten years. He claims it got easier as the Internet started growing. I asked how he could have orchestrated me walking into that liquor store that night and he said it was fate.

"I don't believe in coincidences, Jake."

"I said fate, genius, not coincidence." He scowled at me.

I didn't buy it, but I figured I'd fight it out another time, another place.

"Well, shit, if the last couple of weeks were a long song I'd say this was the drum solo." I said, forcing a smile.

Jake's eyes smiled ever so slightly as he polished off his second beer. "The shoot-out was the drum solo. This is more like the crescendo."

"Right on, half-brother," I said. We clinked bottles. "So, what is it you do again?"

THE END

Drumroll Please

If you enjoyed *Crescendo* you truly won't want to miss *Drumroll Please,* Lou Crasher's next action packed adventure novel from Jonathan Brown. Crasher gets his P.I. license and partners up with British 'tankers' Oliver and Xavier. The trio rejoices when they land their first big case: find a missing Chihuahua. What should be a simple walk in the 'doggie' park quickly turns sideways and nearly ends the Mortimer-Crasher agency before it even begins.

Pick up *Drumroll Please* at all of the usual (and unusual) outlets.

www.jonathanbrownauthor.com

CPSIA information can be obtained at www.ICGtesting.com
Printed in the USA
LVOW08s0803070813

346605LV00001B/1/P